THE
LOST COVE

MARSHALL SEDDON

NFB
NFB Publishing/Amelia Press
119 Dorchester Road
Buffalo, New York 14213

For more information visit Nfbpublishing.com

Also by MARSHALL SEDDON

THE SLEEPER STREET GANG

THE SHADOW OF FOREVER: A NORSE SAGA

for my family

CHAPTER ONE

Two men struggled through deep, powdery white sand, waddling almost, pushing, and pulling at the gurney, whose wheels sank deep into the sand and refused to roll at all. The sun was fully up, and it beat down on the glaring sand, blinding the men, who squinted out from their sweat soaked and stinging eyes. Gulls circled, laughing, and crabs scurried in the sand. An osprey screed overhead. The smell of the humid salt air of the beach, mixed with the rot of seaweed and stench of burnt flesh was overpowering. By the time they reached the small group that had gathered, they were both sweating profusely and wondering how they could get the gurney back to the ambulance weighted down by a body.

"Damn, that old boy's a sight, isn't he?" someone said.

"That's for sure. Boating accident then?"

"Looks like. Someone called in a boat fire late last evening. Sherriff's boat went out, but the fire was too hot for them to get near. Finally burned itself out and sank. They searched for survivors all night, and they've been out all mornin'. Nothin' 'till this one washed in on the tide. Shell collector found him and called it in. She's pretty upset."

"I bet. He's burned to a crisp."

The two EMTs began bagging the body and a reporter was throwing up a little way off.

"Nothing more for us here then Chief?" The rookie lieutenant said, a handkerchief over his mouth and nose. He was in a hurry to get away before he embarrassed himself by throwing up like the reporter.

"Don't think so Lieutenant. You got enough details for your report?" the chief asked, chomping on a cigar, and sloshing a styrofoam cup of coffee. This wasn't the first time he'd seen a dead body washed up on the beach.

The lieutenant looked at his clipboard. "I think so."

"Go ahead back to the station and write it up then. Boating accident. They'll try to get some fingerprints at the morgue for an ID."

The lieutenant got in his unit, turned off the lights and backed the cruiser partway up the sand track that served as a road to the beach. He turned the vehicle around at a grassy area, stopped, opened his door, and threw up. Helluva thing to see before breakfast, he thought.

CHAPTER TWO

Aɴ ᴏʟᴅ Vᴏʟᴠᴏ chugged down the interstate, its over-heated engine threatening to stall at any moment. It shuddered and shook as its driver negotiated the sweeping turns of the crowded highway. It was rush hour and Interstate 4 was bumper to bumper and door to door at seventy-five miles an hour. The hot stink of diesel and gas fumes and the noise of churning engines and singing tires was overwhelming, but closing the windows was not an option. As hot as it was outside the car would have become an oven with them closed, the air conditioner having quit some years ago.

"You'd make better time if you took the bridge."

"You know I hate bridges; they terrify me."

"I know, and I know why. But, if you're going to get up so late, you shouldn't take the long way around. And bye-the-way, bridges are hard things to avoid in the Greater Tampa Area." The last phrase was said with a dramatic news anchor's voice. Drew Andrews was late to work again, and his brother Peter had come along for the ride. Again.

"You should pass that truck; you've been stuck behind him forever."

Drew gritted his teeth and looked in his mirror for a chance to change lanes. The truck ahead of him was some sort of utility vehicle, towing a trailer. Coiled electrical cords and road markers bounced and swung from its sides. The bright morning sun glinted off the metal of the truck and the windows and sides of the other vehicles on the road. He would have been content to just sit behind the truck and be a few minutes later but Peter was insistent.

"Pass him on the next inside curve, Kiddo." Peter had been an avid NASCAR fan and drove like it, causing Drew to white knuckle the sissy strap over the passenger door when he used to ride with him. Goaded by Peter, Drew checked his rear-view mirror for an opening and, at the next inside curve, pulled into the lane on his left. He managed to pull up alongside the careening truck-and-trailer combination, but when he attempted to pass, his old Volvo refused to respond.

"I told you to get this POS tuned up! Or trade it in for a better car. I would have."

"Right," Drew said. A big pickup truck had pulled up behind him and was tailgating him, but he couldn't coax any more power out of the chugging and shuddering car. He couldn't pull ahead, and he couldn't fade back behind the utility truck. He was trapped between the swaying utility truck on his right and a concrete barrier to his left, with the charging pickup truck directly behind him. "This is a fine mess you've gotten us into," he said as the driver of the truck behind him honked impatiently. Drew took his foot off the gas and let the car slow. The truck behind him gave several angry horn blasts but then reluctantly let him ease back behind the utility trailer.

"Nice move," Peter said, laughing. *"I'd have had us there by now."*

"Right, you were always such a great driver."

"I'd have taken the bridge."

"You did take the bridge, as I remember."

"Very funny. What is it I should have said? Sorry for dropping in on you like this."

"Just stop giving me directions on my driving. You're distracting me and I'm late enough as it is. I don't need to get in an accident on top of it all."

"No worries for me! I suppose you want me to wait in the car when we get there."

"That'd be nice. Maybe get lost for the day while you're at it."

"Fat chance Kiddo!"

Drew hated it when Peter called him Kiddo.

He arrived at the parking lot and was forced to park a considerable distance away, the lot being almost full by now. He was sweating when he finally reached the door and could smell the stale beer from last night running out of his pores. At the main desk, Drew said hello to Shirley, the receptionist, and waited for Danny Frame to sign out. He was a new hire on the police beat and he was looking particularly wan. He finished signing out, nodded once to Drew and ran for the door.

"Saw a dead body on the beach this morning," Shirley said when Danny was out of earshot. "Pretty messy, from what I'm told. He's been sick all morning."

Drew shuddered slightly as he signed in. "Glad it wasn't me."

"The reporter or the body?"

Very funny, Drew thought. He smiled at Shirley and headed towards the elevator, but there was a line, as usual, so he took the stairs. The stairwell, reeking of spilt coffee, stale cigarettes, and mold, almost made him gag. He took the stairs two at a time, walked into the noisy pressroom and headed towards his cube, hoping not to be noticed. Sadly, it was not to be.

"Hey Honcho!" Joe Crimmons shouted from his cube. Joe called everyone Honcho, even the women. He was the head of the sports beat and liked to affect the demeanor of a coach. He chewed gum constantly and always shouted. Now he was shouting at Drew, the newest of his reporters, and everyone noticed.

"Morning, Joe," Drew said with a dismissive wave. He tried to continue on, but Joe was not to be denied.

"Big Man wants to see you, Honcho." He said, snapping his gum. "Told me on the phone a half-hour ago; said: 'send Andrews up when he gets in.'" He leaned back in his chair and folded his arms, coach-like, snapping his gum with a grin. "Half hour ago," he said again.

"Tell him to blow it out his ass!" Peter suggested.

"Blow it out your ass!" Drew muttered under his breath as he continued to his cube.

"What?" Crimmons demanded.

"I said I had to stop for gas," Drew said. "There was a line."

"Yeah, that's not what I heard!" Crimmons said. "You'd better watch your mouth; you'd be cleaning out your locker if I was in charge here."

"It's not a locker," Drew said as he sat down. "It's called a desk."

There was a smattering of laughter from the other reporters. "Leave the kid alone," one of them said in a tired voice.

Drew looked at the hand-printed note on his desk. "Big Man wants to see you, pronto!" The printing was scrawled and rough and obviously the work of Joe Crimmons. Drew crumpled it up and tossed it into his wastebasket. He shot a disdainful look at the grinning Crimmons, pushed his chair back, stood up and walked towards the stairs.

"Tell the Big Man I said Hi," Crimmons shouted as Drew opened the door to the stairwell. Drew turned and blew a kiss to him.

"Ass-hole," Drew muttered as he took the stairs two at a time again, hoping to burn off some of his anxiety, and some more of last night's beer. At the landing he stopped, smoothed his hair, tucked in his shirt and caught his breath.

"Should have gotten up earlier," Peter scolded. *"And gotten a haircut."*

"What do I need a haircut for? I'm probably going to be fired anyway." Drew was painfully aware that to be called into Bunny – *Mister* - Bunstall's office usually signaled a pink slip. Bunny liked to do things in person, face to face.

"Don't forget to ask for a letter of recommendation. They usually do that for someone pink-slipped."

"You would know, you got enough of them!" Drew hoped that he hadn't said that out loud. He opened the door.

Soft music played as he surveyed the expansive waiting room. The wall in front of him was covered with various awards that Mr. Bunstall had accumulated over the years: plaques, a large gold key to the city, pictures of him with various politicians and celebrities, and framed awards and honors the newspaper had won. To his right several people sat in overstuffed chairs, waiting for interviews. To his left, next to the door to Bunstall's office, Missus Ida Zimmer sat at a large oak desk. A vase containing fragrant fresh-cut flowers stood on each end. She had grey hair pulled back in a bun and wore a pair of reading glasses on a chain around her neck. She was Mr. Bunstall's long-time secretary and receptionist.

"Well, Mister Andrews," Missus Zimmer said. "I see you've finally made it into work."

The voice was familiar to Drew, although he rarely saw the lady in person. He had heard it just this morning, not even an hour ago, when she called to see if he was awake and coming into work.

Drew cleared his throat. "Yes mam," he said brightly, flashing the best smile he could muster. He turned towards the waiting area.

"Mister Bunstall will see you right away," she said, nodding towards his door. "He's been waiting," she added.

Drew hesitated at the door to Bunstall's office. The last time he was in it, he was being hired. Now, six months later, it looked as though he was going to be fired. What's the point, he thought to himself? Why play out the theater of being fired Bunny's way? He would have much rather just gotten a pink slip in his mailbox, gathered his things and slipped out the door.

"Bunny Bunstall likes to do things a certain way, you know that. He'll let you down easy, assure you that you have a bright future somewhere else and explain to you how your style – do you have a style? – is just not consistent with the editorial policy of the Brantwood Journal. He'll thank you for your efforts over the last few months and then show you the door."

Right, Drew thought. Bunny Bunstall was the consummate professional. He did things his way because it was the right way to do things.

"Just don't forget to get a letter of recommendation."

"Right, right, got it," Drew said as he turned the knob on the big oak door. He noticed Missus Zimmer looking at him funny as he pushed the door open and realized that he had spoken out loud again.

Bunny Bunstall's office featured floor-to-ceiling glass on two sides looking out over the city's bustling main street on one side and Brantwood

Commons on the other. The third wall contained a full bar with several stools and a flat screen TV. The floor was hardwood parquet.

Mister Bunstall sat at his desk, his back to the room and facing the window that looked out over the commons. All Drew could see of him was the back of his three-piece suit and his mane of white hair, which flared out from his skull. Two chairs faced the desk. Teejay Edmunds, the political and cultural editor, sat in one of them. He was leaning back comfortably, dressed in a seer-sucker suit, bow tie and straw boater, french-inhaling a cigarette in a holder. The smoke curled up towards the ceiling past his meticulously trimmed van dyke beard, harkening back to his days spent in New Orleans. He looked appraisingly at Drew as he approached the desk. "Young man," he said without getting up. He didn't extend his hand for a shake and Drew was glad that he hadn't extended his. Drew nodded towards him but didn't say anything. Bunny Bunstall swiveled in his chair to face Drew.

Bunny Bunstall was in his early eighties, but you wouldn't know it. He wore a light gray three-piece suit, a crisp white shirt, and a dark blue silk tie. His face was thin, almost gaunt and his parchment-like skin was drawn tightly across his prominent cheekbones. But it was his eyes that caught Drew's attention: they were clear blue and sharply focused on him.

"Robert J. Andrews" he said with an easy smile. He looked Drew up and down once and then gestured at the view of the city.

"Beautiful, isn't it? Brantwood was named after John Ruskin's home in England. Ruskin was a utopian socialist who inspired many city planners, including John J. Bunstall, the founder of Brantwood, my great, great grandfather."

"Yessir," Drew said. "I grew up playing in that park. I grew up here." He stuttered a little on the last phrase, acutely aware that everyone in Brantwood knew what had happened to his family.

"Yes, you did," Bunny said. "Good upbringing, baseball, tennis and golf in high school; then off to college, where you majored in journalism, political science, and partying with your frat brothers."

"Frats have overblown reputations," Drew said, regaining his composure. "We often took Mondays off."

"Do you enjoy working with Joe Crimmons?" Bunny asked mildly. He opened a wooden humidor box and extracted a hand-rolled cigar, letting Drew consider the question and form a response.

"Yessir," Drew said after what he hoped wasn't too much of a hesitation. "He certainly knows his stuff."

Bunny laughed again and snipped off the end of the cigar. "Yeah, I think he's pretty much an asshole too." He lit the cigar and drew deeply. A fragrant plume of smoke rose towards the ceiling. "But he writes well and gives me some good betting tips, so I endure him."

"Yessir," Drew said.

Bunny looked at the smoldering cigar approvingly. "These are Cubans. Best cigars I've ever had. I have a source," he said with a wink."

"Yessir," Drew said. He noticed that the two men each had a tumbler of whisky, neat.

"*See? These guys have style. Look at how they dress: expensive suits, nice shoes, good haircuts, imported cigars and top shelf whisky – probably single-malt scotch. You'd do well to pay attention to your own appearance. Their dress and mannerisms convey a certain sense of confidence and class. What do you think they think of you?*"

Not much, I'm sure, Drew thought. It had been six months since he had stood in this exact spot, interviewing for a job. He had a fresh haircut and a new sport coat then. Now, as he stood before Bunny and Teejay, he realized that he had the same haircut and jacket, each six months older.

"Where do you see yourself in five years," Bunny asked. "Still writing up middle school Volleyball games?"

"No," Drew said. "I'd like to do more investigative reporting and photojournalism. Hopefully here," he added, taking a chance.

"*He's getting ready to suggest employment at another paper. Make sure to ask him for a letter of recommendation.*"

"There's plenty of room for advancement here," Bunny said. "If you're a team player. I've seen too many reporters go rogue, chasing after some cause or trying to run down some conspiracy theory. We don't need crusaders here."

"No sir," Drew said. "No crusaders."

Bunny laughed. "I'll get to the point. I'm transferring you to the political section. You'll be working under Teejay Edmunds."

Drew was so shocked at not being fired he almost lost his balance. He quickly grabbed the back of the empty chair in front of him as if he meant to. Although he wasn't being fired, a transfer was, in his mind, a demotion, a last chance before a final dismissal. "I don't understand Sir," he said, stammering a little. "Are my articles not up to snuff? Did Crimmons complain about me?"

Bunny waved his cigar as if trying to dispel Drew's doubts. "Relax," he said. "It's not a demotion. I like your articles. They're well-written and cover all aspects of the games you report on; with a little humor thrown in. Since George Cousins left for a job with the Tampa Bay Times, Teejay is short a reporter. We talked it over, and we think you might make a good replacement, with enough grooming, that is." He looked over at Teejay, who nodded, albeit with a distasteful glance at Drew's appearance. His eyes went down to his shoes and back up again.

"See! Did you see him give you the once over?"

Drew struggled not to respond to his brother. Teejay noticed Drew's hesitation. "Is that okay with you, young man? Or would you rather stay in Joe Crimmon's section?"

"No, no, I'm fine with that," Drew stammered. "I just hope that I can live up to your expectations."

Teejay looked at him for a moment more and then looked at Bunny, his eyebrows raised a little.

Bunny cleared his throat. "I also have a special task in mind for you; a mission, if you will."

"Sir?' Drew said.

"Take a seat," Bunny said. Drew sat in the second chair, glancing a little nervously at his new boss, Teejay Edmunds, who was evaluating him through half-lidded eyes, the smoke from his cigarette curling up into his nostrils as he inhaled.

"You know that the governor, Tommy Thompson, is probably headed to Washington." Bunny said. "He's on the Party's shortlist for vice president. Rumors are strong that Senator Frank Sheridan, the Party's nominee for president, is going to name Thompson as his running mate soon."

"Yessir," Drew said. He stopped himself from saying "everybody knows that" just in time. Bunny was a known kingmaker in the city, the county, and even the state. Nothing went on in politics that Bunny didn't know about and, rumor had it, his influence extended to many high-level decisions within the Party.

"You may not know it, but we helped put Tommy Thompson in the state capitol," Bunny said, enjoying his cigar. "And we'll help him all we can in his Washington adventure. When the governor's chair is empty, I want one of our people in it. I've decided that John McNair is the man for the job."

"The mayor," Drew said. "I see it: war hero and progressive mayor; nice looking family. I think he could do quite well in the gubernatorial."

"We think so too," Bunny said, drawing gently on his cigar. "But he needs some work, and that's where you come in."

"Sir?" Drew said, a little taken aback. "I..."

Bunny stopped him with a wave of his hand. "Some journalistic work. He needs to be in the news more, and in a favorable light. He's notoriously private, so I need someone to get close to him. Someone who can gain his trust."

Bunny paused a moment to let his words sink in. He took a sip of his scotch and looked over at Teejay for a moment. Then he continued.

"You'll be working closely with Teejay and reporting directly to me. I want news stories, back stories, photographs, that sort of thing. I also need him vetted."

Drew felt like a deer caught in the headlights of an oncoming car and he was sure that his face showed it.

Bunny laughed. "Coming at you a little fast, am I?" he said. "People – especially my wife – tell me I do that." He set his cigar in an ashtray and put both hands on his desk, leaning slightly forward as he did so. "You went to USF, so did he. You were both in the same fraternity. You play golf, tennis, and racquetball. So does he."

"John McNair is at least fifteen years older than I am," Drew said. "I have no idea how I could make a connection with him."

Bunny stopped him again, a mischievous twinkle in his eye. It was not lost on Drew that Bunny was having a good time at his expense.

"So, here it is," Bunny said, suddenly transformed into the icy business-man he was most known for. "You're to hang around campus as much as you can. I've had you registered for a couple of grad courses. You don't have to attend. Missus Zimmer has all the paperwork and a student ID. See her on your way out. Go to that college bar, The Library, and make some friends. Stop by the frat house when you feel comfortable. Find out every-thing you can about John McNair's past. We don't need any surprises. We'll clean up what we can if we have to and get NDAs if we need to. Everything. You understand?"

Drew nodded.

"Next," Bunny said, his words coming sharp as lasers. "I want you to follow him to every event he attends. Get some favorable pictures. He be-longs to the Brantwood Country Club and golfs on Tuesdays and Thurs-days when he can. He also plays racquetball and tennis. Get your game on. Missus Zimmer has your membership card on her desk. He attends the Brantwood Fellowship on Sundays. You're familiar with the church?"

Familiar with the Brantwood Fellowship? How could anyone in Brant-wood not be. It was a non-denominational megachurch housed in a former athletic stadium. Completely refurbished and redesigned, it stood on a rise above the city and the bay, its modern white masonry and glass exterior, towering steeple and massive gold cross gleamed in the sun like a beacon. At night it was lit by hundreds of lights, making it look like a sparkling gem. The pastor and his wife, Corey and Elizabeth Deschamps, were national celebrities who made guest appearances on dozens of talk shows, religious fundraisers and news broadcasts. Their pictures graced the covers of magazines, newspapers, billboards and benches and busses. They had a nationally syndicated Sunday sermon broadcast all over the country. Thousands of people traveled hundreds of miles to attend the sermons every week, given by the handsome and charismatic minister. Drew had never been.

"Yes sir, quite a show, I'm told." Drew managed.

"You'll be there every Sunday, dressed appropriately," Bunny said, giving Drew another appraising look.

It was Drew's turn to be icy. He might be immature, but he was no patsy. He felt like he was somehow being set up but didn't know how or why. "How did I get all of this?" he said.

"Hmm?" Bunny said.

"How did I get enough money to belong to a country club? People know me. And they know how much a freshman reporter makes."

Bunny allowed himself a slight chortle. "We've got that covered," he said. "You got a healthy endowment from a rich aunt who wants to kick-start your career by putting you in all the right places. She knows that contacts are everything in this business and wants to see you do well. We've given her a small write-up in the next Sunday Supplement concerning her tireless and generous efforts in humanitarian causes. In the interview she mentions her aspiring young nephew."

"But sir, my aunt died, and she wasn't rich."

Bunny stopped him with another, now familiar wave of his hand. "You took no courses in fiction in college?" He asked with a raised eyebrow.

Drew swallowed hard and nodded.

Bunny laughed at the young man's discomfiture. "Get yourself some clothes," he said. "Missus Zimmer has a card for you. My personal tailor. Couple of suits, some polo shirts and khaki pants and shorts, that type of thing. You'll have a line of credit. Do some research. Wear what he wears, but not exactly. Wash your shirts and steam iron them. You don't want them to look too new."

"Yessir," Drew managed. He knew that he looked bewildered and knew that Bunny was enjoying it.

"You're staying at your apartment near campus?"

Drew nodded.

"What are you driving?"

Drew swallowed hard; it was obvious that Bunny already knew that he was driving an old Volvo with a muffler problem. He said nothing.

Bunny laughed, leaned back in his chair and picked up his cigar again. "Missus Zimmer also has my wife's card for you. Call the number and arrange to meet her at my garage. She'll find something a little more appropriate for you to drive."

"Thank you, sir," Drew managed without too much of a stammer.

"Now, on to other matters," Bunny said, he looked once at Drew and then once at Teejay. "Our reporter was too sick this morning to get anything out of Mick Murphy, and I don't want to cash in a favor by calling him. When you go to the James, find out what you can about the body that washed up on the beach this morning. My instincts tell me that there was more to it than a simple boat fire."

"Will do," Teejay said. He glanced over at Drew. "Go get your stuff moved. I'll see you in a few minutes. Oh, bye-the-way, the mayor drinks Heineken, and he likes the Yankees."

"Yessir," Drew said weakly as he stood and walked to the door. "I'll try to remember that." He opened the door, closed it behind him and walked up to Missus Zimmer's desk like a chastened student approaching the front desk in school.

"Here you are," she said, handing him a packet. "Don't screw this up," she said with a scolding look on her face. "You don't want to get on the wrong side of Bunny Bunstall."

"Yes mam," Drew said.

"Yankees!" Drew mumbled to himself as he walked down the stairwell, the packet tucked under his arm. "I hate the Yankees!"

"Learn to love 'em," Peter said.

Drew had a thought. He went past the pressroom door and down to the basement where he retrieved a large cardboard box from a pile waiting to be broken down, then he walked back upstairs to the pressroom door. As he opened it and entered the room, he heard a loud "Whoop!" from Joe Crimmon's direction.

"Whad' I tell ya!" Crimmons exclaimed as Drew walked across the floor, cardboard box in hand. Drew tried to muster as much dejection in his manner as he could.

"Clean out your locker, Honcho." Crimmons said gleefully, popping his gum. He turned to the rest of the people in the room and announced loudly: "Pay up, assholes! Daddy's got a hot date tonight!"

"Leave the kid alone, Crimmons," someone said acidly. People began lining up, paying Crimmons for the bets they'd laid.

"Sorry, Kid" someone said, patting him on the back as he walked by.

"You'll be better off not having assholes like Crimmons to harass you," another said.

Drew had just finished filling his cardboard box when he noticed that everyone was slowly getting back to work. It was always, well, almost always, sad when someone got pink slipped.

Drew hefted his box and headed towards the door, maintaining the look of dejection he'd managed to hold for the last few minutes.

"Hey, where are you going, Kid?" Teejay exclaimed from his desk. "The political section's over here!"

Drew smiled and changed direction. He stole a glance at Joe Crimmons. The big man sat with his mouth open, staring at Teejay in disbelief. His shirt had risen above his pants, exposing a fish-belly beer gut. Drew closed his eyes once to imprint image on his mind. Somebody began clapping and others picked it up. Soon, he was getting a standing ovation. Except for Joe.

"Get settled," Teejay said as Drew arrived at his new desk. "We've got lunch in fifteen."

CHAPTER THREE

"WHAT WENT WRONG WITH the extraction?" The man said mildly. A microphone on his desk was pointed at another man, who sat leaning forward, his elbows on his knees. He was a little shaken. It was his partner and his investigation, and something had gone horribly wrong.

"He must have gotten made. I got the extraction code late in the afternoon and put the plan into motion immediately. But it was probably already too late."

"Your extraction plan was?"

"He'd get a burn on his arm and call for an ambulance. I'd come in with the EMTs and bring him home. At gunpoint, if necessary."

"Hm, fast, effective and foolproof. Almost."

"His phone went dark right after I got the code. He didn't even have time to make the 911 call and, without one, the EMTs couldn't enter the facility. I had to hope that he would find a way to make the call, but it never came."

"Alright, I want you to stay on this with extreme interest. You have contacts in the city?"

He shrugged. "A couple of EMT's we were using for the extraction. We've got some minor stuff on them; sufficient to make them nervous enough to cooperate. I got to them through DMs. They don't know what I look like or sound like. They share a cabin at a refurbished fishing camp attached to a tavern out in the boonies. Couple of goofballs that take pics at accident sites and show them around at the bar. One of the regulars is the son of the owner of the plant. We might be able to lean on him."

"I trust you'll do everything you can. No stone unturned."

He stood and wiped his sweaty hands on his pants. "You can count on it."

"Whoever did this will be expecting us to come at them hard and will be extremely watchful. Lay back a bit and observe everything. When you find out who did it, let me know. We'll give you every resource you need."

He nodded at the Director once, turned and walked to the door.

"One way or the other," the Director reiterated. "You have complete immunity on this. Do whatever is necessary. I don't like losing agents any more than you do."

He turned the knob on the door, looked over his shoulder and nodded. He opened the door and walked out.

CHAPTER FOUR

Lᴜɴᴄʜ ᴡᴀs ᴀᴛ Tʜᴇ Jᴀᴍᴇs, an Irish Pub named for James Joyce. It was across the street from the courthouse and catered to judges, lawyers, cops, and reporters on their lunch breaks. Drew remembered having had lunch there with his father once, during better days. On the drive over, Peter lectured him extensively on his behavior during the interview.

"You fidgeted and stammered, like a kid caught stealing candy!"

"You wouldn't have? Those are the two biggest personalities at the paper, and in the town!"

"Still, they put their pants on…"

"I know, I know, but what could I have done differently?"

"Acted more confident, more professional. Walk in, say good morning, shake their hands, sit down and ask them 'what can I do for you."

Drew laughed out loud, drawing a weird look from the driver in the next lane. "Right, I get it. 'Hey Teej, Hi Bun, how they hangin'? Help myself to a glass of scotch, light a joint. Sit down and put my feet up on Bunny's desk."

"It's what I would have done."

Drew laughed out loud again as he pulled into a parking space half a block down from The James. It was a bright morning, hot and humid and he was sweating again. He walked past a shop that sold dresses, a newsstand with several metal boxes containing the morning papers, and a portable hot dog stand under an umbrella. A small line had formed in front of the stand, and he had to make his way through it. Seagulls circled and hopped on the hot cement, looking for stray bits of food. He saw the owner slathering mustard on a hot dog in a bun and handing it to a customer. The pleasant smell of the cooking hot dogs reminded him of playing baseball in the park when he was a kid. A nice memory from an earlier time.

When he arrived at the tavern Teejay was waiting for him at the door (valet parking?) It was a stone building with a large oak door and a green awning. Teejay opened the door and gestured for Drew to enter. "After you, young man."

The bar was bustling, glasses were clinking, and there was a cacophony of voices, shouting, laughing, and whispering. The heady smell of whisky suffused the tavern, its dark wood beams, bar, and furniture evoking its Tudor decor. Where's the smoke? There should be smoke – cigars and cigarettes – but of course there's no smoking in bars anymore. Smoke would make the scene complete: back-room politics with deals made and broken in whispers.

"*Welcome to your new world, Kiddo. I hope you're ready for it.*"

Teejay made his way towards the bar, Drew following behind, like a little kid trying to keep up with a grown-up. Teejay had a handshake and a smile for everyone he passed. He introduced Drew to them with a quick: "My protégé, R.J. Andrews." Everyone seemed friendly enough and maybe just a little drunk. Sheesh, Drew thought. It's only eleven O'clock.

"*You can't drink all day unless you start early,*"

"You'd know," Drew thought back. Teejay looked at him funny. Had he said it out loud?

"What'll it be, young man?" Teejay said in his slightly affected New Orleans accent as they reached the bar. The bartender, a short, stocky man with flame-red hair and beard, wore a white shirt, a black tie, and a friendly smile. Teejay called him Sean and put a bill on the bar. He turned to Drew.

"Name your poison."

"Beer. A Heineken," Drew said, remembering what the mayor drank. Teejay nodded approvingly.

They mingled. Teejay introduced him around to more people. There was Mick Murphy, the chief of police, Will Tyler, the city court judge, and assorted lawyers, politicians, and businessmen; Drew could sense that they were all in the loop, whatever exactly the loop was. He realized now that it was his job to figure out the tangled web that was Brantwood's political world. It reminded him of the ancient story of the Gordian knot. It was so tangled that no one could untie it. Legend had it that whoever solved the knot would rule the world. Alexander the Great looked at it, drew his sword and cut it. It occurred to him that Bunny had solved the Gordian Knot of Brantwood.

"Or is he the one that tied it in the first place?"

Drew drifted around for a while, nodding, and smiling. But he could sense that no one considered him important enough to buttonhole. Teejay could see that his new protégé was cast adrift and decided to throw him a lifeline. He motioned for Drew to join him.

"This is how it works, Kid," Teejay said, a secretive tone creeping into his voice. "You get to know these guys, treat them right in your write-ups and they'll give you all kinds of great stuff, although much of it you can't print."

"Why not?" Drew said.

"Because that's not how it's done. You make your friends look good and your enemies look bad. Quid pro quo."

"I get it," Drew said. "But what about an impartial press?"

"That's an impartial *jury*," Teejay said. "The press can do whatever it wants. But a newspaper's business isn't reporting the news. A newspaper's business is selling papers."

"Yeah, I'm familiar with Hearst and Pulitzer. But I thought our paper held its reporters to a higher standard than yellow journalism."

"And it does, Kid. News is a part of the political process; always has been, always will be. Politicians have their agendas and newspapers do too. It becomes a matter of how we portray events and in what context. But equally important is how our readers see the events we report on. We don't alter the facts, that would be irresponsible. But we do consider our readers' sensibilities when we report; otherwise, we lose them."

"Don't report what they don't want to read?" Drew said, a little taken aback at the direction the conversation was taking.

Teejay sipped his Manhattan and tilted his glass towards Drew, emphasizing his point. "FDR was a cripple, but you never saw pictures of him with his braces. There was economic depression and war and the public wanted to see a strong president. Kennedy had multiple affairs, but they were never reported on 'till long after his death."

"So, what's our narrative?" Drew asked. "What's our moral compass at the Journal?"

"Bunny," Teejay said. "He's the owner and senior editor. Nothing gets printed that doesn't cross his desk."

Drew nodded and sipped his beer. The noise in the room was almost deafening but he could see that Teejay kept his ear cocked for scraps of useful information. Teejay was the type of person who noticed things that others didn't.

"This is a network for most, a place to make deals or curry favor with a lawyer or judge. And it's not always what's said – it's often what *isn't*. See that guy there – don't look directly – the one talking with the zoning officer, Bob Draggett?"

Drew pretended to rub his forehead and stole a glance. He recognized the man right away. He was Guy Francesco, a local real estate developer. Drew had seen his face on billboards all over town under a banner that read: "Bellissima Estates – Make Your Dream Happen."

"Recognize him? Teejay said.

Drew nodded.

Teejay leaned in closer. "Draggett's been acting nervous all morning. He's usually the first to run up and glad hand me, trying to give me his narrative on some deal he's working on. But today, he's been avoiding me like the plague. I'd like to know why. The word is that Francesco needs to drain some low ground for more houses, but I already knew that. Something else is going on with him." Teejay caught Draggett's eye and tilted his glass towards him in a mock toast. Draggett nervously returned the gesture, but then quickly glanced away.

"Did you see that?" Teejay said. "He's nervous as hell."

"Do you suspect that he knows that you know about the land drainage?" Drew asked.

Teejay shook his head. "He told me about it last week. Francesco got the land cheap but it's wet. Trouble is, he would need to alter a feeder stream to do it. Part of the stream flows through the city border and city environmental regulations won't allow it."

"If the city won't allow it, what good will talking to the zoning officer do? Draggett can't ignore those regs."

"The land will be drained," Teejay explained. "Probably at night by some private sub-contractor. If he's caught Francesco will pay his fine. Houses will be built, people will buy and, when the stream reverts to its natural flow, their sump pumps will run continuously."

"Okay, got it," Drew said. "But, at the risk of sounding naïve, why talk to Draggett at all?"

"Kid, money, information and influence change hands all the time in this town. It greases wheels and keeps things moving forward. If it's discovered that a stream has been altered, there'll be a fine on the subcontractor which will be quickly paid. But there'll be no investigation by the city. Bob Draggett will see to it if Francesco can meet his price."

"Sounds corrupt," Drew said, immediately regretting having said it.

"Think ahead, stupid, don't blurt things out."

"Define corruption."

"Taking money or favors to ignore a violation."

"The seller gets paid for marginal land that was unused, the building contractors' profit, the workers get paid, Francesco sells houses to willing buyers who won't have to fire up their sump-pumps for years to come, and the city collects taxes."

"And Draggett gets enough of a payoff to keep his failing hardware store going for a few more months."

"There you have it, Kid. Life goes on. Unless somebody crosses Bunny."

Drew raised a quizzical eyebrow.

"That's his power. Information. He saves it like cash and uses it only when he has to."

"And if someone doesn't play along?"

"Expose` with a banner headline."

Drew took a deep breath. He looked around the room with new eyes.

"I know what you're thinking, Kid," Teejay said. "I was once young and idealistic too. But this city has flourished under Bunny's influence: good jobs, clean streets, nice parks and thriving businesses. So what if a few corners are cut, a few regulations ignored, a few laws bent?" Teejay paused and took a thoughtful sip of his drink. He looked Drew in the eye. "What does it say beneath our banner?"

"All the news that's fit to print," Drew answered. He hesitated a moment as the light bulb in his head flickered. "And who decides what's fit to print?"

"Exactly, Bunny Bunstall." Teejay said. He clinked his glass against Drew's bottle and drank off the contents. Drew did the same. He had the unsettling feeling that he was becoming part of something that he wasn't prepared for. Teejay moved around the room, a comment or joke for everyone he encountered. Drew drifted, nodding, and smiling and trying not to seem like a clueless freshman reporter.

A little later, Drew recognized one of his high school buddies, Jack Truax, now a lieutenant with the city police department.

"Hey, Truax," Drew said as he greeted his old friend. He was medium built and carried a certain military bearing left over from his time in the MPs. Truax smiled and shook his hand.

"I knew you'd end up working for some paper," he said. "You always had a camera and a notepad in school."

"Got me out of a lot of classes," Drew said. "No teacher wants an impromptu picture and quote for the school newspaper. They'd run away when they saw me coming."

"That's because of your cartoons. Remember how pissed Mr. Williams was when you drew him asleep at his desk? What was the caption?"

Drew shook his head, remembering. "Are snores measured in metric or standard?"

"Yeah, that was it. Laughed my ass off at that one. He was a real tool."

Truax had been a wrestler, Drew remembered. Totally dedicated. He was always in the gym working out. "When I'm in the shower, after a workout, I wonder what my upcoming opponent is doing," he often said. "Is he in the shower too, or is he still working out? That's why a lot of times I'll go back into the gym for a couple more sets."

The two talked about old times for a little while longer. Then Drew changed the subject.

"How is it, working for Mick Murphy?"

Truax gave him a funny look. "Don't quote me, but he's got more deals going than Drew Carey. He's got the judge in his pocket, along with half the city council members. Everybody in the department thinks he's got something on them."

"What do you think?"

"I'm not paid to think. But half the investigations I put on his desk never leave it. I asked him once, when I first made lieutenant, about one of the cases I'd submitted. "On going," he said. "Need more evidence before we can bring it before the judge." Truax laughed and sipped his soda water – he was on duty. "I never asked again," he said.

"So, you must be sitting on a lot of juicy stuff," Drew said casually. He liked Truax well and found him to be a trustworthy friend. The two had gotten away with a few harmless escapades in high school, skipping class, pulling pranks, that sort of thing, and they had often covered for each other when things got sticky. He began to think that maybe they could cooperate a little now; nothing illegal or unethical, just a few heads up now and then. He looked expectantly at his friend, wondering if his mind was traveling the same path.

"Yeah," Truax said thoughtfully. "I've got a lot of stuff that can't be printed yet, stuff that you could get a scoop on when an investigation starts or when an indictment is about to be served. We had a big one this morning," he added softly, looking around slightly to see if he was being overheard.

"We're off the record here," Drew said, noticing his friend's hesitation.

He knew that this was not the last time he'd use that phrase. A quid pro quo would be in order, of course, again, nothing illegal or unethical, but something that might help sway an issue in the court of public opinion.

"That's it, Kiddo! Now you're starting to think like Bunny. 'All the news that fits!'

"All the news that's fit," Drew said, not meaning to say it out loud. Truax nodded, mistaking Drew's meaning. "Look, that body we found this morning at the beach? The one your guy covered. Turns out he was an undercover FBI agent."

"No shit! What was he investigating?"

"No idea. An agent was at the morgue when we got there. He was pretty upset. The guy must have called for an extraction from whatever he was doing. Must have had his cover blown somehow." He gave Drew a serious look. "That can't be printed but keep your ear to the ground."

"Got you," Drew said. "I'm learning a lot about what can be printed and what can't."

They parted company, promising to get together for a few beers some time.

CHAPTER FIVE

A MAZE OF MANGROVES hung over the car as it proceeded slowly down a single lane road, leaves and branches brushing it on the curves. The tires crunched on the crushed seashell pavement and the sun flashed through breaks in the trees. Surprised ibis and herons took flight and raccoons and an occasional armadillo clattered into the brush. The driver opened his window and stuck his head partway out to look ahead at the narrow, curving road. Hot air invaded the cabin and flooded it with the stink of the salt marsh.

"Are you sure you know where this place is Al?" the woman sitting in the passenger seat asked the driver. "We've been out in these mangroves for a while."

"Pretty sure, Cindy," he said. "Based on the information I got. It's off the grid, so the GPS doesn't work. But I think I can find it."

They were a couple on vacation and out for lunch. They rode in a mid-sized SUV with a loaded cargo rack on the top. Several stickers on the back window announced places they had visited. There was a series of white outlines of different sized children's silhouettes and a soccer ball. They were both married, but not to each other.

After a while they rounded a bend in the road which led to a small parking lot, paved with white crushed shell. Behind it there was a group of small cabins and thatched sun shelters. There was a one-story building with a deck and pane-glass windows that looked out over a large cove. Above the doorway there was a hand painted sign on a weathered plank, "You Found It! The Lost Cove!"

They parked the car, got out and walked across the crunching crushed seashells in a simmering heat that took your breath away. A large woman with a red face and strawberry hair piled on her head in an impossible twist opened the door and came out onto the landing.

"Are you lost or did someone prank you into thinking this was a restaurant?" she shouted. "If you were, I'd suggest you turn around now, before it's too late!"

Al put on a carefree face and smiled. "So, you're the cook then?"

The woman laughed, a cackle. "Well, you might as well come in, now that you're here," she said. "I'm Janice and it's my job to make sure you don't forget me." She stood aside for them to enter. She smelled strongly of perfume, tequila and clove cigarettes.

Inside was a series of interconnected rooms that used to be part of a private residence. Thick wads of dollar bills covered the walls, each with an inscription in various colors of sharpies. A U-shaped bar looked out over the cove. The bay could be seen through gaps in the distance. Janice took them to the bar and shouted at the bartender, who was standing right in front of her. "Customers!" she said in an exaggerated fashion that implied that customers were a rarity. The bartender smiled and said, "Welcome to the Lost Cove. I'm Chaz Tasker, can I get you something to drink?"

Al ordered a Red Stripe and Cindy ordered a martini.

"Who do we see about renting a cabin," Al said. He sipped his beer and looked around the room casually.

"I can do that for you," Chaz said. "It's off-season, so we've got a few vacancies. I'll have Stacy show you them and you can take your pick. How long will you be staying?"

"A few days, at least," Al said. "Maybe a week or two. We've heard good things, haven't we Hon?"

Cindy nodded. "Nice place to relax and great seafood."

"You heard right," Chaz said with an easy smile. He extended his hand to Al, who shook it.

"Nice to meet you, Chaz," he said. He settled on a stool and watched the Fishing Channel, which was being played on a large flatscreen above the bar. Cindy enjoyed the view of the cove, with its dock and parked boats. A little while later young girl a little past college age, approached them. She was dressed in shorts and a tank top and a ball cap with a blonde ponytail out the back. "Hi, I'm Stacy," she said with a smile. "Chaz messaged me that you're interested in a cabin?"

"That's right," Cindy said. "We're on vacation for a while. My parents have the kids." She finished her martini, smiled and stood.

"I understand," Stacy said. "Right this way." She walked to the door and held it open for them, a ring of keys in her hand. Cindy and Al followed.

"Cabins five, seven and twelve are all vacant until next Monday. They're reserved after that. Fishing tournament. Number fourteen hasn't been reserved yet."

"Let's see number fourteen," Al said. "We might stay a little while, if Cindy's parents can keep their wits, that is."

Stacy laughed and walked them over to number fourteen. It had a screened-in porch with a view of the cove, the dock, and the restaurant.

"Perfect," Al said. Cindy gave him a look and nodded.

Stacy walked up to the porch, opened the screen door, walked in, and unlocked the main door. She clicked on the lights and held the door open for them. Inside was a cozy living room with a couch, a coffee table and a couple of sitting chairs. A TV sat on a stand. There was a small dining area, a kitchenette and two bedrooms. It was stuffy and smelled faintly of cleaning fluid. She twisted the knob of the air-conditioner and clicked on the fan. Cool air rushed into the room.

Cindy smiled. "We'll take it," she said, looking expectantly at Al.

"Two weeks," he said. "Think that'll be okay with your parents?"

"Sure," she said. "They're taking the kids to Disney," she explained, looking at Stacy. "We'll pay for the two weeks and if we have to leave early, we'll leave early." She sincerely hoped that they could get their work done as quickly as possible. It was a challenge to look like a happy housewife after what had happened. They took the key, walked over to the car, got in, started the engine, and drove it over to the cabin. They got settled and returned to the restaurant. After another drink at the bar, Janice seated them at a table by the window.

"Any recommendations?" Cindy asked. She looked down at a small slip of hand-lettered paper.

"Yeah, get out while you can," Janice said, cackling. Pleased with herself, she walked over to her perch on a stool by the door. A few minutes later, Stacy walked up to the table. She was wearing no apron and had neither an order pad nor a pen. "I'll take care of your orders when you're ready," she said. "Can I recommend a few items? The Key West Pink Shrimp is fresh this morning, it's done with a lime-chili glaze and served with saffron rice, The Jerk Chicken is one of our specialties, it comes with red beans and rice. The Grouper, Mahi, Tuna and Snapper are all harpooned, not netted. And let's not forget our famous Conch Fritters, served with a Caribbean dipping sauce."

"I'm surprised you don't have more items on the menu," Cindy said.

Al gave Cindy a sharp look and looked back at Stacy. "My wife can be a little picky," he said.

"If I was picky, I wouldn't be here with you," Cindy said. It was hard to tell if her comment was a rebuke or a joke.

"Oh, these are just the specials," Stacy said without skipping a beat. "You can get just about anything you want off menu. We've got steaks, chops, burgers, pasta. You name it. Rich Reynolds, our chef, will make anything you want to order." She paused for a moment to let that sink in. "Another round of drinks?" she said turning towards the bar without waiting for an answer.

When she returned with the drinks, they were ready to order.

"I do have one question though, before we start," Al said. He looked around as if to see if anyone was listening. "Janice is a hoot, but is she hard to work for?"

"Oh, I don't work for her, she works for me. My parents own the place. Janice runs it when we're traveling, which is often. She was working here when they bought it and she kind of came with the place."

They ordered their food, with Cindy making many adjustments. Stacy smiled and nodded but wrote nothing down. Twenty minutes later, she returned with the orders exactly as requested. As they ate a seaplane came in for a landing. Al knew it to be a completely refurbished DeHavilland Beaver, a plane built for pond jumping, which Willard had done in Alaska before being recruited to work for Jack Van Ness. It taxied over to the dock and two workers with large two-wheeled carts approached the plane. One of them was dressed in pink shorts, a pink tank top and pink sneakers. The pilot climbed out of the cockpit and jumped lightly onto the dock. He was tan and fit with a shock of unruly yellow hair just starting to go grey and a bright, snaggle toothed grin. He looked to Al more like a beach bum than someone who used to work for Jack Van Ness.

"My father," Stacy explained as she came to check on their meals. "Just in from Key West with a load of fresh seafood."

"Nice plane," Al said. "A Beaver?"

"Yep," Stacy said. "It's a ball to fly. It can take off or land on a dime."

"You fly?" Cindy asked, trying to sound incredulous.

"Had my license since I was sixteen," Stacy said. "Food okay?"

"Delicious," Cindy said. Al nodded his agreement.

CHAPTER SIX

Drew emerged from The James, blinded by the harsh afternoon sunlight. After two hours in the dark pub, his eyes weren't accustomed to the brightness. He squinted. "Find anything out about that body?" Drew said, certain that Teejay had. He had seen him talking to Mick Murphy for quite a while.

Teejay shook his head. "Murphy was very evasive about it. He's like that. There must be a quid pro quo for him, and I had nothing to give him. Must be something to it though, or he wouldn't have acted that way."

"FBI," Drew said. "Doing some kind of under-cover work."

Teejay raised his eyebrows and looked at Drew. "What was he investigating?"

"Don't know...yet. I'll let you know when I find out."

Teejay knew enough not to ask Drew his source, and Drew knew enough not to reveal it.

"Well, good work," Teejay said, clapping Drew on the shoulder. "Maybe Bunny's instincts about you were right after all."

"Maybe," Drew said, a little insulted by the comment. But he let it go. He had much yet to do and the hours were draining away from the day.

"Take the afternoon off and get some things done," Teejay said as they parted company.

Drew found his car and drove to The New York Store where Bunny had given him a line of credit. It was a high-end men's clothing store that Drew had never been in, and he was a little nervous about it. Coming from a middle-class family, Drew had always had a chip on his shoulder when he was around people of a higher status. He knew it was silly to resent them their privilege, but it still rankled him to see their expensive cars, their designer clothing, and their luxury homes in exclusive neighborhoods. The way they walked, talked, and carried themselves bespoke a certain elitism meant to separate them from ordinary people like himself. Soon Peter was back in his head again.

"A line of credit, membership in a posh country club and a car to borrow. You've finally hit the big time, Kiddo! Now it's your turn to look down your nose at us common folk."

"You had the same opportunity," Drew said. "You were in college and on your way to an engineering degree, but you couldn't keep it together."

"You're only barely keeping it together yourself, and you didn't see what I saw."

"True, but I'm aware of what happened. Remember how they took me out of class that day? It was an art class, I remember. We were learning how to use oil-based paint; the smell still triggers my memory of the principal standing at the door, gesturing for me to come out into the hall. "Drew, your aunt is here," she said without explaining. The long walk down the hall without knowing what had happened but realizing that somehow my life had changed. Then Aunt Jane in the office, "Drew, I'm afraid I have some terrible news. What she said next haunts me to this day."

"Right, who takes the news of their parent's deaths lightly. But the guilt of having caused it, that's what haunts me."

"You shouldn't blame yourself; she would have found out anyway. She was probably already suspicious." Drew felt a tightening in his chest and his breathing became labored. Talks with Peter and the memories that came along with them always put him in a state of anxiety. He tried control his breathing and concentrate on his driving. A memory came to mind of an early fall day. There was a fresh breeze that brought the salt-water smell of the ocean; the sky was sunny and there were a few cotton ball clouds drifting over the palms. He began to relax a little and the tightness in his chest eased. His breathing returned to normal. Peter – early, healthy Peter – and he were tossing a frisbee back and forth. Was there a dog running back and forth, trying to intercept the frisbee? Sure, why not? When you're making up pleasant memories to crowd out the painful ones, you can have a dog. A Golden Retriever? Drew laughed. Yeah, a Golden Retriever with a red bandana tied around its neck. Name? How about Rex? No, too cliché. Tucker, that's what I'll call him. Drew smiled as he pulled into a parking space near the store.

Inside, Drew picked out some khakis, polo shirts of different colors, and white dress shirts. The manager, whose name was Jerry, and who was short, bald, and efficient, fitted him for his dress clothes, which would be ready by Thursday, he promised. Shoes! I need shoes too, he thought. He picked out a pair of black leather dress shoes, a pair of brown leather loafers and a pair of deck shoes. After an hour or so, Drew thanked the manager, who was busy totaling the purchases. Jerry called him Mister Andrews and thanked him back. Drew left and headed towards the Bunstall Estate.

Drew knew Mrs. Bunstall to be a legend in her own right. Who didn't? Her maiden name was Gloria Dodson, and she was the daughter of the international fashion magnate, Charles Dodson. He was twice divorced and doted on his daughter. He sent her to all the best private schools and colleges where she studied finance, art, acting and, her passion, equestrianism. She was beautiful and soon began modeling her father's brand. Before long she became the face of the company and was featured in every major fashion magazine in the country; her fame even landed her a few acting roles. She had a very public romance and marriage with a famous baseball player, which got her even more attention from the press. She and her husband began taking up charitable causes and launched a foundation, the Dodson Fund. Unfortunately, the marriage that seemed so perfect dissolved when the baseball player got caught with an underage girl while on a team road trip. When the marriage foundered, so did the foundation. That's when Bunny Bunstall came into the picture.

Bunny had a foundation of his own and, having met Gloria on several occasions at charitable events, heard of her situation. He suggested that they merge the two funds. They got on well and, as Bunny was single again for the third time, they merged also. Gloria managed the foundation and the estate. She worked closely with the city's parks commission and oversaw beautification programs and the development of parks and walkways. She was seen as an icon of culture in Brantwood, and her husband gave her much favorable press in the Brantwood Journal. But dark rumors swirled. It was said that she and Bunny had an open marriage and that each had secret affairs. Drew, of course, had heard the office rumors about Bunny's private elevator that ran from his garage in the basement of the Journal to the suite of rooms that were adjacent to his office. It was whispered that he spent most of his weeknights there, welcoming a succession of beautiful escorts to keep him company. Gloria, thirty years his junior, had yet to have her beauty touched by age. She spent her time working on her fund, managing the lavish Bunstall estate and riding her magnificent stable of thoroughbred horses. One could only imagine that she had her own stable of lovers too. Or so it was said.

Drew parked his car near the carriage house where Mrs. Bunstall had an office. He checked his phone and saw that he was right on time, for a change. As he looked around, he saw another building with a corral and a large field enclosed by hundreds of yards of white fencing. Several horses grazed languidly in the distance. The smell of horse, hay and manure was strong in the air.

As he went to ring the bell next to the door a voice came through a speaker, "Come in, Mr. Andrews," a woman's voice said. "It's unlocked."

As he entered, he saw that he was in a large and well-appointed carriage house room. There were comfortable chairs, a bar and a refrigerator and a large screen TV. The walls tastefully displayed paintings of horses. He noticed that the paintings were signed 'Gloria Dodson.' There was an easel set up next to a window that overlooked the pasture. Drew absently hoped that she used acrylics instead of oils. She was sitting in a chair, a flute of champagne in one hand and a riding crop in the other. She was easily the most beautiful woman Drew had ever seen.

"You hit the jackpot, Buddy! Careful though, she looks as though she could burn you down."

Shut up! Drew said, for once remembering not to speak to Peter out loud. Peter laughed.

"Help yourself to a drink, if you like," Mrs. Bunstall said. Drew noticed that her voice was low and husky, the results of a hard ride, he thought. She gestured towards the bar with the riding crop. She was dressed in riding clothes: short black jacket, white jodhpurs, and black riding boots. Her hair was loose, and her helmet sat on the table in front of her. Her face was tinged with red, and she appeared slightly out of breath.

That's what I need, Drew said to himself. Another drink.

"I'd have one," Peter insisted.

Sure, you would, Drew thought. You'd have two. He went to the well-stocked refrigerator, selected a beer, and twisted off the cap.

"Have a seat, Mr. Andrews," Mrs. Bunstall said. "And please call me Gloria." Drew took a sip of his beer and sat down across the table from her. He noticed that she smelled of horse and a faint, musky perfume.

"I'm afraid you'll have to excuse me," she said. "I've just come in from a ride and I'm a little unkempt."

"Not at all," Drew managed, shifting nervously in his chair. He took another long swallow to ease his nerves and wash away the tight feeling that had somehow appeared in his throat.

"What kind of car do you like?" she asked, looking at him appraisingly.

"Well," Drew began, thinking the question over. "I guess a Porsche. Someday I'd like to own one."

Mrs. Bunstall chortled lightly, almost spitting out her champagne. "Yes," she said, regaining her composure. "Porches are nice. Bunny has several. But what you need is a car that is sporty but not flashy, one that says money but not too much and not your own. An endowment from your aunt, am I right?"

Drew felt his face flush. He thought her question had been small talk, not a request. There was a mischievous twinkle in her eyes. She picked up her phone and hit a button. "Mel, please get one of the MGs ready for Mr. Andrews," she said into the phone. "One of the older ones. British Racing Green."

Clicking off with a "thanks Mel," she finished her champagne and stood. "I might as well give you the nickel tour of Bunny's cars while we wait," she said casually. "Come with me."

Gloria walked through the door to the garage and pulled the lever of a large electrical switch. A bank of lights banged on in succession, revealing a line of cars facing a center walkway, their hoods and windshields sparkling in the light. As they walked, her boot heels clicked on the concrete floor, and she slapped her leg lightly with the riding crop. The smell of oil, gasoline, and industrial cleaner filled the air. Gloria pointed out Corvettes, Aston Martins, Porches, Lamborghinis, and several other cars whose names he did not know and would never remember. "He's quite a collector," she said, her voice still husky from her ride. She waved to a mechanic who was climbing into one of the MGs. He waved back, started the car, and drove through a large open double door to what Drew guessed was the mechanic's shop. The doors banged closed behind him.

"Mel's the best mechanic around and he keeps the fleet in running order," she said as she continued the tour, explaining the merits of each car and when and where Bunny purchased it.

"Ah," she said, arriving at a sleek black limousine. It was impossibly long, and the curve of the bumpers melded into the hood with its vertical louvered silver grille and round headlights. "Here's his pride and joy. It's a 1962 Rolls Royce Phantom V. It accommodates seven passengers and has a fully stocked mini bar. He only uses it for special occasions. Would you like to look inside?"

Her voice was husky and seemed inviting and Drew thought that, if he was misreading a signal, he might try something eminently foolish with his employer's wife. She smiled as if to say, "your move."

"No," he stammered. "No thanks. Beautiful car though," he managed. She laughed and tossed her hair back and slapped her leg twice with the crop.

"Well then, Mr. Andrews, I suppose that we should see if Mel has the MG ready."

As he drove the little car down the long driveway leading from the Bunstall Estate, Peter was in his head again.

"You'll never get a chance like that again! Did you see that look? Unmistakable! You'll be regretting this day for as long time, Kiddo. I thought you had more sand than that."

"More sand?" Drew said out loud. "Try to put a move on the publisher's wife? Good way to get fired, if not arrested."

"We both know you're wrong. And what did she say when you left? "Stop by anytime," she said. And what was up with that riding crop? Kinky!"

"Shut up," Drew said. He fiddled with the radio and found a hard rock station. He turned the volume all the way up.

CHAPTER SEVEN

GLORIA BUNSTALL WATCHED YOUNG Drew drive away in the green MG and wondered if he had any idea what was in store for him. She laughed lightly to herself. Another one of Bunny's projects, she thought. Young, naïve, malleable, and willing, even eager, to be groomed. She'd seen it before. Bunny would shower the young man with clothes, money, and the anticipation of a glamorous life as a reporter for the Journal. If he responded, and who wouldn't, he'd soon be dressing, drinking, and acting like the others Bunny had developed.

Her thoughts turned to George Cousins, the reporter who had left for the Tampa Bay Times. He had been young, naïve, and malleable too when he first joined the Journal. It wasn't long before he was doing things the Bunstall way; reporting what fit Bunny's narrative, regardless of what had really happened. He rose fast, pleased Bunny and got noticed by the Tampa Bay Times. Bunny was only too glad to have the young man move on to a more prestigious outlet where he could continue to rise. But there was a cost. He owed Bunny and Bunny was not one to forget what he had done for the young man's career. Inside information, breaking stories and impending investigations would flow Bunny's way, and if Bunny needed a story written to support his agenda, George Cousins was his man. In his rush to please Bunny, George had buried stories, glossed over details, and even fabricated facts. Bunny had enough on George to ruin his career with one expose and George knew it. It was like a spy operation: Bunny now had a mole in the Tampa Bay Times, as he had in several other journals.

Teejay Edmunds was a fixture at the Journal and would one day rise to senior editor when Bunny retired – or died at his desk. Since Bunny had no children, it would be Teejay, his nephew who took over – perpetuating Bunny's agenda, of course. In the meantime, Teejay would mentor young Drew and mold him into the type of reporter that Bunny required. That Drew had resisted Gloria's obvious advances only underscored the young man's naivete. Give him time, she thought. Give him time.

CHAPTER EIGHT

Drew SPENT THE AFTERNOON, after a shower and a nap, steaming and hanging his new clothes. New clothes, he thought. How long has it been? Not just a new shirt to replace one with coffee stains, but a pile of them. And pants and shoes. He wore his new shoes around to break them in and vowed to buy something he had forgotten earlier: underwear and socks. But by far the most difficult purchase of the day was a New York Yankees hat. Maybe he'd never have to wear it, he hoped. Maybe, if he even got to speak with the mayor, the subject of baseball wouldn't come up. But he had to be ready. He had already begun researching and memorizing current and past Yankees players and memorable games. But he was worried about sounding convincing when it came to classic victories over the Red Sox, of which there were many.

"You have to love the Yankees now. Full commitment. Anything less will appear obvious. Plus, they're a much better franchise."

"That's right," Drew said aloud. "I forgot that you were a Yankees fan! You must be enjoying this!"

"I am! Can't wait to see you in that hat!"

At around six-thirty he drove his newly borrowed MG towards the Lost Cove. Teejay had told him to meet him there, that there would be people he had met at the James and people from the staff. "It's a good placed to make connections and get bits of information." Drew had been invited there before, of course, but working sports, he always had a high school or college game of some sort to cover. It was not easily reached from town, so Teejay had drawn a crude map on a slip of paper.

Drew headed into a maze of mangroves, but the map was next to useless and soon he was hopelessly lost. There were no stores or gas stations where he could ask directions and the only other roads were gated and private. After half-a-dozen dead ends he was ready to just give up on the idea. But then, rounding a bend in the road and looking for a place to turn around, he stumbled on it. "You Found It!" a hand-painted sign proclaimed. "The Lost Cove." A small parking lot was almost full, and he had to park back by the cabins. As he walked across the lot, a large woman emerged from the building and waved to him. She wore a loose purple muumuu and had a mass of strawberry blonde hair twisted on top of her head, held there with what looked like chopsticks. Her face was red, and her fleshy arms wobbled as she spoke, like over-stuffed worms.

"Hey Captain," she shouted. "Where's Tennille?"

Drew looked around, puzzled. What was she shouting about? The large lady stood in the doorway, laughing.

"All's you need is a captain's hat, a scarf and a blue blazer to complete the look," she said. She was blocking the door and he had to stop in front of her.

"You don't have a clue what I'm talking about, do you? Well, I'm Janice," she said without explanation. "You must be Drew. Teejay said you'd be stopping by. Don't mind me, I just like breaking people's balls. C'mon in."

She walked into the restaurant, which appeared dark in comparison to the bright light outside. There was the heady aroma of hamburgers, French fries, and cooked seafood. As he walked in it took a minute for his eyes to get accustomed. Janice was already at the bar, shouting to the busy bartender. "Hey Chaz, get my friend, the captain here, a beer, pronto."

Chaz reached into a cooler, withdrew a Red Stripe and uncapped it. "Glass?" he said. Drew noticed that the man had a black leather eyepatch and a white scar running down the side of his face. He turned his back and walked off with a limp without waiting for an answer.

Drew took a long swallow of the cold lager, sat down on a barstool, and pushed his ball cap back on his head. "So, what's with the captain stuff?" he asked Janice point-blank.

"Don't get your diaper in a bunch, Honey," Janice said. "Like I said, I like to break balls."

"Oh, I don't care about that," Drew said. He took another long pull on his beer. "I just didn't get the joke."

A couple of patrons in earshot tittered. "You're not the only one," one of them said. More laughter.

"Well, lemme 'splain," Janice said.

"Yeah, please do," someone said. "We'd all like to know." More laughter ensued, but the crowd got quiet as Janice glared at them.

"Shut up, all a ya!" she said with a shake of her head and an exaggerated eye roll. She turned back to Drew. "Bunch of idiots," she said loudly. "See, back in the Seventies, there was a pop duo that called themselves 'The Captain and Tennille.' There was a promotion picture of the two of them, a man, and a woman, in a car like the one you drove up in. The Captain wore a blue blazer, a scarf and a white captain's hat. I thought you were going for that look."

"They weren't in no car, and the hat was blue," someone said loudly. Drew recognized the voice and shuddered. It was Joe Crimmons.

Janice moved her eyes from side to side as if pondering some weighty question. "Oh yeah," she said. "Well, if they were in a car, it would be one like his," she said, pointing her thumb hitch-hiker style at Drew.

"What is it?" someone asked.

"MG," Drew said, trying to sound indifferent. "An old one," he added.

"Sweet," the man said. "What color?"

"British Racing Green," Drew said. He looked around the bar and noticed some familiar faces from the press room. He nodded to a few and they nodded back. Friendly place, Drew thought; except for Janice and Joe. Chaz walked up to Drew's seat and placed another Red Stripe in front of him.

"Guy over there bought you this," he said, gesturing towards a young man sitting farther down the bar. Drew recognized him as Jason McCarthy, a buddy from college. He walked over. He and Jason shook hands and clinked bottle necks.

"Did you ever graduate?" Drew asked. Jason was notorious for passing just enough of his courses to stay enrolled in school for another semester. "Gradual School," he called it.

"Are you kidding?" he said. "I finally got expelled for bad behavior and low GPA. Took a course and got certified as an EMT. Love it – never a dull moment. Had a rough one this morning though. Guy's body washed up on the beach."

Drew's ears perked up. "You were on that call?"

"Yeah, he was a real mess. Burns over ninety percent of his body." Jason shook his head and laughed a little. "Your guy was puking all over the place."

"Ooh, I heard it was bad. Boat fire, right?"

Jason shook his head again and took a sip of beer. "Those burns were from no boat fire. They were chemical. We see them all the time at the chemical plant, we get called in there two or three times a week. They handle some really nasty stuff in that place."

"How did he end up on the beach?"

"Don't know. Everybody thinks he was burned in a boat fire. That's how the coroner wrote it up anyway. They never ask us anything."

"Right," Drew said, mentally filing the new information. It puzzled him that both Mick Murphy and the coroner would be so quick to judge it a death from a boat fire. They both must have seen chemical burns before. And then there was the fact that the man was an FBI undercover agent. What was he investigating? Something about the incident didn't seem right. Teejay seemed surprised to find out that the man was FBI, but wouldn't Mick Murphy have told him? He was glad now that he hadn't revealed his source. He was beginning to realize that his new job was a lot more complex than covering high school sports.

Jason talked a bit more about his job and then asked Drew about his situation.

"I managed to get a degree in journalism and got a job at the Journal. I just got transferred from sports to the political section."

"I know," Jason said. "And you've been assigned to get close to the mayor and get some good stories and photos."

Drew glanced over at Joe Crimmons who was trading barbs with Janice at the other end of the bar. "A loose lip will sink a ship," he said.

"I didn't know it was a secret mission," Jason said.

"It's not," Drew said. "It's just that I've got to get a bunch of new clothes to look respectable at the Club."

"The Club?"

"Check this out," Drew said. He pulled out his wallet and extracted a brand-new membership card to the Brantwood Country Club.

"Slick," Jason said with a low whistle. "Hey, while you've got your wallet out..."

Drew bought another round and the two caught up a little.

"Still play rugby?" Drew asked.

"Pope wear a funny hat?" Jason said. "Practices are still Tuesdays and Thursdays, same time, same field. Come by."

"I might, thanks," Drew said. But the mayor played golf on Tuesdays and Thursdays, he thought.

"Still living at your old apartment?" Jason asked.

"Yeah, temporarily," Drew said. "You?"

"I rent a cabin here," Jason said. "It works out real nice, cheap and close to the beach. I help out here a little to get a break on the rent."

Just then a server walked by, carrying a tray of food. Drew recognized her from school, she was Stacy Willard, the owner of the Cove's daughter, as he remembered.

"Hey Stace," Jason said. "Look who I found." She turned and looked at Drew for a moment. "Oh... Drew," she said, suddenly recognizing him. "I'll be back in a minute."

Much more than a minute later, at least two beers, to be exact, Stacy walked up to the bar and accepted a beer from Chaz, who had it waiting.

"Off duty," she said as she hopped up onto Jason's lap and gave him a playful peck on the cheek. "What's new?" she said to Drew as she took a sip from her beer bottle.

"Uh, not much," Drew said, a little surprised that Stacy was sitting on Jason's lap. In college she had a long-time boyfriend whose name Drew couldn't remember. Jason was notorious for having a string of girlfriends who were constantly breaking up with him because of his "immature rugby behavior." Stacy didn't strike Drew as a fit for him. But then again, stranger things have happened, he thought.

"Whatever happened to what's her name, the girl you were dating?" she asked.

"She came to her senses," Jason answered for him. "Went off and married a soap salesman, as I remember."

"Right," Drew said. "That's what I'd call him, a soap salesman."

"If I remember right, he was a purchasing agent for the Henkel Corporation, manufacturer of Dial Soap, among other things," Jason said. "Three-figure salary, I'm told." He looked at Drew with a mock sheepish expression. "Too soon?"

Just then there was a bit of a commotion as Will Willard entered the room. Drew knew of him, of course; everyone did. Beneath his surfer's blonde hair and tan lay a man of many rumors. Some said that he had worked as a government security contractor in the Middle East or as a mercenary in Africa. Still others whispered that he had made a fortune running contraband from locations in the Caribbean, Central and South America. Whatever he had done, he had retired with enough money to buy the Lost Cove and a refurbished float plane. He tossed a green bottle to Chaz who deftly caught it. He turned it over once in his hand and glanced the label. "Ah, mezcal," he said appreciatively. He opened the bottle and began filling shot glasses. Patrons got closer to the bar.

"Hey, I want to see the import label on that bottle," Janice exclaimed as she pushed her way front and center.

Will laughed. "You won't find one, that's why we have to drink it fast." He looked around the room suspiciously. "Any cops in the house?" Actually, there were two locals and one sheriff's deputy. Will knew them well. They stepped up to the bar along with everyone else.

Will's wife Daphne emerged from the kitchen with a large platter of conch fritters and a bowl of cut limes. She set the platter and bowl down on the bar and people began helping themselves. It was a daily routine when Will and Daphne were in town. They traveled often, seeking exotic recipes and items for import. The giveaways were their way of advertising.

Will walked over to where Drew, Stacy and Jason were. Stacy slid off Jason's lap and gave Will a hug. "Hi, Daddy," she said.

Will returned the hug and gave her a peck on the forehead. He turned to Drew.

"You must be Drew," he said, sticking out his hand. Drew took it and shook.

"Yessir," Drew said. "The same."

"You're the reporter who's shadowing the mayor," Will said. "Or at least that's what Joe Crimmons tells me."

"Yessir," Drew said, a little at loss for words.

"The mayor's a good man," Will said. "Or at least he appears to be. You can never tell with these politicians."

"Right," Drew said, regaining his composure a little. He took a swig from his beer. "Pundits, preachers and politicians, they're all cut from the same cloth. I'm thinking of writing a song."

"I like it," Will said. "Be careful, I might steal it."

Chaz brought over shot glasses and some limes and salt. He poured the mezcal and they all drank.

"Whew," Drew said. "That's got some kick."

"Straight out of Oaxaca," Will said. "I'm taking orders," he added in a stage whisper.

"Who's your friend?" Daphne asked as she approached the group from behind the bar.

"This is Drew," Stacy said. "He's a reporter."

"Well, pleased to meet you," she said, extending a hand across the bar. She had a friendly smile and a twinkle in her eye.

"Did you tell our new reporter friend our rule?" Daphne asked Stacy with a smile.

"No not yet," Stacy said. She looked directly at Drew. "See that sign above the bar?" Drew looked to where she was pointing. There was a large wooden plaque with a hand-painted rose and the inscription: "Remember, you are Under the Rose." "It's a reference to bars in ancient Rome. Roman bars were designated by a rose over the doorway. It was an unwritten rule that anything said in the bar stayed in the bar. 'Sub Rosa,' Latin for "Under the Rose."

"Got it," Drew said.

"Pinkey-swear," she said, holding out her little finger. Drew hooked it with his and they shook.

A little later Will left to check on his plane and Daphne went back to the kitchen. The three talked for a while, sipping at their beers. Suddenly Janice stood up from her perch at the window next to the door. "Here comes trouble!" she announced loudly, opening the door.

"Broooce, Broooce!" A chant suddenly went up from several patrons as a tall man with wavy dark hair entered the bar with a girl on each arm.

"Bruce Morley," Stacy explained. "His father owns Morley Chemical."

"I know, he was a couple of years ahead of me in high school," Drew said. "Yellow Corvette, tassel loafers, lots of hangers-on."

"He's one of my father's, um...clients," Stacy said. "He has a big house on the beach just up the road. Throws lavish parties. He often has the restaurant cater. Big spender, big tipper."

"You don't sound impressed," Drew said.

"I'm not," Stacy said. "Big poser."

Drew laughed.

"Hell hath no fury," Jason said with a mischievous grin.

"Shut up Jason," she said hotly. She turned to Drew and nodded. "Yeah,

I dated him for a while. Super nice and attentive at first; bought me lots of stuff, took me lots of places. A lot of fun, really. But then he got bored and turned his attentions to someone else."

"Sounds like a pattern," Drew said. "A serial dater." He gave Jason a hard look, who threw his hands up in mock surrender.

"He never really hurt me," Stacy said defensively. "My father would have killed him if he had. I knew what I was getting into; I knew his record. My father tolerates him, my mother hates him. He still comes around, as if nothing happened."

Just then Bruce noticed the group and walked over, a big smile on his face.

"Red Sawks!" Bruce exclaimed as he noticed Drew's hat. "No way! Let me buy you a drink!" He threw a big bill on the bar in front of Chaz and said: "Set these three up and keep 'em coming!" He came closer and put his arm around Stacy.

"Stacy," he said. "How did I ever let you slip away? How have you been?"

"Just fine without you," Stacy said, gently but firmly slipping out from under his arm.

"Oh, don't be like that," Bruce said, feigning a sad look. "You broke my heart! Please tell me there's still a chance. I'll do anything!"

"Do you realize how close you are to getting kicked in the nuts?" Stacy said.

"Oh, come on now, you wouldn't do that to Brucie," he said, making a kissy face. But he deftly stepped away and threw his arm around Jason to cover the action.

"How's Jason?" he said with a conspirational smile. "You still dating that cute little brunette from Tallahassee?"

Jason smiled," No, she dumped me," he said.

"Too bad," Bruce said. "Got her number?"

Everyone laughed. Bruce might have been a bit of a cad, but he was fun.

Jason introduced Drew and Bruce said: "Oh, you're the guy who's supposed to shadow the mayor, right?"

"Right," Drew said.

"He's a Yankees fan, you know," Bruce said. "Those guys hate the Sawx." It turned out that Bruce had spent some time in Boston and had acquired a Boston accent that he wouldn't let go of. He loved all the Boston sports teams and would often fly a new girlfriend and a few friends to a game to impress her. He had a Cessna Denali, which seated six.

"Yeah, well I guess I'll have to find a different hat," Drew said. He didn't mention the brand-new Yankees hat tucked into his brand-new gym bag. He also didn't notice the couple tucked away at a corner table, sharing a pleasant bottle of wine and idly watching the on-goings as they chatted.

CHAPTER NINE

DREW ANDREWS WOKE TO a harsh alarm and resisted the urge to hit the snooze button for a third time. He had a big day ahead and he was going to have to handle it with a mezcal hangover. He showered, shaved and stared balefully at a container of hair product. Reluctantly he rubbed a dime-sized glob of it between his hands. "Okay," he said to himself. "Here goes." He smoothed the product into his hair and combed it back. "Ugg," he said out loud. He rinsed it out and vowed to get a haircut later.

He looked at the pile of new clothes he had bought on Bunny's tab and selected a pair of khakis and a blue polo shirt. He hung them next to the shower and turned it on hot to steam out the fold lines. Meanwhile, he made coffee and looked at his scribbled schedule. It was tailored to intersect with what was known of the mayor's schedule as much as possible.

First, he had to report to Teejay at the Journal; he still had to do his regular job. But today, instead of lunch at the James, he was going to the club to play a little racquetball, have a light lunch at the club's bar and then play a round of golf. For that he had his brand-new Yankees hat in his gym bag. "Ugg!" he said again.

After golf, he had another fitting scheduled at Bunny's tailor: suit, sports jacket, and tuxedo. Next, he was to go on campus, establish himself as a grad student, and begin digging on any dirt he could find on John Mc-Nair. Maybe I should wear the tux to that, he thought. The image gave him a well-needed laugh. Reasonably ready for the day, he left the house and climbed into the MG. Driving to work with the top down, he put "Love Will Keep Us together" on his playlist. The Captain and Tennille gave him another laugh and he sang along with the chorus.

"Do you really have to play that crap?"

"Hey," Drew shouted over the music. "I have to play the role, remember?"

"Your singing voice is terrible."

"No one here to hear it but you," Drew shouted. He launched back into the song, hoping to drown out Peter's voice. But it was no use, he chattered at him the rest of the way to the Journal.

"You can't get rid of me that easily."

He parked and got out of the car and walked across the hot asphalt with its puddles of sticky oil and scampering, squawking seagulls. He was forced to hit the dank stairwell again, with its familiar smells and slippery steps.

"Hey, Honcho!" Joe Crimmons exclaimed loudly as Drew entered the noisy pressroom. Crimmons looked meaningfully at his watch. "Almost on time, for a change," he announced. "Close, but no cigar!"

"Blow it out your ass," Drew said as he passed Crimmons. A few reporters who heard it laughed.

"Yeah, back 'atcha," Crimmons said. "How's the head? You were hitting that tequila pretty hard last night at the Cove."

"It's called "mezcal," Drew said in a mock-haughty tone that had a pronounced lisp. Another laugh from the reporters – and from Crimmons.

"Yeah, well, be careful around that cute little waitress," Crimmons said. "If you do her wrong, Will is liable to slit your throat and dump you in the sea – if Daphne doesn't do it first!"

"Don't worry, I'm not her type," Drew said as he walked towards Teejay's section. But she sure is mine, he thought to himself.

"I thought you were going to be at the Cove last night," Drew said after he and Teejay had exchanged Good Mornings.

"I was at a concert," Teejay said matter-of-factly. "It was a solo piano program, all Chopin. The pianist was brilliant, although a little heavy on the pedal during the cadenza." He handed Drew a very poorly typed sheet – he still liked to do his work on an old Royal typewriter, clacking away at the keys with two fingers. "Here," he said. "Clean this up and have a hard copy on my desk by nine. We've got to work up a biography on Governor Thompson for Friday's edition. He's coming into town next weekend and Bunny wants the full treatment. His wife is an important supporter of Mrs. Bunstall's favorite charities. I'll need you to get me as much as you can off the internet. Quotes, anecdotes, initiatives, legislative history and record. You know, the usual stuff."

Drew said that he did. So that's how it works, he thought. I do all the work and Teejay gets the byline.

"On my desk by ten, Kid," Teejay said as Drew walked towards his cube.

"Yessir, Chief," Drew said.

At precisely ten o'clock, Drew laid the bio information on Teejay's desk, even though he had completed it a half hour earlier.

"Thanks, Kid," Teejay said, glancing at the page. "Good work. The review was good too. I just might keep you around for a while."

"Gosh, I hope so Chief," Drew said, doing his best Jimmy Olsen impression, the cub reporter on the Daily Planet in Superman comics. Teejay got it and laughed.

"Don't call me Chief," he said. "I'm heading down to the James, you coming?"

Drew shook his head. "No, I'm going to the club for some racquetball, a quick lunch and then it's off to the golf course for eighteen." He affected a snarky, preppy tone as he said it.

Teejay laughed. "Well, say hi to the mayor for me," he said as he grabbed his keys and stood. "I'll have one for you at the James. See you tonight at the Cove?"

"Sure," Drew said. Wouldn't miss it for the world, he thought.

CHAPTER TEN

 T HE RACQUETBALL ECHOED loudly as it smacked off the wall and car-
omed towards the back wall. Drew lunged at it and managed to catch it
just as it was about to hit the floor. He was sweating heavily and working
the ball as hard as he could. His sneakers squeaked as he pursued the ball.
The sweat smelled of stale beer and mezcal. Good, Drew thought. Sweat
it out. It had been a long time since he'd played racquetball and he was a
little rusty. But he loved the game and was once pretty decent at it. He was
playing alone in one of the club's eight courts. The floor was hardwood, the
walls were made from high impact tongue and groove laminate and the
back wall was glass, with glass doors. There was a three-tier set of benches
for viewing. When he signed in, he had chosen the court adjacent to one
being used by a certain J. McNair.

There was a lot of banging, muttered curses and loud 'oofs' coming from
the court. Drew kept working the ball until he heard the men in the next
court finish their game and open the door. He hit the ball a couple of more
times and opened his door. He glanced over at the two sweating men as
he exited and sat down on a bench. He nodded to them, and they nodded
back. He noticed that they had no racquets. Handball, he thought. Hard-
core. They were in deep conversation about the game and paid him no
more mind. Drew knew the mayor, of course but the other man looked
vaguely familiar. Then it came to him, he had been sitting at the end of the

bar at the Cove, talking with Chaz when Chaz wasn't busy. Chaz referred to him as "Top." Drew knew the man's real name was Ned Butcher and that he was an old army buddy of McNair's who served as a sometimes bodyguard. He also noticed that he had only one arm.

Suddenly there was a bit of a commotion as two guys entered the area. They were talking a little loudly, betting on who would score more points. One of them, the taller one with wavy dark hair noticed him.

"Hey, Boston," he exclaimed, pointing a finger at Drew. "I know you; you were the guy wearing the Red Sox hat at the Cove last night."

Drew waved. It was Bruce Morley, blowing his cover as a Yankees fan. Oh well, Drew thought, I wonder if I can get my money back for the hat?

The Mayor and Ned left, and Bruce and his partner opened the door to their court. "We'll have to play sometime," he said to Drew. "I didn't know you belonged to the club."

"Yeah," Drew said absently. Bruce nodded and entered the court, followed by his partner who then shut the door.

"All that hard work at being a Yankees fan for naught!"

"Shut up," Drew said

LATER, Drew hit campus for a while; it had only been a year since he had graduated, and things hadn't changed much. He walked by his old frat house and waved to a small group that had gathered on the porch enjoying a keg. He waved and they waved back. One of them, a guy he recognized as an underclassman he vaguely knew, signaled for him to join them. He walked up to the porch, introduced himself and accepted a foamy beer in a red plastic cup. "Doing some grad work," he said as everyone introduced themselves back. He finished his beer and promised to stop by later. "Got a seminar in fifteen," he said.

He walked around a little more and then stopped by the Library, the main student bar. He recognized the bartender whose name was Ray; he had been there as long as anyone could remember. He was muscular with a thick neck, red beard and red hair tied back in a ponytail. Ray also served as a bouncer at night and checked the proof of age of the young students who came through the door. A large yellow traffic sign hung on the wall behind his station which had been altered to say: "Yield Right of Ray." He had a German Shepherd that helped him screen under-age drinkers. The running legend was that the big dog could smell fear and would bite any-one trying to pass for legal. Drew could attest to that personally.

"Hi Ray," Drew said as he took a seat at the bar. He ordered a beer and looked around. The place hadn't changed much, he thought; there was hand-painted graffiti all over the walls, beer signs, street signs and pictures of college sports teams. The place had once been an old hotel called the Colonial Inn but had been converted to a bar years ago. The rooms were cut up and filled with picnic tables, scarred from years of initial carving There was a pool table and several pin-ball machines, foosball tables and dart boards. Blues music crackled out of some battered speakers. There was the smell of stale beer and cleaning liquid.

Ray brought Drew the beer he had ordered. "I remember you," he said. "You're Drew Andrews. You're a reporter now and are supposed to shadow and vet the mayor in case he decides to run for governor; that is, if the gov-ernor gets tapped as VP at the convention."

Drew stared at Ray, who seemed to be enjoying himself immensely. Drew didn't even ask.

"All right, I'm having a little bit of fun with you," Ray said. "Jason was in earlier, bird-dogging some college girl. He told me the story. He's a good kid so I told him I'd tell you everything I can remember. Don't worry, there's no one around here who even knows John McNair or would care to know that you're here to vet him – or his past any way."

Drew was relieved and took a long sip of beer. Jason! He thought. That dog! He laughed a little to himself and settled back to hear the story.

"Alright," Ray said. "What I remember about John is about what I re-member about you and most of the other students who come here to sow their oats. He drank a lot of beer, partied a lot and got into a few minor scrapes which his father got him out of. Immature, so-so student and almost flunked out a couple of times. We all know that he straightened out in the army, came back a war hero and finished grad school cum laude."

"What about women, or boys," Drew asked point-blank. "Any outstanding paternity suits, drunken gropings, that sort of thing, something that could come back to haunt him?"

"Are you kidding?" Ray said. "He was in love with one girl the whole time, and she seemed to be in love with him. The two were inseparable."

"What happened?" Drew asked.

"When he joined the army, she took up with another guy and dumped him. I heard she wrote him a 'Dear John' letter while he was deployed. Thing is, she was cheating on him the whole time."

"No shit," Drew said.

"And I'll tell you another thing that no one else knows, around here anyway." He leaned over and, even though there were only a couple of guys playing pool in the back, whispered in Drew's ear.

Drew rocked back on his barstool his eyes wide. "No shit!" was all he could think to say.

That evening The Cove was a little subdued: Stacy and her parents had gone off on some trip, searching for the best recipe for jerk chicken. At least that was what Chaz told him. Jason was nowhere to be found and even Janice and Joe Crimmons were a little on the quiet side. Drew sat with Teejay, and they chatted about local politics, the mayor's initiatives, and the bio on Governor Thompson. Teejay asked him what he had found out about McNair's college days. Drew told him everything Ray had told him, saving the best for last.

"No shit!" Teejay exclaimed. "That explains a lot. Keep that under your hat. I'll let you tell Bunny yourself. After a while they parted company and Drew called it an early night, still amazed at what he'd heard.

CHAPTER ELEVEN

IT WAS STILL DARK as Drew drove to work. He had decided to be earlier for a change; he was sick of Missus Zimmer's icy, sarcastic voice waking him with: "Are you planning on coming in to work today?" He was sick of Joe Crimmons saying, "Hey Honcho, late again I see!" And to be honest, he was tired of trying to make lame excuses that didn't ring true. "If you're ten minutes early, you're five minutes late," his mother often counseled him when he was a kid.

As he drove, he thought about Peter being in his head all the time. He knew that it was just an imaginary thing, but it seemed so real. Sometimes he actually *heard* his voice. Why, he wondered? Was he cracking up? Was he getting to be like Peter? Had Peter heard voices in his head too? He tried to banish the thoughts by conjuring another fabricated memory. This time he was walking through the zoo, tagging along behind Peter, who turned and smiled and gestured for him to keep up. "They're feeding the Giraffes," he said. "We have to hurry, or we'll miss it." The sky was clear and blue, and the breeze carried the aroma of cotton candy. There was calliope music coming from a merry go round.

But then the image of his mother came to him, interrupting the Giraffe feeding. She was sitting at the kitchen table, tears in her eyes. Peter was sitting there too. "Boys, I have something terrible to tell you," she said. Suddenly Drew realized that this memory was real. He shook his head to cast it out, but he couldn't shake the sinking feeling that had come over him that day, his heart gripped by some invisible hand that wouldn't let go. He felt it again and remembered the moment as if it was now. He saw again the horrified look on Peter's face as he realized that he had caused the moment to happen.

"You shouldn't blame yourself," Drew said out loud. "You didn't know. You couldn't have known."

"But I should have known that something was wrong. I should have sensed it."

"But I was the one who brought it up, remember?"

"Right, you should have kept your mouth shut."

"Enough!" Drew said aloud. "I've got to go to work."

"I'll be around."

"I'm sure you will."

As he arrived at the Journal's parking lot, the sun was just breaking through the gloom of dawn. To his surprise he found that he didn't have to circle the lot looking for a parking place.

"You're early Mr. Andrews," Shirley said as he walked into the lobby. "Would you like some coffee?" She poured him a cup from a carafe without waiting for an answer. "There's donuts and coffee cake, if you like," she said as she handed him the cup. She gestured towards a counter where there were several open boxes and containers.

"Thanks, Shirley," he said. He grabbed a donut and glanced at the clock. In his haste to be early he had overshot the mark by half an hour. "Have a nice day," Shirley said pleasantly as he headed towards the stairs. On second thought, he turned towards the elevator which was usually crowed when he came in. There was no line. He walked over and pressed the button.

As he walked into the press room, he immediately noted the absence of hustle and bustle he was used to hearing when he came in; and, a bonus, Joe Crimmons was not at his desk. Other than a few good mornings and waves, he was left to his own devices as he got seated at his cube. He noticed that Teejay hadn't come in yet. He clicked his computer on and pulled up his work on Governor Thompson's bio. There was a lot to sort through.

"Simplify, simplify," Peter said, causing Drew to laugh out loud. A couple of reporters in earshot looked at him in surprise. They quickly looked away when he noticed them. "Keep it together," he said to himself under his breath. He gritted his teeth and tried to concentrate on his work.

A little while later Teejay arrived. He looked surprised when he saw Drew but didn't say anything more than a friendly "good morning young man." He sat down at his desk and started working on something.

It amused Drew that Joe Crimmons didn't notice him as the big man came in and plopped down at his desk, shooting his mouth off to anyone who would listen, punctuating his remarks with: "Am I right! Am I right!" He was simultaneously on the phone, on his computer and in conversation with one of his reporters. Drew felt sorry for the new kid who had replaced him in Sports; Crimmons was constantly berating him about something. You could hear it across the room. Oh well, the kid was paying his dues, Drew thought.

Teejay got a phone call and said, "Yes, right away, Ida. Yes, he's here, I'll bring him along."

"Hey, Drew," Teejay said. "Bunny wants to see us, right away."

Drew nodded and stood.

"Good thing you came in early," Teejay said as they walked towards the elevator.

Bunny had an impatient look on his face as they walked in. "Alright," he said. "Teejay says you've got something for me that he wouldn't tell me himself. Said he wanted you to get full credit."

Teejay sat down in one of the chairs facing Bunny's desk.

Bunny leaned back in his chair and smiled. He nodded towards the bar. "Three fingers, neat," he said. He reached in a box and pulled out three cigars. "These are Cubans," he said, expertly snipping the ends. "I get them from a guy who flies them in special."

Drew returned with the scotch. Bunny motioned for Drew to sit and lit the cigars with a black cylindrical desktop lighter that emitted four blue flames.

"Will," Drew said as he drew on his cigar.

"What?" Bunny said.

"Will Willard flies them in," Drew said, trying desperately not to cough. "The guy who owns the Lost Cove."

Bunny nodded approvingly. "You've done your due diligence, that's what a good investigative reporter does. Go on."

Drew told him everything that Ray had told him about McNair and then said, "the girl he was dating was named Liz Young. The guy she left McNair for was named Fred Walowitz."

"Was?" Bunny said.

"He changed it," Drew said. "To Corey Deschamps, who later married Liz Young."

"No shit!" Bunny exclaimed, nearly choking on his scotch. "Elizabeth Deschamps! That explains a lot!" He sat back and looked at his cigar as if expecting an answer to an unasked question.

"She writes a weekly column in the paper," Bunny explained. "Mostly religious stuff but also some local commentary. She seems to be battling my wife for leadership of the cultural initiatives in the city. Gloria hates her for it – female jealousy. Gloria has always worked well with John, and he has pushed her projects forward. But Mrs. Deschamps seems to always find problems with them, whether its benches in the park, a fence around the commons or flowers and signage at the city entrance. Now I see that it might not be Gloria that Mrs. Deschamps is getting to but rather her old boyfriend."

"Could be sir," Drew said. An image of Gloria Bunstall and the Rolls Royce limo popped into his head. He hoped the old man couldn't read his mind. Bunny gave him a funny look.

"How's the car?" he said. Drew almost choked on his scotch.

"The car?"

"Yes, the car," Bunny said. "Gloria told me she gave you the green MG."

"Oh, yessir, the MG," Drew said. "It's just fine."

"And my collection? I hope Gloria gave you the tour."

"Yes sir, she did. Beautiful collection."

"How about that Rolls Royce Phantom?"

"Beautiful car, sir, a real gem."

"Yes, she is, isn't she?"

"Yes, she is sir." Drew caught himself just as he was about to say: "The car, I mean."

"And the clothes are alright?"

"Yessir," Drew said, glad to be changing the subject.

"We've got a big weekend coming up with the governor's visit," Bunny said. "Make sure you try on your suit, sport jacket and tux. Wear them around, get comfortable in them. We don't want you looking clumsy. Wear the shoes as much as you can, break them in. Study some old movies, watch how men move and stand."

"I will sir." Drew said. "I won't let you down."

"Elizabeth Deschamps and John McNair," Bunny said, shaking his head. "Keep that under your hat. A secret like that is like gold, as long as it remains a secret."

"Now gentlemen," Bunny said. "On to serious business. Here's what's at play. The governor is probably headed to Washington, and we hope that John will be headed to the state capital. The governor will be here next weekend. There'll be the fundraiser for his wife's foundation on Friday, dinner at my house on Saturday and then the Corey Deschamps show on Sunday. I want you both on you're A-games. Teejay, you know the governor, so I want you to shadow him. Drew, you seem to be making progress with the mayor, so I want you to shadow him. I want to do a Sunday Supplement featuring his visit. Pictures, interviews...the works."

"Yessir," Drew said. Teejay nodded.

"Emphasize the ladies and their efforts and initiatives. Don't ignore Mrs. Deschamps but portray her as someone more involved with church matters. Same thing with Corey. We love him, we're glad he's here, but he doesn't drive the narrative. Bringing the megachurch to Brantwood was my idea and it has served as a shot in the arm to the city, not to mention the purchase of my old white elephant of a lacrosse stadium. But lately, the Deschamps have been pushing a little too hard for my taste. There needs to be some separation."

"It's our city," Drew said. Teejay looked at him askance, but Bunny punched the air with his cigar.

"Precisely!" He exclaimed. "Our city!"

Drew worked on the Thompson bio for the rest of the morning. The man was amazing. He played football at Florida State and was drafted by the Dolphins. He played three seasons at tight end until a knee injury during the playoffs ended his career. He went back to school and got a law degree at the University of Miami. After graduation, he got a position at a prestigious law firm. He married Susan Haskell, the daughter of the wealthy industrialist-turned-philanthropist Armstrong Haskell and together they had four children.

After his marriage, Tommy Thompson seemed to catch fire. He began serving on advisory boards of environmental and economic foundations. His expertise was exceptional, and he soon drew the attention of the governor who brought him into his administration as chairman of the Council of the Arts. Thompson urged the governor to establish a museum of art, which would fund itself through tourism. Susan was a gifted grant-writer and a persuasive fund raiser. Together they were able to procure an art collection that became famous throughout the country.

When the current governor announced his intention to retire, he put his stamp on Tommy. Susan enthusiastically supported her husband's candidacy and before long they had moved into the governor's mansion. Tommy's interdisciplinary approach to governing and his practical problem-solving skills soon established him as one of the more effective governors in the nation. He initiated a massive expansion of the State University System, pushed forward an aggressive infrastructure program, modernized the telecommunication network, and attracted businesses from other states with tax abatements. At the same time, he pleased conservatives by restructuring the state's cumbersome bureaucracy, and initiating a welfare reform program, which emphasized job training and placement. He eliminated redundant environmental regulations and replaced them with a streamlined system that protected the environment but didn't hamstring businesses with costly delays.

Realizing that there was a lot to unpack in all the information he had gathered, Drew set upon a course that would portray Thompson as a Teddy Roosevelt progressive who pursued a program Drew dubbed: "Reform, Restructure and Rebuild." When he placed the rough draft on Teejay's desk at eleven, his boss was pleased.

"Good job," Teejay said as he rose to leave for the James.

"Thanks Chief," Drew said.

"Don't call me Chief," Teejay said. "Coming?"

"Right behind you," Drew said. "I'll drive."

But as they approached Drew's MG in the parking lot, Drew got a surprise. Sitting on his fender in shorts and a tank top was Stacy, her hair hidden beneath an old baseball cap. Parked next to the MG was a topless Jeep with big beach tires and a couple of paddleboards strapped to a rack.

"Okay if I borrow Drew for the afternoon Teejay?" Stacy asked.

Teejay Laughed. "Go ahead kid, I'll hold down the fort at the James." He walked off towards his own car.

Drew looked inquisitively at Stacy, who was wearing a mischievous smile.

"I want to go on a little adventure, and I need a photographer," she said. "Do you have a camera?"

Drew laughed. He had a couple. They were state-of-the-art DSLRs, courtesy of the Journal. He fished them out of his trunk, along with a canvas camera bag.

Stacy nodded approvingly and jumped into her Jeep. "Hop in," she said as she turned the key and started the engine.

Drew did and Stacy hit the accelerator just as he was getting seated. His cameras and bag fell in a jumble at his feet.

"We just got back from Jamaica," Stacy said as she drove. She had the disconcerting habit of looking straight at Drew as she spoke, disregarding traffic. She drove fast and treated stop signs and traffic lights as mere suggestions. "Ever been there?" she asked.

"No," Drew said, trying to appear nonchalant at her driving. "Heard a lot about it, though."

"All true," she said, swerving slightly to avoid the open door of a parked car. "Beautiful country, if you know where you're going. Great coffee, great rum and great weed. We sailed around the coast, looking for restaurants that serve jerk chicken. They all do, of course, but Daphne was looking for the Holy Grail; the best of the best."

Stacy breezed through a stop light, causing a chorus of blaring horns, which she ignored. "We finally found it near Negril. Little out-of-the-way place with a thatched roof and a couple of picnic tables. Family operation. The food was fantastic. Dad speaks Patois, and he bought the jerk chicken recipe from an old lady who was the matriarch of her family. Paid a lot of money for it too, which is something he does." She laughed as she took a corner on two wheels. "He probably could have gotten it for free, but those people, they're so cool, but they're so poor. At least by our standards."

So far Drew hadn't said a word and was white knuckling the door and dashboard. The Jeep sped up a back road through some mangroves, paved with crushed white shells. After a while they emerged onto a beach and turned right, speeding along the white sand.

"To the left is the main beach," Stacy explained. "Big houses, restaurants and bars along the beach – you know, the strip."

Drew nodded. Of course, he knew. He'd grown up in Brantwood and had gone to the beach often as a kid. Later he and his friends had gotten fake IDs and hit the beach bars.

"To the right is a large nature preserve. It's only accessible at low tide because of the thick mangroves. Beautiful; pristine." As she spoke, she pulled out a joint and lit it. She took a deep hit and passed it over to Drew. "Do you indulge?" She asked. Drew took it and inhaled. It was strong and fragrant.

"Jamaican," Stacy said.

"Wow," Drew said.

They got the paddle boards off the rack and carried them to the water. "My father indulges in a little commerce from time to time," Stacy explained. "But only for preferred customers who understand that it's not for resale, strictly personal consumption. He won't deal with pills, powders or guns. It's like: 'You want Cuban cigars? How many? You want Jamaican coffee? How much? Key West Pink Shrimp? Sure, how many pounds?' You know that sort of thing." She laughed, shaking her head a little. "He's got some baggage from the past. I'm not sure what, but I know that he made a lot of money, enough to buy the Cove and lay low." She laughed again.

Drew was surprised at Stacy's openness about her father's business. For all she knew, he could have been an undercover cop. "Isn't he worried that his...commerce will get him arrested. I mean, it's right under their noses."

"Under whose noses? The police chief, the sheriff, the judge and half the cops in town buy stuff from him. He's too small time for the FBI; there would be no profit in arresting him." She stopped for a moment, thinking. "I guess he does it just to keep his chops up, you know, keep the adrenaline running."

They went back to the Jeep and grabbed the paddles and a couple of dry boxes, which Stacy clipped on the decks. "You can put your cameras in here if you want," Stacy said. "Have you paddled an SUP before?"

Drew shook his head no. "Kayaks, canoes, but not a paddleboard."

"They're easy," she said as she pushed her board out into the light surf. "Just follow me and do as I do. If you get nervous you can kneel or sit on the dry box," she added.

I'll be damned if I kneel or sit, Drew thought to himself. He pushed his board out and jumped on it as Stacy had. It wobbled crazily and Drew went into a crouch, like a surfer. The board settled somewhat, and he stood again. He dug in with his paddle and tried desperately to keep his balance. And to keep up with Stacy.

"You'll get the hang of it," she said over her shoulder.

"Right," Drew said, trying not to sound out of breath. "Where are we going, anyway?"

"Snake Island," Stacy said.

CHAPTER TWELVE

THERE WAS A LIGHT breeze, and the sky was clear blue as Stacy and Drew paddled out into the bay. A couple of dolphins decided to tag along with them, and their blue-gray skin glistened as they gracefully surfaced and dived; their mouths locked in pleasant grins as they clicked and whirred at each other.

After a while, Stacy told Drew about their destination. "In 1921, a hurricane hit this region. It separated the island from the mainland, and it's now only accessible by sea. It's about a mile long, ringed by a beach, and backed by mangroves; the interior is a thick slash pine forest. Few people bother going there because there are so many other beaches nearby. That's why we're going: it's untouched, pristine and I want wildlife photos and videos for my collection. You don't mind?"

Drew looked over at of Stacy, easily paddling her board in the sun. Mind? Why would I mind, he thought? But he said: "No, not at all. I needed an afternoon off anyway."

"Watch it, stupid! She just wants you to take some pictures for her. Don't read anything into it. You know how you are!"

"How am I?" Drew said angrily.

"Did you say something?" Stacy asked over her shoulder.

"No, Nothing," Drew stammered. "Just commenting on what a nice day it is."

"Yeah, isn't it beautiful?" She continued paddling and thought about what Drew was in for. She liked him, maybe a little too much. Was this her way of getting rid of him before things went too far? She maintained a tough exterior but inside she was deathly afraid of a commitment that would end up as all her other relationships had. She knew about his brother, of course, and his parents. Who didn't? She wondered if the whole trauma had somehow messed with his mind. He did seem distracted at times and sometimes talked to himself under his breath, but, other than that, he seemed fine. And he had agreed to come along on her adventure without asking anything about it. Well, we'll see how he handles meeting Nefertiti, she thought wryly.

As they approached the island, Drew could see that it was long, narrow and a little twisty. "I see why it's called "Snake Island," he said. Stacy gave him a funny look and laughed.

"We're going to see a lot of wildlife, I hope," she said as they stepped onto the white sand beach and pulled their boards above the tide line. "Have your cameras ready."

Drew pulled his cameras – one with a wide-angle lens and one with a zoom – out of the dry box, along with his camera bag. Stacy pulled a thin metal pole with a hook on the end out of hers. She extended it and started walking up a scant trail. Drew, encumbered by his cameras, followed clumsily. After a while Stacy stopped.

"See that? Up in the tree," she said pointing. An osprey was in a nest and feeding on a large fish.

"Got it," Drew said. He aimed his telephoto and adjusted it. He took a couple of stills and then pressed "video."

"See what I mean?" Stacy said. "You see them a lot on platforms on telephone poles, but not natural, not like this."

"Great shots," Drew said, his enthusiasm building. It had been a long time since he had taken any kind of pictures except team photos, grip and grin events and portraits of dignitaries.

"Over there," Stacy said as they moved on. "See it? It's a Gopher tortoise."

Drew did and got several shots and a video of the cumbersome animal as is lumbered through some brush.

"They dig burrows all over the place," Stacy said. "Other animals, frogs, snakes and even owls, use them for shelter."

Drew got shots of an eagle soaring high above them and some pictures of an armadillo as they proceeded up an incline in the trail.

"Ah, here we are," Stacy said, stopping at a jumble of rocks and underbrush. "Get your camera ready." She looked around for a little while, gently parting the underbrush and peering intently. Then she found something that interested her, but Drew couldn't see what it was.

"Start recording," Stacy said softly as she pulled lightly at something with her left hand. She held her hook with her right. Drew gasped when he saw what it was. Stacy drew a large Diamondback rattlesnake out of the brush. She softly hooked it with her pole and turned ever so slightly to face Drew.

"Beautiful, isn't she?" Stacy said. "I think she's sleeping, but you can't tell, because their eyes are always open." She turned the snake as it slowly writhed, coiling slightly but not aggressively. "I come here as often as I can to handle the snakes so that they'll trust me. They're used to me now; they know my touch and my scent. See how she tastes the air with her tongue?" She pointed the snake's head directly at Drew and pushed it forward. He could clearly see the snake's heat-sensing pits through his lens. The eyes, slanted with vertical black pupils, seemed to be staring straight at him.

"She's heavier than the last time I handled her," Stacy said quietly. "I think she's full of eggs. She'll carry them for a while longer, they'll hatch inside her and then she'll give live birth." She gently set the big snake down, headfirst, and it slowly – and thankfully, Drew thought – slithered back into the underbrush.

"Her name's Nefertiti, after the Egyptian Queen," Stacy said. She stood and grinned. "Nice job," she added. "I can never get anybody to come out here and record." She looked at Drew, who had sweated through his shirt and appeared a little bit shaken.

"I took some grad courses in herpetology after college," Stacy explained.

"I came to love the creatures, they're so misunderstood. I've got several of my own in my ophidiarium. I raised them from babies that I got from the university; I would never take them from the wild."

"Right," Drew said, hoping she wasn't going to be visiting her other friends. She seemed to read his mind.

"That's enough for today," she said. "I'll come back another time to see the others." She turned and lightly skipped and ran down the trail, clearly pleased with her encounter with Nefertiti.

When Drew got to the beach Stacy was out in the water swimming. She stopped as he approached. "Time for a swim," she said. "I was getting all sweaty. C'mon in." Drew noticed her clothes in a pile on her board.

"Don't worry, I won't look," she said coyly. She turned around and faced out to sea.

Drew shucked his sweaty clothes and plunged in. The water was clear and warm and refreshing, and the salt smell suffused his nostrils. They swam around for a while, laughing and splashing. Stacy did a surface dive and came up behind Drew. As he turned, she wrapped her arms around his neck and kissed him.

Oh my god, Drew thought. If I don't drown, I'll be snake-bit.

CHAPTER THIRTEEN

Janice Crimmons stood in the doorway of the Cove watching two figures approach from the parking lot. She always sat in a particular spot in the bar that gave her a view of the lot. She smoked clove cigarettes and blew the smoke out the open window, watching. It was important to her to see visitors as they pulled in; it gave her a chance to greet them at the door.

"Here comes trouble," she announced as the men got close. She stood, blocking the doorway protectively. "Don't be bringing any body parts or blood-borne pathogens in here," she said. She, like everyone else in the bar, had heard the sirens wailing a couple of hours earlier. The scanner behind the bar had announced a bad accident at a crossroads A little while later it was announced that both roads were closed.

Both men laughed. "Don't worry," Jason said. "We left the best for the hazmat guys."

"Hazmat?" Janice asked. "What happened?"

"We'll tell you – if you buy us a beer," Pinky said with a grin. He was a short man with a wide gap between his front teeth. Although only in his early thirties, he had already lost most of the hair on the top of his head. Rather than compensating with a comb-over or a ball cap, he simply shaved his head. Being naturally red headed, it gave his head a somewhat pinkish coloration; hence his nickname, "Pinky." A jokester, he had embraced the nickname by dressing in pink, wearing pink Converse sneakers and carrying his smartphone in a pink case. He had his Jeep painted the same color and even painted his beloved paddleboard pink.

"Pinky's got pics," Jason said with a wink and a smile. Jason and Pinky shared one of the cabins on the Lost Cove's grounds. Jason was medium built but wiry and had a broken nose and chipped teeth from playing rugby. "Wait 'till you see what you won't see on the news."

Janice was an incorrigible collector of local intrigue and was a sucker for bits of gossip, secrets and conspiracy theories. "Well then," she said with a broad grin. "C'mon in." She stepped aside and opened the door.

"So, what have you got, sweetie," Janice said, rubbing Pinky's head as if for good luck. Pinky pulled out his phone.

"Check this out," he said, hitting a couple of buttons. He looked around furtively in an exaggerated manner; There were patrons at tables in the seating section enjoying the Early Bird Special, all talking a little loudly over the music playing on the sound system. A woman from a table in the back was at the bar, ordering a bottle of wine. At the bar there were a few well-known regulars and all of them knew the unwritten rule of the Cove; they were under the rose.

Janice, along with several others, crowded in to see the pictures. "Ewww," she exclaimed. "Is that a body?"

Pinky nodded enthusiastically. "Used to be. Guy ran a stop sign and hit a chemical truck. It unloaded on him. He was probably already dead from the collision, but the chemicals finished the job. Melted him. Hazmat guys had to scrape him up with a shovel."

"Do your superiors know you have these pictures?" Janice said, she already knew what the answer was. This wasn't the first time Pinky had taken pictures at an accident site. It was strictly against procedure, and, if caught, he would receive a write-up, suspension or even be fired. But Pinky didn't care; he was skilled at taking the pictures, usually from the hip, with his phone hidden from view. It was a matter of pride with him.

"There'd be hell to pay if they caught me," Pinky said. "But they won't. I'm too slick for them." He giggled a little, enjoying his little joke. He waited a moment as people began to drift away.

"But wait, there's more!" He said in a TV announcer's voice. Everyone turned back to his phone. There, pictured through a jumble of EMTs, firemen, Hazmat personnel and police, was the truck. On its side, in large letters was, "Morley Chemical."

"Oh, that changes everything," Janice said. "How much do you suppose old man Morley will pay the family of the poor guy to keep things quiet?"

"Why the guy?" Chaz asked. "He hit the truck, right?"

"He may have still been alive when the chemicals hit him," Pinky said. "Hard to tell...impossible to tell. But if there's an investigation because of a lawsuit of wrongful death, well..."

"What Pinky is trying to say – or *not* trying to say," Janice said, giving Pinky a look. "Is that Morley's chemicals could have been illegally transported."

"But what about all the cops, the EMTs, the hazmat guys, they all saw the truck," Chaz said. "They have to have identified the chemical."

"Not really," Pinky said. "The truck has to have a manifest. The chemical listed on it would be a legal one. Without a test, ordered by an investigation, no one would know. Or care."

"Have you ever been by that plant?" Jason asked the group. He was getting a little tired of Pinky getting all the attention just because he had the pictures. After all, he had been at the accident site too.

"I try to avoid it," Janice said. "The air stinks around there; plus, it's fenced up and guarded tighter than a military base. I hear they take pictures of every car that goes by and run the plates to see if anyone's spying."

"I've heard that too," Chaz said. He was wiping the bar even though it didn't need it. He wanted to be part of the conversation. "Morley has somebody run them for him."

"Yeah, well you ought to see it from the inside," Jason said. "We go in there almost every week." He took a long sip of his beer to heighten the effect of his statement. "Chemical burns, toxic dust inhalation, burnt eyes, burnt lungs...I can't imagine the long-term effects of working there."

"Don't they wear protective gear, you know, suits, gloves, goggles, respirators, that sort of thing?" Chaz asked.

Jason shook his head. "Their equipment is old, worn and flimsy. One guy that we took out sucked in toxic fumes when his respirator hose broke."

"What about the EPA and OSHA?" someone asked. "Haven't they been called?"

"I heard that someone warns Morley about inspections ahead of time," Jason said. "So that he can bring the plant into compliance before the inspectors get there."

"Workers sign NDAs," Pinky said. "The head of security, some guy named Haden, takes care of that. He makes us sign them every time we go in there."

"If you signed non-disclosure agreements, how come you're disclosing right now?" Chaz asked.

"Disclosure means filing a complaint," Jason said. "We're just *telling* about it."

"You sure about that?" Joe Crimmons asked. "It'll be your asses if Morely finds out."

"Who's gonna tell him?" Pinky said. "It'd be hearsay anyway. Wouldn't hold up in a court of law."

"Well, for starters, his son Bruce, who comes in here a lot," Joe said. "And who says it would end up in court? There are other ways to handle a loose set of lips."

"Nah, Bruce doesn't have anything to do with the business," Jason said. "Besides, he doesn't get along with his father anyway."

The discussion continued for a while, everyone guessing at the circumstances of the chemical accident. Why did the driver blow through the traffic light? Was he drunk? Was it even a he? But after a time, the participants ran out of theories and out of interest. Most of them returned to their drinks. Janice returned to her post at the window and lit another clove cigarette.

More tourists and fishermen arrived at the restaurant, along with several regulars, including Teejay Edmunds. Janice welcomed them all with her insulting humor. As the regulars bellied up to the bar, Pinky discretely showed anyone who showed an even passing interest his pictures, hoping to at least get another free drink out of it.

Daphne emerged from the kitchen with two large platters of chicken wings. "Got a new recipe for jerk seasoning," she said, setting the platters down on the bar. "Let me know what you think."

"Try them with this sauce," Will said. He put several small bowls next to the platters. "It's cilantro-lime with a little honey and cayenne pepper."

"So, your trip was a success," Teejay said, sampling a wing dipped in Will's sauce.

"You tell me," Will said.

Teejay took a bite and then sat back, his eyes wide and sweat forming on his forehead. "Whew, that'll get your attention!" he said. He took a big sip of beer from a bottle that Chaz had just slid in front of him. He wiped his brow and selected a second wing. "Plenty of heat, but it doesn't cover up the other flavors. Just the right amount of allspice, cloves and cinnamon. Do I detect fresh thyme as well?"

"Hey, I paid good money for that recipe," Will said. "Don't give it away to this bunch of pirates! They'd sell their mothers for a pint of rum!"

Everyone laughed. Teejay looked accusingly at Will. "You went all the way to Jamaica and didn't bring back any rum? You're holding out on me, Mr. Willard!"

"I can't get anything past you, can I?" Will said. He reached under the bar and pulled out an unlabeled clear bottle filled with a deep amber liquid. He uncorked it and turned to Chaz, who was already lining shot glasses up on the bar. "I got a few cases from a guy I know who runs a private pot still," Will said as he poured. "Robust, with plenty of funk."

Will held his glass up when everyone had been served. "Chee-yers!" He said with a singsong patois accent.

"Cheers!" Everyone said as they drank. Teejay leaned over the bar and said something softly to Will. Will nodded. "How many?" He said with a grin.

"Hey, where's that cute little protégé of yours?" Daphne asked Teejay "Did we scare him away?"

Teejay laughed and said, "You didn't hear? He was abducted earlier. Haven't heard from him since."

Janice cackled from her perch. "Here he comes now! I think his kidnapper will want a reward!" Stacy's Jeep could be clearly heard as it roared into the parking area.

Oh no, Daphne thought with a bemused smile. That didn't take long!

"Well, well, well," Janice said as Drew and Stacy walked towards the restaurant. "Look what the cat dragged in!"

Stacy hissed like a cat and raked the air with her hands splayed out like claws. Janice guffawed.

"Look what I caught today, Daddy," Stacy said as they walked into the bar. "Can I keep him?"

Déjà vu Will thought. He looked over at Daphne, who was choking up and shaking her head, clearly amused. It was the same phrase that she had used on a boat, many years ago.

Stacy walked up to the bar and handed Drew's memory card to Chaz. "Can you put this on the big TV?" she said.

"I don't know if I'm ready for this," Janice said with a broad grin. "There's kids in this restaurant."

The first image was a video of Stacy walking up the hill ahead of him. Oops, forgot about that, Drew thought. There was a smattering of laughter as Jason whispered loudly: "You dog!"

Stacy looked over at Drew and shook her head. "Sorry," he said. "I was checking the light meter." Somebody snickered. Then came the osprey nest and the gopher tortoise.

"Nice shots," Teejay said.

"You ain't seen nothin' yet," Drew said. Next came the video of Stacy handling the big Diamondback rattler.

"Holy shit!" Pinky said. "How do you know to do that?'

"She studied herpetology at the university," Daphne said, totally engrossed by the scene. "She never could get anybody to with her to Snake Island, let alone record it."

"Oh. Maaaan," Jason said as Stacy put the big snake's head up to the lens. "How did you keep a steady hand?" he asked Drew.

"I was more afraid of what Stacy would do to me if I ran away than I was of the snake," Drew said, drawing a big laugh.

Later, Teejay took Drew aside. "You've got to do an article on Snake Island," he said. "Get an interview with Stacy and include some of your stills. I bet Bunny would love it, and you know Gloria and her interest in environmental issues."

Oh, yeah, Gloria, Drew thought.

"And don't forget about church on Sunday. Ever seen the Corey Deschamps Show?"

"No," Drew said. "Heard about it, never been."

"Well, you're going this Sunday. You can sit with Bunny and me. The mayor always attends. His wife thinks it's good for his image. It must irk McNair to have to sit through a service presented by the man that Elizabeth left him for."

"I hear Corey puts on quite a show," Drew said. Teejay chuckled.

"What are you laughing at?" Drew said.

"You hit the nail on the head. That's exactly what it is, a show," Teejay explained. "Written, choreographed and exactingly rehearsed by Elizabeth. She's the real show. She even wrote his books and handles the marketing of the church's merchandise. It's no secret around Brantwood that she created Corey Deschamps and the Brantwood Fellowship."

CHAPTER FOURTEEN

T HE SOFT BRUSH FLITTED over his face and eyelids like the tiny tenta-cles of an exploring insect. His nose wrinkled involuntarily. "Almost done," she said. The smell of fresh-cut flowers, hairspray and powder filled his head. He felt a sense of anticipation beginning to build in him, a sense that his transformation was almost complete. He loved that moment, when he could stride forth, confident and composed; his former self left behind like the hull of a cicada.

He couldn't remember when he hadn't liked getting made up. When he was little, his older sister would sometimes use their mother's makeup and lipstick and wigs to turn him into a little girl. Then he began to do it on his own. Sometimes his mother would catch him, letting out as horrifying shriek. "You little queer!" she would exclaim before going on to call him worse things, slapping him the while. But she was wrong. He didn't want to become a girl, he wanted to escape his timid, insecure self and become something else. He didn't understand why only women could make that transformation and, since there was no male avenue for such a thing, he followed the female model. As he grew older, his makeup sessions became more secretive, with his door locked and his mother banging angrily on it. Then, in elementary school, he discovered acting. His first role was as a tree. He wore a suit painted to look like bark and a tall hat of branches and leaves. His face was painted brown, and his forehead was painted green. He loved it. After that he took every part he could get in every play and production he could find. He didn't care about speaking roles or even a mention in the program. His only requirement was that he could wear makeup.

"Hold still now, Mister Deschamps," Rachel scolded in a friendly manner. "We're almost done." Rachel was his make-up artist and she had two assistants who bustled about the dressing room, inspecting, and advising. It was crucial, the make-up. Too much and it would cake-up under the harsh klieg lights of the stage. Too little and his face would look sweaty and shiny, throwing off the light meters of the video cameras set up to capture every angle of the production.

"Please call me Corey," he said, for the hundredth time. She smiled but didn't say anything. Both of them knew that she would never do any such thing. He was to be referred to as "Mr. Deschamps" or "Sir." To not do so would invite a stern rebuke, if not an outright firing, and everyone knew it. Rachel deftly brushed at his cheeks and held a mirror for his inspection. He smiled softly at his reflection, his perfectly capped and bleached teeth glinting in the light. He deepened his smile to reveal his dimples and put a playful twinkle in his eye.

"You're a genius, Rachel," he said as he stood to his full six-foot four height. The move frustrated his hairdresser Henri as he tried to apply one more spritz of product to Corey's perfectly coiffed mane. "Ahh, someone get me a stool!" Henri shouted in mock exasperation. But Henri didn't mind; he was in love with Corey Deschamps, and he didn't care who knew it. The problem was that Corey didn't share Henri's lifestyle and, although he laughed off Henri's constant lurid suggestions, he never acceded to them. "Doesn't hurt to try," Henri often said when scolded by Rachel or someone else on the team. "You never know."

"We'll have to go with what we've got," Corey said playfully. "The show must go on!" The comment drew a laugh from the make-up team. They were all in good moods, everything was set, and Corey was ready to go on as soon as he got the call. He looked briefly in the full-length mirror by the stage door. He smiled at the figure he cut, tall and fit and confident. The p-90 workouts appeared to be working, he thought as he straightened his back and squared his shoulders. He admired his tailored silk suit, adjusted his tie, and waited for his introduction.

He could hear the band, especially the thumping bass, through the dressing room walls. They were playing his theme song, written by Grammy-winning songwriter Carmen Diaz on commission. The bandleader was Curtis Green, a Grammy winner himself. It was a funky song with a strong bass line and a powerful backbeat. The wailing notes of a guitar rose to the arched ceiling as backup singers sang in harmony. The stage manager stood by the stage door, ready to open it. He grinned broadly when Corey met his gaze, smiled, and nodded. He was ready. As the door opened the full sound of the band rushed into the dressing room like a boisterous group of guests bursting into a quiet party.

The band settled into a groove. "Ladies and gentlemen," Jimbo Onthank announced. "Are you ready?" He stood off to the side of the stage behind a podium with a big announcer's mic, the life of any party. The crowd cheered and clapped in response. He was the perfect lead-in man for Corey, and he knew it; he was always ready with a quick laugh, chortle, or sigh. "Oh, ho *ho,*" was his trademark phrase, which always brought a mirthful raised eyebrow from Corey. It was a real crowd pleaser.

"Are you ready?" Jimbo asked again, his rich voice evoking a wrestling ring announcer's. The crowd cheered again.

"I give you *Mister Cor-ee Day-Shamps!*"

The band kicked into the theme again and Corey slid through the door and Jagger-jogged out onto the stage. The crowd roared. He flashed his trademark smile and pointed to several people in the audience. He looked over at Curtis, who smiled and waved and then raised his hand high. He cut the song off by sweeping his hand down and closing his fist, like he was grabbing some invisible insect.

The room went silent for a brief moment. Corey raised both hands high and threw his head back.

"Can you feel him?" He shouted. The crowd murmured. "Can you feel his presence?" Corey insisted. The people responded by raising their hands and tilting their heads back.

"Can I get an amen?" Corey shouted.

"Amen!" The crowd answered.

"I said, can I get an Amen?" He shouted again.

"Amen!" people in the crowd shouted as one. They loved Corey and he could feel their collective power; he drank their adulation in, and it fueled and animated him. They filled each one of the sixteen thousand seats in the megachurch every week, some driving hundreds of miles to experience his sermons. Thousands of others sat at home, watching on syndicated cable, and wishing they were at the Brantwood Fellowship in person.

The band kicked in again and Corey slid back and forth on the slick stage, moving adroitly, with just a hint of a hip-shake and shoulder-roll. It wasn't dancing, but it was pretty close. He had spent several Sundays attending gospel churches on the South Side where the ministers danced and sang their way through services, and funky bands kicked the rhythm. People danced in the aisles. His congregation was far too white for that.

He turned often to the band, encouraging them to kick it up as he raised his hands and exhorted the crowd with amens and halleluiahs. But mostly he faced the cameras, which were set up along the front and sides of the massive stage. As the band quieted, he began his sermon slowly and softly, nodding his head frequently to emphasize a point or to offer a bit of scripture. His voice gradually gained tone, timbre and volume, eliciting enthusiastic "amens" from the congregation. He had a teleprompter in case he needed it, but he never did. He had the sermon memorized and every bit of it had been thoroughly rehearsed, recorded, critiqued and rehearsed again. Nothing was left to chance. Elizabeth insisted.

As Corey marched through his sermon he noticed, from time to time, his wife sitting in her usual seat with a perfectly practiced smile on her face. It was something he tried not to do, notice her. When he did, it threw his delivery off ever so slightly. Not enough for anyone in the audience to notice but enough to elicit tight lips and a frown from her. He knew that even the slightest stutter, stammer or catch in his voice would result in a severe tongue lashing at Monday morning's critique of the show. Elizabeth insisted on perfection and was intolerant of any slip-up, no matter how small or inconsequential. "Your audience pays us a lot to watch your show, and you owe it to them to deliver a flawless performance," she often said. She was right, of course; Elizabeth was always right. But still, Corey felt that he could do a lot better without the fetters that her exactingly constructed and rehearsed sermons imposed on him. His own inner critic told him that his delivery was stilted and wooden. Sometimes he felt like just letting loose and allowing the spirit to lift him, as it did in many of the televangelists he studied. But to go off script, even in the slightest, would result in a psychological beating that would return him to the quivering mass of insecurities that his cosmetics masked.

CHAPTER FIFTEEN

Elizabeth Deschamps did not consider herself an opinionated person, although others did. An opinion, in her view, was an uncertain belief; a conclusion about something that a person had come to based on their own perspective. Strongly held opinions led to judgements that weren't always accurate. Of course, in her position as the wife of a popular televangelist, she was expected to embody a certain stereotype. That stereotype was a strict, moral, and judgmental woman who was certain of her convictions. She dressed accordingly, acted accordingly, and wrote accordingly in her "Daily Prayer" column. But Elizabeth Deschamps was, beneath her purposely overdone makeup, hair and glittering sequined dresses, anything but the persona she had so carefully created.

At an early age she had discovered an uncanny ability to see character flaws in other people; they seemed to stand out to her, like neon lights flashing. She often laughed to herself when she noticed them in a person. The Seven Deadly Sins: pride, greed, wrath, envy, lust, gluttony, and sloth. People were driven by such flaws, and that made them weak. Elizabeth saw weakness as an opening; a way to manipulate and exploit a person. Everyone she encountered was susceptible to her need for control. It was the only way she could address her own weakness.

Ever since she was a kid, Elizabeth – then Lizzy – had feared abandonment. She had grown up in a broken home. Her father, a workaholic, was usually away on business in some distant city; he seemed always to be leaving just as soon as he came home. Then, one day, he ceased coming back at all. Her mother, for reasons known only to her, decided to become a raving alcoholic and then get herself committed to a mental hospital from which she never emerged. Lizzy spent the rest of her childhood shuffling between a series of abusive aunts and lascivious uncles. In college her one stable relationship, after a series of disastrous ones, fell apart when one sunny afternoon he had stopped by her apartment and caught her in bed with another guy. It was an inconsequential affair that meant nothing to her, she explained, but he didn't understand; despite her continued affection for him he became indifferent and distant and then he left too. She never forgave him for it and a simmering hatred remained in her breast even after all these years. Her life seemed to be marked by instability, entropy, and chaos. But as Nietzsche said: "One must face chaos to give birth to a star."

She was happy today, or at least reasonably so. She sat in front of the soundboard, the best place to hear the true sound of the production and to view the lighting. Because the soundboard was on a platform just below the second tier of seats, it gave her a perch from which to observe the congregation in front of her. It also prevented anyone from sitting behind her - Elizabeth disliked having her back to anyone, an old quirk. In front of her sat a group of people who donated the most money to the church. They were designated "gold cross" members and they got valet parking, reserved seating, and access to the church's fitness center and upstairs bistro. In other words, every convenience the church had to offer. Their importance to her was critical.

As she surveyed the crowd, she also noticed men of substance that were outside her orbit of control. These men she termed "untouchables," men that, try as she might, she could not bend to her will. She hated them for it. Chief among them was the mayor of Brantwood, John McNair; he irked her more than any of the others. Eagle Scout, war hero, straight arrow John McNair with his pretty little wife, square jaw, and unwavering moral compass. She knew that he attended church only because his wife thought that a man in his position should. Plus, she knew that his wife, along with most of the women and half the men in the congregation, had a crush on Corey. His attraction to women was a big part of his charm. Elizabeth knew that John McNair disdained church and considered Corey a sham of the first order. Although he outwardly comported himself with dignity and affected a keen interest in Corey's sermons, she knew that he was enduring the service with stoic forbearance.

Wrenching her thoughts away from John McNair, Elizabeth concentrated on the show. She watched as Corey began his sermon and she admired the way he followed the script. He looked good, projected his voice well, and he moved about the stage with confidence and command. Born to the stage, it was said. She had written and revised the sermon a dozen times over the course of the week and Corey had studied and rehearsed his lines over and over. The dress rehearsal the day before had gone well, and Elizabeth was certain that it would play well to the large in-house audience and to the thousands who were tuned into the syndicated broadcast. But still a nagging worry troubled her. Corey was a wild card in her deck, a thing that could, in an instant, upend her carefully constructed system. She had hired the band and the announcer and the make-up crew and the sound and lights team. Any one of them could be replaced in a heartbeat if they displeased her. But Corey was the star, the face of the Brantwood Fellowship and, as such, he couldn't be replaced.

She knew that everything had an arc: a rise, but then a fall. She met the future Corey Deschamps in a theatre class and transformed him into a popular televangelist. But how long would her creation last? When would the inevitable fall come? She had created him but, like Frankenstein's Monster, he was unpredictable. She controlled him now but would there come a time when he would break the psychological chains that she had constructed? Would he one day feel the conviction of his message and become what everyone except Elizabeth believed him to be, the charismatic leader of a major megachurch? Or would he stumble and fall? One scandal, one ill-advised comment in an interview or one poorly perceived off-script remark during a sermon could sink the massive ship that was the Brantwood Fellowship. If the ship foundered, she didn't intend to go down with it. But Elizabeth had discovered early on that there was a problem: she had no lifeboat.

Although the Fellowship brought in huge amounts of money in the form of tithes, donations, book sales and royalties from syndication, she was still up to her ears in debt. The church itself had cost a fortune to purchase and refurbish. Upkeep and overhead added to the deficit and financing the debt every month only added to the problem. No one, least of all Corey, knew it, but the church was always only weeks away from bankruptcy. That's when Ben Fitzgibbons stepped in.

Ben Fitzgibbons was the Chief Financial Officer of the prestigious Thompson Fund, a charitable organization that was the pride and joy of Susan Thompson, Governor Tommy Thompson's wife. Elizabeth had reached out to Susan, asking for an endowment that would help put the church on a sound financial footing. She appealed to Susan's Christian values, emphasizing the similar goals of the Thompson Fund and the Brantwood Fellowship: to foster a commitment to faith, community, and patriotism in the people of the state. Susan had been only too happy to agree. "I'll send the fund's CFO to work out the details with you," she said. She gave Elizabeth his number and name: Ben Fitzgibbons. Elizabeth had been shocked when she heard it. She had known him when everyone called him "Doctor Fitz."

When he showed up at her office, he was a little older, with a little less hair and he was shorter than she remembered. But he still had that arrogant manner he had had when she first knew him as a business professor at college. He had always been nervous but now he was even more so, his eyes flitted and he sniffled a lot, his nose twitching like a rabbit's. Classic mannerisms of a coke addict, Elizabeth thought.

Susan had allotted a generous endowment for which she only asked that the Thompson Fund be mentioned at some time during Corey's sermons. No problem. Then, Fitzgibbons had mentioned a deal that would benefit them both, if carried out correctly and discretely.

"Your church takes in a lot of cash in donations, does it not?" he asked, needlessly.

Elizabeth nodded 'of course,' without saying it.

"I have certain clients who have cash that they obtained, shall we say, in ways not consistent with the law as we know it. It would be perfectly innocent on your part if, without your knowledge, people were donating money to your church that was…" He searched for a word.

"Dirty," Elizabeth said, her anger rising. "You're suggesting that I launder money through the church. If caught, the scandal would ruin me!"

"If caught," Fitzgibbons said. "Which won't happen." He raised his hands slightly in a calming gesture and said, "hear me out."

Elizabeth was willing to listen. After all, there had to be something in it for her. This might be my lifeboat, she thought. If she had been a prayerful person, she might have thought this was an answer to her prayers. She nodded for Fitz to go on.

"You find people in your employ who are willing to be paid in cash to avoid taxes. Band members would be the most likely, but also cleaners, kitchen people, yard workers and people who you pay consulting fees to. Use the money I bring to pay them. The money you take in in donations and checks, less your percentage, goes into an offshore account which I can draw on for my clients. Clean money. Everyone wins."

Elizabeth was thinking. The mention of consulting fees had piqued her interest, but she didn't mention it.

"I can walk you through the bookkeeping aspect of it," he went on. "There's no way anyone could discover it if you do it right."

"What's my percentage?" she asked. He named it and she upped it. He took it. Must be a big coke habit, she thought.

The scheme was more successful than she had ever dreamed. What she had thought would be a minor operation turned out to be major. Fitz evidently had some big-time clients who were pulling in a lot of money that needed to be laundered. Every Sunday, he would show up at the church with suitcases full of cash and every week she would send it out in pay to her employees and consultants. The money she took in from tithes and donations went on the books and into his offshore account - and into her own. Her lifeboat was turning out to be a yacht.

But there was a problem. Ben Fitzgibbons was another wild card outside of her control. If his coke habit got away from him, if the FBI took an interest in him, if Susan Thompson became suspicious, if one of his clients became unhappy with him skimming too much, if… too many ifs, she thought. Yet, like a gambler who is on a winning streak and lets her bets ride, Elizabeth kept the arrangement going. I'll know when to quit, she told herself. I can read Ben Fitzgibbons like a book. I'll know if somethings going on with him.

And so now Elizabeth sat in her seat in the church, watching Corey perform and assessing the complex system she had constructed. The money that came in was paid out to a series of church members who then willingly (was that the right word?) donated the exact amount back to the church. She had carefully cultivated her stable of donors. They were men of substance in the community and had many business contacts themselves. If any of the dirty money was discovered, it would be virtually impossible to trace back to them. And literally impossible to trace back to the church.

Today, Elizabeth had an especially important recruit to pursue. He was a city council member who was also the city's zoning officer. An important vote was coming up and she needed to turn him in order to defeat it. She smiled and waved as he glanced back at her from his seat, which she had arranged to be in the VIP section. "We need upstanding citizens to be a part of our church," she had told him when she called him at his hardware store. She was aware that the store, one that had been in his family for generations, was on the verge of bankruptcy.

"The church buys a great deal of hardware, and we like to buy from church members," she told him as a tease. His name was Bob Draggett and he had eagerly accepted her invitation. Come into my parlor, said the spider to the fly, she thought as he turned around in his seat.

CHAPTER SIXTEEN

"I KNOW WHAT YOU'RE doing." The stranger's voice was soft and matter of fact as he stood in the doorway.

"Who are you and what are you doing here?"

"I know what you're doing." Again, the voice soft, almost monotonal. He stepped forward and gently closed the door behind him.

"How did you get past security?" He began to reach for the intercom.

"Don't do that." Soft voice, impersonal tone. "I know what you're doing."

"You said that! What is it you think I'm doing?" His voice was rising a little. Was it anger or fear? The stranger seemed vaguely threatening, even though he was smiling. But the smile was devoid of emotion. It reminded him of a python as it stared at its prey, slowly constricting until the animal could no longer draw breath.

The stranger didn't answer. He was medium built and fit, in a vaguely military sort of way, with Khaki pants and a short sleeve shirt unbuttoned at the collar, revealing a deep tan. His eyes, ringed slightly in white from wearing sunglasses, were humorless and assessing.

He had been sitting at his desk in his office, working on his computer. He had felt rather than heard the door open and he had turned to see the stranger standing where no one should have been standing. Security was tight in the offices of the Thompson Fund. He began to again demand how the man had gotten in and what he wanted when it suddenly occurred to him that he had been discovered. The realization hit him with a thud.

"Here's what I want," the man said when he knew Fitzgibbons had become aware of his situation. "I have a client who needs your services. Same percentage as your other clients. A courier will drop off the money at the Brantwood Fellowship on the same day that you drop your money off. It will be returned to us through a numbered account." He handed Fitzgibbons a card with a code printed on it.

Fitzgibbons took the card. How did this man know what he – they – were doing? How had he been discovered? But the man didn't seem ready to reveal the answers. "Is there anything else?" he asked, a little bit weakly.

"Two things. A couple of my men will take over the governor's security detail. We need to keep an eye on the good governor." Fitzgibbons knew that the men's real assignment was to keep an eye on *him*.

"Two?" he asked.

"Get your coke habit under control."

CHAPTER SEVENTEEN

Henri floated into the room on a cloud of cologne, the last one of the team to arrive. He was holding a struggling miniature poodle named Charlemagne, although he usually just called him "Sharly." Monday mornings always put him in a foul mood because every Monday morning Elizabeth held a meeting to critique the previous day's production. She seldom had a good word for anyone on the team. "I've had the worst morning," he said, glancing at her. "Honestly, I don't know why these meetings have to be so *early*," he huffed. "Sharly needs his morning walk."

Elizabeth again said nothing but gave him a sharp look. She didn't like Henri's petulant little outbursts and wanted him to know it. He huffed a little more and averted his gaze, trying to calm Charlemagne, who was yapping excitedly in his defense. She hated his high-strung poodle and had made it clear many times that he didn't belong backstage or in a meeting, but Henri maintained that he was an emotional support animal and crucial to his mental well-being. "I would fall to pieces if Sharly wasn't with me," he often said. So, Elizabeth tolerated the little animal, and Henri's outbursts. But she frequently entertained a fantasy where she wrung the little animal's neck while Henri watched.

The meetings were important to Elizabeth, and she prepared for them assiduously, going over the recording of the sermon Sunday evening, her notebook in her lap and her pencil poised to make notes. In her hand was the script of the sermon, which had been developed during the week previous and rehearsed many times. Corey was a good performer and followed the script well, but during a sermon that lasted a good two hours, there would always be times when he flubbed a line and tried to make up for it by going off-script. These were the dangerous moments, in her view; the moments when he might make a joke or a comment that would be seized upon by his detractors on social media platforms. "De Sham is at it again," they would text with glee, usually attaching some insulting meme to the comment and trolling other detractors. Elizabeth never responded to the trolls but many of Corey's followers did, and lengthy and angry threads often resulted.

Elizabeth looked around the room. Everyone was in place and ready, she thought, except for Corey. Finally, ten minutes late, Corey stepped into the room wearing a designer athletic suit, boutique sneakers and a towel loosely wrapped around his neck. His hair was wet and tousled, the result of a recent shower after a vigorous workout. Eyes sparking, he looked around the room with a smile that spoke of confidence and certainty. Everyone applauded. He smiled and drank in the adulation of his team. Curtis Greene took off his headphones and stood. "You da man!" He exclaimed. "Right on!" Jimbo Onthank boomed. Corey tried to look sheepish, but it didn't work. He loved – no, craved – the attention. He grinned broadly and wiped his face with the towel. He took his usual seat, one over from Elizabeth, who shot him her usual annoyed look at his tardiness.

"Sorry," he managed. There was a hint of a stutter in his voice. Only Elizabeth knew of his own weaknesses.

"Let's get started," Elizabeth said. She used a remote to bring up the video of the previous day's service. She stopped it midway through the band's signature intro. She rewound it. "Hear that?" she said. She played it again. "Did you hear that, Curtis? That trumpet player cracked a note!" She played it again, and then again. There's something unnerving about hearing a bad note played over and over.

And so it went. For over two hours. No one was immune from criticism

except, Corey, who would suffer another two hours of micro-managed criticism after the others left. It wouldn't do to criticize him in front of them.
His ego was too fragile.

Elizabeth encountered Corey Deschamps while taking a theatre class
in college in order to satisfy an elective requirement. Of course, then he
wasn't Corey; Corey Deschamps would be constructed later. His name was
Derf Walowitz, and he was pudgy and pasty-faced and timid. The class was
studying Shakespeare's play, Henry V. Parts had been assigned by lot and
the lead, Henry, had been drawn by Derf. Several students had snickered
into their hands. "Type-casting," someone muttered sarcastically.

But Derf gamely practiced his parts and when, during the next class, he
stood to deliver Henry's famous speech before the Battle of Agincourt, a
transformation occurred. He began haltingly, stuttering slightly and stum-
bling over his words: "Wa… what's he that wishes so?" Titters and rolled
eyes from the audience. Then, a little more firmly, "My cousin Westmore-
land? No, my fair cousin. If we are marked to die, we are enough to do our
country loss." Then, taking a deep breath, he forged on, "And if to live the
fewer men the greater share of Honor God's will!" With the last phrase,
Derf seemed suddenly to light up. His eyes sparkled, his voice strength-
ened in tone and timbre; he began moving around the stage, gesticulating with his hands. In Elizabeth's eyes, he had transformed into Henry. He
continued that way through the rest of the speech, ending with the famous
line: "Gentlemen in England now-a-bed shall think themselves accursed
they were not here, and hold their manhoods cheap whiles any speaks that
fought with us on Saint Crispin's Day!"

The audience was stunned. Someone clapped; then someone else. Soon
the entire audience was on its feet in a rousing standing ovation. As she
stood, clapping with the rest of the class, a plan began to grow in Elizabeth's
mind.

It wasn't difficult to seduce Derf, he wasn't used to much female attention. She convinced him that he was the first man she had ever been with
and he believed her. I guess the theater class lessons must be working, she

thought at the time. Once fully ensnared, Elizabeth convinced him to go on a strict diet and exercise program, get his teeth capped and change his name.

"What's wrong with my name?" he said when she brought it up.

"Seriously," Elizabeth countered. "Derf Walowitz? You need something snappy."

She came up with Corey for "core values" and Deschamps for the very obvious and not too subtle aural connection with "the champ."

Derf was unconvinced and reluctant, that is until Elizabeth put on a full court sexual press that left him exhausted and compliant. A simple trip to the courthouse was all it took to change his name.

The next part was the most challenging. Elizabeth saw no future, or at least no profitable future, in theatre. Bit parts in Off-Broadway productions on the outside chance that he might eventually get bigger parts was not part of her plan. No, she thought, Corey's acting talents would be best suited to preaching. As a child one of her aunts had dragged her to a series of tent revivals. The preachers were engaging, charismatic and, most importantly, not part of a specific denomination that would require years of study at an accredited bible school. She put Corey on a crash course of bible study. "If you're going to be a preacher, you've got to know the bible inside and out. Quotes and verses." Corey had never been very religious, but he did his best. And Elizabeth used sex as carrot and stick, giving liberally or withholding until he reached the level she required. Corey never questioned where she had learned her sexual wiles.

Elizabeth and Corey Deschamps spent every Sunday attending church services of every sort. Catholic, Methodist, Lutheran, Baptist, Non-Denominational and others. They even went to several black gospel services. Corey was amazed at the audience participation at those. He loved the music, and he loved the way the preachers moved and swayed.

Finally, Elizabeth brought Corey to her hometown church. It was a little chapel with just a few dozen worshippers. The pastor, Louis Smalls, had started the church in an old grange hall decades ago. He was old, and his voice was shaky and weak. People listened to his uninspired sermons dutifully, but indifferently. Perfect, Elizabeth thought. She introduced her husband, dressed down for the occasion, as a newly ordained minister looking for a church where he could help and learn.

Louis enthusiastically took the young man under his wing and soon gave him a chance at his first sermon. Although a little shaky, it was a success and soon Corey was filling in for the old pastor more and more. Elizabeth helped with the books and recruited better musicians to play in the worship group. Membership swelled as did the offerings and tithes. When the old minister suffered a fatal heart attack, Corey took over in full.

The rest, as they say, was history. The little church's congregation grew from a few dozen to hundreds. Corey wrote inspirational books, penned by Elizabeth. The church's coffers were growing by the day; they soon needed a new venue.

Elizabeth reached out to the city fathers of several locations in the vicinity. She didn't want to abandon their local worshippers, so it had to be within an hour's drive. She got an enthusiastic response from a Mister John Bunstall, the owner and executive editor of The Brantwood Journal, a newspaper located in a town about 45 minutes-drive away. It seemed that Mr. Bunstall had invested in an indoor stadium for a professional lacrosse team. The team was good, but the league wasn't, and when it folded, Bunny Bunstall was left holding a brand-new white elephant. It sat vacant for two years until Elizabeth called. Bunny was eager to unload the stadium. Plus, a megachurch would be a shot in the arm for his city's economy. Figures were discussed and settled upon. The big church drew in crowds from all over the state and those crowds stayed in local hotels and ate in local restaurants.

Now, sitting in the screening room, Elizabeth looked over her team and wondered if she had sufficiently cowed them with her harsh assessment of their performances. She was tempted to fire one of them, just to send a message to the others. But which one? Curtis Greene would be first on her list; he had a cocky attitude; she could get that sax player, Alphonso Jordan, to run the band. Keyboard players were a dime a dozen, so Curtis wouldn't be hard to replace. Or maybe she should fire Henri, he was getting under her nerves anyway with that little white rat of a dog barking all the time. Jay Rosen's assistant was champing at the bit to take over sound and lights. The only one, besides Jimbo Onthank, that hadn't caused a problem was Rachel. Everybody liked her, so her firing would really shake the rest of them up. She'd have to think it over. As she dismissed the team she looked over at Corey, who knew that his critique was next.

CHAPTER EIGHTEEN

Mourning doves cooed and a mockingbird trilled as spears of the sun's first rays began poking up through the tangle of palmettos and palms, intruding on the pre-dawn gloom. Virgil and Sally Yarber were having breakfast together, as they always did. They were both early risers and it gave them joy to see the first glimmers of God's new day. They clasped hands together and shared a prayer. Their one disappointment in life was that they had, up to now, not been able to conceive. God had, for some un-revealed reason, chosen to not bless them with children. Time was running out. They had discussed adoption, but with the new megachurch taking away from their already meagre congregation, money was too tight. Virgil was under intense pressure from the bishop, who was concerned that the Community Chapel was becoming economically unsustainable. Knowing that losing his little chapel would devastate her husband, Sally had taken a job at the megachurch in the business office. Before being led to enter bible college, she had gotten her MBA at USF and had been working towards certification as a certified public accountant. At the Brantwood Fellowship she advanced rapidly and before long Elizabeth had made her made her the Chief Financial Officer and her personal assistant. She had the codes to the church's computers and a key to Elizabeth's private office. Her salary was good, but still only barely enough to keep Virgil's little chapel in the black.

Sally hated working for that arrogant...well, that arrogant *lady,* Elizabeth

Descamps. But she had no choice. At least not one that would keep her in town and together with Virgil. She had begged him to petition the bishop for a church in another diocese, but he wouldn't consider it. "I can't leave my worshippers," Virgil said more than once. "A shepherd does not abandon his flock just because the wolves have taken some of them. Remember Acts 20:28:30: "For I know this, that after my departure savage wolves will come in among you, not sparing the flock."

Sally never ceased to be amazed at Virgil's command of scripture; he was never at a loss for a passage that reinforced his point of view. So, as the chapel's fortunes began to ebb, she applied for a position "in the belly of the beast," as Virgil put it. That she was able to advance to the position of personal assistant to Katherine Deschamps on the basis of her merit was small solace. What irony, Sally thought. Because Mrs. Deschamps relied on Sally for scripture quotes, and Sally got most of them from Virgil, his message was going out into the world after all, although through a less than ideal vessel. She prayed constantly for a miracle to deliver them from their predicament.

Then one day the miracle happened. It came riding in on a bicycle.

Sally had seen the bicyclist many times while looking out their front window, praying. But on one particular morning the bicyclist turned and came back, stopping at the sidewalk in front of their house. He seemed to be pondering something as he sat there, staring at the front door. Finally, he dismounted and leaned the bike up against the large oak tree whose roots had cracked the sidewalk over the years. He walked up to the door, his cleated bike shoes clacking on the broken sidewalk. He hesitated for a moment, as if collecting himself; then he rang the bell.

"Sally?" Virgil said from his small office, which was a little cubby off the dining room.

"I'll get it," Sally said. She set her teacup down and walked to the door. "Yes?" She said as she opened the door. "Can I help you?" Probably a flat tire and needs to use the phone, she thought.

"Is the minister in?" The man asked softly, almost a whisper. He still had his helmet and glasses on, and he wore a neck gaiter, covering his mouth and nose from the wind, dust, and bugs.

"I'll see if he's available," she said. She walked over to the office door and knocked lightly. Virgil was hard at work, searching his bible for suitable passages that he could use in next Sunday's sermon. Papers with his chicken-scratched scribblings were scattered all over the desk. He looked up.

"We have a visitor," she said. "He asked if you were available. I can arrange an appointment if you like."

Virgil rose, wiping his hands absently on his faded jeans. "Non-sense," he said with a troubled smile. "How often do we get visitors?" He walked into the living room and regarded his visitor, who had removed his helmet, sunglasses and gaiter, with shock. The visitor was Corey Deschamps.

"Please, Mr. Deschamps," Virgil said, shaking Corey's gloved hand. "Welcome. Have a seat," he said, gesturing to a threadbare sofa on which a cat sat. "Sally, would you bring us some refreshment? What would you like, Mr. Descamps? Coffee, tea, soda?"

"Nothing, thanks," Corey said, sitting down heavily. The cat meowed and scampered off. He pulled his gloves off, one finger at a time and stared sadly at the floor. Why did you come here, he asked himself? Why didn't you ride on by, like usual? What led you to stop your ride and ring their bell? It occurred to him that these people must hate him for intruding on their comfortable existence. He knew Sally, of course; she was always at Elizabeth's side, taking notes. He knew that she must have taken the job out of desperation, why else would she work for the competition? What good would stopping at their house do? Still here he was, and he had no idea why. He put his face in his hands and began gently crying.

Virgil saw the desperation in the man sitting before him. He looked at Sally and, without saying anything, the two knelt on either side of Corey and placed their hands comfortingly on his shoulders. They prayed. As they prayed Corey's soft tears turned to sobs. He was wracked with convulsions of shame and self-pity. Finally, he shook them off and stood, his fists clenched and his expression one of anger.

"I'm a sham!" He exclaimed. "A fake! A phony! Everything I say is script-ed, everything I write is written for me. My sermon is nothing but theatre, crafted to extract money from the hopeless, the desperate and the hopeful." He looked at the minister and his wife for a moment, bemused expres-sions on their faces. "I, I'm sorry I intruded," he said, gathering himself. He snatched up his helmet and glasses and headed towards the door.

"Wait!" Virgil said. "Please don't leave! God sent you here for a reason. Let's find out what it is."

Corey stopped and turned. "I don't understand," he stammered.

"We need to pray over this," Virgil said softly. "Together. God will reveal his purpose through prayer."

Corey clutched his helmet and glasses and looked sadly, first at Virgil, then at Sally. "I can't," he said.

"Yes, you can," Virgil said softly. "Please sit," he insisted. He took Corey's helmet and glasses and gestured to the couch. Corey sat, but looked at the two imploringly.

"No, I can't," he said again. "I don't know how to pray."

Virgil laughed gently. The minister of a major megachurch doesn't know how to pray, he thought sadly. As a young man, he had done a lot of read-ing on Christ, his disciples, and the early Christian movement. How far away from those spiritual early beginnings have we drifted? He felt, in his own humble way, a little like Martin Luther, a major influence of his. He saw how some ministers had become corrupt, avaricious and ostentatious in the display of their wealth. He thought again about Corey's bike and Lycra outfit. Their cost would feed a poor family for many weeks. He also thought about time. How many members of Corey's vast congregation needed prayer and comfort while he was tooling around town on such an expensive bike? But as he looked at the pathetic wretch of a man before him, a bit of scripture came to him, as it often did. It was Mark 8:36: "What profits a man if he gains the whole world but loses his own soul." Virgil suddenly realized that God had set him a task. "Let me show you how to pray," he said, kneeling next to Corey.

Over the next several weeks, Corey stopped by almost every day. He opened his heart to Virgil, Sally and, eventually, to God. He confessed to his abiding hatred for Elizabeth.

"She controls every aspect of my life," he said one day. "I have everything I need, but she decides what I need, always the best, of course. Like my bike. It cost a fortune. I only mentioned that I used to like riding, and she decided that it would be good exercise for me. The next day the bike was delivered, along with all the riding gear I have. She even decided on a block of time for me to ride in my daily schedule." He laughed to himself. "If only she knew I was spending much of it here." He managed a weak laugh and continued, "I have no money; if I say I'd like to go to the store or order something, she does it for me. "Why go out and chance meeting your congregants unprepared," she always says."

It seemed to Virgil that Elizabeth had such a controlling personality that it had become an addiction for her. He reasoned that such a person could become extremely dangerous, demanding control of people even to her own detriment. Her cloying control of Corey had become an obsession with her and, like a python constricting its prey, Elizabeth was squeezing the life out of Corey, not physically, but spiritually. Virgil could tell that Corey was at a breaking point and it worried him. There was no telling what Elizabeth might do if he bucked her. Would she further tighten her coils, or would she herself snap? He decided then and there to add her to his prayer list.

The bible study meetings with Corey made progress. Corey had a tremendous memory and knew dozens of verses by heart. But he only knew the words, not the meanings. Virgil and Sally spent much time discussing those meanings with him and he proved an adept student. He asked insightful questions and wasn't satisfied with pat answers or generalities. Virgil began to feel challenged, and he upped his own game. Soon, the meetings came to be more than just the duties that every minister pursues among his worshippers. They became learning experiences for himself. Sally felt the same way.

"With a little help, Corey could become more of what he pretends to be than he is," she said one day. "Imagine the number of souls he could touch, with the right guidance." Working for Elizabeth, Sally had not only a good idea of the number of people that were on his mailing list; she knew the exact figure. Elizabeth was a staunch micro-manager but, like many of her ilk, she had no desire to work on the actual details of things. That was Sally's department, she worked on the church's mailing lists, purchase orders, bills, and finances. She also edited and critiqued the weekly sermons. Because of that, Sally was able to insert bible verses and interpretations that the three of them came up with during their meetings. As a result, Corey came to feel more in control of his own sermons.

One day, while the three were discussing the concept of "render unto Caesar the things that are Caesar's" Virgil casually said. "Like the bishop breathing down my neck."

"What do you mean?" Corey asked, puzzled.

"Oh, nothing," Virgil said, regretting his slip immediately. It was a curse for him, he knew, speaking too quickly. Sally always told him that he was too honest, that remaining silent is not necessarily a lie.

Corey wasn't satisfied with "oh, nothing." He looked at Sally for explanation.

"The bishop is constantly threatening to shut the Community Chapel down because of the paltry amount we take in from donations and tithes."

Virgil tried to stop her from going further. Church business had no place in Bible study. "Now, Sally," he began. But Sally was not to be stopped.

"It's true and you know it, Virgil," she said. She turned to Corey. "The Community Chapel is on probation. If we don't bring the church into the black, they'll close it."

Corey thought for a moment, his brow furrowed. Then he spoke, haltingly at first. "You know I can't attend your services on Sundays," he began. "And Elizabeth would have a fit if she found out I was here. But would you consider me to be a member of your church nonetheless?"

"Of course," Virgil said. "I felt that way the first day you walked in here.

You were a lost sheep," he added, laughing a little, and missing Corey's direction.

"Then I want to tithe," he said firmly. "One tenth of my net worth, right? Isn't that customary?"

"Elizabeth would never stand for that," Sally said, not believing what she had just heard.

"Right," Corey said. "But she doesn't have to know. You run the books. Can't you massage them a little? Maybe through some consulting fees. I know you can."

Sally laughed and shook her head, her eyes twinkling. "You have no idea what your net worth is, do you?"

"No, I don't," Corey said, a little miffed at being made fun of.

"Sorry," Sally said. She had forgotten for a moment how thin Corey's skin was. "It's just that, well, we don't need anything near what that figure would be."

"How much do you need?" Corey said, angry at himself for being so prickly.

Sally mentioned a figure.

Corey nodded without hesitation. "But increase that number by fifty percent. Your chapel needs new furniture."

Now, sitting in their breakfast nook, Sally couldn't help but laugh at the notion that the few people who attended the chapel heard essentially the same sermon as the thousands who sat in the megachurch or watched on satellite TV. A different delivery, admittedly, but the same sermon. She was pleased with the renovations that Corey's secret tithe had financed. Refinished, pews, new stained-glass windows, new draperies, new sound system and even new instruments for the worship band; although, sadly, better instruments didn't make better musicians.

But a gnawing guilt still ate at her. She knew that, someday, Elizabeth might find out about the consulting fees paid to Virgil. If she did, there was no way that she could prove that Corey was behind the payments. Although the man had made great progress towards re-establishing his individuality, there was no guarantee that he wouldn't panic and disavow his connection to the payments. If he stood behind his commitment and admitted that the tithe had been his idea, Elizabeth would stop the payments, fire Sally and their little chapel would go under. But, if Corey didn't stand his ground, if he caved, she would go to jail for embezzlement. She said a prayer that they wouldn't be discovered – again.

CHAPTER NINETEEN

THE WATERS OF THE gulf glistened as Will Willard piloted his plane southward. It was an old De Haviland Beaver, fully refitted. Will loved the plane and it was here that he felt most at home, flying free and under the radar. Of course, he had filed a flight plan with the FAA, just to be safe. But still he flew low, the sensation of speed greater near the ocean's surface.

His destination today was Key West, where he had a shipment of seafood and produce waiting at a private dock. The plane felt good under his experienced hand; responsive and eager, more like a living thing than a machine. It was finely tuned and the engine purred smoothly. Pelicans, ospreys, and seagulls flew just below him, and in the clear blue water he could see dolphins, sharks, and rays cruising. He felt as one with the animals, carefree and unfettered by the confines of human society. Lyrics from an old song by Stephen Stills occurred to him as he flew: "I don't do business that don't make me smile, I love my aeroplane 'cause she got style. I'm a treetop flyer."

A couple of hours later he saw the island, its trees and roofs shining above the bright blue water like a rough-cut gem. He landed and taxied up to the dock, where workers were waiting to load the plane and refuel it. Will called to them by name and walked over to a flimsy office with a corrugated tin roof and malfunctioning air conditioner; it smelled of seawater, rotting seaweed, fish guts, and cigarette smoke. The dockmaster sat at a dusty desk, sweating and smoking a cigarette. His name was Barney and he smiled at Will in a friendly manner.

"How was the flight over?" he asked, blowing a stream of smoke in the general direction of an open window. There was nothing about a windless, sunny day that could cause Will any difficulty. But, then again, if the weather had been stormy, with windshear lashing at the plane and visibility next to nothing, Will would have had the same answer: "smooth." Will was the best pilot that Barney had ever encountered, and he had encountered many. He could fly in any kind of weather, day, or night. In earlier times there had sometimes been a degree of urgency to some of Will's flights, but he had handled them with the cool aplomb of someone used to operating under pressure. It seemed at times that Will welcomed that pressure, in Barney's opinion.

They discussed business for a while and then Will excused himself and went to a shed where he kept an old Indian motorcycle. He carried a canvas duffel bag, which he strapped to the cargo rack and then pulled the bike out. It was fueled and ready. He checked the gauges, gave it a kickstart and headed towards the city.

He motored slowly down Duval Street, taking in the sights. As often as he came here, he never tired of the quaint 19th century architecture and the shotgun and conch houses spread everywhere. In years past, he and Daphne often stayed in a bungalow by the beach, owned by her father and within walking distance of downtown. He passed the Green Parrot, Sloppy Joe's, and a couple of other iconic bars. Pulling into an open parking space, he walked a little way up the street to Rocco's, a little out-of-the-way place that had the best conch fritters in town. As he walked through the door he was immediately greeted by the owner, a man named Flip DeFlippo. He tall, thin and, loud, having had his hearing damaged by an IED in Afghanistan. "Will! Long time no see!" he boomed with a grin. A few of the locals seated at the bar turned and waved to him, laughing at Flip's greeting; Will had been there only two days ago.

He ordered conch fritters and a Dogfish Head beer.

"How's Daphne?" Flip boomed as he served Will the beer.

"Great, how's Peggy?" Will said, referring to Flip's wife. She was short, fat and louder than Flip. When the two of them were together and had had a couple of drinks, it was said that they could be heard two blocks away.

"Mean as a snake," Flip said, making an effort to soften his voice.

"What?" Will said. "I can't hear you." He only mouthed the words and the rest of the clientele burst out laughing.

Just then Peggy came walking out from the kitchen with an order for another customer. She was the cook.

"I heard that, Flip," Peggy shouted. She set the platter down with a loud clatter and stared hotly at Hal.

Hal threw his hands up in mock surrender. Peggy let out a laugh and leaned over the bar to give Will a kiss. "How's Daphne and Stacy?"

"Good," Will said, sipping his beer. "Stacy's got a new boyfriend, a reporter."

"Shall I start a pool to see how long this one lasts?" she said, looking around at the patrons, all of whom knew Stacy.

"Hey, this one might stick," Will said. "She took him out to Snake Island to get some pictures."

"And he's still with her?" Peggy asked.

Will shook his head with a laugh. He ate his meal and left a bill on the bar. He also left the canvas duffel, which contained a considerable amount of money. "Tell Van I said 'hi,'" he told Flip. Flip had been another runner for Van Ness who had also retired. Little did Will know that the money he had left in the duffel would circle through Van to Fitzgibbons and then back to Brantwood via Elizabeth Deschamps.

Will rode his motorcycle back to the docks. The dock workers were just finishing loading the plane and Will checked the invoice against the cargo and paid Barney with cash and a wink.

"Customs agents can't count for shit," Barney said with a laugh. He shook hands with Will and said, "see you in a couple of days."

The rusty fishing trawler crawled along at half speed, its engine chugging loudly. Smoke billowed out of the smokestack in large black puffs that were timed with the ship's arhythmic engine. The captain, a man named Jeremiah Andrewshot, was dressed in greasy fisherman's clothes. He had a three-day stubble of beard, a black knit cap and a cigar clenched in his teeth. His crew of six wore worker's overalls, assorted ball caps and white rubber boots. They had just pulled their nets and had an unimpressive catch flopping in the hold. It was a convincing cover.

Captain Jerry, as he was called, was scanning the horizon with a pair of high-powered binoculars. He was looking for a floatplane this time; there had been three boats earlier. He swept the horizon slowly and methodically, looking not only for the floatplane but for any unwelcome boats or planes - he saw none. Then, flying low, almost skimming the surface, he saw it: Will Willard's Beaver.

Will spotted the trawler and flew over it once, waggling his wings as he passed the vessel. A sailor on the upper deck saw him and signaled all clear. Will landed and taxied up to the ship. A couple of sailors threw ropes and Will secured the plane to a makeshift deck extension just above the water line. He jumped onto it and clambered up the ladder.

"Permission to come abord," Will said as he climbed onto the deck.

"Will!" Captain Jerry said, grabbing his hand in a friendly handshake. "Good to see you again."

Will had a soft-sided cooler in his hands and handed it over to Jerry. "Some Key West shrimp for you and the boys," he said. "You do know how to do a seafood boil, I hope."

Jerry laughed and looked inside the cooler. He smiled appreciatively. "You betcha. Can you take some of these fish off my hands?" He gestured towards the meagre hold of flapping fish.

Will laughed. "No, I'm full up," he said. "I have just enough room for what you've brought me."

Jerry grinned. "Load him up, boys!" He shouted as he gestured to his crew, which was already approaching the plane with assorted boxes, crates and bales. The two went over the inventory vocally, not wanting any paper-work to serve as a record of the deal.

The crew knew the drill and removed several iced containers of seafood, put the cargo in and then replaced the seafood. Will gave them a thumbs up when they had finished. He handed an envelope of cash to Jerry, who paid him the compliment of not checking it. The two had been doing business this way for a long time.

"Give my regards to Van," Will said as he climbed down the ladder and stood on the dock next to his plane. The whole process had taken less than twenty minutes.

"I will," Jerry said with a wave.

Will climbed into the cockpit and got the shock of his life. There, sitting in the passenger's seat, was Buddy, his old partner from the Van Ness days. He was grinning, happy to have surprised his old campanero. He was a little thinner on top and a little grayer and he was a little thicker in the middle. But it was definitely Buddy.

"Long time," Buddy said, sticking out his hand. Will took it and shook it warmly, despite the surprise. He pulled the plane away from the trawler, gunned his engine and took off, waggling his wings at Captain Jerry, who was most likely enjoying the joke.

"So, what have you been up to, these last twenty odd years?" Will said. He knew that Buddy would tell him the reason he was aboard in due time and he knew better than to demand an answer, despite his right to demand one.

"I've been laying low, as you have," Buddy said. "Doing a little side work for Van now and then. That's about it."

Will flew on, not saying a word. Buddy laughed to himself. Will was always a cool one, he thought. Cool under pressure, and cool under fire. Most men would have at least shown a little surprise at Buddy's unexpected appearance in the plane, but Will acted as if he had expected Buddy to be waiting for him. He appeared pleasantly interested in Buddy's life but not at all interested in Buddy's mission. He watched as Will piloted the plane as if he hadn't a care in the world. Finally, he spoke up. He knew he could trust Will implicitly.

"Van's been laundering money through the CFO at the Thompson Fund, a guy named Ben Fitzgibbons, without Mrs. Thompson's knowledge. We think he's been skimming. The money goes in but is very slow in coming out. He claims that the money is tied up in the fund and that he has to be careful. He may be legit, but, well, in this business it pays to be watchful. There's a lot of money at stake and if he gets paranoid, he may run. There's an indication that other people are using him as well. He probably has built up a very large nest egg for himself, if he hasn't put it all up his nose. We've been watching him closely and we have a couple of good hackers, but we don't want to spook him. We suspect that the Feds are starting to snoop; Van doesn't want a connection tied to him." He paused for a minute, waiting for Will to ask the question "what does that have to do with me?" but he stayed mum. Buddy went on: "There seems to be some kind of connection between the Thompson Fund and The Brantwood Fellowship. I'm supposed to find out what it is."

"The Thompson Fund did some heavy funding at the startup of the Fellowship," Will said. "But that's public record."

"Right," Buddy said. "But money has been flowing in some strange ways that we can't figure out. We put a tail on Fitzgibbons and found out that he drives all the way from the capital to Brantwood every Sunday to attend Corey Deschamp's sermon. From everything that we've gathered, Fitzgibbons was never a religious man. He may be using the Brantwood Fellowship as he is the Thompson Fund."

Will nodded that he understood. "But I don't see how you can get in there to find anything out. Elizabeth Deschamps runs a tight ship and she's got some powerful friends."

"She also has a lady working for her, on the books, that's been doing a little skimming herself. Her name is Sally Yarber and she's the wife of the minister of a little chapel that suddenly became flush with cash. All kinds of new renovations, that type of thing. I need to get in touch with her."

Will shot Buddy a hard look.

Buddy threw his hands up. "Don't worry, there'll be no rough stuff. We don't care how   much she's taken from the Fellowship, that's not our concern. But I think she might be able to help us."

"No rough stuff," Will said emphatically.

"No rough stuff," Buddy said. "Scout's honor. We just need to get a look at the books."

Will laughed. "Scout's honor, eh! I bet you can't even make the scout's hand signal!"

Buddy held up two fingers in a V shape.

"That's what I thought," Will said. "I suppose you'll be staying with us?"

"I thought you'd never ask."

CHAPTER TWENTY

Drew took the stairs to the pressroom two at a time. Late again! He thought, chastising himself. So much for the early arrival routine he had sworn to maintain.

"Getting caught up again, just like you'd said you'd never do,"

"It's casual," Drew said.

"Sure, it is, that's how it begins. Then, before you know it, she'll dump you just like that girl who left you for the soap salesman!"

"Not this time," Drew said. "I'm keeping it strictly casual."

As he opened the door to the noisy pressroom he was greeted by a familiar booming voice. "Hey, Honcho!" Joe Crimmons said, snapping his gum and looking at his watch meaningfully. "I saw your car in the lot and thought you'd finally become a team player; finally decided to get here early. Guess I was wrong!"

Just then the pressroom door opened again, and Danny Frame stumbled in, holding a Styrofoam coffee cup in one hand and a sheaf of papers in the other. He was assigned to the police beat, which meant he got calls at all hours to go and cover every fender-bender, domestic disturbance, and petty robbery the city had to offer.

"Oh, another shirker!" Joe boomed, clearly enjoying the young man's discomfiture. "A team like this couldn't beat Saint Mary's School for the Blind!"

"Hey, that's offensive!" Mary Jo Collunge snapped. She was the Food and Wine Editor, a section that had only one employee, herself. She was politically correct and insisted that everyone else be too. She considered Joe Crimmons a throwback to the bad old days of bullying coaches and male empowerment and she called him out every chance she got. She had filed a dozen complaints about Joe's offensive language to HR, but the complaints seemed to die there. She was convinced that Joe's gambling tips to Bunny were the cause.

"How can that be offensive," Joe asked sarcastically. "There isn't a Saint Mary's School for the Blind."

"It's offensive to sightless people," Mary Jo said.

"But there's no sightless people here, so how can anybody be offended?"

Mary Jo fumed but said nothing else. She had made her point, at least to the other people within earshot.

Danny used the exchange to slip past Joe. "Hey, that was a sweet Jeep I saw you get out of," he said to Drew. "And a sweet little driver too! What's her name?"

"Don't know," Drew said. "I was hitch-hiking."

"Right," Danny said. "So, do you always kiss drivers goodbye when you hitch-hike?"

The comment drew a smattering of laughter. "Always," Drew said. "By the way, can I catch a ride with you this afternoon?"

More laughter. Drew headed towards his desk, but he knew that the damage had been done. Joe Crimmons had sharp ears and he was certain to tell Janice. Oh well, he thought. Janice probably had things figured out anyway.

"Hey kid," Teejay said as Drew sat down. "Check this out!" He tossed a couple of sheets on Drew's desk. It was the ready-for-copy draft of the Thompson bio. Drew read the banner: "Tommy Thompson, a Man for His Time." Below it, in smaller print, was the by-line: Teejay Edmunds with A.J. Andrews.

"Hey, thanks for the by-line," Drew said. He hadn't expected to see his name on it even though he had written the entire thing.

"You wrote some of it, Kid." Teejay said, a little superciliously, Drew thought.

"Get used to being used, Kiddo."

Drew started to tell Peter not to call him Kiddo, but all that came out was a soft, stuttered "do...do...don't ..."

"What? Teejay said.

"Nothing," Drew said, shaking his head dismissively.

"Bunny called down and said he liked it," Teejay said.

"That's great," Drew said. But he said it without the enthusiasm Teejay had expected. It seemed to him something was troubling the young lad.

"Is everything all right?" Teejay asked. Better to get right to it, he thought. He was an astute reader of moods and Drew's was a decidedly unhappy one.

"Yeah," Drew said a little hesitantly. "The club thing isn't going so well. I don't seem to be able to gain any traction on the mayor. When I see him, he just gives me a little dismissive smile and goes about his business. I wear my old college shirts to the courts, but he doesn't seem to notice. And his partner, Ned, looks at me like he'd like nothing better than to wring my neck."

"Maybe you're trying too hard," Teejay counseled. "McNair probably knows that you were assigned to cover him and is reluctant to give you an opening. The reason you were chosen was that you have things in common with him. Relax, don't appear too eager to please; John McNair likes his privacy, and he guards it like money. Bunny wants to see more of a human side of the mayor, you know, the stuff that a politician never shows. You'll only get it if you earn his trust – somehow."

"Right," Drew said. "I get it. The whole thing seems a little contrived to me anyway, the clothes, the club membership, the car. I'm sure that he can see right through me."

"Well, I'd advise you to keep at it; you never know when you might have a breakthrough. But don't worry. We all know how private John McNair is."

CHAPTER TWENTY-ONE

As Drew drove to the club, he thought about his conversation with Teejay. Maybe he *was* trying too hard. He was never much of a country club guy and he felt silly driving the little imported car and wearing an expensive golf shirt. He laughed to himself, relaxing a little. Maybe Janice was right, maybe I should get a captain's hat and a scarf.

"Just don't sing!"

"What do you care?"

"Why do you ignore me when she's around?"

"Jealous?"

Drew drove up to the entrance of the club, flashed his card at the gate and parked in the lot, not really caring about the assignment Bunny had given him anymore. He carried his designer gym bag into the fitness area and signed up for a court. He could hear McNair and Ned banging away in court number three. Today, he decided to get a court farther away from them. A brisk workout might do him some good.

"Hey Boston," a voice boomed as he opened the door to his court. He recognized it immediately as Bruce Morley's. He turned a gave a half-hearted wave.

Bruce walked swiftly up to him. "My partner didn't show up. (partner came out as 'paht-nah' in a Boston accent) Are you playing alone?"

"Yeah, you want to play?"

"Sure, go warm up while I get my gear on."

A few minutes later Bruce stepped into the court, dressed in Lycra shirt and shorts with a Lacoste symbol and goggles and gloves shoes and a tear-drop racquet. He warmed up a little and they started playing.

Drew was rusty and it very quickly became clear that Bruce was a cut above him; more than a cut, truth be told. He was quick to the ball, accurate and fast with his shots. He accompanied each rollout with a little victory yelp. But Drew soon discovered that Bruce shied away from center court; he avoided the inevitable contact that occurred there. Drew established himself in the center and began expanding his zone of control. Bruce was forced to play from the outside and rear. When he did venture into the center, Drew made sure he paid for it. He didn't use cheap shots, but he went after the ball as if Bruce wasn't there, which led to several jarring collisions.

But Bruce did manage to win, and he let out a series of yelps when he did. Sweating hard, Drew offered Bruce his hand. "Nice game," he said.

Bruce took it and shook. "You play rough," he said with a smile. He looked at Drew's faded T-shirt which read: "Give Blood, Play Rugby." "I might have known," Bruce said. "Hey, by the way, I'm throwing a beach party tonight at my place. Drop by if you like. Stacy will be there," he added.

Why would Stacy be there, Drew wondered? He showered, changed and walked upstairs to the bar. One beer and I'm out, he vowed. He was tired of Bunny's charade. It was all getting to be a little too much.

"Told you! She's probably rekindling with Bruce. You should have hit him harder when you had the chance."

"I did get in a few good shots though, right?" Drew said just before opening the door to the main dining room, which overlooked the golf course on one side and the bay on the other. John McNair and Ned Butch-er were sitting at the bar, enjoying a cold beer. A golf game played on the large screen TV. Drew walked nonchalantly to the other end of the bar. The bartender, an efficient fellow dressed in black pants, a white shirt, and a black bowtie, brought him a Heineken and a tall pilsner glass. "Thanks Chris," Drew said, remembering the man's name. He went for his club card to show his number, but the bartender said. "185, right?" Drew nodded. Bunny's personal tab. Things weren't all bad. He sipped his beer out of the bottle and half-heartedly watched the golf game.

After a while, Drew saw McNair walk off to take a call. My cue to leave, Drew thought. But Ned signaled Chris and said: "Two tequilas," and motioned towards Drew. He stood and walked over to where Drew was sitting. Drew was surprised to see that Ned was not as big as he thought him to be. In fact, he was only medium built. But he was wiry and compact and moved with an economy of motion that suggested a life spent in the military. When he arrived at Drew's stool, he seemed to suddenly grow, not in size but in presence. Here was a man accustomed to leading men into extreme danger, Drew thought. Chris set two shot glasses of tequila on the bar in front of them.

Ned regarded Drew with sharp, steel-grey eyes. Drew found himself struggling to meet them. "*Those eyes, like those of a hawk! Don't look away, he'll think that you're weak! Which you are! We both know that.*" Drew forced himself to meet the man's gaze and hold it.

Ned nodded once casually and then looked away. "I know what you're doing," he said softly. His voice was low and gravelly, worn by years of barking orders. He took his shot glass, tapped it once on the bar and drank it. Drew did the same. He waited for Ned to explain.

"Bunny gave you a club membership, a car, enrolled you in a couple of grad classes and gave you a line of credit at his tailor. He hopes that your obvious similarities will get John to open up his private life to you so that you can get exclusive pictures and quotes for his paper. He also hopes that you can find any skeletons that could prove problematical as he advances to the governorship. What you don't know is Bunny's purpose." He turned and looked directly at Drew and waited for a response.

Drew felt as if he were being interrogated and was about to crack. His charade was totally revealed and now he felt as foolish as a kid caught stealing candy. He didn't know what Ned meant or what he expected him to say. He sat silently.

"Then you don't know," Ned said. There was the slightest look of relief on his face which he quickly banished. "Let me explain. Bunny's a good man, by and large, but he has his agenda. He views himself as a kingmaker and he wants to put the best people he can in office. He views John as one of those good people, and he's right. But he wants to control John, as he does the other politicians that he has helped put in place. He helps them, they owe him. He finds dirt on them and buries it, they owe him. If they cross him, he can burn them, and they know it. It's *his* show. You understand?"

Drew nodded, embarrassed at the role he had been playing. He felt like a patsy, set up and used.

Ned seemed to read his mind. "Don't feel bad, kid," he said. "You're not the first, and you won't be the last. And, like I said, Bunny's intentions are generally good, from what I've seen at least. John could easily go along with Bunny's program and lots of good things could result. But then there would come a day when someone needs a favor, someone needs everyone to look the other way. Someone wants something that John is not willing to give."

"What's that?' Drew said impulsively.

Ned gave him a long hard look. "His integrity," he said.

A while later, McNair returned from his phone call. Ned and Drew were sitting comfortably, sipping beer and watching golf. He looked the two of them over for a moment and then said, "You guys feel like hitting nine? I've got a meeting at four, but I could definitely squeeze in nine."

Drew was a little shocked at the invitation. He suddenly realized that he had passed some kind of test and he guessed that McNair's phone call was just theatre, giving Ned a chance to assess him. The fact that he was still sitting at the bar meant that he had passed the assessment.

"Sure," Drew said. "I'd like that. I'll get my clubs."

On the course they talked easily, sports mostly. Drew swallowed hard when McNair asked him which baseball team he liked. "Red Sox," he said, a little nervous about what the response would be. Ned and John shared a laugh.

"Then what's that Yankees cap doing in your gym bag?" John said.

Drew felt his face flush, which made Ned and John laugh even harder. "While you were busy vetting me, you didn't think we weren't vetting you?" John said. "Don't forget, I was in counter-intelligence for a while."

Drew reached down, unzipped his gym bag and took out the Yankees hat. "I picked up the wrong hat at the store. I was hoping to get my money back, but then I realized that it was Bunny's money." He handed the hat to McNair who looked it over for a moment.

"Just my size," he said. He adjusted the plastic sizing tabs in the back and put it on. He smiled, readjusted the tabs, ripped off the price tags and bent the rim to his satisfaction. He put it on and grinned. "Tell Bunny I said thanks."

As they played on, Drew was amazed at how well Ned played with only one arm. His drives were powerful and long, his fairway play was masterful, and his putting was precise. John, it turned out, had been an excellent golfer in college and even had a shot at joining the pro-circuit until he opted for the army. Drew was rusty and felt outclassed, but he gamely hung in there. At the seventh hole they had to wait for the foursome ahead of them. Ned reached into a cooler and pulled out three beers.

"So," John said casually. "What did you find out about me at the Library? Is Ray still there?"

Drew was taken aback. He realized that he had indeed been vetted and, evidently, pretty thoroughly. "Yep. Ray's still there. He's a fixture, isn't he?"

John waited for an answer. Drew knew he was on the spot. He decided to answer honestly.

"You were immature, partied a lot, squeaked by on your courses and got in a little minor trouble that your father got you out of." He stopped and allowed himself a laugh. "Sounded an awful lot like my own college experience."

John still waited.

"And you dated a girl named Liz Young, who left you while you were in the army for a guy named Derf Walowitz."

John looked genuinely pained for a moment, remembering an old wound. What was it like to get a Dear John letter while in combat, thousands of miles from home? What kind of person would do that to a man? Drew glanced over at Ned and saw him look down at the ground, feeling his friend's pain; again.

"You've told no one?" John asked. Drew could see that it hurt him to ask. He again swallowed hard.

"I told Teejay and Bunny," Drew said. "No one else. They told me to keep it under my hat."

McNair and Ned looked at each other meaningfully. Drew realized that they suspected that he had told Bunny and Teejay. Another test, he thought. Talking with these guys was like walking through a minefield. Then he realized that these guys *had* walked through minefields.

After that, though, the conversation became more relaxed and the questions became less pointed. John laughed and joked about some of his silly college exploits and close scrapes with the law. "I stole a clock out of the police station once," he said, laughing. "I was drunk as hell and did it on a dare. I hung it on the frat house wall."

"The big clock in the rec room?" Drew asked.

"It's still there?' John said incredulously. "Amazing!"

Later, at the bar, John excused himself again. Ned turned and looked directly at Drew, his steel grey eyes sharp and focused. Drew got the feeling that Ned had looked at many young soldiers that way.

"Look," he said, his words measured and clear. "You're a photo-journalist. Act like one. Soldiers expect their non-coms and officers to dress and act in keeping with their rank. John's a natural leader and a good one, believe me. When he was in the service, he wore his uniform proudly whether it was combat fatigues or dress greens. Now his uniforms of the day are blazers, business suits and tuxedos. Photo-journalists don't run around in expensive golf shirts."

"Then I take it you don't like my little green car."

"You look better in a Jeep."

DREW thought a lot about what had been said that afternoon as he drove back to The Journal. His worry now was what kinds of things he should report to Teejay and Bunny and which things were private and off-limits. He also wondered what Bruce meant when he invited him to the beach party. The phrase "Stacy will be there," kept running through his mind. In what capacity would she be there? As Bruce's date in a rekindled relationship? As the date of some other guy? He wanted to call her about it, but she had made it clear that she didn't like calls and texts; besides, would she think him jealous and weak if he did?

"You should call her. She's probably sitting by her phone right now, waiting."

"People don't sit by their phones," Drew said. "That's in the movies."

"Yeah, sitting by her phone – in Bruce's bedroom!"

An image popped into Drew's head. He banished it. "Leave me alone, will you? I've got a lot on my mind and I don't have room for you in there."

"Oh, right. Sorry to drop in on you like this."

Drew didn't want to appear the fool by showing up at the party like some kind of forsaken lover. He decided that it would be best to skip the party and the Cove as well. He could use a night off anyway. He took the stairs to the pressroom two-at-a-time, hoping to leave Peter behind.

"Hey, Honcho," Joe Crimmons said as Drew walked into the pressroom. His voice somehow didn't have the usual bullying, sarcastic edge to it.

"Hi, Joe," Drew said as he walked by. He tried to sound as pleasant as he could.

"Nice job on the Thompson bio," Joe said. "You might make the team after all."

"Thanks, Joe," Drew said. "That means a lot, coming from you."

"Still a wiseass," Joe muttered as Drew headed towards his desk. A couple of people snickered, drawing a hard look from Joe.

As Drew sat down, Teejay came over, holding a first-run copy of the day's newspaper. "Bunny liked the bio, but suggested we get run our own pictures of the governor for the follow-up article," Teejay said, tossing the paper down on Drew's desk. He noticed that the photo credit was from the AP.

"I'll try to get some good shots," Drew said.

"Good," Teejay said. "You're all set then? Got everything you need?"

"Yep, I'm all set," Drew said.

"Any progress on the mayor?" Teejay asked.

"I managed to get invited to play nine holes with him earlier," Drew said casually.

Teejay arched his eyebrows appreciatively. "Good job," he said. "Progress. Any usable quotes?"

"A few," Drew said. "I didn't press too hard. I did find one thing out though."

Teejay looked at him expectantly

"He's a damn good golfer," Drew said.

Teejay laughed. "Stop the presses!"

"Ned Butcher's pretty good too," Drew said. "And he only has one arm."

"Well, keep up the good work Kid," Teejay said, heading back to his desk.

"Thanks, Chief," Drew said.

"Cove's closed tonight," Joe Crimmons said as Drew headed towards the door an hour later.

Drew looked at him for an explanation.

"Bruce Morley's throwing a big beach party and the whole staff of the Cove is catering. Will is flying in all kinds of stuff for a luau. Should be fun. All the regulars at the Cove are invited," he added.

Drew didn't know if he was a regular yet, but he had been invited. "See you there," he said.

"Know where it is?' Joe asked.

Who didn't know where Bruce Morley's beach house was?

CHAPTER TWENTY-TWO

A HOT BREEZE BLEW gently over the white sand beach bringing with it the salt smell of the sea and a whiff of woodsmoke coming from a fire in a large pit in the sand. A tiki bar was filled with bottles of rum, tequila, vodka, and bourbon. There was wine and a keg of craft beer. A 55-gallon blue plastic drum was filled with a concoction Daphne called "Pineapple Goddamn," consisting of rum, fruit juice, strawberries the size of apples and large chunks of melon and pineapple. She'd seen people get falling down wasted just from eating the fruit.

Stacy was a little disappointed that Drew hadn't called or texted. Sure, she thought, she had told him that she didn't like being called or pestered with texts, but didn't he know that she meant: "call me or text me?" Oh well, it wouldn't be the first time that a budding romance had fizzled out on her. Maybe it was the hike on Snake Island that put him off, or the tour of the snake room at her cabin. Maybe she had come on a little too strong and a little too soon. But then he didn't seem to have minded.

Stacy was puzzled by her attraction to Drew. He was younger than most of her boyfriends, close to her own age for a change. He was unsure of himself and a little naïve. But then he was enthusiastic during their adventures and, although skittish around her pets, didn't seem put off by her fascination with them. Instead of the usual narcissism of Bruce and the others, he was self-effacing and even vulnerable around her. She found herself wishing that he had come to the party but resisted the temptation to call or text him. She was busy anyway, plus, she was developing a bad mood due to Bruce's antics as the center of attention at his carefully orchestrated party.

He seemed to be everywhere, making sure the party went off without a hitch. He flitted from spot to spot, supervising each activity and making sure that everyone had enough to drink. He had organized a beach volleyball tournament, bag toss games and an ultimate frisbee contest. A band was set up on a flatbed trailer and played trop rock while servers circulated with trays of drinks and hors de oeuvres. But his main concern today was the large luau pit which Rich Reynolds and his kitchen crew had dug. The pit was circular, four feet deep and eight feet in diameter. Stones had been placed on firewood and the wood had been lit a couple of hours earlier. The stones were still heating and would be ready when Will arrived with the food. Stacy watched as Bruce went from person to person, putting a plastic lei on everyone who didn't have one, saying, "Been laid today?" It was so Bruce, she thought

The party was well underway when the roar of a float plane announced Will's arrival. He landed in the calm waters of Bruce's private lagoon. Pinky and Jason hustled out to pull the plane up to the beach and secure it. They began unloading its cargo into a couple of big carts. As Will climbed down out of the cockpit Bruce walked up to him, a grin on his face. "What'd ya get?" He asked.

"Pork tenderloins, half-chickens, fresh red snapper and grouper, sea scallops, pink shrimp, spiny lobsters and a couple of bushels of fresh sweet corn," Will said, accepting the cold Red Stripe that Bruce had brought him. "Andouille sausage and chorizo."

"Beautiful," Bruce said. The two men clinked bottles and drank.

"What's that?" Will asked, pointing to a very large teepee shaped pile of driftwood.

"The bonfire," Bruce said. He and his friends had been collecting the wood for two weeks.

"No, I mean what's that on the top, attached to that pole?"

"Oh," Bruce said, "It's a pair of black panties my now ex-girlfriend found under my bed."

The two men watched them flap in the breeze like a flag.

DREW motored his MG up the beach road, his radio blaring "Love Will Keep Us Together." As a joke, he'd worn a pair of white pants, a white shirt, and a blue blazer. Around his neck was a red silk scarf. To top off the look, he had on sunglasses and a white captain's hat that he'd picked up at a tourist store along the beach strip. He turned up the private drive that led to Bruce Morley's beach house, the engine on the MG purring. Cars were parked along the road and people were walking towards the house on the road. Drew beeped his horn and waved as he passed them.

He pulled up to the entrance where he was certain Janice would station herself. He was right and he watched her double over in laughter as he got out of the car. As he breezed past her, he tossed her the keys as if she was the valet. She deftly caught them and stuck her other hand out for a tip. He ignored her and proceeded towards the bar; he kept his left hand in his jacket pocket and his right hand raised in a parade wave. He walked up to the tiki bar and, ignoring Stacy, said to Chaz: "I'm looking for Tennille? I'm told she'd be here?"

"I'll be your Tennille," Janice said, walking up to the bar. She slapped Drew on the butt and reached beyond him for a tall, iced glass with a piece of sugar cane for a stir stick. Janice had developed a fondness for mojitos; she thought they paired well with her clove cigarettes and was never too far from either.

Bruce noticed the group and walked over. "What's with the get-up?" he asked Drew in a friendly manner.

"He's trying to curry favor with the mayor," Janice said, answering for him. "He thinks that's how y'all dress over at the club."

"Haw," Bruce exclaimed loudly, looking around surreptitiously to see if he was being noticed. "I've seen old Drew at the club, and he looks the part okay. But he's a Sawx fan and I don't know how that will play with our good mayor. He's a Yankees fan."

"I hope to convert him," Drew said casually. Then, taking a superior tone, he said, "I hope to bring some light to that dark area in which Yankees fans live."

"Haw haw!" Bruce said, a little too loudly, in Drew's opinion. "Well said! Well said!"

The group laughed. Stacy playfully grabbed Drew's Captain's hat and put it on.

"It looks a lot better on her than it does on you!"

Drew ignored Peter and wrapped the red scarf around Stacy's neck. She did a little twirling dance with her hands intertwined above her head. The crowd clapped along with beat the band was providing.

Teejay and Tracy, his long-time platonic date, showed up and, not having seen the Captain and Tennile bit, Teejay complimented Drew on his new look. "That's more like it, young man," he said approvingly.

"Why, thank you," Drew said in affected voice, his lower jaw jutting out as he did so. Teejay looked puzzled. But Tracy laughed lustily.

"You're right," she said. "He *is* a wiseass." She gave Drew an exaggerated lascivious leer. "We'll have to talk later. We might have something in common."

Stacy leaned forward, jutting her neck out, and hissed, her hands raised like claws. The move sent the group into a big laugh. "Easy now girls," Teejay cautioned. "There's plenty of me to go around."

Not to be outdone, Bruce stepped forward and put his arms around both Stacy and Tracy. "Ladies, let Brucie introduce you to a little concoction I call "Pineapple Goddamn." He led them towards the big blue plastic drum.

By late afternoon, everyone was fairly well drunk and had gorged themselves on the feast Rich had prepared. The band turned up and played rock as people danced in the white sand. Shouts from the games punctuated the air. Chaz, Stacy, and Daphne hustled to keep the drinks flowing. Drew changed into his khaki shorts and a t-shirt and was snapping cameos of the revelers. Many of them struck comical poses when they saw the camera pointed at them. It was a good party.

Later, as the sun was about to set, Bruce prepared his coup-de-grace: the lighting of the bonfire. He climbed to the top of the driftwood teepee with a can of gasoline and soaked the pile. Then he poured more gas into a trench that ran about thirty yards from the teepee.

"Brooce! Brooce! Brooce!" Went the chant from the crowd. Bruce popped a flare and tossed it into the trench. The gas in the trench caught fire and shot towards the teepee. With a loud "whoosh," the teepee caught fire. The crowd cheered. But then, anticlimactically, the fire fizzled out. Undeterred, Bruce climbed the teepee again with a fresh can of gas. Pinky, cheering only moments before, suddenly became hysterical. Jason joined him.

"Stop!" Both men shouted. "Get down!" They began pushing and shoving at the crowd. "Get back!" they shouted to the surprised people. But it was no use, the crowd stared and then cheered as Bruce uncapped the gas can and began pouring. Just then a tiny spark at the bottom of the teepee flickered.

"Jump!" Someone yelled. A woman screamed. Bruce looked down in horror. In one motion, he threw the gas can towards the lagoon and then dove. Another loud "whoosh" sent flames surging up the teepee.

Jason and Pinky sprinted out into the shallow water where Bruce had landed, and Will sprinted towards his plane. As they carried Bruce out of the water people saw that he appeared dazed but alive. "I'm okay," he managed as they reached the shore. Jason and Pinky hustled him to the plane, which Will had fired up. As they gingerly placed him in the passenger area, burnt flesh could be seen hanging from the backs of his legs.

Pinky and Jason pushed the plane into the lagoon, turned it and then jumped in. Will gunned the engine and took off, headed to the landing strip near the burn center at Saint Joseph's Hospital.

"He didn't look too good," Stacy said. Drew noticed that there were tears in her eyes.

CHAPTER TWENTY-THREE

Drew was getting on the elevator when Joe Crimmons came through the front door. Drew held the elevator door open for him.

"Thanks, Andrews," Joe said as he stepped onto the elevator. "Did you see the game last night?"

"No, I missed it."

"Umpire missed a call in the ninth! Saeli definitely broke his wrist on a curveball but the ump called it ball four. Bases loaded, DeJoe comes up and hits a two-out grand slam! Put 'em up by one, but we couldn't get a hit to save our lives! Coach got ejected and is appealing, but you know how that goes."

"Sucks," Drew said as the elevator door opened onto the pressroom.

Crimmons laughed, shaking his head. "My job today is making that umpire's name mud. I just have to come up with a banner."

"How 'bout "Grand Theft Baseball," Drew said off the top of his head.

"Hey," Joe said. "I like it! How did I ever let you go?" He added.

"You let me slip right through your fingers," Drew said.

"Yeah," Joe said, missing the sarcasm. "Teejay holds a lot of sway around here. I figure he robbed me."

Robbed? Drew thought. You were betting on me getting fired! But he decided to take the high road. "We can still work together once in a while. Let me know if I can do anything for you."

Joe again missed the sarcasm. "Yeah," he said. "I'd like that."

Drew walked to his desk, shaking his head.

A while later, Teejay came into the pressroom and walked up to Drew's desk.

"Just talked with Bunny," he said. "He wants you to head over to Saint Joe's and interview Bruce Morley. He said to give you this." He handed Drew a card. "Please give my representative, A.J. Andrews, every courtesy." It was signed by Bunny.

DREW made the drive to the hospital through heavy traffic. The little green MG was zippy but small and as he weaved through the towering trucks, SUVs, and RVs he felt like a little bug, ready to be squashed. It was on drives like this that Peter came to him most powerfully, coaching and criticizing his driving. *"Pass that van on the right, there's an opening.* Drew hated passing people on the right and hesitated. *"Lost your chance, hot shot,"* Peter said as the gap closed. "Yeah, like you lost all your chances," Drew said out loud. *"Don't you think I know it? If only you had kept your mouth shut! I wouldn't have had to explain. Things would have been a lot different."*

"But how were we to know?" Drew said. "How were *you* to know?"

"Still, I might not have fallen that day."

"Fallen? Is that how you put it?" Drew was referencing Peter's suicide. Distraught, strung out, unemployed and facing an upcoming DUI court date that would likely send him to jail again, Peter had jumped off the Skyway Bridge one fine day. He made a mess of it, though. He hadn't noticed that there was a fishing boat directly below him and, instead of smacking into the concrete-hard water surface, he'd ended up in the bait well of the boat, tossing the anglers out of their seats and onto the deck of the bouncing boat. A shower of silvery baitfish from the well descended on the scene. Somebody in another boat caught the whole thing on his phone and, for a week or so, Peter was a prime star of social media.

Family and friends were devastated, of course, and everyone agreed that they should have seen it coming after what had happened to his parents.

The funeral was a somber affair, with everyone saying all the right things and ignoring the undercurrents of blame, resentment, guilt, and accusation. Drew had always been susceptible to feelings of guilt. Peter was five years older than Drew and after *that day* he and Drew parted company. Yet, after *the event* (nobody used the word "suicide"), Peter started coming into his thoughts more and more. Drew listened because he felt guilty about not being a better brother to him when he was alive. Catholics call it a sin of omission, you could have done more, but didn't.

"*If only you had kept your mouth shut,*" Peter said again. It bothered Drew to hear it, since it was what he had kept saying over and over around the time of their parent's funerals, which they didn't attend.

"You can't blame yourself," Drew said out loud, passing a series of slow-moving vehicles as he did so. "You didn't know anything. You couldn't have foreseen what would happen."

"*Still, what happened wouldn't have if you had kept your mouth shut. Better still, if I hadn't had that chance encounter with Jim Osborne, I wouldn't have had anything to say that evening at the dinner table.*"

"If it's any solace, I feel pretty guilty about it all too," Drew said, easing the MG onto the exit ramp. "I might have been able to stop it."

"*You were at school when it happened. Besides, who would have thought that she'd do it?*"

True, Drew thought. Who would have known? Who would have guessed? One day Peter had come home with the news that he'd run into Jim Osborne, an old school friend whose cousin was visiting from Atlanta. He told Drew what seemed to be an incredible story. That evening as they were sitting at the dinner table with their parents, Drew brought it up.

"Hey," Drew said. "Tell Mom and Dad that story about Jim Osborne's cousin."

Peter looked a little uncomfortable, like he hadn't meant Drew to mention it.

"What about Jim Osborne?" his mother said insistently. Her lips were tight, and she had a tense look about her.

"Oh, nothing," Peter said. "Just ran into him, that's all."

"Tell me," his mother said, pressing him. Drew remembered later that their father seemed uncomfortable. He shifted in his chair and cleared his throat as if he were about to speak.

Peter, leveling a stare at Drew for bringing it up, went on to explain, a little haltingly.

"Jim was with his cousin from Atlanta who I had never met. He acted like he knew me and shook my hand warmly. 'Hey Norm,' he said to me, 'what are you doing in Tampa?' I told him my name wasn't Norm and he laughed, like I was pranking him, so I showed him my driver's license. 'No shit!' he said. 'You're a dead-ringer for a friend of mine named Norm Allen.' Strange, right?"

Drew never forgot the strange pallor that came over his father that evening, or the accusatory look his mother gave him. You could have cut the silence with a knife and Peter and Drew had uncomfortably gone to their rooms. A loud argument between their parents ensued with their father finally slamming out the door. Their mother called them to the table and explained between fits of sobs and copious tears. "Boys, I have something terrible to tell you. Your father confessed something that I've suspected for a long time. He has a second family in Atlanta. They think his name is Norm Allen. There are kids, almost grown. One of them is named Norm, after him."

Shocked, the two brothers tried to calm their mother, but it was no use. "I knew something was wrong," she explained, still crying softly. "He was always gone and when he was home, he was always making mysterious phone calls. Business, he told me when I became suspicious. But a woman can tell when a man is talking to another woman. I thought it was a casual affair that he would eventually end and so, for your sake, I stayed with him. I had no idea he was married to the woman and had another house and children!"

During the evening something seemed to snap in her. Her sobs turned into a strange, frightening bitterness and she sat up all night talking to herself with Peter trying desperately to bring her out of it.

Drew was at school the next day when it happened, but Peter was there. He had been sleeping when he heard the doorbell ring. Moments later there was the loud report of a pistol. He ran downstairs and saw his mother standing over his father, holding his father's pistol. "I'm sorry," she said and then put the pistol to her head.

Peter never recovered from the shock of the scene and, although he had multiple therapy sessions, he spiraled downward into a world consumed by alcohol and drugs. Soon the therapy sessions turned into a series of longer and longer rehab stays and then jail. He and Drew lost touch. Drew moved in with an aunt to finish high school and then took a small apartment to attend college. Peter disappeared into the depths of the inner city only to call out of the blue one day.

"I finally feel free of it all. I feel as if a huge burden has been lifted from my shoulders. I almost feel like I can fly."

Drew told him he was happy for him and suggested that they get together sometime soon. Later that day Peter jumped off the Skyway Bridge.

"You should call them, you know. You should have called them a long time ago."

"Who?" Drew said as he drove the remaining block to the hospital. He knew full well who Peter was referring to.

"Dad's other family, that's who. You've at least got another brother that we know about. His name is..."

"I know, I know. Norm Allen. But he never called either of us." Drew often wondered about his father's other family in Atlanta. How had they taken the news? Had they gone to their father's funeral? Drew and Peter hadn't. Nor had they gone to their mother's. It was just too much at the time.

THE hospital parking lot was large but full and he had to walk through a summer shower to get to the main entrance. By the time he got there he was soaked.

"Patient's name?" The bored looking receptionist asked at the visitor's sign-in.

"Bruce Morley," Drew said. The receptionist scrolled down through the patient list for a few moments.

"No visitors," the receptionist said, popping her gum. She looked up briefly and there was a spark of pity in her eyes as she noticed Drew's wet condition. "Sorry," she said. "Did you drive a long way?"

"Yeah," Drew said. "But that's OK. Can I have his room number? I'd like to send up some flowers."

"234-C," the receptionist said. Drew thanked her and headed towards the gift shop. But when he saw her addressing the next visitor, he headed towards the stairs.

After wandering around the big hospital for a while, Drew finally found the burn unit. The double doors to the facility were locked and required a visitor to state name and patient for it to be buzzed open. He leaned against the wall and pretended to study his phone until a pair of visitors opened the door from inside to leave. He slipped into the facility behind them and walked with a sense of purpose down the hallway, past the large nurse's unit.

"Sir?" A female voice said firmly. "Can I help you?" He waved her off and continued, hoping he was headed in the right direction.

"Sir!" The voice repeated more loudly and firmly. "You have to sign in!"

Drew continued and turned down a hallway that had numbered rooms. He found 234-C and gently pushed the door open. Inside he saw a patient, face down on a hospital bed, hooked to an array of wires and tubes. Monitors beeped and flashed. A nurse dressed in scrubs turned and looked at Drew in surprise.

"Who the hell are you?" A deep male voice demanded. Drew turned his head to see a couple sitting side by side, holding hands. The man was large, with an imposing personality. Drew recognized him as Leonard Morley. Drew pulled Bunny's card from his pocket and handed it to Morley. Morley stared at it for a moment and handed it to his wife.

"I specified no visitors and definitely no goddamn reporters!" He said in a voice that belonged to a man who was used to giving orders and having them obeyed.

"Sir," the nurse said to Drew. "I'm afraid I'm going to have to ask you to leave." She shot a nervous glance at Leonard Morley who was glaring angrily at Drew.

A moan came from the man on the bed. It was Bruce. Everyone turned to look. "I had the nurse call Bunny this morning," he said, his voice muffled by the pillow and shaky with pain. "I asked him to send Drew to do an article on me."

"Why the hell would you do that?" The elder Morley demanded.

"Because what I did was stupid and could have cost lives. Will told me that if I hadn't thrown the gas can clear it would have exploded like a bomb. I want Drew to get the story out so that others don't make the same mistake."

An act of contrition, Drew thought. Surprising for a guy like Bruce. But then maybe there were some deep-seated issues behind his personality; his father's aggressive demeanor and his mother's coddling nature may have been the cause of Bruce's ego-driven behavior.

"I want you out of here right now," Leonard Morley shouted, rising to his full height, and clenching his fists. "And I want you to give Bruce another dose of pain killer," he said to the nurse.

"Sir," she said, her voice trembling. "I already told you that..."

A man dressed in scrubs appeared in the doorway. He was flanked by two uniformed security guards. "Is there a problem here?" He asked, looking directly at Morley.

"You're goddamn right there is!" Morley said, his voice now booming. "I want you to clear this goddamn reporter out of here. Right away!"

"Let him stay!" Bruce said, as loud as the pain would let him. "I want him to stay! Tell him, Mother!"

Bruce's mother, previously silent, suddenly stood and took her husband's arm firmly. "Let him stay," she said. "Bruce wants him to!" She said it with the firm voice of a person who was the only one to ever challenge Leonard Morley.

Leonard Morley gave one fierce look around at the people in the room as if to say, "This isn't over!" And then walked out past the security guards, who appeared relieved.

"Your card," Mrs. Morley said as she passed Drew. She handed him Bunny's card. "Don't be too long, and don't paint him the fool."

Drew nodded and pocketed the card with a nod.

Drew moved up close to Bruce's face to hear him better. "You're in a lot of pain, aren't you?" he said.

Bruce groaned. "You have no idea. They have to scrape away all the dead skin every morning. I'm hoarse from screaming."

Drew nodded and, not knowing what to do, patted Bruce's arm.

"Look," Bruce said. "Here's what I want. Here's what I would like," he said, correcting himself. "I'd like you to take some pictures of my legs and lower back. Do you have pictures from last night?"

"I always have my camera," Drew said.

"Pictures of me pouring the gas. Pictures of me sailing through the air?"

"Yes, I do."

"Can you do an article on the dangers of starting fires with gasoline? You know, like a public service announcement?"

"Sure," Drew said. "Bunny will want it in the Sunday Supplement."

"Good," Bruce said. He had the nurse remove the bandages from his legs and he groaned and winced as they were pulled away from the burned flesh. Drew blanched at the sight but managed to take a series of shots from different angles. He also got one of Bruce sitting up a little and grinning, flashing a thumbs up. "At least my face is okay, he said with just a shred of the old Bruce cockiness. Then he collapsed back into his pillow as the nurse injected another syringe into his open tube.

Later when Drew had left, Bruce's parents returned. His father was livid.

"How could you let that reporter in here?" He demanded. His wife tried to calm him, but he shushed her. "Do you realize what kind of attention that article will bring on my company? I've told you many times, the less attention drawn to us, the better! Now you're going to appear in the Sunday Supplement!" He paused for a moment, collecting himself. Then he continued. "I think not, Bruce. I'm going to have Bunny kill that story." He paused for another moment, then, in a softer voice, he said: "Sometimes you don't make sense to me, Son."

Bruce turned over with a moan and confronted his father, something that he had never done before.

"The article will bring attention," Bruce said, a little shakily. "But it will be positive attention. You can kill it if you want, but news isn't spread just in the media anymore. You can have it bent all you want, but it still gets out. How about that accident with the chemical truck? You don't think that didn't get out? The guy was friggin' *melted* for god's sake! And it was a Morley Chemical truck! I don't know what was in the truck, but there were EMTs, Hazmat guys and cops all over the scene. You don't think some of them won't talk? Threaten them all you want, have them sign NDAs. People will still *know*! If not on social media, the information will spread by word of mouth. Eventually someone from the EPA will hear about it and they'll investigate. If they find out that you're doing something illegal, they'll prosecute. Then where will your precious company be?"

Leonard levelled a withering gaze at his son. "I tried to bring you into the company," he said. "I gave you every opportunity to get involved, I even gave you computer access codes so that you could work from home. But you would have none of it. You're part of a different generation, enabled and entitled. You don't understand the value of hard work and the principle of true competition. "Winner take all" is the credo I learned to live by. I built this company up despite a fierce group of competitors who were all trying to take me down. Everyone talks about "clean competition" and "fair play," but in the reality that is the real world, competition is a knife fight in a dive bar. I have no use for fair play or clean competition; nor do I have any use for the rules that government imposes on businesses. They were written by politicians who were owned by special interests and geared to tilt the table in their favor. I learned that lesson too, and I bought many politicians over the years, all of whom were beholden to me; that's how the real world works!"

It wasn't greed that drove Leonard Morley, nor was it money. Life was a battle and he fought hard, asking no quarter and granting none. He ascribed to no ideology other than Darwin's. He lived simply and worked hard. He had a nice house, but it wasn't a mansion. He didn't have a fleet of expensive cars and yachts. He took no expensive vacations. But his son did and now he was questioning how he ran his business – a business that he knew nothing about.

"When you heal up and come home, we'll talk about the business; it's high time we did. Until then, your allowance is cut off. And I will kill this stupid story, you can count on that!"

He grabbed his complaining wife by the elbow and hustled her out the door past a very surprised nurse.

CHAPTER TWENTY-FOUR

Bruce woke to the sound of beeping monitors. The pain in his legs had brought him out of his stupor and he reached for the buzzer for the nurse. It wasn't there. He felt around on the bed for it.

"Looking for this?" a man said. Bruce turned as much as he could and saw a vaguely familiar couple sitting in two plastic chairs next to the bed. The man was holding the buzzer. He lifted it slightly for Bruce to see. Bruce groaned.

"Who are you?" he mumbled.

"Let's just say that we're two friends, concerned for you welfare."

"Well, ring up the nurse," Bruce said with just a touch of his usual arrogance. He winced in pain.

"I will," the man said. "But not until we've had our conversation. Whatever they're giving you puts you out for a while."

"How long have you been here?" Bruce said. The man looked at his watch and shrugged. He looked over at the woman.

"We got here shortly after your parents left," the woman said. She looked at Bruce with a touch of sympathy in her eyes. "You've been out for a while. Don't worry, we've got nothing else to do and we shouldn't be here long now that you're awake."

"Awake and in a lot of pain," Bruce said. He was growing impatient with his mysterious visitors and wanted nothing more than to be put out again.

"I'll make this as quick and painless as I can," the man said. "I'm sorry that we aren't meeting under better circumstances, but your little pyrotechnic display made that impossible."

Bruce groaned.

The man opened a manilla folder and tossed the contents in front of Bruce. Bruce tried to read it, but it had fallen slightly sideways and leaning back to bring it into focus proved too much. He let his face fall back into the pillow. "What is it?" he said, his vision swimming. The pain in his legs was becoming unbearable and he longed for nothing more than the nurse hitting his IV with another dose of painkiller.

"DEA investigation," the man said. "They've got you on transporting narcotics – cocaine – with intention to sell."

Bruce pulled himself up and out of his pillow, suddenly awake and aware. He looked over at the couple incredulously. "You're DEA?" he said. He felt his heart beginning to beat furiously in his chest. His head swam with the realization of his situation.

"No," the man said. "FBI." He flashed his badge in Bruce's face. The woman flashed no badge but nodded.

"You're looking at five to ten at least. Loss of your pilot's license and confiscation of your plane. Ever done any hard time?"

"No. What the hell do you want from me?"

The man picked up the sheaf of documents and sat back. "I can make this all go away," he said. "I just need a little cooperation."

Bruce just groaned.

"We're investigating a chemical supplier that Morley Chemical buys from. Stolen chemicals. Your father doesn't know, the manifest of the chemicals has been forged. Your father is not at risk, but we want to find the identity of the supplier. We just need the code for Morley Chemical's manifest. No one will ever know that it came from you, and the company will not be investigated for any wrongdoing. We're after the supplier, no one else."

"Can I get that in writing?" Bruce said.

"Sure, if you want a paper trail. But I don't think you do. Our hackers will make it look like they stumbled on the code. We'll pop the supplier and no one, but the three of us, will be the wiser. You'll keep your freedom – and your Denali."

Bruce moaned again and gave him the code. "Now can you call the nurse?"

Al stood with the packet from the DEA, most of which he had forged. Cindy called the nurse and the two left the hospital.

"You're a really good liar," Cindy said as they walked across the parking lot to their car.

"Just don't tell my wife," Al said.

CHAPTER TWENTY-FIVE

Virgil Yarber finished his weekday service to a small group of loyal parishioners who stood and sang the final hymn as he went to the door. He always did that, greeted everyone as they came in and said goodbye as they left. He knew them all by name. He knew about their families, their jobs, their health, and their troubles. He had known them for all the years that they attended the Community Chapel; except for the last one, a nondescript man in his fifties, who lingered until everyone else had gone.

"Thanks for coming today," Virgil said to the man with a handshake. "God go with you."

But instead of letting go of the handshake, the man put his other hand on Virgil's elbow.

"Can we speak for a few moments?" the man said. His tone was soft but insistent.

"Certainly," Virgil said. "What about?"

The man let go of Virgil's hand. "Inside?" he said. Without waiting he stepped into the little chapel's foyer, such as it was. Virgil followed, somewhat puzzled.

The man was gazing around at the newly refurbished chapel, a look of approval on his face. "You've done quite a bit of upgrading recently," he said, his hands clasped behind his back and staring up at the ceiling.

"Yes, we have," Virgil said. "I'm glad you approve."

"Tell me," the man said. "How is it that such a little ministry can afford such expensive work?"

Virgil was somewhat taken aback by the question. It almost sounded like an accusation. "Well," he said, stammering a little. "God has sent us an anonymous benefactor." He said nothing else, and an uncomfortable silence followed as the stranger smiled, his eyebrows arched as if waiting for further explanation. Just then Sally emerged from the little side room that served as an office. She had been listening.

"Excuse me," she said. "Who are you and to what do we owe this unexpected visit?"

"My name is unimportant, and I only require a little of your time," the man said. "You are Sally Yarber, and you do the books for the Community Chapel, am I right?"

"I don't see that this is any of your business," Virgil said, snapping out of his funk. Who was this man to demand explanations about the chapel? Was he an agent of the bishop? If so, he should have identified himself. But there he stood, questioning his wife. He began to feel anger rise in his breast, an uncommon thing for him. He screwed up his courage. "I think you should leave now," he said as firmly as possible.

The stranger smiled but made no move to depart. He looked directly at Sally, withdrawing an envelope from an inside pocket on his sport coat. "The man I work for would like to become a benefactor to your chapel," he said. "I assure you, there is nothing untoward about his offer. But he does require that I speak to you privately, to preserve his anonymity." He looked meaningfully at Virgil, who started to speak. Sally stopped him. She had the feeling that this man knew something about her massaging the books at the Brantwood Fellowship, as Corey had termed it. She looked in the envelope, raised her eyebrows and handed it to her husband.

"I think that the least we can do is give this man a few moments to explain himself," she said as pleasantly as she could. A sense of dread was gripping her. Who was this man, she wondered? How does he know about us? What does he want? She looked askance at the man, who seemed not unfriendly. She turned to her husband. "Virgil, could you put the envelope in the safe for me?"

Virgil reluctantly but obediently walked towards the back of the church, where the safe was kept.

Sally gestured towards the little office from which she had emerged. "Shall we?" she said. The man nodded.

"After you," he said politely. They walked in and sat.

The man, his hands held comfortably in his lap, began. "My employer, your new benefactor, has become aware that there are certain, shall we say, irregularities in the finances of the Brantwood Fellowship." Sally started to speak but he stopped her with a wave of his hand. "Your activities have no interest to us," he said. "They are small in comparison. The irregularities that we have found, if discovered by the authorities, might lead to an investigation that would be threatening to my employer. And to you. We need to discover what is going on and put a stop to it."

Sally sucked in her breath. Discovered! Just what she was afraid of. Why had she accepted Corey's help? Why had she been so greedy? "What can I do?" she finally said. She felt trapped and there was no way out but to cooperate. But how?

"I need to see the books of the Brantwood Fellowship's finances," the man said.

"That's impossible," Sally said. "Elizabeth watches that office like a hawk, there are surveillance cameras everywhere. There's no way you could get in there, even with my help."

The stranger smiled again. "But you have access to her office, and to her computer. I'm told that you have the only other key to the office and that you have all of the access codes and passwords to her computer."

Sally stared at the man, shocked. Who could have told him these things, she wondered? Virgil knew nothing. The only other person that would know these things was Scott Meade, the assistant minister in charge of activities, but he...her thought trailed off at the sudden realization. The stranger smiled again, reading her mind.

"His name is Scott," he said. "It's surprising how much, in the hands of a skilled interrogator, a large private donation can loosen a person's tongue. Don't judge him, he only thought we were making small talk. The donation was to the sports program and was to be kept confidential. He was overjoyed at the prospect of new uniforms."

Sally shook her head sadly. This man had come prepared, she thought. And he was good.

"Even if I gave you all those things, there's still no way I can get you in and out without you being discovered."

The man smiled and took a small flash drive from his pocket. He handed it to her. "Just make a copy," he said. "One financial quarter will be fine."

CHAPTER TWENTY-SIX

"I SEE YOU'RE STILL DRIVING that little car," Stacy said as Drew pulled into the parking lot of the Cove.

"It runs a lot better than my Volvo," he said. He was a little surprised at her demeanor. She seemed a little impatient, something he hadn't seen in her before. He was late, he knew, but up to now, that hadn't been a problem.

"Late again, Kiddo! A good way to ruin another relationship."

"You sound..." Drew said out loud, catching himself just before saying jealous.

Stacy mistook his meaning. "No, I'm not annoyed," she said lightly, trying to mask her feelings. It was a problem with her, she realized. She hated to be kept waiting. Thus far, Drew had been nothing but fun, but he *was* late a lot. It was the type of thing that rarely got better, in her experience. But, then again, time was only a concept, her mother liked to say. Stacy laughed to herself. A cosmic struggle between tardiness and impatience. Who would win? Stay tuned.

"What's funny?" Drew said. He was worried that his constant babbling to a voice in his head was getting out of hand. Now Stacy was laughing at him.

"Nothing," Stacy said. "Just a random thought; nothing important. Let's take that little Tennille-mobile of yours for a ride, there's something I want to show you."

They traveled southeast for an hour or so, Stacy driving with the top down and the engine purring. She had Drew's captain's hat on. Stacy found Drew easy to talk to, a trait most men lacked, in her opinion. Most of them spoke endlessly about themselves, hoping to score points with her. They talked of their jobs and their wealth and their possessions and told her their opinions. When they asked her a question it was perfunctory, as if they already knew the answer she was supposed to give and expected her to give it. When she answered - if she answered – they seemed not to listen but rather appeared to be thinking ahead about the next thing to say. Bruce Morley was like that and she often wondered why she had gotten involved with him in the first place. But then, most of her boyfriends had been that way. It made her wonder if it was some flaw in her own personality. Drew was different. He *listened*. His questions and comments seemed to be constructed to bring out a thoughtful response from her, or an irreverent comment or joke. He laughed easily and didn't seem at all put off by her famous pouts and moods. Then again, he didn't do or say the types of things that put her into such a state. And he didn't seem to mind her snakes, she thought with a laugh.

Stacy liked to drive fast, and Drew found himself gripping the little handhold on the door and he hoped she couldn't see him doing it. She looked straight at him when she spoke, only watching the road through her peripheral vision. When he was with Stacy, Peter seemed to fade away. It was like the thought of her crowded him out; warm and fuzzy and friendly, it enveloped him like the musky smell of an exotic perfume. It was a feeling he hadn't had for a long time, and he was a little apprehensive. Normally Peter would be warning him to pull back, to not be taken in by something that would end up leaving him disappointed.

After a while Stacy turned off the main highway and onto a long straight road that followed a drainage ditch in the middle of a big swamp. Mangroves, cypress, and mahogany trees lined the road, with vines and creepers twining upwards on them. Here and there clumps of Spanish moss were draped on branches like casually thrown silk scarves. Wild orchids glittered in the sun, splashes of unlikely colors amidst the green, brown and grey. They followed the road for a long time until they reached a little store with a faded sign that advertised "Airboat Rides" with a telephone number under it. They parked and walked in.

The store was more like an old truck stop than anything. There was a small counter behind which a short, stout woman stood, dressed in traditional Indian clothing. She had black hair tied in braids, high cheekbones, and ruddy skin. "Help you?" she said, her voice crackling slightly from a lifetime of cigarettes. She held one in a wizened old hand, its long ash threatening to fall among the ashes and butts of others in a battered old tin ashtray. She smelled strongly of them along with the aroma of fried food and sweat.

"We're looking for Dan," Stacy said with a smile.

"Oh," the woman said, squinting. "I remember you, you're Stacy. Sorry, the eyes aren't so good anymore. He'll be back in a bit, he's out back, working on his airboat. You hungry?"

Drew looked up at an old menu that advertised Fry Bread, Gator Tail, Hush Puppies, Frog's Legs and Softee, among the usual burgers, chicken fingers and fries. "What's Softee?" Drew asked.

"It's a native soft drink made from rice," the old woman said. "Want to try some?"

Without waiting for an answer, she poured a glass from a large plastic pitcher sitting behind the counter. She handed it to Drew. He took a sip.

"How do you like it?" The old woman asked.

Drew swished it around in his mouth, thinking about how to spit it out, and where. It had the consistency of thick broth and tasted like rice water gone bad. Girding himself, he swallowed and said "refreshing."

The old woman and Stacy broke out laughing. Drew thought that maybe he'd been pranked with some dishwater.

"It's not for everyone," the old woman said. When she laughed, she showed a set of yellowed teeth on her lower jaw. She had no teeth on her upper. She took the glass and drank off the rest with obvious gusto, she smacked her lips and smiled contentedly.

"Could you dig us out a couple of beers, Nancy?" Stacy said, still laughing.

Nancy fished around in a battered old green Coleman cooler with a rusty bottle opener on the side and came out with two bottles of cold beer. She uncapped them and set them on the counter. "Any food?" She asked. Drew looked up at the menu again and shook his head. "Had a late lunch," he said a little weakly.

Nancy laughed again and when she did it came out as a cackle.

While they waited Drew looked around the section of the store entitled "Gift Shop." It had the usual tourist items, some quite dusty. There were alligator heads, post cards, coffee mugs, t-shirts, and ball caps. Pictures and paintings, faded by the sun and time, depicted Indian huts and natives wrestling alligators, spearing fish, and paddling dugout canoes.

A while later a man, who Drew assumed was Dan, walked into the store through a back door.

"Almost set," he announced to no one in particular. He had on a greasy ballcap, several days-worth of beard stubble and an equally greasy work shirt and pants. He kissed Nancy on the forehead. "Hi, ma," he said. Drew noticed that he had the same high cheekbones, ruddy skin, and black hair as his mother. He wiped his hands on a rag and put his hand out to Drew.

"Vincent," he said. Drew saw that he only had a thumb and pinkie on his hand. He took it awkwardly and shook.

"Drew," Drew said. "Nice to meet you."

"Lost these to an old bull gator I wasn't careful enough about," Vincent said, holding his hand up for Drew to examine. "My own fault," he added.

Vincent turned to Stacy and grinned. He too was missing teeth. "Hi Stace," he said. "Dan's almost done."

"Hi, Vincent," she said in response. "How's Mary?"

"Mean as a snake," Vincent said, giving her a peck on the forehead. "If only I'd met you first," he said jokingly. A moment later, the loud roar of an engine drowned out any further conversation.

"Sounds good!" Vincent shouted. "Just a fouled carburetor, turns out!"

A moment later the engine cut off. Stacy finished her beer and dropped a bill on the counter. "Thanks Nancy," she said as she walked out the back door. Drew followed.

On the dock, next to an old wooden deck that doubled as a dining area for the restaurant, stood a handsome young man wearing long khaki pants, a black t-shirt with the letters JREC and a rattlesnake's rattle as a logo. He flashed a broad grin. "Stacy, you made it!" he said. He opened his inked and well-muscled arms to give Stacy a hug. She went up to him, accepted the hug and stood on her tiptoes to give him a kiss. She turned, still enveloped in his arms, and said, "Dan this is Drew, the guy I told you about."

Dan walked over to Drew with a friendly smile and shook his hand. He flashed a perfect set of white teeth and said, "I hear you're quite a photographer,"

"I try," Drew said, silently trying to figure out the situation. The two of them seemed like old friends and maybe more. He could feel Peter trying to crowd into his thoughts again and banished him with a "forget it!"

Stacy looked at him kind of funny and then turned to Dan. "How's Janet?"

"Great," Dan said. "I told her you were coming, and she said to say hi."

"And the kids?" Stacy added.

"Do you mean the rug rats or the snakes?"

"Timmy and Josie, smartass," Stacy said, referring to Dan's two children. She turned to Drew. "You should see his snake room, it's twice the size of mine!"

"It's coming along," Dan said. "Little Cleo almost nipped me the other day though. I need to spend more time with her. She's still a little nervous."

"Cleo's a rescue," Stacy explained. "Cops called Dan to an apartment they raided where they found a tank with a juvenile female Diamondback. She'd been taunted and was mean."

"She'll be alright," Dan said. "Just needs a little more time."

"Dan is an associate professor at John Ruskin Environmental College," Stacy explained. "He's working on his doctorate in Conservation Biology with a research focus on herpetology. I was one of his students."

"One of my best," Dan said. "I work at the Miccosukee Indian Village on weekends doing alligator demonstrations. It's just down the road. Nancy and Vincent let me keep my airboat here in return for Vincent using it to book airboat rides."

"And I keep it in tip-top shape," Vincent said proudly. He jumped deftly onto the airboat and took the driver's seat. "Ready when you are," he said, a little impatient to get started. He had a few rides scheduled for later in the day.

The group clambered aboard, Drew a little clumsily with his cameras and bag. Dan grabbed his hand and helped him. The little boat was flat-bottomed and stable, but it still wobbled a little and Drew took a seat, pretending to check his cameras. Stacy and Dan stood on either side of Vincent, prepared to make observations and give directions. Vincent started the engine and the big propeller, encased in a protective wire cage, whirred loudly. Vincent engaged the throttle and sent the boat in a tight turn, heading towards one of the channels that interlaced the region like links in a farm fence.

They raced across the swamp, sometimes almost flying over grassy areas that only held a few inches of muddy water. Herons, wood storks and ibis took flight. A pair of ospreys could be seen circling on columns of air high above in the cloudless sky and they screed at each other as they searched for prey. The air was filled with buzzing insects and the pungent smell of rotting detritus. Stacy crouched down to give Drew a running commentary on the flora and fauna they were seeing as he clicked away on his cameras, shifting from one set up with a wide-angle lens to a second with a zoom.

"We'll see alligators, snakes, deer and racoons," she shouted. "Maybe even a panther, if we're lucky." She went on to describe the swamp's ecosystem in detail far beyond Drew's understanding, emphasizing the impact of man and the fragile existence of the many endangered species living there. "There's only about a hundred panthers left in the region," she said with a look on her face that projected sadness, anger, and concern. Drew could only nod in agreement as he continued shooting.

Finally, they came to an isolated levy with a faint trail in the center. "Here we are," Stacy said. Vincent cut the engine and anchored the boat. The four adventurers walked down the trail single file, Drew bringing up the rear, clattering along with his cameras. "Shh," Stacy said with an exited smile. Drew noticed that Dan was barefoot.

They passed a hummock where a large Diamondback was coiled, buzzing its tail in warning. They were a little too close for comfort in Drew's opinion and he would have counseled a hasty retreat, but Dan stepped forward with a snake hook and lifted the big reptile expertly, grabbing it by the tail and holding it out to keep it from striking. Drew had seen Stacy do the same maneuver many times, but it still made him nervous. He had set his camera to video and concentrated on not shaking too much.

"This is Old Willy," Dan said, turning the snake for inspection. "Seems healthy enough," he continued. "I figure he's about ten years old, judging from the rattles. They add two or three a year, but they sometimes break off. We lose a lot of them to hunters, environmental degradation and competition from pythons, which are invasive." He gently set the snake down and they watched it crawl off into the underbrush.

Later they came upon a large alligator basking in the sun. A couple of glossy ibis were pecking away in the shallows and they took off when the group approached. The big gator seemed not to notice.

"Ah, here we are," Dan said. He turned to Drew. "Camera ready?" Drew nodded. Without hesitation, Dan waded into the swamp, approached the gator from behind and pounced onto the gator's back. He grabbed it under the jaws with both hands and lifted. The gator thrashed its tail and flailed with its claws, but Dan had it firmly under control.

"This technique was developed by the Miccosukee Indians for hunting," Dan explained. He held the gator still by putting its jaw under his chin. He pulled out a tag and stapled it to the underside of its cheek. "They have a closing strength that's a couple of thousand pounds per square inch strong, but almost no opening strength at all," he explained. He stood and jumped aside as the big tail slashed back and forth. After a minute or two the gator squirmed harmlessly away.

"I put a GPS chip in his cheek so that we can track his movements," Dan explained. "I've got a dozen or so tagged and saw this one from a distance a few days ago." He looked at Drew, who was still crouched with his camera. "Did you get all that?" he asked in a friendly manner.

Drew held his camera up as if for inspection. "The whole thing," he said, shaking his head. "That was one of the most amazing things I've ever seen," he added.

Dan laughed lightly. "Alligators are only a foot tall in their minds," he said. "They're only aggressive when they feel threatened or are defending a nest. Otherwise, they're really pretty docile."

Yeah, right, Drew thought. Then how do you explain Vincent's missing fingers? But he didn't say anything.

The group walked back down the levee towards the boat, talking about the environment of the swamp the whole way. Drew kept his camera at the ready and took many shots as they walked. Suddenly, without warning, Stacy leaped aggressively into a deep pool. She disappeared beneath the swirling, muddy water. Drew didn't know if he should try to help her or record the incident. No one else seemed concerned, especially Dan, who watched the water with great interest. Drew aimed his camera at the pool and waited. A moment later, Stacy surfaced, a huge snake wrapped around her shoulders.

"I've got it!" She exclaimed. "I can't believe it! I caught a Burmese Python!"

The snake, unhappy at being captured, bit her on the arm several times. She ignored it and struggled up the bank where Dan managed to get ahold of its head, while Vincent lifted its body off of Stacy's shoulders.

"It's a beauty, isn't it?" Stacy said as Drew continued to record. The snake was large, maybe six or eight feet long, with tan blotches outlined with black and separated by light tan lines. The head featured dark wedges behind the eyes and on top. Its wet skin glistened beautifully in the sun.

"Too bad," Dan said. "But it's necessary." He held the snake's head down on the ground and Vincent put a single bullet in its brain with a pistol that

Drew hadn't noticed him carrying. The snake writhed for a few minutes and then lay still. Vincent carried it to the boat and put it in the back.

"They're invasive," Stacy explained. "People who had them as pets released them years ago when they got too big to keep. They found their way into the 'Glades and took hold. They've all but wiped out the native racoons, rabbits and squirrels and are working on the deer and smaller gators. There's concern that they might carry parasites that will infect native snakes. They're ambush predators and more skillful than native species."

"Vincent will get a nice bounty for this one," Dan said. There was a note of sadness in his voice as he spoke.

"I need all the help I can get anyway, the hunting's not been good lately," Vincent said.

"I saw a lot of deer sign today," Stacy said casually.

"Oh, there's plenty of game," Vincent said. "But their guts are messed up. I'm not even sure if they're safe to eat anymore, although we still do. But their livers, one of the tastiest parts, have turned to mush. I think it's the water."

"Yeah, there's been a lot of run-off for a lot of years," Stacy said with a sad look. "Sewage, pesticides, agricultural run-off, industry – they all contribute. The pollution affects animal and plant life. When it gets into the ocean it causes an algae bloom."

"Red Tide," Drew said.

Stacy nodded. "Karenia Brevis. It's killed thousands of fish and wiped-out huge areas of seagrass. Manatees are dying of starvation by the hundreds."

"It's especially bad off Three Mile Creek, up your way," Vincent said. "It's pollution from the chemical factory. There's also a lot of construction going on; they're clearing a big area north of the creek," he added.

"Morley Chemical," Stacy said, a little vitriol creeping into her tone. "I wonder what's up with that. You're not supposed to cut mangroves without a permit. I doubt he has one."

"Won't the City fine him?" Drew asked. He knew that Stacy had dated

Bruce Morley. Maybe she had a problem with his father. Or he had a problem with her.

"It's actually in the county," she said. "Morley convinced the city to re-district a few years ago, to avoid new state regulations on pollution. He had to submit a viable plan to the state, which he did. But it was tied into the city sewer system. Morley then pressured the city council members in his pocket to redistrict the Three Mile Creek area. The gerrymander put his factory outside city limits."

"Clever," Dan said. "Since he'd been approved, he didn't have to re-apply and he didn't have to spend the money to install the pollution abatement system. So, he continues to pollute, without state or city interference. The mayor, John McNair, had pledged to redistrict and it's coming up for a vote soon. I doubt he'll succeed, Morley has some powerful friends, and they'll stop at nothing to prevent it."

Dan's comment seemed especially bitter to Drew, and he looked to Stacy for an explanation.

Stacy was hesitant and glanced at Dan. He nodded, a pained look on his face.

"One of Dan's good friends was killed the other day," she said. "An accident with a Morley Chemical truck."

"No accident," Dan said. "He was a lawyer, working pro-bono on an environmental lawsuit against the company. One of their holding tanks leaked into the adjoining neighborhood and it had to be evacuated. Thousands of gallons of wastewater flooded the region. The State came in and emptied the rest of the water into the bay, but no blame was put on the company. As I said, Morley has powerful friends."

"I heard about that accident," Drew said. "The report said he ran a stop sign."

"Of course it did," Dan said. "Hard to stop when your brake lines are cut."

Drew looked down at the ground and bit his finger. The accident had been investigated by Mick Murphy and written up in the Journal. A feeling of guilt washed over him, although he had had nothing to do with the article. All the news that's fit, he thought.

The group was quiet as they rode back to the dock in the big airboat. As they were disembarking, Stacy had a thought. "Do you mind?" She said to Drew. Without waiting for an answer, she walked over to Vincent, who was still sitting in the driver's seat. She took off his greasy ball cap and flung it onto the dock and placed Drew's Captain's hat on his head. He grinned from ear to ear.

LATER, Drew and Stacy drove into the parking lot of the Cove and headed for the door.

"Oh, here comes the Captain and Tennille," Janice boomed from her spot by the door.

"Hi, Janice," Stacy said brightly as she breezed past the big woman. "C'mon in, Drew's got something you might like to see."

"Ooh, I love sex tapes," Janice said. She followed them in.

"Hook this up, would you Chaz?" Drew said, handing Chaz his camera. Chaz took it and began fiddling with some plug ins.

"It's not been edited yet, so it's pretty raw," Drew said apologetically. The video and pictures from the trip in the Everglades flickered on the flat screen TV over the bar. Everyone gathered to watch. Chaz gave Drew the remote and he fast forwarded to the video of Dan and the Diamondback.

"Wow," Joe Crimmons said. "That guy's hardcore!"

"You ain't seen nothin' yet," Drew said. He brought up the sequence with the big gator.

"He can jump on me anytime!" Janice exclaimed when she saw Dan leap onto the gator's back. "How'd you let him slip through your fingers Stacy?"

Stacy shot her a hot look but didn't say anything.

"Now," Drew said. "Drum roll please!" He fast forwarded to the part where Stacy jumped into the pool and caught the python. Just then Will walked into the room and saw the event.

"Jesus, Stacy," he exclaimed. "You're not wearing a PFD!"

The small crowd erupted in laughter and applause. Stacy did a mock courtesy, sweeping the floor with her hand dramatically. "Had to kill it," she said sadly. "It's invasive. Beautiful snake though," she added wistfully.

"Couldn't you relocate it?" Chaz asked. He had a soft spot for animals and had fostered several dogs and cats.

Stacy shook her head. "They find their way back," she said. "They tracked one that traveled twenty-two miles. But there's nowhere you can put them where they won't be a danger. They eat racoons, rabbits and squirrels, but, if they got into populated areas, domestic animals would be at risk. They're too big and numerous to be homed as pets," she added sadly.

"Is there a bounty?" Chaz asked. He was always looking for a little side money.

"Yep," Stacy said. "Up to a few hundred dollars for the big ones. But they're hard to find. Most hunters go out at night and drive down the levees, hoping to catch them on land. They actually have a yearly contest, sponsored by the State Conservation Department. They get dozens. But experts agree that it's only a small fraction of the true population."

CHAPTER TWENTY-SEVEN

THE HORSE, A GREY stallion, cleared the fence cleanly and galloped forward, the rider's crop just touching his flank. It was a perfect morning for riding: cool with a light breeze that ruffled the plants and trees at the wood line. The horse's name was Wellington, after the great general who defeated Napoleon at Waterloo. Gloria Bunstall called him "Duke." He was a powerful steed with his own mind, and it was all Gloria could do to keep him under control. She loved it. She loved feeling the breeze in her face, she loved galloping across the fields, and she loved having the big horse between her legs. By the time they reached the stables both horse and rider were lathered and breathing hard.

"Thanks Tommy," she said to the stable boy as she dismounted and handed the reins to him. "Be sure to give him a good rubdown," she added as she took off her helmet and shook out her hair. He'd probably like to give me a good rubdown, she thought as she watched him pat the horse's muzzle. He was nineteen, tall, well-built and, judging by the glance he stole at her, more than willing. She had been tempted many times after a hard ride, but an affair with the stable boy? How cliché. Plus, a boy didn't understand the rules of discretion. He would come to expect her attentions every day and might even fall in love. He almost certainly would brag to his friends. No, she preferred her liaisons to be with men mature enough not to ruin a good thing.

After her ride, Gloria showered and changed into some casual clothes instead of her usual business suit. She made a phone call and went over to the car garage. "Is the Porsche 911 gassed and ready?" she asked Mel, the mechanic.

"They all are, Mrs. Bunstall," he said, a little proudly. "Which one would you like?"

"The blue Carrera," she said. Miami blue, she thought. It seemed appropriate because Miami was where she was heading.

The Carrera felt good on the highway, the well-tuned engine purring. Miami was a couple of hundred miles away, but she was in no hurry. She decided to take the more scenic Tamiami Trail rather than the crowded interstate. It wound down along the coast and then across the Everglades. Alligator Alley, it was called. Gloria was a fast driver, but she didn't worry about tickets. As soon as a cop saw her name, he usually let her go with a warning. If she did get a ticket, she simply made a call to Susan Thompson.

Earlier, when the inclination had struck her, she had called and made a reservation at the Four Seasons Surf Club for a King Room. She loved Miami, she loved the view of the city and the beach from her room so, every so often, she would travel there for a getaway. The getaway usually coincided with the arrival of Barry Richards, who played saxophone in a touring jazz quartet. Tonight, they were booked at Ralph's, a popular high-end bar a short walk from the hotel.

She and Barry had met in college when they were freshmen and they had immediately fallen deeply in love. Together, they discovered the wonders of sex, learning by intuition, discussion, and experimentation. They were together for three years, until Barry got an offer from a bandleader who was performing at the college. During an afternoon workshop he heard Barry play and offered him a gig on the spot. "Something like this only comes along once in a lifetime, or never for most musicians," Barry had explained to her when he told her of his decision to leave. She was devastated and begged him not to go, but, deep down, she knew that if he did pass up the offer, he would always feel a sense of regret. He left, she finished school and moved home. Years later she got a call. He was in town with his own band and would like her to come to the club where they were playing. She went and they immediately fell back in love. But, since they were both married and he was still on the road, there was no chance that they could get back together. So, instead, whenever he was playing somewhere nearby, she would go and meet him.

A few hours later Gloria pulled up to the hotel, grabbed her overnight bag and tossed the keys to the grinning valet. "Nice car," he said, opening the door. She noticed that he stole a glance at her as she walked up the entry way. She gave a little hip-shake to further make his day.

In her room she opened the bottle of champagne that she had room service send up and poured herself a flute. She looked out the window and admired the Miami skyline and the white sands of the beach that stretched for miles. After a time, she went downstairs and walked to Ralph's. It was a bar along the strip and was lit by a large neon sign that read: "Ralph's Jazz Bar." Below it, in smaller letters it proclaimed: "Music Every Night."

The band was just setting up and Barry, who had been looking for her, rushed over and gave her a hug. She felt good in his arms, familiar even after all these years. He smiled warmly and said: "Missed you," softly in her ear. She went to the bar and ordered a chardonnay and watched and listened as the band tuned up and started it's set. The selections were familiar to her: tunes by Miles, Trane, Cannon, Horace, Herbie and others. She had heard them a million times while she was dating Barry. The band was excellent, and they played quite a few original compositions.

During the break, when the rest of the band went outside for some air, Barry joined Gloria at the bar. "Same old stuff," he said. "Sorry, it's all I know." He said the last phrase with a broad grin. Gloria slapped him playfully on the arm.

"I hear Curtis Green is leading the house band at your megachurch," Barry said. He ordered a beer and took a sip.

"Not my church," Gloria said, a little bitterness creeping into her tone. "I rarely attend."

"Why not?" Barry said. "I would think that the music would be excellent. I played with Curtis a few years back, and he's top shelf. He used to be the leader of the "Better Late Than Never" show."

"I know," Gloria said. "I used to watch that show occasionally. Really funny. Too bad about the scandal though." She got quiet for a moment, regarding the wine in her glass, and thinking of what to say. "It's just that that whole show annoys me," she went on. "Corey Deschamps dances around and flashes his teeth and dimples while throwing out platitudes like confetti at a parade. No substance."

"People like him, though," Barry said. "He's a syndicated national celebrity. And right from your little town!" He said the last phrase dramatically. She slapped his arm again, regaining her good humor. She took a sip of wine.

"It's Deschamp's wife, Elizabeth," she said. "She runs the whole show. Everything. Scripts the sermons, directs the band, the lighting and the sound."

"So?" Barry said.

"What bothers me about Elizabeth is that she bucks every effort I make at any kind of beautification project or charitable endeavor in the city. It's like she's determined to take the city over through her own fund."

"Ah ha!" Barry said in a fake mocking tone. "Maybe you two should fight it out on the village green. A cat fight for the ages! You could sell tickets!"

Gloria almost spit out her wine. She slapped his arm much harder this time. "You are such a jerk! How did I ever put up with you?"

Barry reeled back defensively. "Hey! C'mon now baby! Don't be like that! You know you love me!"

The band, back from their break, cracked up, along with a few of the patrons.

Towards the end of the last set, Barry sang "Change is Gonna' Come" by Sam Cooke. It had been her favorite song back when Barry had been in a college band called: "Hard Times." He sang it straight at her, with emotion. She almost burst into tears.

Later, back at the hotel, the two availed themselves of the king-sized bed. They explored each other as they had in the early days and then some.

"You've learned some new moves," Barry said, laying back on his pillow and out of breath.

"As have you, my dear," Gloria said, stroking his chest.

In the morning they breakfasted on omelets and mimosas in the hotel's five-star restaurant. Barry looked around at the surroundings. "You sure have done well for yourself," he said.

"I live comfortably," Gloria said, shrugging. "My inheritance, my alimony and my husband's money. I run the Fund and the household. I have an open charge account."

"And you're happy?" Barry said.

Gloria gave him a sharp look. "You don't get to ask that question," she said, her lips tight over her teeth. "You left me, remember?"

Barry apologized and the conversation turned to more pleasant things.

"Where to next?" Gloria asked.

"Orlando," Barry said. "You could always...

Gloria cut him off with a wave of her hand and a smile. "One night with you is enough for me," she said. "I'm not as young as I used to be. Besides, you could easily become a habit."

CHAPTER TWENTY-EIGHT

THE ELEVATOR GLIDED UP to the fourth floor and dinged. "After you," Teejay said to Drew as the door opened. "I thought you were going to get a haircut," he added as he looked critically at the young man's mop of unkempt hair. "And didn't Bunny give you a line of credit for some new clothes?" Teejay himself was always nattily dressed and groomed and it surprised him when others didn't hold themselves to a higher standard. Oh well, he thought. It probably was an effect of having worked for Joe Crimmons, the man was a haberdasher's nightmare.

"Sorry," Drew mumbled as they walked up to Mrs. Zimmer's desk. She waved them by with a perfunctory "he's waiting." Drew hadn't expected to be called into Bunny's office so early and he hadn't had time to go home and change when he left Stacy's cottage. Now he would have to endure the critical eye of Bunny Bunstall, who had bankrolled his expected makeover.

"They must think you're a pure fool! You've been handed everything you ever wanted and you're fuckin' it up! And you're letting that little girl into your head too! She's distracting you and now look, you're going into Bunny's office looking like a slob!"

How do you know it's everything I ever wanted? Maybe I want something different. "Did you ever think of that?"

"What?" Teejay said as he opened the door to Bunny's office.

Drew just shook his head and said, "nothing."

"Gentlemen," Bunny said as the two walked into his office. "We have a problem." No scotch, no cigars, no pleasant banter. He Bunny was again the cold-blooded businessman. Drew noticed for the first time that Bunny's desk acted as a barrier behind which he did his business. A big oak fortress from which to fight his battles. As he sat, Drew realized that the two chairs in front of the desk were shorter than normal chairs, and the backs were slanted so as to render the sitters vulnerable. *"Is there a pistol in one of the drawers, or is that too cliché? A button that when pressed sends the sitters into a deep pit?"* Drew shook his head to clear it of Peter. Teejay gave him a funny look. You okay Kid? it said, but he didn't say anything.

"We thought we'd bring you in on this," Bunny said to Drew. "You've proven yourself to have, shall we say, *instincts* about things. We're looking for a motive as to why a city commissioner would change his vote on the fence bill. Elizabeth Deschamps thinks that the fence would be an ugly eyesore and opposes the fence almost every day in her column and on her prayer podcast. We all know the real reason why she opposes it: she wants her church to be involved the in the refurbishing of the fountains, cupola, benches, and walkways. I've even heard rumors that she wants the square renamed: "The Brantwood Fellowship Park" in return for the work, which would be financed by her church and done by church volunteers. Gloria is livid. She sees it as an aggressive takeover that will lead to the church dominating the city with its brand. I get her purpose, but I just can't figure out what she's using for leverage on Draggett."

"Man," Drew interjected. "When that new hotel, restaurant and sports complex get built, this town is going to look like Dollywood in Sevierville." He was referring to Dolly Parton's hometown in Tennessee. Her brand seemed to be on everything in the city and surrounding region.

"Francesco might be the developer she plans on using," Teejay said. "That would explain why he's cozying up to Draggett; he might need to drain some marginal land for the project. You know, get Draggett to look the other way when he does it."

A realization struck Drew like a blow. He sat up and sucked in his breath audibly. Bunny and Teejay looked at him in surprise.

"What is it boy?" Bunny said impatiently. "Spit it out."

Drew cleared his throat. His heart pounded and he stammered a little as he began to speak. "A source of mine told me that Leonard Morley is clearing land along Three Mile Creek. He's dredging the creek bed and cutting mangroves. Multiple environmental violations but no one seems to care, least of all the government."

Bunny slapped his desk with both hands and came halfway out of his chair. "By God, boy! I knew there was a reason why I brought you in today!"

Teejay and Drew looked at each other in shocked surprise.

"Twenty years ago, the State passed legislation requiring any factory or business that was dumping into feeder streams to come up with a viable plan to clean up their runoff. Morley Chemical is on Three Mile Creek, which is a feeder stream. The company submitted a plan that would filter the water and tie it into the city sewer system. The state approved the plan. It was going to cost Morley hundreds of thousands of dollars to implement it and thousands more every year to maintain. But the plan was never put into practice. Morley used every bit of political leverage he could muster to get the city to redistrict, putting Three Mile Creek - and Morley Chemical - outside city limits. When John McNair was elected mayor, he began building a coalition to support a reversal of the gerrymander. He attached a rider to the fence bill, mandating a commission to investigate redistricting. Morley can't go public with his opposition; it would draw too much attention to his environmental violations."

"If Elizabeth Deschamps is looking at Three Mile Creek for her development, the current districting would save her a lot of money." Teejay said thoughtfully. "There's no tax on the church, of course, but there will be taxes on her hotel, sports complex, and restaurant. If that's true, all three of them, Francesco, Morley and Deschamps, have a vested interest in keeping the region outside city lines. The city will lose out on millions of dollars of tax revenue over the years."

Bunny sat quietly for a moment, staring out the window at the commons. "Brantwood Fellowship Park!" he said forcefully. "I'll be damned if I let that happen! And Morley made the mistake of crossing me. Gloria told me that he pulled his donations from the Dodson Fund and, presumably, put those same funds into the Brantwood Fellowship. Now we know why."

Bunny looked appraisingly at his two reporters for a moment, letting the thought sink in. Then he leaned forward, his hands planted firmly on his desk. A decision had been made.

"Teejay, I want you to get in touch with Mick Murphy. Find out what he's got on Draggett, I'm sure he's got plenty. You'll write up a breaking story from an anonymous source on an ongoing investigation into bribery, graft and corruption involving a city councilman. Don't name Draggett but make sure everyone knows it's him. Mick will follow up with an indictment that will force Draggett to resign. McNair gets to appoint a replacement in such a case, which should guarantee passage of the fence bill."

He turned his attention to Drew. "Leonard Morley needs to be taken down a notch. I want you to work up an expose on Morley Chemical and the pollution it emits into Three Mile Creek. And make sure to mention the gerrymander that allowed it to happen. We'll turn public opinion in favor of the fence bill, and the redistricting rider will pass with it, by God!"

The two reporters stood, their assignments firmly in mind. Bunny turned and looked back at the commons. "Brantwood Fellowship Commons my ass," he muttered.

In the hallway, Drew made a quick call to Stacy. He knew that if anyone could get him into Morley Chemical for some pictures it would be her. He explained his idea.

"Get some pictures of Morley's chemical factory for an exposé?" she said, a little excitement creeping into her voice. "I'd love to, and I know just how to do it. That old bastard's been polluting our bay for years."

CHAPTER TWENTY-NINE

W HEN HE GOT TO the Cove, Stacy was nowhere to be seen. He parked and walked towards the door. Janice, smoking a clove cigarette, stepped out.

"She's waiting for you down at the boat dock," she announced. "What's the big hurry?"

"Got a deadline," Drew said, slinging his cameras and bag over his shoulder.

As he approached the docks, Drew noticed a flurry of activity. There was a fishing tournament going on during the next week and contestants were getting their boats ready, checking their gear, and heading out into the bay to scout the area. The boats, most of them, were fantastic. They had large multiple outboard engines, rod holders lined up on top and off the stern, and lots of electronic gear that Drew guessed would be depth finders, fish finders and underwater cameras. He knew that tournaments paid big prizes to winning competitors. The anglers, with jackets and hats festooned with names and logos from sponsors, revved their engines and, ignoring wake rules in the channel, roared out into the bay.

Drew knew that, if they were going on a boat ride, Stacy would probably be using one of the boats in Will's collection. Word had it that it was extensive and included modern boats and restored classics. He expected a Boston Whaler or a Chris Craft but, when he got to the dock, he saw Stacy standing in a dented and rusty aluminum Jon boat with a single battered engine that looked like it had seen its day many years ago.

Stacy noticed his questioning look.

"We need to be unobtrusive," Stacy said. "The boat is part of our cover."

Drew climbed aboard. "So, what's our cover?"

Stacy just grinned and gunned the surprisingly powerful engine before he had a chance to sit. He flopped back on to a bench, his cameras and camera bag jumbling along with him. "Hey!" he yelled over the sputtering engine. Stacy laughed at her joke.

"This is quite a boat," Drew said as they motored out into the bay and cut speed. "Part of your father's collection?"

"I borrowed this from Jimmy, one of the dockhands. I wanted something commonly seen in the slack water. Here," she said, tossing him a pair of well-worn white rubber boots. "I borrowed these too. They should fit you."

Drew looked at the boots and wrinkled his nose.

"You can go barefoot if you don't like the boots," Stacy said. "But I wouldn't recommend it."

"Any chance I can find out what our cover is?" Drew asked, pulling his shoes off and slipping into the boots. They were several sizes too big, but they would work.

"We're going to a swamp to get some pictures," she said coyly. "Why else would I bring you along."

"Pictures of what?" Drew said, fiddling with his camera and aiming it at Stacy.

"Stop that! I don't have my make up on!" She said, holding her hand up to block the shot.

"Right," Drew said. "Since when did you start wearing makeup? And you didn't answer my question."

"Morley's chemical plant is surrounded by fences and guards," she said. "The main channel of the creek is bordered by roads that are patrolled, so we can't take the boat straight up the creek. To the south of the creek is a swamp that's on Morley's land but probably not patrolled. We need a reason for being there in case we're discovered. I'm doing grad work for the college and need some pictures, that's why you're along."

"And what are we looking for?" Drew said.

"Agkistrodon conanti," Stacy said.

"What?"

"Agkistrodon conanti, otherwise known as the Florida Cottonmouth. 'Round here we call 'em Water Moccasins," she said in an exaggerated Southern accent.

I might have known, Drew thought. She was taking him on another snake hunt. What he knew about Water Moccasins he didn't like: aggressive, deadly, and so well camouflaged that you couldn't see one until you stepped on it. At least rattlers warned you, he thought. But, as he had been told as a kid, you didn't have to worry about Water Moccasins unless you went into a swamp.

He looked at Stacy, who seemed to be having a good time at his expense. "You've turned a curious shade of white," she said. "Almost the same color as a Moccasin's mouth."

Drew fiddled with his cameras, pretending not to hear. What was it about this girl that attracted him, he wondered? She crashed through brush looking for Diamondbacks that she had names for, she dove into the Everglades after a Burmese Python, and now she was about to traipse through a swamp looking for Water Moccasins. But the excitement that was palpable on her face and in her actions answered his question. Even though he had a fair degree of trepidation about plunging into the swamp, he felt lucky to be along for the ride. Plus, he might get some really good shots.

To the south of the creek there was a thick mangrove salt marsh. Stacy used her phone's GPS map to negotiate the various channels and mangrove tunnels upstream. Eventually the mangroves gave way to a cypress swamp. The tall trees, covered with Spanish Moss, towered above them. The boat, being flat-bottomed, made good progress but eventually fallen trees, cypress knees and grass hummocks brought them to a halt.

"We walk from here," Stacy said matter-of-factly. She tethered the boat to a sapling and climbed out, grabbing a small knapsack and snake hook as she did. Drew scrambled after her, his cameras and camera bag swinging wildly as he struggled to keep up. They walked for a long time. Finally, Stacy stopped in a small copse of cypress trees.

"Notice anything wrong?" She said as Drew caught up, a little out of breath. He looked around.

"Other than charging through a snake infested swamp, I would say no."

"No birds," Stacy said. "No frogs, no fish jumping. Amphibians are the first to go when there's pollution." She sniffed the air and wrinkled her nose. "Do you smell that? The chemicals?"

Drew sniffed. There was a distinct chemical taint to the air. "What is it?" He asked.

"I don't know," Stacy said. "But I aim to find out. She took a small glass vial out of her backpack and dipped it into the water. She sealed it, took out a label and a sharpie and wrote something on it. She returned it to the backpack. "Let's keep going," she said. Without waiting, she pressed on into the dark, fetid swamp.

After a while, Stacy suddenly stopped, crouched, and peered into a spongy mass of grass and dead leaves. "Do you see him?" She said, she moved stealthily forward and then turned to Drew. "Get your camera ready," she said with a wave of her hand, beckoning him closer.

Drew checked his camera and inched forward, trying to see what she was seeing. At first, he saw nothing, then, imperceptible at first, he saw movement. The dark brown scales of a thick snake glinted slightly as it moved. Stacy turned and grinned. She reached out with her hook and lifted the snake's head a little. It coiled and flicked its tongue.

"He seems a little sluggish," Stacy said, Suddenly the snake reared its head back in a strike position. Stacy moved it away with her hook. "That's more like it," she said. "Now he's awake. Are you getting this?"

"Yep," Drew said nervously. He had never been that close to a Water Moccasin before. Come to think of it, he had never seen one in the wild at all.

"Isn't he beautiful?" Stacy said, letting him slide slightly over the hook and turning him slightly so that Drew could get a good angle. He had his camera on video, and he was getting some really good shots. He inched closer, repositioning himself a little. The snake pulled its head back even further.

"You do know that you're in his strike range, right?" Stacy said. There was even a slight bit of worry in her voice, a rare thing. Drew immediately pulled back.

Stacy moved the snake around a little bit until he opened his mouth, baring his fangs and showing his famous white mouth. Stacy swiftly shifted the hook and lifted, so that he couldn't strike. "Okay, that's enough," she said. "He's getting pissed. Did you get enough shots?"

"More than enough," Drew said.

"Good," she said. "Now, if it wouldn't be too much trouble, take my backpack, set it on its legs and open the top." Keeping her eyes and hook on the snake, Stacy shrugged out of her backpack with Drew helping. It had self-standing legs, like a backpack for carrying a toddler. Drew extended the legs, set it firmly on the ground and opened the top. He noticed that the pack was made of durable nylon with a thick rubberized interior. There were small slit vents around the top.

"You might want to stand back a little," Stacy advised. Drew did and aimed his lens. Stacy positioned the hook at the snake's middle and gently lifted. As the snake came up, a ray of sunshine hit it. The dark body of the snake glistened, and Drew could see its large, triangular head and its elliptical eyes, which reminded Drew of a cat's eye. The body was marked with dark crossbands over dark brown and yellow scales. The belly was yellowish white with dark spots here and there.

"Beautiful, isn't it?" Stacy said as she carefully lowered the snake into the backpack. "It's a juvenile and I'd like to have Dan take a look at it. It may be sick. If so, he can treat it and release it somewhere else. This water is tainted." She closed the top, put the backpack on and stood.

"Now, let's head upstream a little farther," She said. "You should be able to get some good pictures of the chemical plant."

Stacy took off at her usual pace and Drew followed, sloshing and slipping. It struck him by the way she walked that she spent a lot of time trekking through the wilderness, something he did little of. Although he tried follow in her footsteps, he hadn't acquired the gait that she used, and he felt clumsy by comparison.

After a while they came to an earthen levee topped by a natural undergrowth of palmettos, small bushes, and a few scruffy pines. A dirt road veered around it, following the main channel of the creek.

"This is it," Stacy said, crouching a little. "The end of the swamp. I want you to take a peek over the levee; but keep low and don't make any sound."

Drew was beginning to feel a little uneasy. As dangerous as snakes were, they were harmless compared to humans. He got his cameras ready and crawled part way up the side of the levee. The undergrowth was thick, and he hoped there were no snakes in it. As he reached the top, he pushed a big palmetto leaf aside. There, on a raised section of the creek bank, was a large chemical facility. Smoke poured from chimneys and he could see hard-hatted workers walking to and fro. There were semis, backed up to loading docks and tanker trucks sitting next to large holding tanks. All of the trucks and the smokestacks were emblazoned with the company name: "Morley Chemical."

Drew took several photos of the facility and then turned his attention to the large pipes jutting out over the creek. Each one of them was spewing waste from the factory directly into the water. After he had gotten enough shots he slid back down the bank, but when he got to the bottom, he found Stacy missing. He walked towards the creek road and saw her at the bank, dipping a water sample bottle into the creek. She finished, capped the bottle and slid it into her backpack with the others – and the snake. She donned her backpack and walked swiftly towards Drew.

"Let's get out of here," she said. "We both got what we came for."

Just then a large, covered four-seater ATV rounded the bend next to the levee. It slid to a halt in front of them.

"Let me do all the talking," Stacy said quickly. "You're my photographer and you don't know anything."

"Right," Drew said, his heart in his throat.

Two men, wearing green uniforms and green hardhats that read: "Morley Chemical," got out of the vehicle and approached them. Drew noticed that both men were wearing sidearms.

"What are you doing here?" One of the men demanded. The second man said something into a communication device clipped to his shirt. The device crackled a response that Drew couldn't understand.

Stacy pulled an ID card from her waist pouch and handed it to him. "I'm doing research for the John Ruskin Environmental College," she said. "This is my photographer."

"Do you have a permit to be on company grounds?" the man asked, handing the card back to her.

"I applied for one a couple of months ago and haven't heard back," she said, tucking the card back into her pouch. "I'm working on a grad project and need to research an untouched section of native swamp. This fits the bill. I couldn't afford to wait any longer, there's a deadline."

The guard appeared convinced and was about to get back in the ATV when the second man stopped him.

"Boss wants to see them," he said curtly. He turned to Stacy and Drew and said, "get in."

"No need for that," Stacy said firmly. "We didn't mean to come so far upstream. I got what I was looking for, we'll just leave."

"I don't think so," the second man said. There was a touch of menace in his tone. He held the rear door open and gestured for them to get in.

On the ride up to the facility, Stacy tried to convince the guards that none of this was necessary, but she was only met with stubborn silence. The guards had their orders. Drew kept quiet and fiddled with his cameras, as usual.

A guard, dressed identically as the two ATV guards, opened a large gate as they approached. They drove up to a small stucco building with a sign that read "Morley Chemical – Security." The guards got out and escorted Drew and Stacy inside.

The room was filled with surveillance equipment with several technicians working. There was a bank of camera monitors, several computers, microphones and communication devices on battery chargers. Drew noticed a rack of assault rifles on a far wall and another rack of handguns. A man, wearing civilian clothes and an ID badge, approached them. He was fit and compact and had a military bearing about him. He reminded Drew of the CIA officers in a dozen action movies. His ID badge simply said: "Head of Security." There was no name.

Stacy produced her ID and gave him the same explanation that she had given to the two guards.

The man listened and then, without saying a word, disappeared into his office. A few minutes later he emerged. He looked at the two guards who had brought them in. "The big man wants to see them," he said. He turned to Drew and Stacy and said, "let's go."

The five of them walked across the yard in silence and entered what appeared to be a main building by a battered side door. A small metal sign read "Leonard Morley."

The office of Leonard Morley was a surprise. It was dusty and barren, with only a faded out-of-date calendar on the wall, an old clock of the type that was in every nineteen fifties school classroom and a faded poster that read: "Morley Chemical, Your Path to the Future." The room was lit by a flickering fluorescent light and a window that looked like it hadn't been cleaned in decades. There were no curtains, no shades, no receptionist, no ambient music, and no bar. Everything stood in stark contrast to Bunny Bunstall's opulent headquarters at the Journal. Yet, to Drew, the place had the feeling of immense power.

Leonard Morley sat at an old gray metal desk, cluttered with a few papers and an older telephone. He was wearing a workman's blue shirt with the sleeves rolled up. He looked more like a factory foreman than the owner of one of the biggest companies in the region. He finished a conversation on the phone and looked up. When he saw Stacy, his eyes widened in surprise.

"Hello, Mr. Morley," she said. "How have you been?"

Drew knew that Stacy had once dated Bruce for a while, but he had assumed it was casual. The familiar way she spoke to Morley told a different story.

"Stacy," he said. "What a surprise. You didn't have to sneak in, I would have let you in the front gate and given you a personal tour."

"She told us that she was working on a graduate project for some college," one of the guards said. "Something to do with an untouched swamp."

"Oh, she did, did she?" Morley said with a laugh. "And you believed her?"

"I had no reason not to," the guard said defensively. "She showed us her ID card."

"She was here taking pictures of the factory, especially the outlet pipes and probably taking water samples to boot," Morley said to the guards. "She's what you call an environmental activist." He looked back at Stacy.

"You know everything I do here is legal," he said. "I'm breaking no regulations."

"You're dumping toxic waste directly into a feeder stream," Stacy said, anger creeping into her voice. "The whole swamp is dying."

"And what good is the swamp doing us?" Morley retorted. "My operation provides hundreds of jobs and I provide chemical products that are sold all over the world."

"And killing the swamp, and the bay, in the process," Stacy shot back. She had developed an abiding hatred for Leonard Morley ever since she had dated Bruce. He had once given Stacy a tour of the Morley chemical facility; it was one of the things he did to impress people, especially new girlfriends. Look at this, the tour said. I am heir to all of this. It didn't matter that Bruce knew next to nothing about the facility or what it produced, and it didn't matter that he knew nothing about chemicals. When his father retired, the business would be handed over to him and be run by a bunch of surrogates. When Stacy asked him about details about the chemicals produced there and about the pollution caused by waste from the plant, Bruce had been stymied. That's when he made his second mistake. He took Stacy to his father's office.

Stacy's first impression of Leonard Morley was not a good one. When introduced he only looked up from his desk for a moment in a very distracted way. He was a busy man and had little time for his son's new girlfriend, or for Bruce himself, it seemed. He grunted in recognition of the introduction and looked at Bruce as if to say, "What are you doing here?"

But when their eyes met for a moment, and Stacy saw a bone chilling coldness that belied any redeeming humanity. It reminded her of the cold look of Anthony Hopkins playing a psychopathic killer in "The Silence of the Lambs." She had always wondered how Hopkins had managed to cultivate that look. For Leonard Morley, the look seemed to come naturally. Now, standing in his office, Stacy saw that look again.

"Alright, I've had enough of this," Morley said icily. "The water samples and pictures you have were obtained illegally. My chemists send water samples to the state on a regular basis, as per the environmental laws as they stand. I want yours left here."

Stacy reached into her belt pack and took out two labelled vials. She set them on Morley's desk. He nodded approvingly. "I'll have them tested in our lab," he said. "You can call for the results in a few days."

He turned to Drew, who he suddenly recognized. "You're that goddamn reporter who did the article on Bruce," he said accusingly.

"Yessir," Drew said, trying not to appear nervous. "I filed it this morning. Should be in next week's Sunday Supplement."

"That article will never run." Morley said. "I had Bunny kill it. Makes Bruce look weak," he added.

"But Bruce wanted the article done," Drew said. "He asked me to come to the hospital to do it!"

"Shut up," Morley said, growing tired of the conversation. "I can have you fired with one phone call. Put your stuff on the desk."

Drew set his two cameras and camera bag on the desk. "These are the property of the Journal," he said. "They're on loan. I have to return them. Check them if you like. You'll find no pictures of the factory. Stacy is my friend and she asked me to help her with her graduate project. We just wandered a little too far upstream. I'm sorry," he added.

"Check the camera's pictures," Morley said to one of the guards. "You know how to do that?" The guard nodded.

"Look through his camera bag and check his vest Bob," he said to the CIA looking guy. "You're looking for water samples."

Right," Bob said. He dumped out the contents of Drew's pack and looked through the items. Then he roughly but expertly searched Drew's pockets. "Nothing here," he said, standing back.

The guard who was looking through the cameras finished. "Nothing here either, except a lot of pictures and videos of snakes."

Stacy looked at Drew and tried to hide her surprise.

"Check her backpack," Morley said to the second guard. The man picked it up from where Stacy had set it.

"Don't do that!" Stacy said, alarm in her voice. She started to move towards the man, but Bob stopped her by grabbing her arm.

"Easy," he said. She shook her arm free but the guard with the pack had already unzipped the top. He looked down into it and recoiled, dropping the pack and staggering backwards. "Shit!" he exclaimed. The pack hit the floor and tipped, and the Water Moccasin slithered out, flicking its tongue. The two guards jumped back in surprise. Stacy grabbed her snake hook, caught the snake, and lowered the reptile into the backpack. "Asshole," she muttered at the guard, whose face was ashen.

Leonard Morley, who had not flinched when the snake came out of the pack, suddenly burst into laughter. "This little girl has more balls than the two of you put together," he said, directing his comments at the guards, who looked ready to bolt.

Stacy finished zipping up the pack.

Morley shook his head with a bemused look on his face. "Will Willard's daughter," he said. "Acorns don't fall far from the tree."

Stacy ignored the comment and put the backpack on. "Can we go now?" she said, a disdainful look on her face.

"Get 'em out of here," Morley said to the two guards. He shook his head and laughed again. "Will Willard's daughter," he said, more to himself than anyone else.

"I think we should impound the cameras and backpack," Bob said. Drew noticed that he was re-holstering a pistol. "Just to be safe," he continued. "And have them sign NDAs."

Morley gave the man a hard look. He wasn't used to having his orders questioned. "Go," he said to Stacy, Drew and the guards. "You stay," he said to Bob.

"You're making a mistake," Bob said after they left. He sat down and looked Morley in the eye. "We can't have any loose ends in this operation. If the public gets wind of this, there'll be hell to pay, and I'm not taking a fall because of your stupidity."

Leonard Morley wasn't used to being called stupid, and it showed in his attitude and his tone of voice. He leaned back in his chair; his hands folded across his stomach. "We have enough trouble on our hands with that boating accident that happened the other day," he said. "My sources tell me he was FBI; the Bureau won't believe it was any kind of accident. And now the accident with the environmental lawyer! A couple of your mercs were driving that truck, I'll wager! Drawing undue attention from Will Willard won't help our cause either; the man has connections. Let the kids have their little environmental crusade, the story will never reach print. I have Bunny Bunstall in my pocket."

"I know about Willard's association with Van Ness," Bob said. "The man's using the same connection we are to launder his money. He won't cause us any trouble; and as for the boating accident, no one can make any connection with us. The lawyer had to go, he was getting too close, but we got the story buried, didn't we? My guys do a clean job. But, as I said, we can't have any loose ends, my people won't tolerate it. If we can't keep a lid on this operation, you and I are liable to wind up as loose ends ourselves."

RIDING down the dirt road in the ATV, Drew could see earthmovers clearing land on the other side of the creek. The creek itself had been dredged, widened and diverted in order to facilitate the drainage of the land that was being cleared.

Stacy saw what he was looking at. "Altering a feeder stream, removal of mangroves, destruction of natural habitat; the list gets bigger and bigger," she said. "I doubt he has permits for any of this."

"Even if he got caught and fined, it would only be a tiny fraction of what he will stand to gain from the land sale," Drew said. He had his camera in his lap and was quietly recording the operation.

The guards were only too happy to drop Drew, Stacy and the snake off in the rough vicinity of the boat.

"Have fun in the swamp," one of them said. The other chuckled.

"Maybe you'll find your snake's brother out there," the other guard said. They both had a good laugh as Stacy and Drew splashed off into the swamp.

"I can't believe you didn't get any pics of the factory," Stacy said when they were alone. "Even if the guards erased them, at least you would have tried." There was an accusatory tone to her voice. Drew laughed.

"I can't believe you gave up the water samples so easily," he said with a smirk. "At least you would have tried."

"Those were extra, in case we got caught," Stacy said. "I've got others in the bottom of the pack with the snake."

Drew couldn't keep the charade going any longer. "I sent the factory pics to my home computer and then erased them on the camera while we were being taken to the facility," he said. "I knew the guards wouldn't know that I could do that."

Stacy slapped him on the arm, grinning. "Ass," she said.

"I'm just surprised Morley didn't make us sign non-disclosure agreements," Stacy said. "Anyway, I'll get these samples to Dan and he'll have Dr. Donnelly at the college test them. I hope he can do something for this snake," she added. "He looks pretty sick."

"Did you see those guards jump when he came out of the pack?" Drew said.

Stacy laughed. "They'll probably have to change their shorts!"

CHAPTER THIRTY

"THERE'S A LOT OF STRANGE stuff going on here," Daphne said, clacking keys on her computer. Will, Buddy and Stacy were watching her work. Stacy's mother never ceased to amaze her. Ever since she was old enough, her parents had insisted that she know everything about their businesses. "You're getting a prime education by watching your mother work," Will often said. Daphne had studied business administration in college and had skills in bookkeeping and computer science. When Buddy was able to get a copy of the Brantwood Fellowship's books on a flash drive, Daphne was the person he took it to.

"I've been working on this all morning and I'm finally starting to see a pattern," Daphne continued. "See, here," she said, bringing some entries up. "This column shows payments made to some individuals for consulting, in cash. Now, a big church like the Brantwood Fellowship would get a lot of cash in donations, so, nothing suspicious there. But this column here," She said as she clacked some more keys and brought up another column. "This shows donations paid by church members. See this? The donations are exactly what was paid out in consulting fees."

Buddy whistled softly. "Clean money. Cash deposited in their private bank accounts and paid back by checks or money transfers."

"Right," Daphne said. "People who work for a church often give the money they're paid back as a donation, so, clean books. But here's where it gets interesting. Some of the money goes into the church fund, where it normally would go, but some goes into two different offshore banking accounts."

"Maybe the accounts are insurance, in case the church goes under for some reason," Stacy said. "The government will freeze their domestic accounts if there is suspicion of malfeasance."

"Right," Buddy said. "If Van suspects something, the government won't be far behind."

"Two accounts?" Will said. "One of them is probably Fitzgibbon's and the other is her own. Can you get into them?"

Daphne shook her head. "We've got some codes and passwords, but if I try to use them, she'll get a warning. We don't want her emptying those accounts. But I agree that one of them could be a connection with Fitzgibbons. My question is why she would want to launder money - if she is; there's nothing but circumstantial evidence here at best. If she really is laundering money and she got caught, the scandal would ruin them. She's as straightlaced as they come. She dresses like a librarian and has an ultra-conservative column in the paper."

"Doesn't have much good to say about the bar scene in Brantwood," Will said. "Claims she's going to clean it up one day."

"She's comin' for ya baby," Daphne said with a laugh. She turned to Buddy. "What do you know about Fitzgibbons?"

"Not much to know," he said. "Bachelor's Degree at Buffalo State, MBA at UB and Doctorate at USF. Taught there for a while, then went into business, eventually ending up in Tallahassee as CFO of the Thompson Fund. Good salary, lots of perks. Clean record except for a cocaine habit that brought him into the world of money laundering. He was small time at first, but he was so good that he came to the attention of Van, among others. He either got greedy or desperate for more coke. Hard to tell. Way more money goes in than comes out. He always says that the money is "in transit," and to be patient. But, as you know, Van is not a patient man."

"Did you say that he taught at USF?" Stacy asked.

"Yeah, why?" Buddy said.

"Drew's been spending time there, vetting the mayor for Bunny Bunstall. You know, looking for skeletons that might pop up at the wrong time. Maybe he can find out a little bit about this Fitzgibbons guy."

"He was only there for a short while, but it's worth a try," Buddy said. "I'm drawing a blank so far."

Later that day, Stacy told Drew that she needed some information about some guy named Ben Fitzgibbons who used to teach at USF. She didn't tell him why and he knew enough not to ask.

"Let's go," Drew said, heading towards his car.

"Where are we headed?" Stacy asked. "Admin building?"

"No," Drew said. "The Library."

THE Library was the same as he had left it just a couple of days before. Pool balls clacked in the back, a couple of guys were playing darts and Ray was wiping the bar down.

"Hey Drew," he said as he and Stacy came through the door. "You're becoming a regular again."

Drew introduced Stacy and laid a bill on the bar. "I need a little more information," he said.

Ray ignored the bill and set two Red Stripes on the bar. "I'm a veritable font of information," he said in a dramatic tone. "What can I do you for?"

"Guy named Ben Fitzgibbons," Drew said. "Got his doctorate and taught here a few years ago. Thought you might remember him."

Ray chortled, his eyes dancing. "It was before your time here, but he was the talk of the campus for a while."

Drew looked at him quizzically.

"Yeah, he taught economics and business at USF. He was young and popular with the students. "Doctor Fitz," they called him. His wife caught him in bed with a cute little intern and all hell broke loose. Dumped a hot container of coffee on his balls." He looked over at Stacy. "Sorry," he added.

"I know what balls are," she said, sipping her beer.

"Anyway, the guy had to be treated for third-degree burns. The administration found out about the affair and he was fired."

Stacy looked at Drew and nodded. At least it was something, she thought.

Ray had a twinkle in his eye as Drew took a big sip of beer. "Girl's name was Liz Young," he said. Drew spit out his beer with a loud "pfft." Ray laughed, pleased with his timing. Stacy looked at Drew for an explanation.

"Liz Young got married," Drew said after he regained his composure. He waited a moment until Stacy took a sip of her beer. "To a guy named Cory Deschamps."

It was Stacy's turn to spit out her beer.

CHAPTER THIRTY-ONE

SALLY COULD SEE THAT he was anxious to the point of panic. He paced back and forth, reciting lines, then glancing at the script. "I don't know if this will work," he said, his voice shaking a little.

"We can change the line if you like. Is it too strong, or not strong enough?

"No, no, the line's fine. I mean I don't think that I can do this."

"You don't have to; you can go back to the original script. We can save this for another time."

"No, I want to…I have to. I just don't think that I can."

They were standing on the Community Chapel's stage, the three of them and they were working on an alternate sermon for the upcoming Sunday service. It had been a radical idea, the alternate sermon; it had been decided upon the previous Monday afternoon during his Corey's regular bike ride visit.

"I don't know what to do," he had said when he arrived. He flopped down on the couch and took off his riding gloves, slapping them into the palm of his hand as he spoke. "I can't take it anymore. I've got to do something, or I'll go insane!" Corey's private critique with Elizabeth that morning had been particularly brutal, he told them. Elizabeth had picked him apart ruthlessly, playing the recording over and over and pointing out even the most miniscule flaws until, when she had finally finished, he had staggered out into the morning shaken and trembling. He rode his bike straight to the Yarber's house and threw himself on their mercy. Sally hadn't seen him this distraught since that first day he had come to them.

"She seems to almost take delight in seeing me quiver," he said. "It's not about the sermon or the performance anymore, it's about me. The more I speak up, the more she bears down."

Sally knew exactly what was happening and she knew that the situation would someday come to a head. Elizabeth was obsessive compulsive; she exhibited all the signs of what some people call a control freak. As Elizabeth's personal assistant Sally had seen first-hand her exploitive ways with the members of her team. She was a master of control and she used whatever weapon necessary to maintain it. But there was one flaw in Elizabeth's method and that's what made her so dangerous. Sally reasoned that some deep-seated fear compelled Elizabeth to wage her campaign of manipulation. Fear is a powerful emotion, and it causes people to do desperate things; the most dangerous animal is a cornered one and Corey's quest for independence was threatening to corner Elizabeth. Despite his determination, Elizabeth was a redoubtable fighter and Sally didn't want to be caught in the crossfire when it occurred.

Strangely, it was Virgil who had suggested an alternate script for Sunday's sermon instead of a confrontation. "You need to be your own man," he told Corey. "Although you've been inserting scripture and text into your sermons through Sally, the final script is still Elizabeth's. You need to take control of your ministry. You need to become what your worshippers believe you to be."

"What's that? Corey asked.

"You need to be Corey Deschamps. You need to deliver your own sermon, not hers."

The three of them worked all week on the new script and Sally began to see a determination in Corey that she didn't know he possessed. Although Virgil and Sally did most of the research – the sessions with Corey could only be for a short time, during his scheduled bike ride – it was Corey who made the final decision on the script itself. By the end of the week, it was complete, and Corey was assiduously rehearsing it. But now, on the stage of the little chapel, he was wavering. Virgil offered words of encouragement and it calmed Corey for the moment, but Sally couldn't help wondering which sermon he would give on Sunday, and what Elizabeth would do if he gave the alternate one.

CHAPTER THIRTY-TWO

GLORIA BUNSTALL WATCHED AS the trio of Jimbo Onthank, Corey Deschamps and Elizabeth Deschamps emerged from their limo. Bunny had insisted that Corey be invited to give the benediction at the reception for the governor. "It will look good on the invitation and will help to attract more donors," he had said at the time. The response to the invitations had been overwhelming and Bunny appeared to have been right about adding Corey Deschamps' name to the invitations, along with Jimbo Onthank as M.C. Both the Thompson Fund and her own fund would take in a great deal of money from the reception. Still, she was worried. Elizabeth seemed to have a growing influence on the city council, which endangered her initiatives. She had heard that Bob Draggett had reversed his vote on the fence bill; Teejay's carefully worded article implying that he was tied up in a corruption scandal will put an end to that, she thought. But a searing question remained: how had Elizabeth Deschamps turned him? And then there was Leonard Morley. Citing financial strictures, he had sent her a letter regretting that he would no longer be contributing to her fund. His son, Bruce, usually attended her fundraisers and gave generously. Bruce was in the hospital, she knew, but Leonard had chosen not to send another representative – and there had been no letter of regret for not attending, and no attached check. Had Elizabeth managed to turn Morley too? She was determined to find out, and if so, she would find a way to stop Elizabeth Deschamps. She sipped her champagne and watched as the throng of attendees arrived.

Bunny and Teejay were watching as well, and you could almost cut the tension between them with a knife.

"Where's your boy? He should have been here when we arrived," Bunny said icily.

"I don't know. Maybe he ran into some traffic," Teejay said, trying to sound relaxed.

"That's bullshit and you know it!"

Bunny was livid. As a young man, he had studied men of great success. Great businessmen and political leaders that he admired had certain things in common: they were organized, intelligent, determined and driven to succeed. But, in Bunny's mind, the thing that they all had in common, the thing that brought them success and separated them from the pack was good instincts. Bunny had worked hard at all the virtues that made men great, but he especially worked to cultivate his instincts. He considered it a personal failure when his instincts were wrong, and it seemed to be wrong about A.J. Andrews. He was late. Bunny had specifically told Teejay to make sure that he was here on time and dressed for the occasion.

"The mayor's here, Deschamps is here, we're here and soon Tommy Thompson will be here." He looked askance at Teejay, who had failed him.

Teejay sipped his scotch and didn't say anything. He was angry too, although it had been Bunny's idea to groom the young man in the first place. But it was his job to make certain that Drew had his shit together for the reception. Bunny had invested a lot of money in the boy's make-over and it had seemed like it was working. But here they stood, waiting for the governor, and their photographer was missing.

Suddenly a loud 'crack!" rent the air which sent police and security scurrying. "Just a backfire," one of them reported. There was another backfire, and a faded blue Volvo came chugging up the hill. Finding no parking place, the driver pulled into a diagonal space next to the fenced-in dumpster. Drew Andrews stepped out of the car.

"What the hell!" Bunny exclaimed. "Look at him!" He looked angrily at Teejay "You get down there and fire his ass. And get my cameras back!"

"Yessir," Teejay said. He looked balefully at Drew. He was dressed in jeans, old hiking boots, a khaki shirt and a faded green photographer's vest. He had two cameras and a canvas camera bag slung over his shoulders. On his head was a battered Red Sox ballcap.

Teejay walked as swiftly as his patent leather shoes would let him. Drew noticed him, smiled and waved. He headed up the hill towards the podium, where the mayor and his wife were standing. Teejay was about to shout to stop him when he saw Ned Butcher walk down the hill towards Drew.

"Hey Drew," Teejay heard him shout. "Glad you could make it. We're up here." Drew waved to Teejay again and shrugged as if to say: "Sorry, can't see you now, gotta go."

Teejay watched as Drew arrived at the podium and shook hands with John McNair in a familiar fashion. They shared a joke about something and then, after having been introduced to McNair's wife, Drew unlimbered his cameras and began shooting. Ned seemed to be suggesting angles. Teejay turned and walked up the hill where Bunny was standing as if in shock.

"Forget the order to fire him," he said as Teejay got near. He shook his head in wonderment. "I guess my instincts were right safter all."

Drew couldn't help noticing his boss and his employer, standing together in their tuxes and patent leather shoes, drinking scotch, and watching him. They had to be happy that he was getting close to the mayor and getting some good shots, but he had to wonder what would happen next; what would come after the mayor went off to run for governor and he was back at his cube, writing stories for Teejay.

"You missed your chance! You should be up there with them, wearing a tux, your hair slicked back and a glass of scotch in your hand. There'll be plenty of time for photo ops, Jacki McNair will see to that."

Right, Drew said, trying to remember not to speak out loud. Country club friends, hot car, trophy wife that cheats, expensive vacations; that's what I'm after "Peter."

His eyes widened as he realized he'd said "Peter" out loud. Ned gave him a funny look for just a hint of a moment. Drew busied himself with his cameras.

The mayor was laughing, sharing some joke with Ned. He seemed completely oblivious to Drew and his cameras. Drew caught him tipping his head back, his eyes raised skyward and trying to keep his composure as Ned continued to poke at him. Jacki came over and scolded them playfully. "Behave, you two," he heard her say. Got it, Drew thought as he captured the image. He kept at a low crouch and tried to stay out of the trio's line of sight as much as possible. When one of them did look his way, he stopped shooting and pretended to adjust his camera.

Other photographers were there too, of course, as well as a cameraman from channel 10. Drew tried to keep out of their way as they jostled for position in front of the podium. He didn't want those shots anyway, the posed grip and grins that he was so tired of. What Drew was after was the type of shot you got in your mind's eye when you looked at someone who was relaxed and being himself. He'd photographed too many practiced smiles.

AFTER an hour of drinks and hors d'oeuvres, the diners took their seats. Salads were served and Jimbo Onthank took the microphone. "Oh, ho, ho!" He boomed. "There's more costume jewelry here than at a trailer park social!" There was a smattering of laughter. Jimbo tapped the mic. "Is thing on?" A little more laughter, but not much. Tough crowd, he thought. Bunch of rich tight asses.   Okay, pull out all the stops, Jimbo. "How 'bout that baseball game?" He said, his arms spread wide. "The one the papers are calling "Grand Theft Baseball?" There was a collective moan, along with some booing. That got their attention, Jimbo thought. "That umpire stole our victory! Snatched it right out of our hands!"

"Right!" Somebody shouted. There was a chorus of agreement.

"Well, I'm here to tell ya that life can do that! It can throw you a curve ball when you least expect it! Just when you think you've got something going it can snatch your victory away! You feel robbed! You feel mistreated! And who do you turn to? Well, I've got just the man who can tell you! Ladies and gentlemen, I give you *Mister Corey Deschamps!*"

The crowd broke into applause as Corey jogged up to the podium and took the microphone from Jimbo. He flashed his patented smile and rocked his dimples. He waited a few moments, as Elizabeth had coached him, basking in the applause. Then he began.

"Ladies and gentlemen, we are gathered here today to talk about two things you aren't supposed to talk about at dinner parties: religion and politics!" There was a smattering of laughter and applause. Jimbo did his job, Corey thought. He had warmed the audience up nicely.

"I'll leave the politics to the mayor and the governor – render unto Caesar. But religion, well, that's my job!" He raised his hands, palms up and looked to the sky. "Can you feel him here today? Can you feel him here today?"

"Amen!" A woman's voice answered. "Amen!" Several other people said in response.

Corey shook his head up and down, his eyes closed. "Yes, I feel him! I feel his presence! Yes folks, he is here today to bless us all. Let him guide the words of our public servants as they speak of worldly things. But remember Romans 15:13: May the God of hope fill you with all joy and peace as you trust in him, so that you may overflow with hope by the power of the Holy Spirit!"

"Amen!" the woman's voice came again, stronger and more assertive. Corey knew that it was Elizabeth, of course; everything had been thoroughly rehearsed. "Amen!" came a chorus of voices. Then came the applause. Corey put his hands together in prayer, closed his eyes and looked skyward again. Jimbo grabbed the mic. "Corey Deschamps, ladies and gentlemen!" More applause. Corey stepped away as Jimbo took over.

"Inspirational, as always!" He said, clapping as Corey took his seat next to Elizabeth. She watched impassively as John McNair stood off to the side of the podium, waiting to be announced. He would be nervous, she knew. He hated public speaking. She wondered again how fate had played such a trick on her as to bring them together in the same town and now, today, at the same reception.

She and John had dated in college years ago when she was Liz Young, and he was an immature frat boy. They were in love and couldn't keep their hands off each other. She thought at the time that they would ride off into the sunset together, facing the world and the future as a team. But there was a problem, one that she tried to bring up to John several times; a problem that she could never quite bring herself to confront him with. The problem was that she liked seeing other men. Maybe it was her fear of abandonment. Or maybe it was simply her smoldering libido, which had been awakened by her uncles when she was a teen, but she couldn't help herself when she noticed a man noticing her. "What do you think of open relationships?" she asked him once. He told her that some people rolled that way, but he couldn't imagine being with anyone else but her. Silly, loyal fool! He had no idea that she was suggesting it for them, or at least herself. He thought it was just a rhetorical question.

Then one day he had come over to her apartment early, his class having been cancelled for some reason. She was in bed with a professor at the college, a certain Doctor Fitz, a man that she would one day enjoy a very profitable business arrangement with. John let himself in. She hurriedly dressed in her bathrobe and intercepted him at the door. "Just taking a nap," she lied. "Put a record on, I'll be right in." He had tried to get amorous, but she fended him off with a fabricated headache. John Coltrane was playing as Fitz slipped out the door. John never suspected, or at least so she thought. Had he heard the door? Had he looked out the window to see a stranger leave the apartment and drive away?

"What's going on?" he had asked her after she had dressed. She thought it a strange question at the time and had changed the subject. "Not much," she told him. "Hey, did you hear that Jennine is having an affair? Crazy, right?"

"Does Frank know?" he said. She told him she didn't know and then he asked her if she would ever do such a thing to him. "Don't ever ask me that question again," she told him. She had immediately regretted answering that way. Why had she blurted that out? She explained to him that asking such a question implied distrust. He trusted her, didn't he? Of course, he told her. Sorry for asking, he said.

After that, their relationship seemed to cool. He became indifferent and distant and didn't come around quite as often, which was fine with Fitz. Then one day, just before graduation, he announced that he had joined the army. Not "was thinking of joining the army," but "I've joined the army."

She was speechless. A lifetime of army bases and army brats? It was a life that she had never imagined for herself, and she had imagined many. She still saw him when he returned on leave and she was still in love with him but finally, when he was deployed and she met Derf Walowitz, she realized that there was no way forward for the two of them. She sent him a letter, explaining her situation and apologizing. She never heard from him again; that is until she moved her church to Brantwood and found out, after the purchase of the stadium was complete, that John McNair was the mayor of Brantwood.

John and his wife attended church every Sunday, which she knew was Jacki's idea. It was good for the mayor to be seen in church. She saw him glancing at her occasionally, but she never met his gaze. She was afraid of what would happen if she did.

Now, sitting at an elegant table at a reception for the state governor, she watched Jimbo Onthank welcome him to the podium.

"It is my esteemed honor to welcome to the podium a man you all know well: war hero, former school board member, former city councilman and current mayor of Brantwood. Johhhn McNairrrr!"

The crowd cheered as John rose and walked towards the podium. As he did, he said softly to Ned, "What is this, a wrestling match?"

Ned laughed.

"Thank you, Jim," John said, taking the mic. "You're too kind." He waited a few moments for the crowd to settle down. God, he hated public speaking; he would much rather be in a council meeting, working on some important initiative than standing in front of a bunch of wealthy donors and serving them political pap. He looked at Jacki who smiled and nodded enthusiastically, then he glanced over at Elizabeth Deschamps, who sat immobile, staring straight ahead. Oh well, he thought. Here goes.

"I first met Tommy Thompson when he was our state representative, what was it? Ten years ago, now? It was in a VA hospital where I was recovering from some pretty nasty shrapnel wounds. He had heard that I'd been shipped home and wanted to visit me and thank me for my service. He didn't just stop by for a quick photo op; he sat by my bedside and grilled me on my opinions about veteran's affairs, the VA, and the treatment of veterans in general." John paused for a moment and then, with a slight smile, said, "I told him what I thought."

"He stayed all afternoon, talking politics, sports, and life in general. I soon found that I had a kindred spirit: we shared similar opinions on values, justice and truth. I can think of no finer man to have as governor than Tommy Thompson."

John McNair wasn't a small man, but Tommy Thompson, the former NFL football player, towered over him as he stepped up to the podium. Thompson's voice was deep and rumbly and had an assertiveness born of calling plays since he was in middle school.

"Thanks, John," he said, looking kindly on the mayor. "And thanks for your service. I'd also like to thank all of the veterans here this evening for their service. Could you please stand and be recognized?" No one stood. As I thought, Thompson thought to himself. He looked over at Ned, who had chosen not to stand and was surveying the crowd with a look of disdain. Thompson, who had served in the Army National Guard, threw a quick salute Ned's way. Ned smiled and nodded.

"As you all know, I'm an avowed capitalist who believes in free enterprise, hard work and individual achievement. When our forefathers tamed the frontier, they did it on their own against great odds. They asked for nothing except the right to forge lives for themselves and their families. But the government did help. It provided free land if a settler could build a house and raise a crop – The Homestead Acts. The government incentivized railroad companies to build a transportation network that was the best in the world – The Railroad Acts. It built schools and universities that produced the highest trained workforce in civilization. It protected inventions through patent laws. Municipalities provided police departments, fire departments, garbage removal systems and sewage disposal facilities. And the Nation built the finest military establishment in the world, protecting our borders and interests.

"There were abuses, to be sure. Native Americans were unfairly displaced and mistreated – The Trail of Tears and the genocide of tribes. Human beings were bought and sold like chattel – slavery. Wars were launched in pursuit of bald-faced land grabs – The Mexican War and The Spanish-American War. Workers were exploited – wage slavery. But we drove on, admitting our mistakes and righting them when we could. The Thirteenth Amendment ended slavery. The Bureau of Indian Affairs and the Department of the Interior were set up to deal with Native Americans. The Wagner Act legalized unions and set up a procedure for grievances. Other abuses, monopolies, trusts, and cartels that had destroyed competition were brought under control by legislation and important court decisions.

"We must continue our forward progress through reasonable legislation, initiatives and incentives. That's where the Thompson Fund comes in. It provides scholarships to promising students, beautification projects that attract tourists and permanent settlers in communities throughout the state, programs for the Arts, and greenspace initiatives. All at no cost to the taxpayer. I call the Thompson Fund a win-win proposition and I appreciate your participation in it. Thank you."

The crowd erupted in applause and gave the governor a standing ovation. He smiled, waved and began signing copies of his best-selling book: "The Thompson Effect," a chronicle of the fund's purpose, its trials and its successes. He shook hands, posed for pictures and allowed selfies. At $2,000 a plate, it was incumbent upon the governor to indulge them. After a time, the governor, the mayor and a few notable patrons repaired to a private room in the club for whisky and cigars. Ned motioned to Drew. "C'mon along, Troop, there might be a few more photo ops," he said.

Once inside, Bunny called Drew over to the bar. "I don't know how you did it, but you deserve this." He handed Drew a tumbler of scotch, clinked the glass with his own in a toast and downed the smokey, amber fluid. Drew did the same.

"Just doing my job," Drew said. He glanced over at Ned, who winked.

CHAPTER THIRTY-THREE

STACY LOVED TO FLY, at least as much as her father. She took out Will's Beaver whenever he wasn't using it, which was far too rare an occurrence, in her opinion. Soaring out over the Gulf, the controls of the floatplane light in her hand, she could almost imagine being one of the animals that dipped and weaved and dived and swam just below her. Fun choice, she often thought. Would she like to be a soaring osprey or a cruising dolphin? She would choose when she was given the choice, she decided. But it was still fun to dream.

Today she was headed to the 'Glades again with a sick snake and a few water samples. She found herself wishing that Drew was along, but he was working, if golfing and lunch at the mayor's house constituted working. She liked Drew – a little more than she cared to admit. He had a sense of adventure and had handled himself remarkably well at the chemical factory. She knew about the tragedy of his family, of course; who hadn't? He seemed sometimes distracted and she often caught him talking to himself. Minor quirks, she hoped. But she couldn't help wondering how much damage had been done by the trauma; and how much of it was permanent. Another problem was that he was being trained by Teejay Edmunds and seemed destined to being locked at a desk, writing articles, and sallying forth for grip and grins at business grand openings, political speeches, and cultural events. She had noticed Teejay's obvious approval of Drew's Captain and

Tennile outfit the day of Bruce's party. No wait, strike that, she said to herself, laughing. Bruce's *Barbeque!*

The thought put her to mind of her relationship with Bruce. She had been attracted to him because he liked to fly, and he had a sense of adventure. But she soon found out that Bruce, because of some unknown issue, was afraid of women. Not women in general, but strong women. Was it his mother? She was the only woman able to stand up to Leonard Morely; maybe she had some sort of controlling hold on Bruce. Whatever the reason, Bruce was one of those guys who objectified women so as to neutralize their inherent power. His other girlfriends, before and after, were all beautiful, sexy, attentive and… was *obedient* too strong a word? Compliant. Yes, that's a better word, she thought.

Stacy guided the plane down out of a cloudless sky towards the sea of green that that was the Everglades. White birds dotted the landscape, ibis, egrets, herons and countless other species. As she got closer, she could see Great Blue Herons standing in the shallows, looking like sentries dressed in blue-grey uniforms. She landed on a section of open water, cut the engine and waited. As she did, she marveled again at the huge river of grass that was the Everglades, once untouched and untouchable, it now stood in danger of being destroyed by the great destroyer – mankind. Drainage ditches and roads scarred its pristine visage and industrial pollution, agricultural run-off and raw sewage poisoned its waters. How much longer would it survive before the bulldozers and backhoes put an end to it? She remembered Leonard Morley's speech about unused land being useless land and the benefits mankind provided by clearing and developing it. A line from a song her parents had listened to when she was a child came to mind, "they paved paradise, put up a parking lot." Who was that by? She tried to jog her memory. Oh yeah, Joni Mitchell. "Big Yellow Taxi."

After a short while an airboat came into view, roaring across the grass flats. As it pulled up next to her, she could see Vincent sitting in the pilot's seat, a big grin on his face and a white captain's hat on his head. She climbed out onto one of the plane's pontoons and Dan, standing in the bow, threw her a line.

"What have we here?" Dan said, accepting the backpack.

"Sick snake," Stacy said. "Like I told you on the phone. And some water samples in the side pocket."

Dan and unzipped the top of the pack. Holding his snake hook, he lifted the snake part way out. "Ooh, doesn't look good." The snake coiled slowly as he gently set it back in the pack. He shook his head sadly. "This one may be lucky, I may be able to fix him up, but imagine all of the others, already dead in that swamp."

"Drew's doing an exposé on Morley's operation on Three Mile Creek. It would be good if you could put a rush order on these samples."

"Will do," Dan said, securing the pack to the boat. "And I'm glad Drew is doing an expose, but what good will it do in the long run? It's been done before, in other papers and on other factories. People will read it in the morning and be outraged but, by afternoon, they'll have already forgotten about it."

"Yeah," Stacy said. "Maybe Doc Donnelly can light a fire under those folks at the EPA if he finds something ugly."

"It might be time for a little "Monkey Wrench Gang," Dan said. He was an avowed environmental activist and not afraid to join in protests and demonstrations. He had once driven hundreds of miles to join a protest against the Dakota Access Pipeline and had been arrested several times at environmental demonstrations. One of his heroes was Edward Abbey, who urged environmental activists to peacefully sabotage work sites that threatened the environment.

"What are you going to do, chain yourself to an outlet pipe?" Stacy said.

"Maybe."

"They'll shoot you if you try to get anywhere near that plant," Stacy said. "Trust me, I've been there."

"Don't worry about me," Dan said as he cast off from the plane. "I can take care of myself."

Vincent waved, gunned the engine, and motored the big airboat away.

On the flight back, Stacy couldn't help being concerned about Dan. It wasn't what Dan might do that she was worried about; she was worried about was what Morley's head of security might do if he caught Dan trying to sabotage the factory. The man had eyes colder than any snake she had ever handled.

CHAPTER THIRTY-FOUR

D REW FELT A HEAVY tension bearing down on him, and it made him uncomfortable. He hated deadlines, they made him rush his writing which then sounded pedantic and strained. He liked to take his time, playing with sentence structure and word choice until the narrative flowed smoothly, immersing the reader in the story. As he sat at his desk, poring over the final rushes of his exposé for the Sunday supplement, he noticed Teejay glancing nervously at him. The deadline was five o'clock and it was already 5:20. Bunny had held up the printing schedule so that Drew's article could be included. He would have been done much earlier if he hadn't had to follow the mayor and governor around the golf course in the morning, cover a luncheon hosted at the mayor's house at mid-day and then listen to a bunch of speeches by the governor and mayor at prominent business-es in the city. Such was the life of a cub reporter, he thought wryly as he envisioned Teejay Edmunds as Perry White, Clark Kent's boss at the Daily Planet, chomping on a cigar impatiently.

The golf game had been fun at first and he got lot of great cameos of the governor and mayor, but the morning had stretched out interminably with the deadline looming over him.

Then there was the luncheon, hosted by Jacki McNair on their patio. Again, Drew got many cameos of the mayor throwing frisbees for his two kids and their Golden Retriever. Then a bonus: the governor and mayor played catch with a football. The pictures were gold. He had even had a brief conversation with Jacki, a surprise.

"You're Drew Andrews," Mrs. McNair said during a casual moment. She was a pleasant, good-looking woman of about thirty-five. She looked as though she worked out; she had the toned and muscled shoulders and legs of an athlete.

"What do you think of John?" Jacki asked abruptly. It was a serious question, Drew realized.

"Well," he began, slowly. "War hero, clean record, churchgoer, family man. What's not to like?"

"What do you see as his virtues, and his faults?"

"Courage, decisiveness, a sense of justice. Honesty," Drew said.

"Ah, the last one," Jacki said. "You hesitated. Is it because you're not certain that he is honest, or do you view honesty as a weakness?"

"I...," Drew stammered. He had only paused because he was searching for another word.

"Sorry," Jacki said. "I didn't mean to jump you. It's just that he is honest, to a fault. Maybe it's the Eagle Scout in him. Maybe it's his military training. But he always speaks his mind truthfully, even when it costs him. I often tell him that he doesn't have to lie, he doesn't have to be dishonest. But he doesn't always have to be so damn honest all the time." She laughed a little at her own remark and took another sip of iced tea.

"Bunny understands politics," she continued. "Tommy and Teejay understand politics. But I'm afraid that my wonderful, heroic husband doesn't."

Drew sat silently for a minute, digesting what he'd just heard. It was obvious that Jacki was the driving force behind John McNair's political career. It was also becoming increasingly obvious that, although she was trying desperately to groom John, he didn't much like being groomed. The expensive suits, the country club membership and the black-tie dinners were not his style.

"Who are his constituents?" Drew asked impulsively.

Jacki seemed surprised by the question. "Why, the usual; businessmen, bankers, investors. That's why I have him dress well: you have to fit in with those people."

"Ned calls it the "uniform of the day," Drew said.

Jackie laughed. "So does John when I lay out his clothes or help him with his tie; or when I smooth some product into his unruly hair."

"A little spritz of high-priced cologne," Drew said.

"Exactly," Jacki said.

"But those aren't his constituents," Drew said. He felt that he was going out on a limb, but then she *had* asked him. "Those are his donors. His constituents are working men and women, trying to make ends meet, trying to keep their families together. The people living paycheck to paycheck that see John as someone who understands them and will fight for them. They see him as one of them."

"But don't they see him as a model of what you can achieve?" Jacki asked. "Someone who has made it?"

"Oh, sure," Drew said. "They look up to him and they admire him. But at some point, won't they begin to see him as just another wealthy politician who ensconces himself in a cushy job? Someone who tells them what they want to hear just before every election and then goes back on his promises. Won't he become just another of the country clubbers who look down their noses at the common man?"

Jacki looked at Drew with a funny expression on her face. She got up and fished another beer out of a cooler and handed it to him. "Keep talking," she said.

This was new ground for Drew, and he wasn't certain what he was going to say next. But he forged ahead. "Ever notice that the members of congress from certain districts wear string ties, cowboy boots and country and western suits? Why do they do that? They may have spent years in Washington, but they never lose their regional accent."

Jacki laughed. "How could you miss them? I swear they just stepped out of an episode of Hee Haw!"

"Hicks," Drew said.

"I'm PC, but you hit pretty close to the mark," Jacki said.

"Who votes for hicks?" Drew said, driving his point home.

Jacki looked directly at Drew, a thoughtful look on her face. "I see your point," she said. She thanked him for the conversation and politely excused herself to see to her other guests.

"You freaking idiot! Why can't you keep your mouth shut?"

Drew agreed with Peter for once. He doubted that he'd be invited to any other lunches.

But that afternoon, as the mayor and governor arrived at the first business they were to tour, there was a marked difference in how they were dressed. Gone were the business suits, leather-soled shoes and power ties. John wore a comfortable pair of khakis, worn boat shoes and a faded blue polo shirt. The governor was similarly dressed down.

"What in God's name did you say to Jacki?" Ned asked Drew as they donned yellow helmets for the tour.

"We talked about uniforms of the day," Drew said.

"Job well done, Troop," Ned said with a nod. Then he laughed. "I bet she still dresses him up for the fundraisers."

Later, as he finished up the expose and turned it in, Teejay gave him an impatient look. They were due at the Bunstall estate for drinks, Hors de Oeuvres and dinner at six. Drew hadn't expected to be invited to the dinner and had made plans with Stacy for the evening, but Bunny Bunstall was not to be denied. He wanted Drew there to get cameos again.

CHAPTER THIRTY-FIVE

Teejay was driving. He told Drew that Bunny liked the rough drafts of the Morley expose and was pleased with the pictures. "How in God's name were you able to get them? That place is closed up tighter than a drum. No one without an ID gets through the gate without express permission from Leonard Morley."

"It was a little tricky," Drew admitted. "The head of security looked like he wanted to pull my fingernails out with a pair of pliers."

"Yeah," Teejay said. "Morley called Bunny and wanted to know what the hell was going on. Bunny disavowed any knowledge of your activities, he said you were acting on your own and that you would be disciplined for improper use of company property."

It was Drew's turn to laugh. "Your mission, should you choose to accept it..." he said in a narrator's voice.

"What's the working title of your expose?" Teejay asked.

"Snakes are Venomous, Pollution is Poisonous," Drew said. "I featured a picture of the sick Water Moccasin with the caption "Deadly Snake Finds Its Own Swamp Deadly.""

"I like it," Teejay said. "By the way, the governor liked the bio that you wrote. Both he and the mayor feel comfortable with you around, and so does Jacki."

"I hope so," Drew said. "I mostly try to stay out of the way."

Teejay noticed the way that Drew plied his craft. He was easy going, quiet and undemanding. Where some photographers stalked around, aiming their cameras, and calling out "over here!" or suggesting poses, Drew calmly walked around, seemingly lost in adjustments to his lenses. When he aimed a camera, he looked as though he was checking the aperture or light meter. People rarely knew that he had snapped them, therefore they ceased noticing him altogether. Distraction, Teejay thought. He practiced it himself. From thumbing through his notebook, to examining the brim on his hat to flipping open his cigarette case, he kept whoever he was speaking with slightly distracted and a little off-guard. Just enough to give him an edge.

THE Bunstall Estate was on a small rise overlooking the bay on one side and the city on the other. It was said to be one of the highest elevations in that part of the state. Green fields stretched out below it, fenced in by miles of white plank fencing for Gloria's string of horses. Tall live oaks, draped with Spanish moss were everywhere, providing shade for the horses, which grazed languidly under them. Drew took several shots with his wide-angle lens.

The house was tan brick with a red tile roof in Spanish Colonial style. There were dozens of tall windows on two floors and a third floor featured gabled dormers jutting out from the roof. Drew knew that it been built during the grand days of the late 1800s called by Mark Twain "The Gilded Age." Bunstall had it thoroughly modernized when he bought it, but it retained its colonial character.

When Drew arrived, Ned noticed him and motioned him over to his table, which was off to the side of the main dining area. There was a cold beer in front of him.

"Over here, Troop," he said, gesturing to an empty chair. Drew pulled up the chair and sat down. Ned reached down into a cooler, fished out a can of beer and slid it towards Drew.

"Thanks," Drew said. He cracked it open and took a swig. "What's the op, Top?"

Ned laughed. "You guys who watch war movies have a language all your own," he said, shaking his head. "The Top Sergeant tells the Squad Leaders what the operation is, and they tell the troops."

"Well, what do the troops say to the Top Sergeant then?"

"They don't say shit if they value their ass!" Ned said. He noticed Drew aiming his telephoto at something over his shoulder. He turned and looked as the camera clicked and whirred.

Faster than a snake, Ned turned and snatched the camera from Drew.

"What the…" Drew began.

"Do you know who those guys are?" Ned asked. Drew had been snapping pictures of the governor's two bodyguards who were leaning against the governor's limo, parked a short distance up the hill.

"The governor's bodyguards," Drew said, a little taken aback.

"They're a couple of former mercs who the governor's wife pays to keep him out of trouble. I'm sure you've heard the rumors about our good governor."

Drew nodded.

"They'll stop at nothing to keep the governor's reputation, and the reputation of the Thompson Fund, clean. I doubt very seriously that they would appreciate pictures being taken of them. If they had seen you, you'd have been lucky to get away with only a smashed camera. And that's only because I'm here."

"Thanks," Drew said sarcastically. "Good to know you've got my back. Now, can I have my camera back?"

Ned laughed to himself as he slid the boy's camera across the table. He was young, cocky and inexperienced. He had led hundreds of boys just like him into combat. Not all of them had come back. He had seen some killed or wounded by sticking their heads up at the wrong time, some by not paying attention while walking down a trail, most got hit by just being in the wrong place at the wrong time. Drew had to face none of those physical dangers, but careers could be ruined just as quickly for the unwary, the inexperienced or the unlucky. As he looked over the guests at the dinner party, Ned realized that all of them were survivors. They had kicked, clawed and fought their way to the top of the hill by out-thinking, out-witting or out-lucking the competition. Some had done it by cheating, lying, and back-stabbing. Others, like John, had taken a more noble path.

Ned had watched John McNair take command of his company with the usual skepticism that went with a new commanding officer. There would be a trial period where the new CO would have to establish himself in the men's eyes. He would have to set an example and make examples, being careful to establish fair and even-handed discipline; too harsh and he would be branded a martinet; too lax and he would be considered weak.

When John McNair walked up to his command position in front of the company for his first review, he exuded a sense of decisiveness and purpose.

"Everyone has jobs to do; jobs that you were trained to do; jobs that you've done before. When you know your job well, through training and experience, you will execute it precisely and efficiently. As you know, there's no room for error in combat. A mistake can cost a life; your own or, worse yet, the man next to you. My message to you today is know your job and do it well. I'll to do the same."

The men, standing at ease, shifted a little. They had expected a lot more: talk of teamwork, patriotism, duty, honor and country. The usual. McNair, his hands clasped easily behind him, regarded them for a moment. "Questions?"

A soldier, standing somewhere in the middle of the formation, asked, "How much combat experience do you have, Sir?" There was a slight pause before he said "Sir," making it sound a little insulting. Sergeant Butcher glared at the man. Someone snickered. An insolent grin appeared at the corners of the man's mouth. The Company had been in country for several months and, except for replacements, each man had at least a dozen combat missions under his belt.

"Miller, right?" McNair said mildly.

"Sir, yes Sir!" Miller said, snapping to attention in an exaggerated fashion.

"At ease, Private Miller," McNair said, with only the slightest hint of a laugh in his voice. "I've read your file."

A couple of men laughed. Miller looked around for the culprits angrily, then focused back on the captain. "Yes Sir," he said. "I'm sure you have." Another snicker and an open laugh could be heard in the ranks.

"I've read all your files," McNair said, looking over the group. They became quiet again. "Courage on the battlefield, misbehavior off. Fighting, insubordination; petty stuff mostly, but enough to get you written up and, for some of you, busted. The kinds of things young men do to relieve the intense pressure of combat." He paused for a moment. "How did you feel the first time you went into combat, Miller?"

Miller laughed, shaking his head. "Scared shitless, Sir," he said. "Didn't want to fuck up."

"Well," McNair said. "That's how I feel right about now. This is my first combat assignment, and I hope that I can perform as well as y'all have, according to your files." He looked at the company as if to say, "anymore questions?" There were none.

McNair proved to be a superior commander right away. His orders were clear and precise, his operations were well-planned, and he always used the chain of command: top sergeant to platoon leaders to squad leaders, to troops, leaving specific tasks to the immediate leaders. But it also became quickly apparent that he knew each man's job at least as well as the man himself. He made adjustments and criticisms through the NCOs rather than directly to the men.

In combat situations he was cool and collected, giving no indication that he was personally afraid for himself. He wasn't crazy brave like some men, who seemed to have a death wish when under fire. But he also wasn't afraid to put himself in harm's way if the situation demanded it. More than once he took over the machine gun on his Humvee when the gunner had been wounded or killed. Under fire he moved down the line, reassuring the men and firing himself when a target appeared. That same bravery almost cost him his life one hot afternoon on the plains of Afghanistan.

The company was on a patrol through a series of dusty little villages in Taliban territory. They had seen no movement all day, but when they entered one particular village, there was an unsettling absence of villagers, who normally stood in the heat and the dust, watching the sweating soldiers walk by. Sergeant Chaz Tasker was with the lead squad when they were suddenly ambushed by a large group of Taliban that appeared out of a jumble of rock. They were pinned down and cut off. McNair and Butcher led a counterattack. The fighting was intense, and an RPG had exploded in their midst, killing several and wounding Tasker and Butcher. Wounded himself, McNair had carried the wounded men out of harm's way.

Now, sitting at a table with a young, naïve photojournalist, Ned watched John McNair negotiate the vicious battlefield of politics, where a wrong word or gesture could be as fatal to a career as a landmine could be to a life in combat. John approached his mission as mayor in the city as he did his position as CO in the Army. He was forthright, deliberate and truthful in his initiatives. He didn't make promises he couldn't keep in order to get votes, something that his wife had advised him to do. "To support an idea or program that you know won't pass isn't dishonest," she often said. "It indicates to voters that you're on the right path even if the way forward is temporarily out of reach."

"If the way forward is out of reach, then I owe it to my constituents to tell them that," John countered. "I won't tilt at windmills."

Ned noticed Drew fiddling with his cameras and moving his lips, talking to himself – or someone. He'd seen that kind of behavior before, and it troubled him. He knew about Drew's family, of course. What sort of scars had those events left on the young man? He decided to take the bull by the horns.

"Who's in your head, Troop? He said softly. Drew looked up, surprised.

"No one," he stammered. "Just thinking out loud a little, I guess. Sorry."

"Sorry for what?"

"Sorry that you saw me talking…to myself."

As I thought, Ned thought. He and John had thoroughly vetted the lad knew what was troubling him. Losing your family at a young age is never easy to bear, and the way it had happened must weigh heavy on his mind.

"It's a funny thing, trauma," Ned said. "You see something that you know will haunt you for the rest of your life. It happens unexpectedly, and you can't escape it. You see a soldier that you know, mortally wounded, mumbling his last words to you as you hold his hand. You see the look in his eyes just before the look fades to nothing. When I was young, I held my uncle's hand while he died of an aneurism. He looked at me and said, "I'm going." And he went. That was the first time. I held my wife's hand as she died from cancer. I've seen a dozen men die in combat. You remember that stuff your whole life like it was only moments ago. The memories come back at unexpected times, haunting you, chasing you. But the emotion you feel the most isn't fear, it isn't grief; it's guilt. Guilt that you lived, and they didn't. Guilt that you couldn't do more for them. Guilt that you couldn't make things different somehow."

Drew stared at Ned, this scarred, tough old combat veteran, and wondered how the man had managed to read him so completely.

Don't listen to him, man, he's fucking with you. Sure, he's been through a lot, but he hasn't been through what you have."

Ned saw the kid struggling with what he had just said and realized that he was farther gone than he thought. He had seen the same thing in soldiers with PTSD and knew the struggles they were enduring. Some managed to conquer their feelings, some managed to control them and some sank deeper and deeper into despair. Ned continued.

"The hardest thing to deal with is invented memories. A buddy hears of his friend's death and imagines that he was there. His memories get more and more detailed until he's convinced that he *was* there. He tries to imagine every kind of scenario where something he does stops the event from happening. But he can't make it real, and he becomes more and more delusional."

"Tell him! Tell him the truth! How you should have been there for me; been more of a brother to me. After all I went through! After what I saw!"

Yeah, like the bait well you went through! Drew felt hot, almost feverish; his breathing was coming in short gasps. He wanted desperately for Ned to not see. He felt like running, like a desperate deer, eager to escape the wolves closing in on him. "Sorry to drop in on you like this!"

Drew looked at Ned in surprise. He knew that he had mumbled the last words out loud. He felt panic rising in his breast. Save me! He wanted to shout. Get him out of my head! Shoot him, or I will!

"Easy kid," Ned said. "You'll be okay." But he wasn't so sure. He waited for Drew to compose himself. He saw him struggle, but then he saw him succeed, if only briefly. Ned knew that he only had a moment to pull the kid back from the abyss.

"Peter didn't see your mother shoot your father, so he invented a memory. But he did see her take her own life. The twin memories, one fabricated and one real, tortured him until he took his own life. You didn't see any of it, so you've been inventing memories, tweaking them, massaging them and obsessing over them. Peter comes to you in your head, and you argue and joke with him, hoping that he'll become real. But you're afraid that if he does become real, you'll have lost your mind."

Drew was breathing hard and sweating; he felt as if a giant hand had gripped his heart and was squeezing it. "How do you know all these things?" he managed. "How do you know about my family? How do you know what's going on in my mind?"

"Because I've been through it. They used to call it shell shock, then combat fatigue, and now post-traumatic stress disorder. I was badly wounded in a firefight, I had a severe concussion, multiple shrapnel wounds and had lost an arm. But most importantly, I lost half my squad. I was unconscious and bleeding to death. I was told later that a certain Captain John McNair carried me and the rest of the other wounded men back to safety while under enemy fire.

"But, because I hadn't *seen* the men die, I imagined seeing them die. I played the scene over and over in my head until it became real. Once out of the hospital, I began seeing them in crowds. I began calling out to them.

Then, I let them into my head, and I ended up back in the hospital – the psych ward this time."

Hearing what he'd heard calmed Drew a little. It was good to know that someone else had struggled like he had. But he wondered if a mental hospital was where he was heading. "How did you..."

"Beat it? I didn't. I still get the memories, but only the real ones. I still sometimes see those guys in a crowd, but I laugh, because I know they can't be there. You see, while I was in the hospital, I read a lot. Psychologists, self-help gurus, philosophers. None stuck until I happened upon *Meditations* by Marcus Aurelius, the Roman Emperor. As I read, and re-read, I came to understand the vagaries of fate and how to face them. I finally came to an irrefutable truth. Time is like water. In the present, it's fluid and flowing; the past is ice; frozen, rock hard, unchangeable. The future is vapor, indiscernible, unreadable; it only congeals when it becomes the present. I realized that the present is the only reality. Make up all the narratives you want about the past, but those narratives won't change it. Imagine what might happen in the future and prepare for it, but don't think you can influence all of it. Change what you can, endure what you can't."

Drew began to feel as if a burden was being lifted. His breathing returned to normal, and he no longer felt the gripping sensation in his chest. He took an embarrassed look at Ned, who smiled benignly.

"It's all about Will," he said.

"Determination," Drew said, relaxing a little. "I understand." He expected Peter to chime in with a comment be he was curiously absent.

"Yes, but determination implies something you're *trying* to do. Will is a realization; a triumph if you will."

"Nietzsche," Drew said.

"Butcher," Ned replied.

Later that night Drew had a dream. In it he was playing frisbee with Peter and their dog, Tucker, who was chasing back and forth, trying to intercept the disc. Suddenly the disc sailed over his head. As he turned to get it, he found himself on the railing of the Skyway Bridge. He looked out at the blue sky, dotted with clouds and gulls and pelicans. He smelled the sea air and felt the stinging wind whipping past him, making the hundreds of support wires hum in unison. The sound got louder, and Peter was at his side, holding his hand.

"With me, together!" Peter shouted over the humming wires. "We can fly! We can be free!" And they jumped.

Drew felt the air sucked out of his lungs and he saw a boat below them; they weren't falling towards it; it was rushing up at them. The baitwell, brimming with thousands of shimmering pilchards, swallowed him up, they were soft and cloying as he struggled to get out of their grip. Suddenly, he was standing on the deck, looking at two bored fishermen who were talking with each other. They didn't notice him. "Sorry for dropping in on you like this," he said. They didn't respond or even look at him. He went down into the cabin to look for…what? Peter? The Frisbee? Tucker?

As he walked through the dark cabin, he encountered door after door, each one leading to a series of darker and danker rooms. He felt the dampness of the dripping stone walls and his feet felt the cold of the concrete floor, slick with standing water. The smell of the dampness and the mold and the faint putrescence of a long-dead rodent caught in a forgotten trap filled his nostrils. He recognized the last room as the basement of his house. The stairs leading up to the kitchen ended at a door beneath which was a thin ribbon of yellow light. It beckoned to him. He walked up the slippery wooden steps, gripping the splintery handrail until he reached the door. His hand hesitated over the doorknob, afraid of what was behind it, but in a dream, you always open the door, and he did. There, sitting at the kitchen table and facing him were his father, his mother, and his brother Peter.

"We're sorry for what we did, Andrew," his mother said. His father nodded and Peter smiled. He was petting Tucker, who had the frisbee in his mouth.

"It was never your fault," Peter said. His parents nodded and then faded away as did Peter and the dog. The kitchen light got brighter and brighter and he tried to shield his eyes from it. An echoey voice was shouting his name. He woke to find himself tangled in bedsheets on the floor. Stacy was pulling them off him and asking him if he was alright.

"Yeah, I'm okay," he managed, sitting up and blinking at the harsh glare from the ceiling light.

"You sure?" she said. "You were thrashing around pretty good for a while. "You were yelling something about some damn pilchards."

CHAPTER THIRTY-SIX

Drew was in church, sitting next to Ned Butcher who wore his ever-present vest, concealing his ever-present piece. The room was packed and only the insistence of Bunny and John McNair had persuaded the head usher to allow the two of them admittance. McNair liked to have his former top sergeant around. Drew was puzzled and unhappy. He was puzzled because Teejay had insisted that he attend the service even though he could have just as easily watched the show on cable in the comforts of Stacy's bed. But he was also puzzled that his exposé had a disclaimer under his name: *"The contents of this article, done by an independent reporter, do not reflect the editorial policy of this newspaper."* What did that mean, he wondered? He had called Teejay about it, but Teejay only told him not to worry, that the Journal just needed to keep some legal separation from him. Did that mean they were worried about a lawsuit from Morley? Was Bunny hanging him out to dry? He felt like a patsy, and he told Teejay so. Teejay had just laughed. "Don't worry Kid, Bunny will cover any legal fees if you're sued. You'll still work for us, but on an article-by-article basis. You'll keep your desk but there'll be no set hours; and Bunny said you can keep the cameras."

Drew fumed as he sat in the church, mulling over the situation he had been thrust into. He expected Peter to chime in with some advice or admonishment, but he was strangely silent. Maybe the violent dream had somehow banished him. Strange, Drew thought, he missed him a little now that he was gone. He looked over at Ned, who was stoically enduring what he called the magic show. He thought again about the kinds of trauma the old sergeant had endured in his life and he felt guilty about his own difficulties, which were minor by comparison. He had not seen his parent's bodies because he and Peter had not attended the double funeral; and he hadn't seen Peter's – his was closed casket. He hadn't seen his mother shoot his father and then kill herself as Peter had and he hadn't seen Peter hit the bait well of the fishing boat when he jumped off the Skyway bridge. But he *had* imagined those events many times. And, he now realized, he had been torturing himself with those imagined images. Feeling a sense of relief, he turned his attention to the show.

The band was good, he had to admit. Top notch. He didn't watch much late-night TV but knew that Curtis Green had led the "Better Late than Never Show" band for years until the host had been caught up in an affair and the show had been cancelled. Elizabeth had snapped Curtis up immediately and Curtis had brought along most of his musicians. In addition, Jimbo Onthank, the show's opener and foil, had been hired. It was a winning combination and Drew, never a churchgoer, found himself enjoying the experience.

"I saw your article in the paper this morning," Ned said casually, his gravelly voice rising above the music. "How does it feel to be an independent reporter?"

"I'm not sure," Drew said. "I spoke with Teejay this morning and he assured me that everything was okay, not to worry. He said that there had to be some legal separation between me and the Journal, which made me think that I might be sued. He also said that I'd be working on an article-by-article basis. It felt a little bit like I was being cut loose."

"More like being set free," Ned said. "Or do you like writing the articles that Teejay gets the byline for?"

Drew laughed, feeling a little better.

"You'll have to work harder to get paid, but they'll be stories that you *want* to do," Ned said. "And I'm sure that, knowing Teejay, he'll still have you doing some stories for him. Just make sure you charge him enough."

"I guess I shouldn't worry about being sued," Drew said. "You can't get blood out of a rock."

It was Ned's turn to laugh. He changed the subject.

"Do you know why you're here?" he asked above the chatter of worshippers filing in and the sound of the band.

"Teejay told me to come so I could watch," Drew said idly.

"Couldn't you have done that at home, on cable TV?"

"That occurred to me," Drew said. "I guess he wants me to get some pictures."

"But they won't let you take any pictures, and Teejay knows that." Ned said.

"Then why did he tell me to come and watch?"

"He doesn't want you to watch, he wants you to notice," Ned explained.

Drew looked at him quizzically. Ned smiled.

"Look," Ned said. "You're here for the same reason I am. We can look around, gawk even, if we want to. No one will notice. John can't do that, and neither can Bunny or Teejay. It's all about decorum for them."

"What are we to notice?" Drew asked.

"Everything," Ned said. He was a little surprised that Teejay hadn't explained all this to the young man, but that was just like Teejay: he often assumed too much, in Ned's opinion. He'd seen officers like him, assuming that their orders were fully understood when, in fact, they weren't.

"What did you notice when you arrived?" Ned asked. "Tell me everything."

"Well, the first thing I saw was a humongous parking lot. A traffic volunteer..."

"How did you know he was a traffic volunteer?" Ned said, interrupting sharply.

What is this, another interrogation, Drew thought. "The person was wearing an orange vest; a safety helmet and was waving orange traffic control wands," he said. "And it said "Traffic" on the vest."

"Good," Ned said. "How did you know he was a volunteer?"

"I assumed," Drew said.

"Ah," Ned said. "You *assumed!*"

"How did you know it was a "he," Drew shot back. "I didn't specify gender."

Ned threw his head back and laughed, drawing the attention of a couple of churchgoers in the process. "Good retort," Ned said, still laughing. "Remember that assumptions can become false facts in your mind. They can lead your thinking astray and cause you to miss something that might otherwise be obvious. Now, tell me what happened next."

"He saw my car and directed me to the overflow parking lot. It was a long walk."

"No shuttle?"

"I waved at one, but the driver ignored me."

"Why do you suppose he ignored you?"

"The way I was dressed, maybe," Drew said. Where was Ned going with this? Then he looked around at the churchgoers finding their seats. Then he noticed.

"They have badges," Drew said. Ned smiled.

"The same badges?

Drew looked around again. "No. Some are the rectangular stick-on kind, you know, name tags. Others look more formal and are in the shape of a cross. Some are silver and still others are gold."

"The gold cross members donate the most," Ned said. "They get preferential treatment, the full shot. Valet parking, private coffee bar and lounge. They even have access to the fitness center, it's state-of-the art and open twenty-four hours a day. Except for Sundays, of course."

"The gold cross members seem to be clustered around Elizabeth," Drew observed. "Best seats in the house, except for the VIP section." He noticed Governor Tommy Thompson and Mayor John McNair, sitting together and discussing something. He longed to sneak down there and capture the moment, but he had been warned not to.

"Now," Ned continued. "Do you recognize any gold cross members that are on the city council?"

Drew's eyes widened. Working the political beat, he had to know every council member, and every other public official, for that matter. He saw five council members, the city comptroller, and even the coroner.

"Wow," he said.

Ned nodded. "Anything about any of them that strikes you as strange?'

Drew kept looking around, pondering the question. Well-dressed, well-to-do members of the community. What would be strange? But then he did notice the obsequious way they treated Elizabeth. Drew had been around those guys in the James, the club and at various city functions. They were, for the most part, arrogant and superior acting. But here, in front of Elizabeth, they appeared anxious, edgy, and even a little nervous. Like a pack of whipped dogs, sitting at the feet of their master. He also noticed the absence of Bob Draggett; Teejay's article had forced him to resign from the city council. But why would that cause him to lose his gold cross membership at the church?

NED watched Drew and noticed his affectations: fiddling with his cameras and his phone and seeming to be distracted and even uninterested in what was going on around him. It worked. No one noticed the young man in jeans and khaki shirt with the unkempt hair. He was unimportant to the posers, dressed in their finest and trying to be noticed by the others. Because of that, Drew was able to observe, unnoticed. Ned saw the same thing in Teejay, who wore fancy suits, bow ties, a boater hat and always had a pretty woman on his arm. People were more interested in the trappings than the substance and that allowed Teejay to ply his skills as a reporter, picking up snippets of information, gossip and off-hand remarks.

He himself needed no such affectations. Captain John McNair once described him as a hawk that sat on a perch, surveying the landscape around him. Every animal knew he was there, and no animal wanted to meet his gaze; to do so would invite undue attention in the form of swooping wings and extended talons. Better to leave him to his commanding perch. Ned had a look, born of years of command and combat, that spoke of calm confidence and ability. Where people didn't notice Drew or Teejay because of their mannerisms, people noticed Ned but looked away. With clear, piercing grey eyes he seemed to answer an unspoken question of "what are you looking at?" with an unspoken answer of "I'm looking at you."

Suddenly Ned elbowed Drew. "Pay attention," he said with a laugh. "Here comes the show." Drew watched as the crowd quieted and Jimbo Onthank took up his position off to the side of the main stage.

"Ladies and Gentlemen of the Congregation!" He boomed in his sonorous baritone.

"It's a beautiful day here in Brantwood, isn't it?" The crowd responded with some light applause and a few amens. Jimbo tapped the mic. "Is this thing on?" He asked loudly. A few people laughed. He leaned into the mic and boomed even louder. "It's a beautiful day here in Brantwood, isn't it?" He turned and cocked his ear towards the audience expectantly. People laughed, clapped and cheered. "Yes, it is!" A woman's voice answered.

Jimbo pointed to her. "At least one person gets it," he said. "Thanks honey, I knew I could count on you!" People began openly laughing and clapping. Everyone knew that the woman wasn't Jimbo's wife.

Letting a little Foghorn Leghorn creep into his voice, Jimbo said: "I say, I say, I say, it's a beautiful day today in Brantwood, isn't it?" His voice was loud enough not to need a mic. The people responded with a loud, collective "Yes, it is!" Then a cheer and loud applause.

"That's more like it!" Jimbo boomed. He spread his arms wide and threw his head back as if accepting the crowd's adulation.

Jimbo continued his set-up, goading the crowd, teasing the band and exchanging comments with Curtis Green. When he considered the crowd sufficiently warmed-up he announced Corey.

"Ladies and gentlemen, are you ready?" The crowd cheered. "Are you ready?" The crowd cheered again.

"I give you *Mister Cor-ee Day-Shamps!*"

Corey jogged out onto the stage, flashing his smile and pointing to people in the crowd. "Can you feel him?" He boomed, matching Jimbo's volume and intensity. The crowd cheered even louder. "Can you feel him?" He shouted again. Again, the crowd cheered. "He is here today! Can I get an amen?"

"Amen!" The crowd shouted in unison.

Corey nodded his head solemnly and waited for the crowd to calm down a little. It was time to work his magic.

"Yes, he is here today, with us," Corey said, nodding his head enthusiastically. "As he is with us every day, wherever we are. The Lord of hosts is with us; the God of Jacob is our fortress," he said reassuringly. "God goes with you; he will never leave you nor forsake you; wherever you go, wherever you are!" he said loudly, emphasizing the point. He walked purposely back and forth on the stage, nodding his head and rolling his shoulders. He flashed his signature grin, his dimples showing.

"You are here today, and God is with you," he continued, his voice taking on a serious note. "He is with us!" Do you feel his power?"

"Amen!" Someone shouted. "Amen," the crowd responded.

"It is good that we are all here today," Corey said. "I feel the collective power you all have brought to this great church!"

"Amen!"

"But when you leave, do you leave him here?" Corey asked rhetorically. "No, He goes with you."

Corey looked up and around at the church's rafters and windows. "This church is beautiful, is it not?" The crowd murmured its assent. "This is not God's house, it's a beautiful building, but it's not God's house."

People looked around at each other, unsure of what direction Corey was headed. Drew noticed Elizabeth's jaw tighten and she spoke into her wrist microphone. Jimbo made an 'I don't know' shrug and Curtis Green raised his hands, readying the band to come in. He's going off script, Drew thought, and Elizabeth is getting ready to cut him off. But the crowd roared its approval. He could see her glancing around at the audience nervously.

Will she pull the trigger? Does she dare? A moment later she answered the question by sitting back in her seat and crossing her arms. She nodded 'no' to Jimbo. Curtis Green relaxed. Drew saw Corey hesitate for a moment, shooting a nervous glance, first at his wife and then at Jimbo. Then he smiled and continued.

"God is here because you brought him here. All of you. All of us." Corey paused and looked around meaningfully.

"It is good that we have gathered here," he said. "It is good to share time with fellow believers. Your donations and tithes built this church for just such gatherings. But when I say, at the end of the service, "Go with God," I mean that sincerely. Don't leave him here until you come back next Sunday. Take him with you!"

Corey laughed to himself and stole another look at Elizabeth, who was struggling to contain herself. He knew that she could cut his mic at any time. The band stood ready to play and Jimbo was ready to take over. But the crowd was enthralled, and Corey knew that she realized it. He started to feel a freedom he had once felt long ago, when he put on his mother's makeup and when he was onstage in high school and college. He realized that the freedom had disappeared when he met Elizabeth; not right away, but gradually, like an ebbing tide. As he delivered the sermon, he felt that the tide had turned. He became more and more energized as he continued. Virgil often talked about being lifted up by the spirit when he delivered his own sermons. Was this it?

"Go out into the world and enjoy your life," he continued, his voice rising. "Sing, have fun and enjoy everything God has made for you. Stop praying to God for forgiveness and asking him to intervene in your life. He's not going to answer you. He won't make your job easier or get you a raise or help your favorite team win. He will inspire you to handle the things that challenge you. He will help you to find your strength!"

There was a murmur of affirmation from the crowd. A woman yelled "hallelujah!"

Corey moved around the stage, shaking his hips a little. The band launched into a soft groove behind him. "Stop blaming him!" Corey shout-ed, raising his fist in mock anger. "God didn't bring misery to your life! By giving up on your struggles, you allow misery into it! He gave you the strength to fight and he gave you free will to make decisions, hard as they might be! Wrong as they might be. You are free to create your own life; enjoy it, revel in it! But don't suffer in it, like a dog with his tail between his legs, cowering away in shame and disgrace."

"Be strong and courageous. Do not be frightened, and do not be dis-mayed, for the Lord your God is with you wherever you go. See him in a sunrise, see him in a rainstorm, see him the woods, rivers, lakes, and beaches. See him in the bright shining eyes of a child. Then shall the righ-teous shine forth as the sun in the kingdom of the father. With God all things are possible!

"Respect your peers. Do unto others as you would have them do unto you. Do not judge, do not hate, do not wish ill-will on others. Accept oth-ers as you would have them accept you, with patience, understanding and love. Be not quick in your spirit to become angry, for anger lodges in the hearts of fools.

"Stop praising God, stop thanking him; he knows you are grateful through your actions. Take care of yourself and your health and your rela-tionships and the world. Express your joy! Don't deny who you are, for God made you that way! If someone loves you, love them back. If someone hates you, love them back. What others think of you is none of your business; it is their business!"

Corey looked over at Curtis Green and grinned. "Do you know "John the Revelator?"

"'Deed I do," Curtis said into his mic. He pulled his earpiece out and began the organ intro to an up-tempo gospel tune. It featured a call and response, a field holler. The band took it up.

"Sing if you want, dance if you want!" Corey shouted as Curtis called: "Who's that writin'?" The band answered: "John the Revelator!" "Who's that writin'?" Curtis repeated. "John the Revelator!" came the response again.

Corey joined in and began dancing. The guys playing horns in the band formed a horn line and played along with the lyrics, doing a little dance in unison as they did. People in the church came to their feet and began clapping in tempo. Some sang. Some danced. The room was alive with the spirit of community and shared jubilation. Except for Elizabeth. Drew noticed that she sat stock-still, her hands folded in her lap. A few of the gold cross members seated near her caught themselves and quickly sat.

Curtis quieted the band as Corey spoke breathlessly into the mic. "All as one," he said. "Regardless of race, gender, sexual orientation or political beliefs, all together. As God intended. Thank you all, you've lifted my spirit today and I hope that yours has been lifted too. Go with God, but don't forget to bring him back next week!"

The band picked up the closing anthem. A large number of people lined up to greet Corey and Elizabeth and buy merchandise for sale at a large kiosk, manned by youth volunteers. After greeting Corey and Elizabeth in the reception line, the governor and mayor and other luminaries filed upstairs to the church bistro, where a light breakfast buffet was being served. Drew drifted upstairs as well, following Ned.

"Get pictures if you can," Ned said in a whisper. "All the gold cross members and anyone who seems oriented to Elizabeth. Don't be too obvious but take notice, as I will."

Drew looked at the tough old sergeant quizzically.

"Know your enemy," Ned said with a smile and a wink.

AFTER the reception line, Corey headed to his dressing room to freshen up, change clothes and have his make-up and hair seen to. He didn't see Elizabeth come up behind him. She grabbed him by the elbow in the empty hallway and spun him to face her. Her face was livid and her tongue sharp.

"What the hell was that all about," she demanded. Corey stared at her in surprise, the assault was so strong. Not waiting for an answer, she continued, "All as one? "Regardless of race, gender, sexual orientation or political beliefs? And what was all that stuff about God being everywhere and stop praising him and thanking him? Where did you come up with that? It wasn't in the script!"

Corey felt trapped, cornered. He began visibly shaking. He tried to answer but only managed a trembling, "I, I, I…"

"Our audience is white, Christian and conservative! Dancing in the aisles like a bunch of…" She stopped herself short of saying what she was thinking, but Corey got the meaning.

"Did Curtis Green put you up to this?" She asked, coming to a conclusion that she had been mulling over in her head. "He came in with that soul music right on cue! It was him, wasn't it?"

Corey tried to answer, to defend the band leader, but his tongue was frozen, and his arms were trembling. "No, it was…it was…" he stammered. Elizabeth pounced.

"It was Sally Yarber, wasn't it, that little snake!" she said, her anger hot and laser focused. Don't think I don't know about your little bike rides to the Yarbers every day! That's who put you up to this, isn't it?"

"No," Corey said weakly. "It was…"

Elizabeth softened her tone. "Don't worry," she said soothingly. "I know it's not your fault. You let yourself be led astray." Corey looked like he might cry; exactly the response she wanted. "Go, get changed, we've got guests to greet."

"I… I'm sorry Elizabeth," he said. He turned and walked towards his dressing room.

As she watched him go, she wondered if this was it. Had the arc been completed? Bob Draggett had been caught up in a scandal and resigned, which meant that John McNair would appoint his replacement; the fence bill would pass, and the city would be redistricted. Was it time to get out? Maybe, but all was not lost, at least not yet; if her plan for the afternoon worked, she wouldn't have to worry about the vote. And Sally Yarber and Curtis Green were expendable. She'd fire them and work her wiles on Corey again. That should bring him around, she thought. If not, well, she had a foolproof escape plan in place and on her way out, she'd take the church down and Corey with it.

Jimbo Onthank held court in the bistro as everyone waited for Corey and Elizabeth to enter. Curtis Green played soft gospel music on a white Steinway piano. A few people had plates of food, but most held coffee cups and munched on croissants or beignets. Somehow Teejay had found some scotch for himself, the governor and Bunny. The three stood huddled, talking politics. John McNair stood off to the side with Jacki, reluctant to engage in the kind of backroom talk that was going on.

Drew stood near the back of the room. He had left his cameras and his camera bag by the door and appeared to be taking a series of silly selfies with Ned looking on, shaking his head disapprovingly.

"What would these kids do without their phones," Ned said casually to a well-dressed woman with a gold badge displayed on her dress. She looked at Drew and shook her head with a "tsk."

After a while, Elizabeth entered the room. She was wearing a white high-necked gown with shimmering sequins, a diamond encrusted gold cross around her neck and a tight smile. As she moved around the room exchanging perfunctory handshakes and busses on cheeks, she whispered her apologies for Corey's performance. "He sometimes goes a little off the rails," she said in contrite whispers. "He had ADHD as a child and still takes meds for it. Perhaps he forgot to take them this morning."

"Not a problem," most of them said, nodding their understanding. "Our son, well, he has difficulties also," many said.

But some of them spoke of how invigorated they felt during the end of the service.

"Yes, yes," Elizabeth said to each of them. "The form was certainly inspired. But, well, some of the substance was...unwise."

Again, nods of approval and understanding. Most of the people in the room knew that Elizabeth was the real driving force behind the success of the church. Most ministers, caught up in the Spirit, often went off script. It was not an unusual thing.

To each person she spoke with, Elizabeth handed a personalized prayer card with the church's logo emblazoned on the front along with contact phone numbers and e-mails, tailored to specific needs such as: "Prayers for illness," "Advice for marital problems," and "Instructions for donating." On the back was a list of scripture passages for each day of the week.

Finally, she reached the little triumvirate of Governor Thompson, Bunny Bunstall and Teejay Edmunds.

"I see that you've availed yourselves of the healing balm of Gilead," she said with a laugh. "You scoundrel," she said, looking pointedly at Teejay.

"Guilty as charged," Teejay said, raising his glass a little in a mock toast.

She turned slightly towards Governor Thompson. "I hope you enjoyed our little service this morning, Governor," she said.

"Very much so," Thompson said. "It was quite a show."

"Indeed," Elizabeth said. "Corey seemed to have been lifted by the Spirit."

Teejay laughed lightly. "I didn't know he was familiar with Baruch Spinoza."

Elizabeth looked at him quizzically but didn't respond. She turned her attention to the governor.

"I'm sorry your wife couldn't be here," she said. "I think we might have a lot in common." She handed Thompson a card. "Have her call me."

Thompson looked at the card briefly and put it in his pocket. "I will," he said. "I'm sure she would enjoy talking with you."

She turned her attention to Bunny next. "And the lovely Gloria, a no show again?"

Bunny took a thoughtful sip of his scotch. This happened every week. Both of them knew that the two women were fierce rivals in the charitable foundation arena and detested each other.

"She likes to ride on Sundays," Bunny said. "She believes that God's true house in is nature, in the hills, forests, mountains and streams."

"And what do you believe, Mr. Bunstall"?

"I believe I'll have another scotch," he said, looking at Teejay pointedly. Teejay suppressed a smirk and pulled a flask out of an interior pocket.

"We're being ignored, again," Jacki said to John. "That woman seems to take pleasure in making me feel uncomfortable. Don't you think people notice?"

"Notice what?" John said.

"Notice her giving us – you – the cold shoulder. I've tried so many times to reach out to her, but I never get anything more than a polite, forced smile."

"Nobody notices," John said patiently. He of course knew the reason, but such things are better left forgotten, he reasoned. Besides, if Tommy went to Washington, he would make a run at the state capital. Then they could leave this little Peyton Place far behind them. Corey's entrance forestalled any further conversation.

"Hey, ho!" Jimbo boomed. "The man of the hour!"

Curtis launched into Corey's theme song and everyone applauded. Corey entered the room, dressed all in white. Teejay noticed that he acted differently than he usually did at these things; he seemed to be nervous and Teejay knew why. Corey had gone off script. You could see in Elizabeth's tight, forced smile that she was displeased with him. It was different than his usual message and, although people had clapped and sang and danced enthusiastically, there was no doubt that something very unusual had occurred. Corey moved about the room with his usual vigor, shaking hands, kissing cheeks, and posing for selfies, but his nervous glances towards his wife and her cold demeanor towards him made Teejay think that there would be hell to pay later. He laughed inwardly at his pun and sipped his scotch.

After a while, Corey walked over to the mayor and his wife, another first. He had always studiously avoided them, only giving them perfunctory hellos from a distance. John was convinced that he avoided them on Elizabeth's orders. Corey looked only briefly at John, but then turned and gently put his hands on Jacki's shoulders. "You have a light about you," he said softly. "I can see it." He smiled and took his hands away and turned back to John. "You are a lucky man, to have such a beautiful creature as your wife."

Before John could respond, Teejay Edmunds approached the group. He had been noticing the encounter and knew John's poorly hidden disdain for Corey. It would only take one careless word by Corey to trigger John's famous temper, one of his few flaws.

"Wonderful sermon," Teejay enthused. He shook Corey's hand warmly. "I especially liked your having touched on some of my favorite thoughts about God's real manner."

"How do you mean?" Corey asked. He had always been a little afraid of intellectuals like Teejay; he never quite knew when they were being facetious with him. It was a failing, he knew. What few liberal arts classes he had taken he had only squeaked through. His interests were in acting, nothing more.

Teejay laughed. He enjoyed catching people like Corey off-guard. It amused him to see their uneasiness at a simple question or comment that might expose their lack of knowledge or understanding. But this time he was serious. He was curious about Corey's new approach. "I mean your obvious allusion to the thoughts of one of my own favorite philosophers, Baruch," he said, purposely omitting Spinoza's last name.

"Oh," Corey said. "I like that you're so familiar with Spinoza that you're on a first name basis with him. I myself have only recently become aware of his teachings; perhaps, at a later time, you could enlighten me further."

Teejay burst out laughing. He held his glass up in a mock toast. "Touché!" he said.

Corey laughed in a strange, distracted sort of way, regarding Teejay with half-lidded eyes. The effect was unsettling. He turned away quickly, explaining Spinoza to Jacki.

"Spinoza, you might remember, was an early rationalist who criticized organized religion's interpretation of the Bible," Teejay said. "Scripture should be read by individuals and interpreted by themselves, not church leaders. He believed in God but saw him as the sum substance of the universe. He is present in everything and everything is present in him. 'See him in a sunrise, see him in a rainstorm, see him the woods, rivers, lakes and beaches. See him in the bright shining eyes of a child,' I think I heard you say," he said as he turned back to Corey.

"Very good," Corey said. "It's nice to know that someone was listening."

"And, I assume, Elizabeth was okay with that?" Teejay said softly, rattling the ice in his glass.

"You tell me," Corey said.

Teejay looked over at Elizabeth, who was glaring angrily at the little group from across the room. She looked away immediately when she saw Teejay notice her, but the look was unmistakable. Oooh, Teejay thought. Corey will be lucky not to have his eyes gouged out, if not worse.

LATER, in the parking lot, Teejay walked over to where Drew was standing. Bunny and John were wishing the governor a safe trip back to the capital and he shook their hands as he climbed into the waiting limo.

"Glad you made it," Teejay said. "You sounded a little off put this morning on the phone. I'm glad you're still with us."

"A little heavy on the 'Nawlins accent, don't you think? 'Ahm glayud yo steel weuth us.'"

Drew laughed a little, drawing a strange look from Teejay. Oh, Peter! Drew thought sarcastically. There you are. And I thought you'd left me!

"I'm always available for a little advice. Tell him what you're thinking."

The brief pause gave Drew time to consider a response to Teejay's statement. He also noticed that it made Teejay a little uneasy.

"Well, it can be a little disconcerting to realize that you've been played for a fool," Drew said.

Teejay didn't say anything at first. He withdrew a silver cigarette case out of his pocket, opened it and withdrew a cigarette. He fitted it into his holder and lit it with a gold lighter. He French-inhaled the smoke, put his case and lighter away and regarded the cigarette for a moment. "These are Turkish," he said. "Will Willard gets them for me. Best cigarette tobacco in the world." He looked at Drew through half-lidded eyes.

"What's that got to do with you being set up?"

Drew suddenly laughed when he realized that Teejay had said all he was going to on the subject. Water over the dam, he thought. Time to move on.

"I noticed that a lot of the gold cross members were sticking pretty close to Elizabeth and acting a little nervous this morning," Drew said, ending the impasse. "She seemed upset about something."

"Yeah, I noticed that too," Teejay said. "Look, Bunny told me to have you start working on the governor's visit for the next Sunday Supplement. Feature the governor and John and his family as much as you can, you know, the usual casuals. No pictures of the church, Corey Deschamps or Elizabeth; just a little sidenote that he attended services with John and his wife. I'll get the by-line, but you'll get paid a consulting fee, and get credit – and pay - for your photos," he added.

"Got it," Drew said. 'All the news that's fit to print,' he thought.

Teejay turned to Bunny, who had walked over after saying goodbye to the governor. He nodded once to Drew but didn't say anything.

"Heading home?" Teejay asked mildly.

"Yep, I guess Gloria should be done with her ride by now."

CHAPTER THIRTY-SEVEN

Drew drove out to the Cove, hoping Stacy hadn't already left with Pinky or someone else. He was late again. Janice was sitting in her spot by the door, smoking a clove cigarette as he walked up. She began singing an old Billie Holiday song.

"I don't know why, but I'm feeling so sad,

I long to try something I've never had

Never had no kissin'

Oh, what I've been missin'

Lover man, oh, where can you be?"

"Very funny," Drew said. He made a kissy face at her was he walked by.

"Oh, what I've been missin'" Janice sang again.

Inside, Chaz was behind the bar and a ball game was blaring from the flat screen TV above him. He smiled, uncapped a Red Stripe and slid it across the bar to Drew.

"Long morning?" He asked mildly.

Drew took a sip. "You know it," he said and took another.

"How was the Deschamps show?" Janice said, taking up a stool next to him. "I've never seen it."

Joe Crimmons got up from his seat at the other side of the bar and came over to listen.

Drew chuckled and took another sip of beer. "It's hard to explain," he said. "It's like no church service I've ever been to anyway. The place is packed, the band is rockin' and the MC, big Jimbo Onthank, is warming up the crowd. Then Corey is announced. He comes out sliding, pointing, grinning and shaking his hips."

"What was the sermon like?" Joe asked. His parents had been devout Baptists and he had once fancied himself a minister; until he found that gambling was considered a sin, that is. "What did he talk about?"

"I don't know, exactly," Drew said. "He was firing off scripture, giving advice on life and…"

"Asking for donations and tithes," Joe said, interrupting.

"No, that was the strange part," Drew said. "Corey went on and on about God being everywhere, in the forest and the trees and the mountains and the streams. He never mentioned offerings or tithes, come to think of it."

"Wow," Chaz said. "That's usually the big closer, the offering."

Drew nodded. "Something else, his wife, Elizabeth, seemed pissed about something. Maybe that was it."

"Maybe he went off script," Joe said. "Sometimes ministers do that. They get carried away."

Janice chortled derisively. "What would you know about it? The last time you were in church was our wedding day!"

"Yeah," Joe said. "I saw what misery religion causes that day and never went back!"

Janice cracked up, along with everyone else. The two teased each other incessantly.

"Maybe he did," Drew said. "But the crowd loved it. He had them up dancing and singing at the end. The band was playing some bouncy gospel tune."

"Ooh, all those tighty-whiteys dancing and singing." Janice said. "I'd pay money to see that."

The group shared another laugh. Janice noticed that Drew was stealing glances around the bar, most likely looking for Stacy. She thought about teasing him; about saying that she went off with Pinky again, but she could sense the longing in the young man. It was sad, she thought. To see young people so much in love, for she could see it in Stacy too. She had felt that way once, long ago. It had seemed then that the world would never stop spinning, that she would never stop loving, and being loved. But life moved on and somehow, she got left behind, or he did. She wasn't certain. Since then, she had been through several relationships until she settled on Joe Crimmons, or he settled on her. She wasn't certain. The roar of Will's plane overhead interrupted her thinking.

"Looks like Will's back," Chaz said needlessly. Everyone knew the sound of Will's plane.

Most of the patrons moved to the large window to the left of the bar, where the cove could be seen. Will was taxiing in towards the dock. Daphne, who had climbed out of the cabin and onto a pontoon, threw a line around one of the dock's mooring posts and pulled the plane in. To Drew's immense relief, Stacy climbed out behind her and threw a second mooring rope. Will shut the engine down and gave a thumbs up towards the bar. He knew he was being watched. Will, Daphne and Stacy walked down the dock towards the bar.

"What'd you bring us today, Skipper?" Chaz asked, knowing what the answer would be. He set three beers on the bar.

"The usual contraband." He tossed Chaz a bottle of Jamaican rum and said, "set 'em up."

Chaz set shot glasses on the bar and poured. Everyone stepped up and grabbed a glass. "Salud!" Joe Crimmons said. They drank.

"The ocean's an amazing thing to see from the air, especially at low altitude," Stacy said to Drew casually as they stood at the bar. "You really should come along on one of our trips. That is, if you're not too busy attending church," she added with a sly smile.

"Love to," Drew said, choosing not to defend his attendance at church. After all, he was directed to attend as part of his job. He did wonder how Will managed to get Jamaican rum, Cuban cigars, Key West Shrimp, Bahamian conch, and whatever else he had in those carts, in one trip. He knew the floatplane had a limited range and, besides, airports in those places had FAA regulations. He accepted another beer from Chaz and put a bill on the bar. It was a large one, part of the spending money Bunny had given him to throw around at the Club. He made a circular gesture with his finger, indicating a round for the bar. "Keep the change," he said. This one's on Bunny, he thought.

CHAPTER THIRTY-EIGHT

H E REACHED FOR THE doorknob but hesitated, a surprise for him. He was a determined man, and he had no intention of being denied. Yet he hesitated.

"Open the door when I knock," she had said. "Not before."

He had waited. Obediently? Was that possible for him? Yet here he had stood for a good five minutes, waiting. Then the knock had come, soft and inviting. He turned the doorknob. It resisted at first. A signal? A warning? He had the feeling that if he opened the door, somehow his life would change. He twisted the knob further and gently pushed the door open. What he saw took his breath away.

Just fifteen minutes earlier he had been having a conversation with a woman dressed in a business suit. Her voice was as all-business, her demeanor the same. Earlier she had given him her private number. He called her, and she invited him to a meeting to discuss important matters. "Matters important to our shared initiatives," she said. "Something we can't discuss over the phone?" he said. He was a busy man with a tight schedule. She laughed. "Yes, something we can't do over the phone." Something about her voice made him change his schedule to accommodate her. He had come, expecting a business meeting. She offered him a drink. "Sure, I'll have a scotch, if you got it."

To his surprise – the first of many that afternoon – she opened a cabinet and produced a bottle of single-malt scotch and a cut-glass tumbler. She poured him three fingers and handed him the glass. She left the bottle on a small table and, excusing herself, walked to a door, opened it, and slipped into a darkened room. That's when she turned and told him to wait for her knock.

He sat down in an overstuffed leather chair and drank the scotch, its heady flavor suffusing his body with a pleasant warmth. He poured another. Then he heard the knock.

The woman he saw when he opened the door bore little resemblance to the woman that had left just a few minutes before. Gone were the glasses, tied-up hair, and business suit. The woman that faced him now had her hair loose and she wore nothing but black lingerie and an alluring smile. The room was dimly lit by a dozen flickering candles. Musky incense burned and soft music played in the background. A large four-poster bed stood behind her, covered with silk sheets and pillows. She beckoned to him with an almost imperceptible hand gesture. He entered the room and stepped up to her.

She grabbed his silk tie and pulled him down slightly, blowing gently on his neck as she did. She moaned in his ear ever so softly. Was it her perfume or the scotch that made his head swim?

"Men pride themselves on knowing what a woman wants," she said in a soft whisper. "But they don't know what *they* want. I'll help you find that out."

As she pulled him down onto the bed, he felt his temples throb with excitement. He vaguely wondered what had been in the drink she had given him. Moments later he realized that he really didn't care.

CHAPTER THIRTY-NINE

It was a quiet afternoon at the Cove and Joe Crimmons got Drew to put the pictures taken at the 'Glades again. Chaz put the slide show on auto, showing the pictures Drew had taken. Chaz kept the drinks coming and Drew threw the last of Bunny's spending money on the bar. Good riddance, he thought. He hated to be beholden to anyone – and he wasn't giving the money back.

A while later Daphne brought out a platter of fresh conch fritters and a bowl of new Caribbean sauce she had been toying with. As everyone was helping themselves the police and fire dispatch receiver behind the bar blinked. Chaz turned the speaker up. The slightly garbled message called for EMT to an address that Drew was very familiar with. He grabbed his cameras and started towards the door, then stopped and turned.

"Want to come along?" He asked Stacy. She jumped down from her bar-stool and headed towards the door.

As he drove, Drew explained, "You might have to wait at the car," he said. "You don't have a press pass, but I might be able to pass you off as my assistant. Hell, they might not even let me in. Depends on what the emergency is; could be nothing more than a fall in the shower or shortness of breath." He looked over at Stacy. "I have to be where the action is, though," he said. "My job."

"Is it your job to watch the road?" Stacy said in alarm.

Drew jerked the wheel just in time to keep the car on the road. "Sorry."

When they got to the location Drew was surprised at the number of police cars parked all over the grounds, their lights flashing. An EMT ambulance was parked next to the entrance and people were milling about randomly. He noticed that the Channel 10 News crew was camped out farther down the drive, their lights and cameras undeployed. Drew parked and he and Stacy walked up to the nearest cop, his old friend Jack Truax, who appeared to be part of a police cordon around the building.

"Hi Truax," Drew said, flashing his press credential. "My assistant," he said, referring to Stacy.

Truax put his hand out in front of Drew. "Sorry, Drew," he said. "Can't let anyone through, Chief's orders."

"What happened here?" Drew asked.

"I have no idea," Truax said. "They didn't tell us anything, except to form a cordon and not let anyone through without specific permission." He swept his arm around, indicating the tight perimeter that had been formed. "I think we've got every cop on duty here." He laughed a little. "Be a good time to commit a crime."

Drew noticed Teejay Edmunds up by the ambulance. "That's my boss," Drew said. "Can I go talk with him?"

"Nope," Jack said. "I'll have to shoot you if you try," he added with a laugh. But Drew got the sense that he meant business.

Drew waved to Teejay and got his attention. Teejay walked partway down and said: "He's okay to come this far," to Truax. Drew met him halfway.

"What's going on Teejay?"

"Can't say," Teejay said. "But you won't read about it in the news. Big stuff," he added.

"All the news that's fit," Drew said.

Teejay laughed. "See you at the plant tomorrow." He turned and walked away.

"See you, Truax," Drew said as he walked back. He and Stacy climbed into his car and drove back to The Cove.

Janice was waiting at the door when they returned. "Well, what's the scoop?" She asked.

"No scoop," Drew said. "They froze me out. Wouldn't let me past the police cordon."

"Wow," Janice said. "A big timer like you, frozen out! Hard to believe."

Drew laughed and they went inside.

There was a lot of speculation about the event, but Joe Crimmons put things in perspective.

"Look," he said, popping his gum, "If Bunny Bunstall wants a lid put on something, it stays put. Guess all you want, and one of your guesses might even be right. But we'll never know."

CHAPTER FORTY

Teejay Edmunds stood aside from the crowd of EMTs and cops, talking earnestly with police chief Mick Murphy, county coroner Simon Ross and Bunny Bunstall, who looked a little wan.

"This didn't happen," Bunny said, his voice slightly shaky. "This city will not become a national focus because of a scandal. I've worked – we've all worked – too hard for this to ruin it."

Mick and Teejay nodded their agreement but didn't say anything.

"I want this site cleaned up and I want her cleaned up," Bunny said, glancing at the other room. He seemed to be struggling with his emotions. Then, in typical fashion, he regained control. His voice became calm, even and businesslike. "NDAs for everyone in this area," he said. "Make sure they know that that their jobs depend on their discretion."

Mick nodded. "No problem, Bunny," he said. "Lieutenant Truax already has a clipboard full of them. No one will leave this site without signing one. He's also confiscating all cell-phones, which will be checked and scrubbed if necessary."

"Good," Bunny said. He turned to Simon Ross, the coroner. "Cause of death?"

"Natural causes," Simon said. "Aneurism, obviously. No need for an autopsy."

"You'll write it that way," Bunny said to Teejay. It wasn't a question.

"Short news release, second page," Teejay said. "Channel Ten will get a copy. They'll be told to read it as is, no going off-script."

"See that it's on my desk by noon," Bunny said. "We need to put this thing behind us as soon as possible. People die every day," he added.

The men nodded their agreement. Teejay looked around at the gaggle of cops, EMTs and other officials and wondered if it were possible to keep something like this quiet. The rumor mill had probably already kicked into gear, and word of mouth was all but impossible to trace, NDAs notwithstanding.

CHAPTER FORTY-ONE

J ANICE WATCHED AN OLD JEEP painted pink pull into the parking lot at the Cove. Pinky's Jeep was a familiar sight, he and Jason often rode to work together in it. She wondered if they had any details on the recent events in town. Drew and Stacy had none when they returned an hour earlier. Her question was answered when they pulled straight up to the restaurant instead of parking back at the cabin they shared. They still had on some of their EMT gear.

"Back from an extended honeymoon?" Janice announced loudly.

"You're not going to believe this," Jason said, nodding towards Pinky as they walked through the door. She followed them in, consumed by curiosity. Pinky usually had some graphic pictures on his phone.

"Gather 'round," Pinky said, looking furtively around the bar. There were a few patrons in the dining area, but no one unfamiliar at the bar. Chaz set two beers in front of Jason and Pinky and leaned over the bar to look. Everyone else craned their necks.

"Holy shit!" Chaz exclaimed as Pinky scrolled through the pics. "Is that...?

"Sure is!" Pinky said. "I couldn't believe it myself."

"Kinky," Janice said, looking over his shoulder.

"Bondage Gone Bad!" That's your headline!" Jason said to Drew. "I can see that picture on the front page!" he added. Jason considered himself a jokester of the first order and had been saving his headline for just the right moment. He laughed at his own joke, pleased with himself.

"Yeah, you won't see anything of the sort," Drew said. He was still a little bitter at having been frozen out by Teejay at the site, although he now knew the reason why.

"Too salacious?" Pinky said. He was working on improving his vocabulary and jumped at any chance to insert a new word into a sentence. "Did I use that right?" He asked softly, unsure if he had used the word correctly.

"Close enough," Stacy said. "Why won't we see it?" She pressed Drew.

Drew shook his head dismissively. "When I approached Teejay at the site and he wouldn't let me in, I knew that the story would be killed. Bunny doesn't want any scandal to besmirch the reputation of this fair city!" He said the last phrase in a dramatic manner, holding his index finger up for effect.

"You can't hide something like this, can you?" Stacy asked. "I mean, it'll be on the police blotter, recorded on the 911 call and registered at the hospital – or morgue."

"When we got there, the husband was the only one around," Pinky said as he went through the pictures again for anyone who hadn't had enough. "When Old Man Murphy came in, everything changed. The cops made us sign NDAs and took our phones. Told us we'd lose our jobs if we even whispered anything about it."

"How did you manage to keep your phone?" Stacy asked. She thought about what Pinky had just said: "Told us we'd lose our jobs if we even whispered anything about it." Here were Pinky and Jason openly bragging about the event and even showing off pictures taken at the site.

Pinky grinned. "I dropped it down my pants and said that I left it in the ambulance. Since I hadn't brought it in, I couldn't take any pics, right? Plus, the cop was Jack Truax, he wasn't going to hassle me."

Drew thought about cautioning Pinky and Jason; after all, Bunny and Murphy meant business. But he thought better of it; he would just sound like some tight-ass prude. The disclosure didn't seem to bother Joe Crimmons much, as a matter of fact he was scrolling through the pictures for a third time. Janice noticed too.

"Pervert!" She declared, snatching the phone from his hand, which brought a couple of "hoh, hohs" from the group. His face turned red.

"I wasn't looking at the woman," he said defensively. "I was looking at the husband. He doesn't seem to be that upset, just a little shaken."

"Lemme see," Janice said, thumbing through the pics with renewed interest. "You're right! He's just kind of standing off to the side as if he's not surprised."

"So, he knew his wife was kinky, and maybe got it on with other guys," Jason said. "That fits, because, when we got there he was just standing there, alone."

"No cops?" Drew asked. "That's unusual."

"Not really," Pinky said. "The dispatcher didn't call it an emergency. We usually get those when someone, usually older, dies of natural causes. Sometimes the coroner even gets called first. Sad, but routine. We didn't even have our lights or siren on," he added.

"He said he found her that way," Jason said. "Said that she texted him to come to her office."

"Sounds like a lie to me," Janice said. "Sounds like he killed her, maybe in an act of passion, but then got cleaned up and called 911. Besides, she was handcuffed. How could she text him?"

"Handcuffed and dead," Jason said. He snickered. Everyone gave him a dirty look. "Too soon?"

"Why would he do that?" Pinky asked. He was still confused by the strange chain of events and now things were getting more complicated. "Why would he make that stuff up?"

"He didn't want to face charges," Janice said. "Didn't want the scandal an investigation would bring."

"Won't there be an investigation anyway?" Jason asked. He hoped he wouldn't get called in to testify. He didn't like courtrooms and the confusing, leading questions that would be asked. He had been subpoenaed several times in the course of his career and what initially seemed simple and straightforward seemed to always get convoluted.

"There probably won't be, judging by the NDAs and phone confiscations," Drew said. "Sounds to me like they're going to bury the story."

"But a woman is dead, Drew," Pinky said. He was surprised at the cavalier way that everyone was treating the death, strange as it had been. "Someone choked her to death. Husband or lover, she was killed by someone. I can attest to that," he added.

"That's how David Carradine died," Janice said. Looking around at the group, she realized that no one, except Joe, knew who he was.

"He was a big star of a TV series," she explained. "He hanged himself in a closet, you know, to get off. They ruled it a suicide at first, but after careful examination, it was ruled an accidental death."

"People get off by being choked?" Stacy asked. "I never heard of such a thing."

"Oh yeah," Janice said. "It's a real thing. Kinky."

Everyone looked around at each other, but no one had anything else to say.

CHAPTER FORTY-TWO

THE NEXT DAY, SITTING at his desk, working on the governor's visit, Drew heard Teejay clacking away at his Royal typewriter. After what he'd seen on Pinky's phone, he wondered how Teejay would write the event up. It seemed to him that burying stories was a common practice at the Journal; just like Mick Murphy kept cases on his desk, to be used as he chose, Bunny chose the news that fit his own narrative. He had the police chief and even the coroner in his pocket, not to mention his own reporters. He remembered his meeting with Teejay and Bunny when he first got transferred. What had he said? Something about being a team player and not going rogue, chasing after some crusade. Now he understood. He applied himself to the governor's bio, wondering if he wasn't becoming part of the alternate reality that Bunny created and maintained.

Later, Drew was almost done with the bio when Teejay suddenly exclaimed "What?" into his phone. Heads turned at the uncharacteristic behavior of the usually self-controlled editor.

"Yessir, right away," he said. He hung up his phone and stood, a little shaky, Drew thought. He straightened himself and headed towards the door.

"Drew," he said as he walked past Drew's desk. "Come along and bring your cameras. I'll explain on the way."

Drew grabbed his cameras and his bag and hustled after Teejay.

"Happy Hour at the James get moved up?" Joe Crimmons asked loudly. The remark drew general laughter, but everyone wore curious expressions. Something big was up.

"The governor dropped dead this morning," Teejay explained as he pulled out of the parking lot. "Aides found him dead at his desk. Massive heart attack, they think. He was on the phone at the time, I heard." Teejay knew that the governor was expecting a call from Senator Sheridan and wondered if the call, naming him as the vice-presidential candidate in the upcoming election, had triggered the attack.

"We're headed to the mayor's office, where he'll deliver an address right after the news hits. Channel 10 will be there, of course, but Bunny wants some front-page photos from you. I'll get quotes, you get pics, got it?"

Drew nodded. It was common knowledge that John McNair would run for governor if Thompson resigned in order to campaign with Senator Sheridan. His words today would certainly put him in the national spotlight.

A cordon of police ringed the entrance to the mayor's office. Drew noticed Jack Truax as he and Teejay flashed their press credentials. "Twice in two days," Truax said. "What's up? They haven't told us anything – as usual."

"You'll know when I know," Drew said, a little lamely. He couldn't very well blurt out the news to a line of cops and a crowd of people hanging around, gawking.

Channel 10 was just getting set up and the mayor was behind several officials gathered around a podium, emblazoned with the shield of the mayor. Ned Butcher stood off to the side and motioned for Drew to join him. Teejay joined the gaggle of officials at the podium.

CHAPTER FORTY-THREE

A<small>T THE</small> C<small>OVE</small>, a group of regulars sat around the bar as Will, Daphne, Stacy, and a couple of part-time servers struggled to keep food and drink orders flowing. There was a fishing tournament in town and the bar was full of professional anglers, some of whom had rented cabins for the week. They wore the usual tight-fitting jackets, carrying the logos of the sponsors involved. They wore white or light blue baseball caps with more logos and almost all of them had expensive-looking sunglasses. They were drinking pitchers of beer and eating platters of shrimp, conch and scallops. The TV blared the fishing channel, which was covering the tournament. Every once in a while, a group would cheer as its boat was shown.

Janice circulated among the patrons, dispensing insults and making sure everyone was happy. Chaz filled pitcher after pitcher of light beer as two dishwashers tried to keep up with a large pile of dirty dishes, pitchers and glasses, stacked at the end of the bar. A collective moan went up as national news broke in on the broadcast.

"We interrupt this program to bring you breaking news from the state capitol," the familiar announcer said. "This morning, Governor Tommy Thompson was found dead of an apparent heart attack at his desk. We go over now to Channel 10 News in Brantwood for an address by Mayor John McNair, whom the governor had been visiting just this weekend past."

The room suddenly got very quiet, except for the rattling of dishes in the back room.

"Why wouldn't the lieutenant governor give the address?" Someone asked.

"Two reasons," Joe Crimmons said. He was there for lunch, as usual. "One, he's from the opposition party and hates – hated – the governor. And two, he's in Washington, campaigning for the incumbent president."

Gerald Wrigley, the news anchor for Channel 10, stood at the podium as the crowd in front of the Mayor's office quieted.

"Ladies and Gentlemen," he said. "We've just received the shocking and tragic news of Governor Thompson's untimely passing. Here for a statement is Mayor John McNair."

"Thank you, Gerald," the mayor said as he stepped up to the microphone. "I've known Tommy Thompson for many years and consider him a mentor. I've never known a man more dedicated to the people he served and to the causes that he embraced. Over the weekend, during his visit to Brantwood, we discussed his many plans to make the state safer, more productive and more beautiful. That his mission was cut short is a tragedy, but his legacy is intact and will live on!"

The crowd clapped respectfully, and national news cut back in. "That was Mayor John McNair of Brantwood. Much more on this important news later but, for now, we return you to your regular programming."

The fishing channel came back on and the room buzzed with conversation.

"They found Nelson Rockefeller the same way," Joe Crimmons said with a knowing wink. But no one in the room seemed to know who Nelson Rockefeller was or how he had been found, except for Janice who let forth a dirty laugh.

"Nelson Rockefeller was the governor of New York and vice president under Jerry Ford, back in the seventies," Janice explained. "He was found dead in his office at Rockefeller Center. Heart attack." Janice smiled a coy little smile and kept everyone hanging for a moment. "Later it was rumored that he had died in a townhouse on 54th Street in the company of a 25-year-old woman. Evidently someone moved his body to avoid a scandal, but word leaked out anyway. The late-night shows had a ball with it for a while."

"So, the governor was with a woman?" Pinky asked innocently. "Wow, what a way to go!"

There was a smattering of laughter. Pinky wondered if they were laughing with him or at him.

Janice rubbed his head comfortingly. "Tommy Thompson was a known womanizer," she said. "Might have happened, might not have. We'll never know. But I will agree, there are worse ways to die."

CHAPTER FORTY-FOUR

Teejay and others congratulated John McNair on his statement. A reporter from Channel 10, Cassie Griffith, was trying to break through for some additional comments.

"Not right now, Cassie," John said. "Can you come back a little later for a full interview? I'm still a little bit shaken by the news. I just said goodbye to the man yesterday afternoon." He walked away from the crowd and into the building. Ned followed.

"Rumors are starting already," Ned said as they made their way to a couple of chairs by a window.

"I know," John said. "He was a great guy, but he couldn't keep it in his pants."

"Sounds a little like JFK," Ned said.

"Yeah, but he at least had the good sense not to die in the act," John said. "Any idea who the girl is?"

"Not yet," Ned said. "His two bodyguards are keeping everything quiet. "They've given NDAs to everyone close to the case and have backed them up with threats. You know those types."

"Hmm," John grunted. He accepted a cigarette from Ned and Ned lit it for him with a worn Zippo lighter. "I'm trying to quit, you know," he said. He drew deeply on the cigarette and looked at it appraisingly. "I do miss these," he added. Ned shook a second cigarette from the pack and lit it for himself.

Both men sat silently for a while, smoking.

"I'm surprised Thompson hired those guys," Ned said casually. "They seem pretty hard-core for a guy like Thompson."

"Oh, he didn't hire them," John said. "They were hired by the CFO of the Thompson Fund, a guy named Fitzgibbons. He runs the Thompson Fund for Susan Thompson with an iron hand. Susan worries that Thompson's infidelities will cast a shadow on the fund and so these two guys babysit him wherever he goes and cleans up any messes along the way. Payouts, NDAs and threats, that's their M.O."

"Thompson was okay with that?" Ned said. "He doesn't seem the type. And neither does Susan."

"What they don't know doesn't hurt them. Fitzgibbons and the body-guards keep everything on the QT," John said. "Tommy didn't like them, but he tolerated them in order to keep Susan off his back." He took another long drag on his cigarette and looked at it again. "I guess we all have our weaknesses."

Ned laughed. "They're only weaknesses if they make you weak," he said.

"Profound," John said. "Is that Marcus Aurelius? Nietzsche?"

"No, Ned Butcher," Ned said. "Thompson let his affairs weaken him. He was blinded by them."

"This Fitzsimmons guy troubles me," John said. "He's power-hungry, but that's not unusual in his business. What bothers me is that everything about the Thompson Fund seems a little too clean. You know the old adage: "nothing resembles an honest man more than a cheat.""

"Not much to go on there," Ned said. "But I will admit that your hunches are often right."

OUTSIDE, Jacki stepped up to Cassie with an appointment book. Her hand trembled a little as she wrote in an agreeable time for an interview. What was going to happen now, she wondered? Without the governor to endorse John for the vacant seat in the capitol, the lieutenant governor, Louis Lloyd, would fill the governor's chair until the election. She wondered if the Party would put forth much effort on John's behalf if it looked like he couldn't win.

"I know what you're thinking," Teejay said, walking up to her as she walked away from the throng of reporters. He had known her for a long time and knew her aspirations for her husband.

Jacki looked at him quizzically. Teejay had a knowing smirk on his face that made her laugh. "Tell me, Mr. Edmunds, how you know what I'm thinking." Even though he was a notorious rake and a scoundrel, there was something about Teejay that put her at ease. Of course, he had put her at ease a few years ago, before she met John, and before Teejay met his second wife.

"You have that "all hope is lost" look about you," Teejay said. "I'm not sure you understand what happened here today, so I'll explain it to you." He said the last part in a fake condescending tone that was calculated to bring a response from Jacki. It did. She slapped him on the arm, laughed and said: "You're such a cad! Go ahead, mansplain it to me."

"Louis Lloyd is in Washington now, working on the current president's re-election campaign. He's hoping for a top cabinet position if the president wins a second term and so is campaigning vigorously for him. He's left our state behind. Thompson cared for the state, and so does John. That's how the voters in the state will see it."

"How can you be so sure?" Jacki asked.

"Because that's how I'll write it," Teejay said.

CHAPTER FORTY-FIVE

Sᴀʟʟʏ Yᴀʀʙᴇʀ ᴡᴀᴛᴄʜᴇᴅ ᴀs Corey Deschamps paced around the room, his fists clenched, and his eyes fixed on the ceiling, mumbling desperately. He had been at it for a long time.

"It's all my fault," he said over and over. "I've ruined everything with my selfishness. Elizabeth told me that she knew about our meetings, that she blamed you and Curtiss for the alternate sermon. I tried to tell her that it was my idea, but she wouldn't listen! Now my ministry is ruined, and yours will be too!"

Sally tried to calm him, tried to tell him that, if anyone was to blame, it was Elizabeth. "She had such a controlling nature," she said, a little breathlessly. "She was cloying and controlling and determined to get her way, regardless of how it affected you. You felt trapped; how could you be blamed for what happened?"

Corey had appeared at their door the night before. He had found his wife dead, bound to a bed, dressed in lingerie, and covered with blood. Moments after he had discovered her, the EMTs had shown up, then the cops. He had been questioned, of course, but not charged. Mick Murphy had called the death an accident. He had implied that Corey, caught up in a sexual frenzy, had accidentally choked his wife to death. To avoid a scandal, he had ordered everyone in the room to sign an NDA and turn over their phones. The coroner had signed the death certificate as a death by natural causes. Most likely an aneurism, he said at the time. Corey was free to go. "We'll take care of this," Murphy said, nodding to the coroner. "No need to besmirch the reputation of the church."

He had gone to his house and wandered around it aimlessly, going over the shocking event in his mind over and over. Finally, he had staggered out into the night and wound up at the Yarbers. They had been asleep, but let him come in. They prayed with him and for him and for Elizabeth. Virgil had finally gone back to bed, but Sally stayed up with the distraught man, comforting him as best she could.

As morning came, Virgil woke, dressed, and fixed them breakfast. Corey couldn't eat, and neither could Sally, so caught up in his grief as she was. She had worked for Elizabeth for a long time and knew her well. Her death affected Sally almost as much as it affected him.

"I didn't do it," Corey said over and over. "I got a message to come down to her office. When I got there, the door was open. I walked in and saw that the door to her back room, the room she used for napping and late nights when she was too tired to come home, was also open. I walked in to see her laying there, dead. She, she…was handcuffed to the bed! Then, the EMTs came, smirking to each other. Before they could get her free, the cops came in. One of them started asking me questions and taking notes. But then the police chief arrived and stopped the questions. They all looked at me as if I were a depraved monster to have done such a thing. Now my wife is dead, my ministry is ruined and so is my life. I'm even to cowardly to kill myself'" he added sadly.

Sally decided then and there that it was time to act. She couldn't sit there any longer, watching Corey wallow in self-despair. Things had happened that were no fault of his. A woman was dead, it was true, but the woman had brought her death on herself. That Corey was blaming himself for her death only revealed his inherent weakness, a weakness that Elizabeth had exploited for her own gain. She looked over at Virgil, but he could be of no help either. He was weak too. It was clear that he found Corey somehow culpable in the woman's death or at least guilty in causing the woman to seek solace in another man's arms, however depraved the liaison had been.

"That's enough!" Sally exclaimed. She suddenly found herself standing over the blubbering mess that was Corey Deschamps. "Pull yourself together," she said firmly.

Corey was shocked at the sudden ferocious demeanor of the normally mousy little woman. She had been friendly to him when he needed a friend and was a welcome shoulder to cry on. But the woman standing before him now bore little resemblance to that person. Her eyes were bright and focused, her voice was clear and crisp, and her manner was decisive and insistent.

"Thousands of people have come to depend on you for strength and guidance," she said. "You cultivated their faithfulness. You brought them to your ministry. They are your followers, and you owe it to them to get back on your feet and carry on."

"But I'm a sham," Corey said. "You know that. They call me that behind my back, you know. Elizabeth told me. "Corey De Sham," they say. The big phony with the capped teeth and the styled hair, prancing around the stage every Sunday and spouting whatever platitudes that will make them happy. Do you have any idea how hollow I feel when they cheer and applaud? It's all just theatre! Nothing more!"

"How did you feel when you went off script?" Sally asked. "How did you feel when you quoted Spinoza and heard the people cheer? How did you feel when you had them dancing in the aisles? They weren't praising or worshiping God, they were celebrating! Celebrating the life that God had bestowed upon them!"

"Yeah, right," Corey said, allowing himself a short laugh. Sally's harsh words had forced him out of his self-depreciating funk. Although he was still devastated by Elizabeth's untimely and grotesque end, he began to feel the early glimmerings of a freedom he hadn't felt since he was chubby Derf Walowitz doing Henry V on a small stage in college. Sally's words resonated in his mind. It was true that he enjoyed being on stage every Sunday, people hanging on his every word. But last Sunday had been different. Instead of the exactingly rehearsed sermon that Elizabeth had put him through, he had spoken freely and with a conviction that he had never felt before. And the words he had spoken had come spontaneously, from the pleasant conversations he had had with Virgil and Sally during his clandestine meetings with them. He felt invigorated, much as the early Christians must have felt during their own secret meetings in the days of ancient Rome. They gambled with their lives to attend those meetings, but went to them gladly, convinced that they had found salvation. His sermon on Sunday had been his salvation and he had risked Elizabeth's retribution in the process. Elizabeth had constructed his ministry and she had constructed him. He felt at times like a marionette, dancing as Elizabeth pulled his strings. Now that he was free, he was that same marionette, laying broken on the floor, his limbs and strings scattered and useless and piled around him.

Sally seemed to read his mind. "You need to gather yourself," she said firmly. "Be the man – the spirit - that Elizabeth crushed. Virgil and I can help you with your sermons, as we did last week. I can run the business part of the church; I've been doing most of the work anyway. You didn't kill Elizabeth and you didn't cause her death. You must move on!"

Virgil watched and listened to the exchange. He felt bad for the confused and conflicted young man sitting before him, but he didn't feel his wife's sympathy. He was surprised that his wife was so certain that Corey bore no responsibility for Elizabeth's death; he wasn't so sure that the man hadn't killed her in a depraved act of sex. Or worse, murdered her outright. His hatred for her was well established. That he had been let go to avoid a scandal didn't absolve him. His fits of guilt and self-loathing seemed to be God's punishment – or Karma.

It was fine that Sally was helping the man through his grief, and he admired her for it. But telling him that they could help him with his sermons and that she could run the business of the church seemed a little much, in his opinion. Let the monster that was The Brantwood Fellowship die a natural death, he thought. Maybe he was being selfish, but he longed to get his congregation back. Keeping the megachurch going, even for a little while, seemed to be a fool's errand. And counter to God's will.

Corey stood up and composed himself. He apologized for his behavior and wondered if he could use their bathroom to clean up. He didn't want to go back to his house or the church just yet. After he left the room, Virgil looked questioningly at his wife.

"Why did you offer to help keep his church going?" He asked, dumbfounded. "Though we didn't wish for it, this situation is exactly what we need to get our own ministry back on its feet. Why help him?"

"Virgil," Sally said, a note of impatience in her voice. "Don't you realize what just happened. Can't you look beyond your own situation for once?"

A puzzled look came over Virgil. What was she talking about, he wondered?

"The Brantwood Fellowship just fell into our laps," Sally said. "Along with its star, Corey Deschamps. All that we must do is what we did last week. The three of us will develop the sermons; you give them your way, at your church and Corey will give them his way at the Fellowship. I'll do the books for both churches and you'll get paid a decent consulting fee, which will keep your ministry going."

Virgil looked as if a light bulb had gone off in his head. "You can manage both ministries?" He asked a little dubiously. "Seems like it would be a lot of work."

"It's not any more than I have been doing," Sally said. "And I won't have Elizabeth breathing down my neck every minute, rest her soul. I can manage everything that Elizabeth did, and more."

CHAPTER FORTY-SIX

J ASON AND PINKY WERE holding court the Cove again. Pinky had been contacted by a friend, Jamie Johns, who was an EMT in the capital. He had been one of the first responders to the governor's death. He sent Pinky some pics he had secretly taken at the scene.

"Jamie told me that the governor had been dead for hours before they were called," Pinky said. "He was stiff as a brick and his clothes had been forced on him. The shirt wasn't even buttoned up right."

"Why would they wait so long?" Stacy asked.

"Because he wasn't in his office when he died," Jason said. "He was in bed with some babe. She probably called his bodyguards, and they came and got him."

Joe started to speak, but Drew stopped him with an upraised palm. "Hold on, guys," he said. "Do we know what time the governor died?"

Pinky smiled. "I've got it right here," he said, holding up his phone. "When Jamie and the other EMTs were getting the body ready to transport to the morgue, the coroner filled out his report. One of the bodyguards looked at it and called him stupid. The coroner said "sorry" and crumpled up the document. He pulled out another one and wrote in the time the bodyguard told him. He didn't think to keep the first document right away and, in the confusion, Jamie scooped it up and took a pic, then threw it back down. Here it is."

The picture showed a crumpled and wrinkled document with the governor's name and time of death. It was 2:30, the day before. "Hey, Pinky said. "That's the almost the same time that Elizabeth Deschamps died. Her certificate said 2:45."

"Well, that explains a lot," Janice said loudly. A couple of pro fishermen who were standing at the bar and drinking beer and watching the fishing channel looked over.

"Shh," Pinky said, looking around furtively. The fishermen didn't seem interested and went back to their program.

"That explains Elizabeth's broken windpipe," Stacy said in a whisper. "The governor was a strong man. He crushed it while in the throes of a massive heart attack."

"Yeah," Jason agreed. "His bodyguards came in and took him to the capital. They waited to call it in until the next day so that there would be no apparent connection."

Everyone nodded. Mystery solved. Of course, there would be no investigation on either side, a scandal must be avoided at all costs. Death by natural causes in both cases. Life would go on and another story would be buried, Drew thought. He looked at Stacy and shook his head. "All the news that's fit," he said.

"So, it wasn't Corey, it was the governor who killed Elizabeth Deschamps," Janice said. "Corey discovered her later."

"Right," Jason said. "He was upset, but not hysterical as you would expect someone to be after accidentally killing someone. It all fits now," he added.

"How did she text Corey?" Chaz asked, polishing a glass.

"The bodyguards did it," Jason said. "To set Corey up. They called the EMT dispatcher too, timed to get us there before anyone else. They made a series of phone calls as they drove away, all timed to throw suspicion on Corey and away from the governor and themselves."

"But did she die with the governor, or did someone finish the job later?" Janice said. She had a flair for the dramatic and loved to travel in conspiracy theories.

"Scroll back to the bed," Drew said. "I thought I saw something that struck me as strange."

Pinky did.

"Look at the bedposts," Drew said. "The handcuffs have rubbed the finish off them. And look at her wrists; they're bloody and raw."

"Man," Jason said. "She was still alive after the governor died. Somebody came in later and killed her."

"What'd I say," Janice said, pleased that her conjecture had turned out to be true. "But who, besides the bodyguards, had an interest in seeing her dead?"

"Plenty of people," Pinky blurted. "Because of the recordings."

"What recordings?" Stacy asked.

"Oh, yeah," Pinky said. "I forgot to mention that. Bob Burkhaus, the guy who runs "Bytes and Pieces," you know the electronics store, told me that he had installed hidden cameras all over the church facility. Every room, hallway and doorway, all hooked up to her computer. He had to sign an NDA before he did the installation. Cost a fortune."

"If he signed an NDA, why did he tell you?" Chaz asked.

"He wasn't "disclosing" anything," Pinky said defensively and making air-quotes. "He just let it slip out one day when we were talking about how expensive everything is at that big church. We were hanging out with Jay Rosen, the sound and light guy at the church. He's made a fortune off them, by the way."

Janice laughed lustily, drawing on her clove cigarette. "If she had other lovers in that little sex den of hers, she would have some pretty juicy stuff," she said. "If she managed to entice the governor, I can only imagine what other big shots she got in there."

"Blackmail?" Chaz said. "Why? What would she have to gain?"

"Money," Joe said. "It takes a lot to run a big church like that. She may have been in debt up to her ears." He snapped his gum, satisfied with his assessment.

Drew considered the possibility that she had blackmailed council members to vote for her civic programs, and against the fence bill. She had been stopped, but the question was, had it happened by a chance accident or had it been done on purpose? He doubted that the bodyguards would have killed Elizabeth; they would have called Fitzgibbons for instructions. She was much more valuable to him alive, plus, they had once been lovers. No, someone else had come into the room and finished the job on Elizabeth. The question was, who? He noticed that Stacy had a strange look on her face. Was she thinking the same thing? He had a thought. "Had the computer been messed with?" he asked Pinky. "You know, when you came in or left, through her office, had her computer been tampered with?"

Pinky looked at him questioningly, thinking. "I don't know," he said. We were passing through. But I did have my phone on video, as usual, hidden behind the handle of the gurney."

He scrolled through his pictures and videos. "Here it is," he said. "Pretty shaky, but here's her desktop."

Drew looked over his shoulder. "Can you pause it and go back a little?"

"Sure," Pinky said.

"There it is," Drew said. "The tower's in the right spot, but one of the screws on the cover is missing, and one is not all the way in. Somebody was in a hurry," he added.

"Hey," Pinky said looking closely at the video. "Look at this." He scrolled to a pile of cards strewn carelessly on the desk, as if a neat pile had been knocked over.

"Those are her prayer cards," Drew said. "She hands them out to everyone in the reception line. Off to the side was a single card. Pinky enlarged it. "Governor Thompson," it read.

"If she gave the governor a card after Sunday's service, why would it be in her office?" Stacy said.

"That would prove that he was there Sunday afternoon," Janice said loudly, almost crowing at her revelation. Everyone shook their heads and rolled their eyes.

Pinky was laughing at something. He was hitting keys on his phone's dial pad.

"What are you doing?" Jason asked.

"There's a phone number in the lower right corner of the card. I just dialed it!" He laughed at his own joke.

Suddenly the phone of one of the fishermen standing at the bar went off. "Jesus!" Pinky exclaimed. The man looked at him funny and took his phone out.

"Yeah, Bill," he said. We're just getting ready to leave. Call you later." He put the phone back in his pocket and looked over at Pinky again, a WTF look on his face. Then he turned back to his conversation with his partner.

"Wow, that scared me!" Pinky said. "Did you hear that guy's phone go off, just when I dialed Mrs. Deschamps number?"

"You're an idiot," Jason said. "Now, whoever has her phone has your number, and knows that you called."

Pinky looked hurt; after all, he was just fooling around. A dead woman's phone was a dead woman's phone. Who would bother answering it, let alone be checking it for calls? Jason was as big a jokester as he was, or even more so. He had no doubt that if the situation was reversed, Jason would have done the same thing.

"How would they know who I am?" Pinky said defensively. "Unknown caller" is what they'd see."

"And your number!" Jason said. Just then, Pinky's phone rang. He just about fell off his stool, it gave him such a shock. He looked at the number. It was Stacy's.

"You dog!" Pinky said. He looked at his phone again, with sly interest. "Now I have your number," he said, a lewd expression on his face. "Expect a late-night call!"

The group erupted in laughter.

"You already have it," Stacy said condescendingly, like a tired mother explaining something to her child. "How else could I have called you?"

The conversation devolved into idle banter. Drew said something to Chaz, and he put out some shot glasses, limes and salt. He poured tequila into the glasses, and everyone drank to the memories of Elizabeth Deschamps and Governor Tommy Thompson

CHAPTER FORTY-SEVEN

T EEJAY WAS SITTING IN Bunny's office, a glass of scotch in his hand and a worried look on his face. "I'm afraid this thing is spinning out of control," he said. "Rumors are flying. It won't be long before the tabloids get ahold of this and it won't be long before someone gets offered enough money to break his NDA."

"Relax," Bunny said. He took a long pull on his cigar and waved the smoke away as if it was the rumors that were swirling. "I'll talk with Corey once he's calmed down. We'll get a statement from him that will dispel the rumors, at least to his followers. He'll have to weather the storm, not us. Who knows, he may be able to use the media attention to his advantage. You know the old saying: "In celebrity, there's no such thing as bad press." Plus, the news of the governor's death and his upcoming funeral will eclipse those rumors anyway."

Teejay nodded, but Bunny could tell that he was not convinced. "Get Drew on that Sunday Supplement piece on the governor's visit, it needs to be done before you leave.

"Leave?" Teejay said.

"Leave for the capital. I want you there for the governor's funeral as my representative. The governor's death puts us behind the eight ball in the upcoming gubernatorial. The lieutenant governor will be sworn in as governor and he'll have the upper hand in the election. We need some good press on McNair."

"Yessir," Teejay said, finishing his drink. "When do I leave?"

"The funeral will be Thursday," Bunny said. "I want you there a day ahead of time, so, Wednesday. And see if you can't come up with a few 'gotcha' comments from Louis Lloyd. He's an idiot."

Later, at the James with Drew, Teejay was glad to see that Bunny had been right: there was very little talk about Elizabeth Deschamp's death other than conjecture over whether the church could continue without her. Most of the conversation revolved around the governor's death and John McNair's chances in the upcoming gubernatorial election.

As he surveyed the noisy bar, Drew noticed the actions of some of the men that he had identified as gold cross members of the Brantwood Fellowship. They appeared nervous and unsure of themselves, as if some unknown force was at play. Of course, he had developed a pretty good idea as to how they had gotten their memberships, and what Elizabeth Deschamps had over them. He wondered again who had the hard drive from her computer.

After the James, Drew headed out to the Cove. He had plans to go out to Snake Island again with Stacy. He even found himself looking forward to seeing Nefertiti again. At least snakes had no secrets or hidden agendas, he thought.

When he pulled into the parking lot, he could see that something was amiss. Janice was not at her usual post and Jason was frantically loading his car with everything he could fit in it. He hadn't packed, he was just throwing items into the car helter-skelter. Drew parked and walked over.

"What's up, man," he said as he reached Jason's car. Jason looked up, a pile of dirty clothes in his arms.

"Don't you know man?" He said, a note of panic in his voice.

"No," Drew said. "I don't."

Jason stopped for a minute. "You know that guy, Jamie Johns, the one that sent Pinky the pics from the governor's office? They found him dead in the surf. Caught by a riptide, they said."

"Oh, man, that's terrible," Drew said. Johns' death didn't explain Jason's behavior, though. "Those riptides are killers," he added.

"Yeah, well, he was a really good swimmer, and the tide wasn't that bad," Jason said. Drew was still waiting for some connection with his friend.

"Well, Pinky went missing this morning," Jason explained. "Jack Truax found his jeep parked out at the Point."

"Pinky went out a lot," Drew said. "He could still be out there, fishing." But a dread feeling was starting to come over him. Clearly, Jason was spooked by Johns' death and his friend being missing.

"Pinky never went to the Point," Jason explained. "He always just left from here. That's how I know something is wrong!"

Jason threw a few more things into his car and got behind the wheel. "I'm getting out of here, man!" He exclaimed. "Game over!" He stepped on the gas and sped out of the parking lot.

When Drew walked into the Cove, the place was as silent as a morgue. The TV was off, the fishermen were all out to sea and the tourists hadn't come in yet, it being just past the lunch rush. Janice sat at the bar, silently crying, Chaz stood behind the bar, a wet rag dripping on his pants. Stacy was sitting at the bar, her face as white as a ghost. When she saw Drew, she ran to him and buried her face in his chest. She sobbed uncontrollably.

"Will and Daphne have been out searching," Chaz explained. "Along with the Sheriff's Department and half the town. They found his board a little while ago, shattered. Hit by a boat, most likely," he added.

"Pinky?" Drew asked.

Chaz shook his head. "No sign of him," he said sadly. "They're still looking."

Just then the Will's plane roared over the bar and splashed down in the cove. He taxied it up to the dock. Will got out of the plane and walked up the dock, a grim look on his face. Daphne followed. It was clear that she had been crying.

"The board was over a mile out in the gulf," Will said as he walked into the bar. Chaz pulled a beer out of the cooler, but Will stopped him with a wave of his hand. "Coffee, if you've got some," he said. He looked exhausted. "I'm going back out as soon as the plane is refueled," he said. Drew thought by the look on his face that he didn't hold much hope for finding Pinky alive.

"Pinky never went that far out," Stacy said. She had managed to regain her composure and had an angry look on her face. "Why would anyone ever want to hurt Pinky?" She said: "He wouldn't hurt a fly."

Daphne came over and put her arm around her daughter's shoulders. "It was those damn pictures Pinky was showing around," she said. "Somebody wants this thing to stay buried, this thing about the governor and Elizabeth Deschamps. There was a reason for the NDAs and the phone collection. He never should have taken those pics, and he never should have shown them around," she added bitterly.

"Who in this room would have told anybody?" Janice said, wiping her eyes on her sleeve. She looked around the room and shook her head. She knew the answer was 'no one.'

"One of the fishermen," Chaz said. "The place has been crawling with them for two days. One of them could have overheard us."

"None of them would have had any idea what we were talking about, and none of them would have cared if they had," Janice said. "It must have been someone who got Pinky's friend's phone; the EMT in the capital that drowned. What was his name?"

"Jamie Johns, I think," Stacy said. "But how would anybody know that Pinky was here. The only thing they had was his number."

Everyone looked at each other with expressions of puzzlement and fear.

"Everyone be especially watchful," Will said as he downed a cup of tepid coffee. "I'm going back out for another run. It seems that we're up against some tough customers."

Everyone nodded their agreement. They watched as Will walked out to the plane. Fishing boats were starting to return to the docks. It would be another busy night, and no one felt like working.

WILL gunned the engine and popped over the line of mangroves that enclosed the cove. He flew straight out to where he had found Pinky's board, marked on his GPS. He didn't hold out much hope for finding the lad alive at this point, but he had to try. Pinky never wore a PFD, he knew, and it was a long swim to even the closest islands that dotted that part of the coast. Plus, it looked as if Pinky had been hit by a boat, most likely one of the many fishing boats racing out into the gulf for the fishing contest. It puzzled him that the boater hadn't realized that he'd hit something and turned back to check. But, then again, boats hit manatees all the time and sometimes even dolphins, rays or sharks, cruising near the surface. The contact might have even felt like a rogue wave in the morning fog.

But all the talk at the bar led Will to think that something more sinister had occurred. An FBI agent was dead and now an EMT in Tallahassee. Pinky and Jason were playing with fire by recording scenes from their calls; they had been taking unnecessary chances with their jobs by sharing those recordings. Regardless of what caused this strange chain of events and who was culpable, Will began to be concerned for the safety of his friends – and his daughter.

Much later, running low on gas, Will prepared to return to The Cove. He wondered if he should re-fuel one more time to continue what was increasingly becoming a fruitless task. Then, suddenly, he saw it. The pink shorts and tank top were unmistakable. He banked the plane and landed it as close as he dared.

CHAPTER FORTY-EIGHT

Stacy burst into her cabin, an angry – and frightened – look on her face. Drew, as usual, was fiddling with his cameras. He looked up and noticed that she was soaking wet.

"Take a look at these," she said. Drew couldn't tell if she was shaking from the cold, fear or anger. She handed him her phone, encased in a clear dry bag. Drew looked at the pictures. They were a little dark and grainy but appeared to be the keel of a boat, taken from underneath. There were the usual scrapes, scratches and dings boats got in the shallow waters of the bay. Then he saw it: the keel had a long pink scrape on it. He looked up at Stacy.

"Where did you get this? He asked. "Which boat?"

"It belongs to the two fishermen in Cabin 5," She said, her teeth clenched.

"Take a look at this," Drew said, showing Stacy a picture on his camera. It was of the two bodyguards assigned to Governor Thompson. He had snapped it while sitting at a table with Ned Butcher at the reception at the Bunstall residence. Then he showed her a picture, taken on his phone, of different patrons at The Cove. He centered on two of them and zoomed in. Stacy's eyes widened.

"I thought that the two fishermen looked somehow familiar," Drew said. "They dressed and acted like every other fisherman in the place, so I didn't notice at first. But when Pinky made that phone call and the fisherman's phone went off, I became suspicious and looked through my pictures.

"What would Governor Thompson's bodyguards want with Pinky?" Stacy asked.

"I have no idea," Drew said. "But it's got something to do with the governor's death while in bed with Elizabeth Deschamps."

Stacy's jaw was set in anger. Pinky was a friend of hers and he had evidently been killed by these two men. She aimed to find out why and see to it that they paid for their crime. "I can get a key," she said. "We can slip in while they're having dinner. If we find any evidence that could connect them with Pinky's death, we'll notify the police, and they can get a warrant and have them arrested."

"I think we should wait," Drew said. "I called Ned Butcher and he's on his way here. He'll be able to ID the bodyguards and know what to do next." He felt a little bit like he had the day they'd gone to Snake Island. Snakes can bite you, he thought wryly, but they can't shoot you.

"It won't hurt to look," Stacy said, an angry and determined look on her face that told Drew that she was going, whether he was with her or not. She went off to watch for the bodyguards.

A while later, Stacy returned to the bar, a set of keys and a flashlight in hand. "They just ordered dinner," she said. "We've got some time."

As they slipped through the door of the cabin, Stacy gave Drew a pair of throw-away rubber gloves. "Don't touch anything and keep watch at the window," she said. "I'm going to look around."

Drew stood by the window, watching the restaurant door and feeling ineffectual. He kept running all of the events of the past few days through his head, searching for a motive that would be strong enough to provoke a killing. Sure, Pinky had broken his NDA, but he had no proof of any wrongdoing except the death of Elizabeth Deschamps, an accident of passion. The governor was dead and other than a prayer card, couldn't be linked with her death. Yet an EMT in the capital was dead, their friend Pinky was missing and presumed dead. Jason had fled in a panic that suddenly appeared justified.

"Found it!" Stacy announced in a loud whisper from the other room. Drew went to investigate.

"Here," she said grimly. Her flashlight was trained on an open gym bag. Inside was a pink cellphone. Drew gasped in surprise but had the presence of mind to snap a couple of pictures with his own phone.

"That should do it," Stacy said, closing and zipping the bag. "Let's get out of here."

But as they turned to go the door suddenly opened and two men entered. Each had a pistol trained on Stacy and Drew.

"Don't make a move, don't make a sound," one of them said. "These pistols have silencers and we're not afraid to use them."

One man kept them covered while the other swiftly collected their cellphones, opened the gym bag, and tossed them in. "Let's go," he hissed. "Out the back door."

They went out the back door and down to the dock where the fishermen's boat was moored.

"Get in," one of the men said, his gun trained on them. The other one threw off the mooring ropes and shoved the boat away from the dock. He got behind the wheel and started the big engines. A few minutes later they were motoring out into the bay. Except for the roaring engines, they rode in silence.

Drew looked at the sun, which would set in a half-hour or so. Even if they were missed, and he wasn't certain that they would be, any kind of effective search wouldn't be able to be mounted until the morning. By then, he and Stacy would be dead, and the fishermen long gone. He looked over at Stacy, who had a sad, resigned expression on her face. She mouthed the word 'sorry,' and began to cry softly.

After a while, well out to sea, the driver cut the engines to neutral. He went to the back of the boat and lowered a tandem kayak into the water. He used a rope to bring it alongside the boat. The man with the gun said, "get in."

Stacy and Drew complied, fully knowing the men's plans. The man with the gun untied the kayak and pushed it away. The driver engaged the engines and pulled away in a large circle.

"When I yell jump, jump!" Stacy shouted. "Swim for the bottom and stay down as long as you can. It's our only chance," she added needlessly. The big boat was headed straight for them.

"Jump!" Stacy screamed as the boat was about to hit them broadside. Drew dove for all he was worth. He heard the 'crack' of collision as the speeding boat hit the kayak. He swam as deep as he could and held his breath longer than he thought was possible. He could hear the boat circling for another pass and tried to stay down. After the boat roared overhead, he surfaced for a quick breath of air, his lungs screaming. He saw Stacy briefly. She signaled for him to dive again. He heard the 'whiz' of bullets as they hit the water. They were being shot at, he realized. He grabbed a big a lungful of air and went back down. He heard the boat roar by again and, waiting as long as he could, surfaced. He knew that it was only a matter of time before he was either shot or run over, but he had no other choice. Again, he saw Stacy briefly in the waves generated by the speeding boat. She smiled and gave him a thumbs up and then dove down again. Drew dove down too, wondering how many more dives they could make before one of them was hit. He was rapidly getting too exhausted to stay down for very long. He knew that if he came up too soon, he would provide an excellent target for the gunman.

But this time, as he surfaced, he heard the roar of another engine. He looked up to see Will's plane heading straight for the boat with a vengeance. It skimmed over the water and only banked up and around at the very last second. The driver of the boat veered away and then cut a wide circle. The second man could be seen shooting at the plane.

On the plane, Will heard shots hit the fuselage with loud 'tings.' He turned to his passenger, Ned Butcher. Ned gave Will a hard look and pulled out his forty-five. "Get in as close as you can," he said. Will made a tight circle and headed for the boat, which was frantically zigzagging towards the swimmers again. "Make it count," he shouted needlessly. As they flew past,

Ned shot the boat's two engines out and the boat went dead in the water. Will circled the boat but when the two men raised their pistols, Ned took aim. "Fools!' He exclaimed. He shot twice at each man. They both clutched at their chests and slumped to the deck.

Will landed his plane as close to Stacy and Drew as he could. They both swam up to the plane's pontoons and were helped up into the plane. Will grabbed Stacy as Ned extended a helping hand to Drew.

"Good shooting," Drew said as he climbed into one of the passenger seats. He hoped that Ned wouldn't notice how shaken he was.

"Thanks," Ned said. "I'm a little rusty. It took more shots than it should have. First time under fire?" He added. It was more of a statement than a question. "I pissed my pants the first time," Ned said with a laugh. He looked meaningfully at Drews soaked clothing.

Stacy was sitting in Will's lap, gripping him so tightly that he almost couldn't breathe.

"Ned showed up at the bar, looking for you," Will said to Drew. "Ned ID'd them and told me who they were. I had called Mick Murphy earlier and he told me to sit tight until he got here for an arrest. We were sitting in my office, waiting when we saw the two guys rush down to their cabin and realized that something was wrong. As we ran into the parking lot, we could see the boat racing out to sea with you two on it. Luckily, the plane had been refueled and was ready to take off."

Will taxied over to the bodyguard's boat and Ned climbed onto it. He checked the bodyguard's pulses and did a thumbs down. He would wait with the boat until a police boat came to tow it in.

"How did you know about those guys?" Drew asked Will. "They might have been acting suspiciously, but that's not enough to bring in the cops."

Will turned and smiled. He gunned the plane's engine and took off. "I'll show you," he said, a little mysteriously.

They flew towards a series of islands that Drew suddenly recognized. Will expertly landed near the largest one and taxied to the beach. To Drew's surprise, Pinky walked out of the underbrush and climbed onto the plane.

"Hey," he said, flashing his snaggle-toothed grin. "Y'all look pretty wet!" Stacy rushed to him and gave him a hug

"How did you..." she said.

"Well, a guy grabbed me as I was leaving my cabin," He explained. "He put a gun in my ribs and made me drive out to the point. There was a boat waiting there. He forced me to carry my board out to it and then put it on board. Another guy was behind the wheel. They took me out into the bay. After they searched me and took my phone, they made me get on the board. Then they ran me over!" He shook his head, still shaken by the experience.

"Sounds familiar," Stacy said. He looked at her for an explanation.

"I'll tell you later," she said. "How did you end up on Snake Island?"

"I dove deep and held on to some sea grass 'till I thought my lungs would explode," he said. "I guess they thought I was done for and, anyway, they had me so far out to sea that I'd never be able to swim to shore even if I was still alive. What they didn't know was that we were on the grass flats, only four or five feet deep in a lot of places at low tide. I walked half the way." He chuckled. "What I didn't know was that the nearest island was this snake-infested place!

"I found Pinky and told him to stay put," Will said. "We were waiting for the police when you two idiots decided to take matters into your own hands."

Drew shook his head, accepting the accusation. He really did feel quite stupid now, like a kid caught red-handed stealing apples from a farmer's orchard. "What is this all about?" he asked. "It's got to be more than a woman killed in a sexual tryst."

"I don't know, that's for sure," Will said. "Maybe the cops can tell us more."

"I don't see how those guys thought they could get away with three accidents," Pinky said. "It seems that someone would see the coincidence."

"They didn't care," Will said. "The best anyone could come up with would be circumstantial evidence. There wasn't even enough of that for an arrest." He shook his head thoughtfully. We have a witness to attempted murder, but the suspects are both dead. Ironic."

When they landed and taxied up to the dock, everyone could see several men and women in blue windbreakers with "FBI" and "Police" in large yellow letters on the back. Mick Murphy and Jack Truax walked up the dock, accompanied by two FBI agents who identified themselves as agents Alvin Kefauver, and Cindy Fowler. Will immediately recognized them as the couple that were staying in cabin fourteen.

"What happened here?" Kefauver said, noticing the bullet holes on the plane.

"Thompson's bodyguards tried to kill my daughter and her friend," Will explained. "Had to shoot 'em. They're in a boat being towed in by the police."

"Damn," he said. "No choice?"

Will nodded at the bullet holes in his plane but didn't say anything.

"I would have liked to have interviewed them," Kefauver said. "We had an undercover agent wash up on the beach the other day and they likely had something to do with it." He set his jaw and his eyes turned cold. "I'll find out who ordered the killing and make them pay, you can count on that."

"I believe you," Will said. He called Pinky over and introduced him.

"Isn't he the one that was missing?" Kefauver said, referring to Pinky.

"The same," Will said. "Would have been star witness number one." He shook his head, a puzzled look on his face. "They didn't know Pinky was alive," Will said. "They caught Stacy and Drew in their cabin, but there couldn't have been anything to link them to Pinky's death. Why try to kill them?"

"They weren't worried about being linked to Pinky's death," Kefauver said. "There would have been no corpse, at least not for a few days anyway; and even if one was found, a smear of pink paint on a boat or a pink cellphone wouldn't go very far in a court of law. It would only be circumstantial evidence. No, they were cleaning up after a disastrous weekend that would have led to an investigation; something they desperately didn't want."

"Why?" Stacy asked. She was becoming more confused by the moment. Still shaken by the attempt on her life and the shock of finding Pinky alive, Stacy wanted answers. "What would an investigation into an accidental death have meant?"

"I guess you're owed an explanation," Kefauver said, looking askance at his partner, who nodded. "The investigation is still ongoing, so everything I tell you is strictly confidential – and I'll deny having said it if you tell anyone. But, having said that, I can tell you that our hackers found that a certain local chemical company has been obtaining illegal chemicals, producing military grade poison gas, and selling it to a foreign operator. It appears that the money involved in the transactions was being laundered by the CEO of the Thompson Fund, Ben Fitzgibbons, and the Brantwood Fellowship. An investigation into the coincidental deaths of Elizabeth Deschamps and Tommy Thompson would have exposed the whole operation. We were about to bring in the two bodyguards in for questioning when we saw them run down to their cabin. We didn't know why and didn't see them leave by the back door with you two." Kefauver looked at Cindy meaningfully. "I Would have liked to have interviewed them before we moved on the factory."

"It'll be harder to get warrants now," she said to Kefauver as they walked away

"Who needs warrants," Kefauver said, a grim look on his face.

Fitzgibbons, Drew thought. Where have I heard that name before? Then he remembered: Ray, at the Library said that Fitzgibbons was a big shot in the state capital, CFO of the Thompson Fund. He was the one that Elizabeth Deschamps was having an affair with when she was dating John McNair! That was the connection!

Just then, the Sheriff's boat pulled into the cove and docked. It was towing the bodyguard's boat and, presumably, their bodies. Ned Butcher was sitting upfront with the Deputies.

"Thanks for the ride," he said, stepping onto the dock. The Sheriff's Deputies motored back out into the cove and headed towards the bay.

Ned held what looked like an empty gym bag. "They dumped everything," he said. "Must have done it when they saw us approaching. They were caught red-handed at attempted murder. They had nothing to lose, so they tried to shoot us and run."

Drew used Ned's arrival as an opportunity to take the FBI agent aside. He told him about the connection between Elizabeth and Fitzgibbons. He also told him about the connection between Elizabeth and McNair.

"Wow," Kefauver said. "Does McNair know about her affair with Fitzgibbons?"

"I don't know," Drew said. "But I don't want to be the one to tell him. I think, down deep, he's probably pretty upset about her death, especially the way it happened. At least I would be," he added.

"Pinky had a lot of pics from the office," Drew continued. "One of them showed that the computer had been tampered with, the hard drive was most likely taken by the bodyguards and dumped in the sea. Also, there was a stack of prayer cards on the desktop. One of them had the governor's name on it, along with her personal phone number. There were others. I think that she used a hidden camera to record her trysts to blackmail the men that she lured there. I imagine you will have some serious questions for Mr. Fitzgibbons. Ned told me that he was the one in charge of the governor's security detail."

Kefauver shook his head, "He went missing. They found his car at a parking area on Lake Okeechobee. Blood and a pistol with one round fired. If he fell into the lake, then the gators got him." He smiled and started to walk away. Then he stopped and turned. "In the future, leave the investigating to us professionals," he said. "You and Stacy almost got yourselves killed today."

Drew nodded. No shit, he thought, but he didn't say anything.

CHAPTER FORTY-NINE

T HAT NIGHT A RUMBLING boom shook the town. Dishes clattered and the room shook. Drew jumped out of bed and looked out the window. Stacy joined him. There, on the horizon to the west, a bright orange flame lit the sky, flickering angrily.

"Morley Chemical," Stacy said. "It's burning!"

They quickly dressed and drove in the direction of the fire. Stacy thought of Dan and his comment about the Monkey Wrench Gang. He had called her that morning and told her that the lab results came back from Dr. Donnelly. The chemicals in the water sample were by-products from the manufacture of sarin, the deadly gas that Assad was using against his own people in Syria. She hoped that Dan's casual comment hadn't become a reality.

On the way they were forced to pull over for fire trucks, an ambulance, a hazmat vehicle, and several police cars. The road was blocked a good mile away from the fire, which was burning hotly. Jack Truax was at the roadblock. He stopped them as they approached.

"No farther," he said, holding his hands up and stepping towards them. "It's a chemical fire," he said. "The fumes are being blown out towards the bay for now, but it's still dangerous."

Drew noticed a gas mask dangling from Truax's belt. "What happened, Truax?" Drew asked.

"Explosion and fire at the main complex," he explained. "It's the middle of the night, so no one was at the complex except security. They're all accounted for and safe."

Suddenly an excited man in a hazmat suit shouted through a bullhorn. "Clear the area now! The fire can't be contained, and the wind is shifting! It'll soon reach the storage tanks!"

Police cars, fire trucks and other emergency vehicles were speeding towards them, their sirens blaring and men hanging onto handholds on the big trucks. Drew and Stacy ran to her Jeep, but, by then, the caravan of fire trucks and emergency vehicles was passing them on the narrow road. Stacy gunned her Jeep and took to the brush alongside the road. The Jeep bounced crazily as branches and tall grass whipped at the windshield. Suddenly, a blast erupted from the factory. Drew could see flaming globs of orange, red, yellow, blue and green arcing into the pre-dawn sky out the back of the open Jeep. There was a loud whoosh as the wind from the blast reached them. Drew could feel its heat.

Finally, they came out onto the highway, Stacy veering wildly as she turned onto it. "Head for the fire station," Drew yelled. "That's where the trucks will go." He desperately hoped that no one was caught in the blast and conflagration that followed it. He knew that the fumes, if inhaled, would be deadly.

As they pulled into the firehall's large parking area, a concerned fireman, holding traffic direction lights, guided them off to a side area. The big trucks, police cruisers, hazmat vehicle, EMT truck and ambulances pulled in behind them. Jason, Pinky and the ambulance crews rushed to see if anyone had been injured. Luckily, except for a few superficial burns and some minor smoke inhalation, everyone was alright.

People were milling everywhere, talking excitedly and watching the flames that flickered on the horizon. Drew snapped cameos of the shocked and exhausted first responders while Stacy walked over to where Jason, Pinky and a few other EMTs were clustered.

"Hey Stace," Jason said as she walked up to the group. "What brings you out on a night like this?"

Stacy laughed at his attempt at a joke and gestured with her thumb towards Drew.

"Oh," Jason said. "Always on the job, that guy."

"Just like us," Pinky said with a wry laugh. "I hope he got some pictures of the hazmat guys; they went right into the belly of that beast. I'm surprised no one got hurt."

"Somebody said that old man Morley was in the building," Jason said casually. Pinky shot him a hard look. He knew that Stacy had dated Bruce Morley for a while and thought Jason's comment was insensitive.

Stacy looked at the two EMTs questioningly. "What do you mean?" she asked.

Jason and Pinky exchanged glances. "Well," Pinky began slowly. "There's a rumor going around that old man Morley set the fire himself and got caught in it. Someone saw a burned-out Cadillac next to the building. The kind that Morley drives."

Stacy didn't say anything. She was watching Drew, who had wandered over to where the security guys were standing around. She wondered what he was up to.

"Oh, hey," Drew said, fooling around with his cameras and acting like he had just stumbled upon the guards. "Long time no see."

"Yeah, screw you," one of the men said. "You and that little bitch are the ones who caused this."

Drew assumed a friendly smile and an easygoing manner, like they were old friends. "What do you mean?" he said. He stepped back a little, aiming his camera at the men.

"Get that thing out of my face before I smash it," a second man said.

Drew clicked "video" and stepped back farther. "Okay, okay," he said, lowering the camera but keeping it running. "I'm just here to take pictures. What do you mean I caused this?"

"Hey, he was just the photographer that day," the third man said, calming his friends. "He doesn't know what happened."

The first man, calmer now, explained. "That girl, Stacy, the one that hired you? She got some water samples and sent them to some lab. The lab sent them on to the EPA and recommended that Morley be investigated for banned chemicals."

"What?" Drew said, feigning surprise. After all, he was just a photographer hired to get some pictures of snakes. How would he know that his employer had ulterior motives?

"That's right," the guard continued, warming up a little. "You know how these government agencies are, they'll shut you down for anything; or maybe old man Morley did have something to hide, I don't know. All I know is that Mr. Haden, the head of security, seemed worried that the old man might do something drastic."

"Mr. Haden?" Drew asked mildly, seeming to be more interested in one of his cameras than he was of the guard's story.

"Head of security," the guard said. "He came by earlier today and said that we should be especially watchful tonight. We were just the night crew, and there was no one at all in the compound. "Don't let anyone in tonight, and if someone tries, let me know immediately," he said. Seemed like a strange request at the time. He said something about loose ends. Anyway, we were just watching the camera monitors in the office when suddenly the one at the back gate went out. Pete here," he gestured to the second guard. "Was outside having a smoke. He yelled to us that someone was entering the building at the main complex. We were getting ready to drive over there when the explosion happened."

"The first responders saw a Cadillac parked at the main complex," the guard named Pete said absently. He lit a cigarette and looked around like he was waiting for the police to let them go home.

"Yeah," the first guard said. He too was beginning to look bored. "Morley drives a Caddy."

"Where is he now?" Drew said. He was looking around in his camera bag for something.

"Morley?" the first guard said. "Nobody's seen him. Probably in the factory, burnt to a crisp."

"No," Drew said. "I mean, what's his name, your boss."

"Haden?" Pete said. "Damned if I know. The prick should be here, getting us released."

CHAPTER FIFTY

Daphne was clacking away at the keys of her computer as Will, Buddy and Stacy watched. "Let's see what little nest eggs Fitzgibbons and Elizabeth had salted away for themselves." She entered the code for the first one, but it came up 'access denied.'

"Must be Fitzgibbon's account," Buddy said. "He probably changed the code before he killed himself, although it seems strange that he would do so; he dropped money off every Sunday, so he must have known by the time he got back to Tallahassee that Elizabeth was dead." He gave Daphne the code for the second account. She clacked some keys. 'Access denied' came up again.

"Fitzgibbons must have changed the codes," she said.

"How would he have gotten the code to Elizabeth's?" Will said.

"They were lovers," Daphne said. "Maybe they had each other's codes, you know, in case something happened to one of them."

"It's the only explanation," Buddy said, a look of profound disappointment on his face. He had come back to Brantwood to transfer the money in the two accounts to one of Van's. His boss was not going to be happy.

"Doesn't add up," Will said. "If Fitzgibbons had the codes to both accounts, then he had a boatload of money. He could have gone anywhere. Why would he kill himself?"

"Hard to say," Buddy said. "From what we've gathered, he had some very hard customers breathing down his neck. If any one of them got ahold of him, his death would not have been a pleasant one." He got up and dusted his hands off on his pants and looked at Will. "Any chance I can catch a ride to Miami? I've got to deliver some bad news to Van, and I can't do it by phone. You know how he is."

"The plane is gassed up and ready," Will said. He felt bad for his old friend. He knew that Van trusted him and wouldn't blame him, but Buddy took pride in his work and didn't accept failure easily. He looked over at Daphne, who was still trying permutations of the codes. "Be back in a few hours."

She nodded and said goodbye to Buddy. She knew that Will would be with Buddy when he gave the bad news to Van. It was the way he was.

Stacy went downstairs to the bar and found Drew waiting for her.

"I thought you would be going to Tallahassee for the governor's funeral," she said.

"Wasn't invited," he said. "The Morely estate may still sue me for defamation because of my exposé and Bunny wants to keep some distance, Teejay told me. If I'm going to be an independent reporter, I might as well act the part. I thought I'd drive down to Key West and do an article on the iguanas there. Want to come along?"

"I'll get my things," Stacy said. "How long are we staying?"

"As long as we want," Drew said. "I just got paid for my articles and pictures."

A while later Drew pulled up to Stacy's cabin in the green MG.

"Still have this?" Stacy said. "I'd have thought Bunny would have had you return it by now."

Drew laughed. "Must have slipped his mind." As they pulled out of the lot, Drew cranked the volume on "Love Will Keep Us Together."

CHAPTER FIFTY-ONE

Sunday, 2:30

Elizabeth Deschamp's eyes popped open. Where was she? Her throat was raw and painful, and she tasted blood. It was hard to breathe. She remembered the governor straining on top of her and then clutching his chest and squeezing her throat. She looked over and saw his lifeless body on the floor. Shit! she thought. How am I going to get out of these restraints? She pulled, tugged, and yanked vigorously, but it was no use. She thought of screaming, but who would hear her? Plus, her throat was too sore to even think of screaming. What time is it, she wondered? How long have I been out? She lay there waiting, wondering when the governor's bodyguards would notice that there was something wrong. The ringtone on the governor's phone answered her question.

What would they do when the governor didn't answer? Give him a little more time? But she knew they'd eventually have to come get him. A soft knock on the door in case he was still involved? Probably. She would try to shout for them to break the door down, but she didn't know if her damaged throat would handle the effort. But eventually they would come for him. They'd break the lock on the door and find the governor where he lay. They would check with Fitzgibbons and he would tell them to let her loose. She had more than a dozen men on the line, held there by the recordings she had made in this very room. Each one funneled the money she took in from Fitzgibbons into the church's coffers and from there a split found its way into private offshore accounts. One was held by Fitzsimmons and another was held by her. She controlled the city council and the police. She was too valuable an asset for Fitzgibbons to lose. She had almost had the governor himself under her control, but the idiot had managed to have a heart attack and now he lay dead on the floor. Most of the men that she entertained were quick and apologetic, but Tommy Thompson was virile and powerful, and she felt that she had finally met her match in bed, but then he had arched his back and died. She lay there for a long time remembering another man who had touched her spirit in the same way.

Suddenly she heard a key rattle in the outer office door. There was a soft, inquisitive knock as the door opened a crack. "Come in, she croaked. I need help." The door opened all the way, flooding the darkened room with light. There, framed by the doorway, stood someone she hadn't expected.

"I can explain everything," Elizabeth said, her voice raw and gravelly. "Please undo these restraints and help me."

But the intruder just stood there, staring at the dead body of the governor and at Elizabeth, strapped to the bedposts.

"Get over here and undo these!" Elizabeth insisted. "Now!"

But the intruder still stood, transfixed by the macabre scene before her.

"You don't think I know what you've been doing?" Elizabeth said, growing angry. "I know about your seamy little meetings with Corey! I know about the money! What happened here was an accident, but what you did is illegal! I'll have you arrested! You'll go to jail! You'll be ruined! Now do as I say!"

But, with the last word, a shout, Elizabeth felt her damaged throat tighten. She began to cough and choke. She felt blood rise from her wound. She couldn't breathe. She writhed desperately, thrashing back and forth on the bed. She tried to grab at her throat, but the restraints held her. A moment later everything went black again.

Sally Yarber stood, shocked at what she had just witnessed. She had heard desperate thumps coming from Elizabeth's office and had gone to check. Now she faced her boss, covered in her own blood, her lifeless eyes staring vacantly. On the floor lay the naked, dead body of the governor of the state. Unsure of what to do she stood still for a long time blinking and trying desperately not to vomit. She had seen dead people before, of course, but only in funeral homes; now here were two dead people, one of them her boss, who had been alive only a few moments ago. Then a stark realization struck her: she had to move, or she would be caught up in what had happened. She would be implicated, investigated, and arrested for embezzlement. Who was to say that she hadn't finished Elizabeth off after she found her alive? It would be murder! She knew that she had to take swift action before the bodyguards came to check on their boss.

She took a tissue and wiped her prints from the door handle. She stepped over to Elizabeth's computer and removed the hard drive, her hands shaking. Now, with Elizabeth's computer hard drive safely in hand, she prayed that it would be all she needed to keep her payments to Virgil a secret and to keep her out of jail. "God's will be done," she thought. She left Elizabeth's door open and walked down a corridor to a back door, slipped out into the hot afternoon and walked home.

CHAPTER FIFTY-TWO

CORY DESCHAMPS DANCED OUT onto the stage as the band kicked into his theme song. Jimbo Onthank announced him loudly. "Ladies and gentlemen, *Coree Day shamps*!"

Moving around freely, flashing his signature smile, he felt a new freedom. The church was his and his ministry was whatever he wanted it to be. He danced and he shouted, and he sang, and he felt a joy that he had never felt before. The congregation moved with him, dancing and shouting amens and singing with the chorus. He turned and gave Curtis Green a smile. Curtis grinned and cut the band with a flourish.

"Do you feel him?" Corey shouted. "Do you feel his spirit? He is among us today!" He moved around the stage, nodding as people applauded and shouted "amen!" He was channeling Shakespeare, gesturing, gesticulating, and projecting his voice to the rafters. He looked out and saw Sally sitting where Elizabeth had once sat; but instead of avoiding her visage, he looked straight at her. She was smiling enthusiastically, completely engrossed in the sermon they had developed. Every so often, when he felt the spirit lift him, he went off-script, letting the spirit guide him. Instead of the tight lips and frowns he was used to from Elizabeth, Sally clutched her hands to her bosom and looked to the sky, a rapt expression on her face. At those times he felt as if he was flying with the angels, soaring into the bright light of transcendental bliss, and engaging with the epiphanous nature of the ultimate truth.

THE END

About the Author

Marshall Seddon graduated from Fredonia State University in 1971. He served six years in the New York State National Guard, taught history at Brocton Central School for forty years and was a founding member of the Blackhorse Rugby Football Club. He enjoys fly fishing and playing jazz guitar. He and his wife Heidi live in Fredonia, New York. They have eight children, two golden retrievers and a cat named Twist.

www.ingramcontent.com/pod-product-compliance
Lightning Source LLC
Chambersburg PA
CBHW051244260626
47162CB00002B/601